The Carto

Anne Spillard was born in Leeds, a taught for many years, mostly at sp as a nurse, and then worked as a packer at a Lunch-o-fax warehouse.

Once married, she has a son and a daughter.

She has written plays and stories for the BBC and her stories have appeared in many anthologies and magazines. This is her first novel.

Anne Spillard

The Cartomancer

Pan Books
London, Sydney and Auckland

First published in Great Britain 1987 by
Hamish Hamilton Ltd

This edition published 1989 by Pan Books Ltd,
Cavaye Place, London SW10 9PG

9 8 7 6 5 4 3 2 1

© Anne Spillard 1987

ISBN 0 330 30912 9

Printed and bound in Great Britain by
Richard Clay Ltd, Bungay, Suffolk

For Davey

*New interests
appear on the
horizon*

♡♣♢♠ **Chapter 1** ♡♣♢♠
Nine of Diamonds

Last summer, at this bridge, Hugo and I had seen a
kingfisher. I slowed the car down.

'Last year, at this bridge, Hugo and I saw a kingfisher,'
I said to Vincenza, who was sitting beside me.

As I said it, I wished I hadn't. Vincenza hadn't the
slightest interest in kingfishers, not unless they could fuck
you. But she did like to know things she could pass on to
other people, and soon the whole of Avalon would know
about Hugo.

'Kingfisher,' said Vincenza. She opened her window
and blew cigarette smoke into the clear air. She peered at
the stream through her violet contact lenses.

'Lovely,' she said.

We drove up from the wooded valley where the stream
was, and came out onto open moorland where cotton
grass shivered among the rushes, and the sheep looked
more like limestone rocks than the real boulders did.
Early summer sun brightened the dulled grass of winter
that was only just beginning to green again. The hawthorn

1

trees had not yet unfurled their bread-and-cheese tips, and all that stuff.

Vincenza leant back in her seat and let the sun shine on her make-up. It shone on her open pores too, they stretched themselves like sea anemones on an incoming tide. Vincenza looked best in the winter, except that she was so thin that then she complained all the time of the cold.

She sighed luxuriously. 'On days like this,' she said, 'I feel nostalgic for the Market Square and the redolence of sex.'

I knew someone, a school secretary, who'd been raped in the Market Square, in a shop doorway by the side of Pearson's. I told Vincenza.

'Ah,' she said. Full of meaning. 'Too bad. Turn right down this track.'

We were in the wilds now. The track had potholes full of water. The hawthorns all leaned away over the barbed-wire fence as if they had been cut like that, and the sparse grass beside the track echoed the angle of their oblique-ness. Across the fells we could see Roseberry Tor, the local viewpoint which each of us was learning to identify with homecomings.

We came to Nerina's barn. It had reached that stage in its conversion when it was hard to tell whether it was being dismantled or converted. There were breeze-blocks and cement mixers all over the place.

'She can't come to the door,' said Vincenza. The door was a mahogany affair with a telescopic viewer. Vincenza pushed it open, for it was not locked.

She didn't call out. Quite the opposite, she was at pains to move quietly, whilst not seeming to do so.

I disliked her stealth, so I fell over the umbrella stand. She was amused that I had demolished her game, perhaps because it put us on the same footing. She burst into peals of laughter.

A voice called out from a room leading off the wide wood-panelled entrance hall. 'Who is it?'

'As if you didn't know.' Vincenza pushed open a door,

and we were in a long low room that owed its elegant shape to the recent knocking through of several of the original rooms. Most of the walls were of stone, but there was plenty of white everywhere as well.

Nerina was lying full-length on a cerise-painted Victorian settee upholstered with Heals fabric. Nerina herself was upholstered in a close-hugging T-shirt of subtle design and a skirt of fine lawn that fell in folds like a wedding dress around the sofa.

'My god!' said Vincenza. 'You look like the young Victoria at Balmoral.'

'Was the young Victoria ever *at* Balmoral?' Nerina asked. 'Didn't Albert buy it for her in early middle age?'

'She was twenty-nine when she first saw it,' said Vincenza. 'That's if you count the original castle as her first sight of it. So you see, it's a compliment, as it happens, because that makes her quite a bit younger than us.'

'You really are a pedant,' said Nerina. But she had lost interest in history, and was looking at me. Vincenza noticed this, for she watched everyone all the time.

'Sorry we're late, ducky,' she said. 'We were doing our nature bit. Looking at kingfishers and sheep and things. How can you bear it here? It's miles from anywhere.'

Nerina looked down at the cat she was stroking. 'It has its advantages,' she said. 'And you're always late.' But her voice was indifferent. Other things were on her mind.

'Come to think of it, you look more Barrett Browning than Victoria.' This surprised me, for I had not thought of Vincenza making an effort to ingratiate herself, and now I saw she was devoting herself to the sort of discussion of her friend which achieved exactly that.

'Did Barrett Browning have a pot leg?' asked Nerina. She shifted her plastered leg impatiently, and looked at me. We weren't friends. We weren't enemies either. I knew Vincenza, and so did Nerina, that was all. As Nerina regarded me, I thought she herself was cat-like, her attention focussed on the one who was the least impressed with her, as a cat will sit on your knee if you display indifference, and ignore those who fuss over it.

And so Nerina ignored Vincenza and pulled a face at me.

'All this for a broken big toe,' she said. 'It's so embarrassing.'

This seemed a strange choice of adjective, though events presently explained it.

'You'll have to make your own tea,' she called to Vincenza, who had crossed the room when she saw that her friend was bending her attention in my direction. From the kitchen came the sound of a kettle being filled from a tap.

'Rosehip or mint?' she called, ignoring Nerina's sarcasm.

It was a house of no tea, in other words. I said I wasn't thirsty. Then I felt prudish, so I asked for water.

'You'll get typhoid,' said Nerina. But it was a passing remark, said with little concern, or hope.

I told her I had it all the time. But she didn't smile.

'Just don't give it to me,' she said. 'I've got enough on my plate, thank you very much.'

Other people lived in this nearly-house, but there was no sign of them. Louis would still be at work, and Christian would no doubt presently be brought home on the school bus. But where was Nerina's mother, about whom I had heard so much on the Avalon grapevine?

There was a sudden flurry at the kitchen window, as if small stones were being flung at the glass.

'Oh, my god!' said Nerina. She picked up a *Harpers* and began thumbing through the pages. Then she slowed the action down, turning them slower and slower, but not reading.

'Out! Out!' shrieked a voice from outside.

Nerina ignored it, apart from not reading *Harpers*. I strolled over to the kitchen door to see what was going on. I had the strange feeling that I could do exactly as I pleased, because nobody cared whether I was there or not.

4

I arrived as Vincenza began to open the window. She had her practised social worker look on.

'Well, *hello*!' she said to someone outside. 'You must be Nerina's mother.' She was fly enough not to put her hand out of the window to shake hands. It would have been crushed as the wild fury outside slammed the window shut again.

A lot of words followed, but they cannot be reported by me, as they were in German, and I didn't understand them. Nerina's mother was an Alsatian, which seemed appropriate in the circumstances, I remember thinking.

But Vincenza understood her. She answered soothingly, in English, after listening with professionally assumed attention. Always listen to what the client has to tell you, her attitude said.

'Oh, I don't think so,' she said through the window, when there was a pause. 'Come and have some tea,' she said. 'You must be parched. All that gardening. It's going to look beautiful when you've finished it.'

The old lady was appeased enough to back away from the window. 'I come inside,' she agreed.

She climbed over some drainage pipes stacked against the house wall, opened the window, and clambered in. She stood with one foot in each of the stainless steel sinks, the muddy soles of her wellingtons grating on the smooth new metal. Then she turned her back on us, bending down so that we saw her pink long-johns and the varicosed gap that stretched down to the rolled-over tops of her self-supporting stockings. Her bottom was broad and it pointed its blue Harris tweed in my direction. I stepped back.

'Damn you, Hilde,' Nerina shouted from the other room. 'Get out of the bloody sink. You'll ruin it.'

But Hilde turned on the mixer tap, holding her booted feet under, first one, then the other, swishing the tap from sink to sink. Satisfied, she turned, holding out her hands to Vincenza and me. 'Help me down, my darlings,' she said.

We held her hands and she jumped down onto

5

the quarry-tiled floor. She grimaced, kicking her boots off.

'They are cold, these tiles. Nancy runs a cold house.' (She refused to cooperate with Nerina about her changed name, holding firmly to the old one. 'Daddy and I chose your name. That you cannot take from me.' Vincenza told me that. And Vincenza had laughed. 'Nerina can take anything from anybody,' she had said.)

Now Vincenza (familiar to her parents as Vera) put out the tea things, if such they were, on a tray, and we filed back into the living room. The labels of the infusion bags gave a half-finished air to the tray, I thought. They diminished the aesthetic pleasure of drinking. Nevertheless, I wished I had a cup in my hand, for as the others supped, I sat priggishly on a corner-seat, hardly able to refrain from twiddling my thumbs.

Vincenza took pity on me after a while.

'Come and see the bathroom,' she said, jumping up.

'It still isn't finished.' Nerina turned back to her magazine.

We went up the back staircase, where the roof began to slope over our heads. As we rose, I saw the bathroom, because it had no door.

I saw the bathroom second. First I saw Derek Thackray, Professor of European Studies. I saw all of him, because he was standing full frontal in Nerina's dark green, shaded-through-lime circular double bath.

Vincenza laughed. 'She could have warned us!'

But of course Nerina wouldn't do that.

Derek Thackray reached for a towel. 'Warned you? You have to be warned against me, have you?'

He hardly saw me. I looked beyond him. The roof stretched on endlessly, unplastered, an attic space piled with furniture, boxes. Presently a wall would divide it from the bathroom, but not yet, so the luxury suite perched at the top of the stairs, and Derek Thackray bent and pulled out the plug of the lime-and-avocado bath. He was Galbet, the Lilliputian admiral, stuck in the middle of some swirling marine cocktail of noxious creation. Melon

6

liqueur came into my mind, and I gulped. There was a small pause, in which the other two, without even glancing at each other, enjoyed my, as they construed it, bourgeois dismay in the face of male nakedness.

'Nice, isn't it?' Vincenza turned to me and winked.

'Green isn't my style,' I said, looking in an unfocussed way at Derek Thackray.

We clattered back downstairs.

'Nerina, darling, I would just love to have a bath in your bathroom. Why didn't you tell me it was open to the public?'

We were back in the living room, where the Alsatian was sucking on a *petit four*. I thought how you shove a mackerel in the mouth of a conger eel to stop it biting you. Why did I think of such a thing? For I had heard very little from the Alsatian, though reports of her sayings were legion.

'It's so embarrassing.' Nerina tapped her plaster leg and looked meaningfully at Vincenza. And now I knew why it was embarrassing. Because Derek Thackray was Nerina's lover, and the plaster cast was coming between them.

Nerina was not allowing me into this confidence which she had just made it clear she shared with her friend.

'Derek keeps his boat here, in the barn. He's working on it. Goodness knows if he'll ever finish it.'

'He will, he will,' Vincenza promised, and her tone was cool. When he's finished with you he'll finish his boat, her tone said.

She and Nerina understood each other. Nerina wasn't offended, she laughed, then shrugged and held out her hands expressively. You win a few, you lose a few, her hands said. Her husband was a lecturer without tenure in Derek Thackray's department. I was intrigued. How much more exciting were the activities of this little sub-world than the high spot of our social life so far – college dinners with the regal Cicely Samuelson, one-time head-

7

mistress of a girls' public boarding-school and now warden of Camelot College, to which Edwin, my partner, had been assigned.

'Edwin is something to do with medieval French, isn't he?' They expected him to be dry as dust, a doddering old puffball. Before they met him, you could see the wives wondering how on earth a lecturer in medieval French called Edwin could be good in bed; could possibly exist outside the breeze-block walls of the university, even.

After they'd met him, they stopped wondering. I would stand at his side in my humble way at cocktail parties, while they eddied round him, fancying him, but not quite, because after all he was too handsome. And that was wise of them. I regretted Edwin's handsomeness because I always had to be watching, watching for rivals. He was the vine that had grown by the roadside, and I hid behind my vine armed with a shotgun, expecting wayfarers to feast on the grapes. Yet they didn't. The fruit was so lustrous that they suspected a trap, and I was less at risk in losing a partner than poor Phyllis Thackray was of losing her perfectly ordinary-looking Derek. Derek had to prove himself; Edwin didn't.

Not, as we all know, that appearances count for anything.

Derek flopped down the stairs in his Eastern sandals, reminders of a previous year's sabbatical. He lay on a goat-skin rug in front of the wood-burning stove and grimaced at its arrangement of unlit logs.

No sun warmed this long pale room. The Alsatian, interpreting his look, used it as an excuse to switch on a small fan-heater, the sort that comes free with orders over ten pounds in mail order catalogues. Its busy sound helped us to believe in warmth, though there was no real change in the temperature.

Nerina drew a white cobweb shawl over herself. Such femininity, such frailty. Derek Thackray looked at her with clear longing – or lust, and I thought how easy it was, how you could snare a man with a shawl as delicate as gossamer, easier than trapping lobsters in lobster-pots.

Then I thought maybe I'd got it all wrong, and that Nerina was the one who was snared.

Once I'd sat next to Phyllis Thackray at a party. She'd turned to me occasionally and asked peremptory questions, mostly about Edwin's previous job. She herself had been at Oxford, and she managed to keep her face still as I told her he'd been a principal lecturer at a polytechnic. She didn't ask which one, and I sat there with defiant pride, mingled with the sinking feeling, despite myself, that she classed us as inferior. I'd been sitting at the end of a window-seat, so there was no one else to talk to. Across the room, Edwin was talking to another professor, a fat one with a high blood pressure complexion and bright poppy eyes, or rather, eyes that popped, that were unhealthily shiny. I looked round the room and thought how unattractive the men looked. Most of them bore a remarkable resemblance to Lord Carrington, or, even worse, though possibly not so arid, Kissinger. Edwin's professor, the one he was talking to, had one of those low fat bottoms, his crotch seemed too near the floor, and I wondered where his legs parted – surely not so low down as that? I imagined him walking, straddle-stepped, as if he'd wet his knickers.

Phyllis Thackray was looking sourly across the room at her husband, who was guffawing at a male joke. He was tanned, with a seamed, sailor's face and thick greying hair. He was a womanizer, you could tell that. So when he went to these wife-and-husband parties he left the women alone. That's one sort of womanizer. At these parties, we weren't his sort of women, we didn't send out signals. The Nerinas and Vincenzas didn't often attend this sort of party, it was too boring for them.

Phyllis called across the room, 'Derek, your fly's unzipped.'

She said it with hate, and lit a cigarette fiercely.

Derek, caught in mid-joke, carried on talking and zipped himself up casually, not even looking in her direction.

9

'If I'd been one of his students, he'd have blushed,' said Phyllis. She said it out loud, looking straight ahead, speaking to everybody, or nobody, and I'd been relieved that it was a statement, and didn't require an answer.

'What does it feel like, being a JP?' One of the wives had come up and stood, sherry in hand, and asked her, for she did not circulate, didn't Phyllis. No. People came across the room if they wanted to talk to her.

'It feels the same as usual. What did you think it would feel like?'

'We'll have to stand up when you come into court,' said the wife. 'Doesn't that give you a feeling of power?'

'No.'

'Well, don't you feel uncomfortable, meting out punishment under some of the Tory laws?'

'Look, I'm just there to see the laws carried out.'

'How would you feel if there was a Fascist government and you had to carry out the law?'

'Oh, for heaven's sake,' said Phyllis Thackray. 'Everyone asks the same questions.'

'Does that invalidate them?'

But Phyllis got up, not answering, and began to shoulder her way towards the bar, which was at the other side of the room. She didn't return, possibly because the other wife took her place. 'That worked,' said the other wife, as she sat down. 'My feet are killing me.'

Nerina was speaking to me.

'You used to work here?' she was asking.

But I didn't want to talk about it. 'It was a long time ago,' I said.

They all looked at me for a moment, then they turned away.

Except for Hilde. She said, 'Show me your hands,' and when I held my hands out, she said, 'It was a long time ago, you are right.' For my hands were smooth and white.

Hilde also saw that my hands were ringless. I saw her

10

noting this, and I folded my hands prissily and put them on my lap.

'Hilde, darling.' Vincenza turned her full attention on the Alsatian. 'When are you coming to see me for our booze-up?'

Hilde laughed, a deep booming laugh. 'Any time and all the time I am willing to do that,' she said.

'I'll phone,' said Vincenza. She stood up, and I knew we were going.

Derek Thackray had moved to a pouffe which he had placed beside Nerina, the lady of Shallot.

He smiled an absent goodbye to us, then turned back to the sofa. Nerina bent her long white neck, shallot-like, and her hair fell over his hand.

Hilde came to the door with us. She exchanged looks with Vincenza.

'My dear!' she said, and her eyes tilted upwards. 'All this loving. It is too much!'

Vincenza put her arm round Hilde's shoulders and hugged her. 'You are the perfect mother,' she said. 'What other daughter could entertain her lover with her mother present?'

Hilde's bottom lip stuck out, like a child's.

'Darling, it is not easy,' she said. 'I can tell you.'

Vincenza laughed. 'You'll manage, my darling,' she said.

We walked back to the car.

I was looking at the 'barn', as Nerina had referred to it. It had never been a barn. It was a cowshed, and it was where I had learned to milk my first cow. Now its doors were partly open, and I could see the stone floor, and the sill that had been partitioned for the eight beasts. But the partitions were there no longer.

A huge shadow hovered a few feet above the floor, propped by chocks of timber. Derek Thackray's boat floated in mid-air, its clinker-built hull painted in Cornish blue that came to an arbitrary finish where, I supposed, his tin of paint had run out.

Idle hours of titivating, where Henshaw, or Hens, as I

had called him, had struggled for a living, milking his eight cows by hand, showing me how, till they calved and he could use the machine again.

I had gone by then.

He was bad-tempered and taciturn, yet he had been a good teacher. I was the only one of us who hadn't been afraid of him.

Now, picking my way between slates and window-frames, I heard a voice singing among the soft noises of the long-dead beasts. My own voice. For he had told me the cows would let their milk down more readily if they were contented. And Hens' cows were musical.

What tunes had I sung to them? I tried to remember as we neared my car. There would have been no words. I could never remember the words to tunes.

Hens had been a policeman, before he was a farmer. He'd fallen for a greengrocer's wife, had even gone to live with her. But he had left her, according to his wife, Cissy, because she had refused to darn his socks.

I opened the car door. Strange how little things date you. What woman darned socks nowadays?

Hens had gone back to his wife. Did he think she'd forgiven him? I wondered now. Because she had not. Every meal I helped her with, every time we searched for eggs together, she told me about it, how hard done by she was, how unfaithful Hens had been, what a hussy the greengrocer's wife was.

They had come here to start a new life, relying on Hens' policeman's pension, because he had done his time around then. But it wasn't really a new life, because Cissy chewed the old one over and over, she never forgot it, not, I believe, for one moment. It became a part of her life, a sort of voyeur's fascination, she thought of it over and over, Hens' unfaithfulness. She never spoke of anything else, except her sister's conversion to the Latter-day Saints.

Vincenza sat in the car watching me. 'Difficult to imagine it being a working farm,' she said.

'Difficult to imagine it *not* being,' I said, and this made

12

her look at me harder, for it was the nearest I'd been to showing any assertiveness.

We drove slowly away down the almost derelict track, where we had jogged with the tractor, with our humble couple of churns, every morning and evening.

At the junction with the road the stand which we had cemented for the churns was still there, disused for ever now, I supposed.

Why did Vincenza bother with me? Why did I bother with Vincenza? Why, for that matter, does anyone bother with anybody outside their own family?

So I pondered, as we drove back over the fells, through the wood, and over the bridge, and Vincenza sat chatting on about Nerina, whose privacy she had so respected in her presence.

'You were marvellous,' she told me. 'You were so right that she's uncomfortable in body and spirit.'

For, as Vincenza said to me, where Nerina was concerned the vagina ruled the spirit, and Nerina was having trouble with this sensitive part of her anatomy. (You see how hard it is to be totally exact in novels, at least until you are more experienced than me at writing them. Vincenza didn't say 'vagina', because she rightly preferred Anglo-Saxon words, as I do myself. But I cannot bring myself to write down that crude-sounding word the Saxons apparently used for our private part, so readers will have to substitute it for themselves, if they are seeking true realism.)

Vincenza even went so far as to suggest that Nerina's broken big toe was psychosomatic, a method of deterring Derek Thackray from the otherwise inevitable love-making which at present would be very painful, even impossible, for his suffering would-be mistress. 'It's gone all hard and dried-up, sort of shrunk,' Vincenza said, affecting sympathy. 'Poor Nerina has to use a ghastly device to sort of stretch it every few hours.'

'It would show up on X-ray, if she hadn't really broken it,' I said, referring, of course, to the big toe.

This was getting too practical for Vincenza in her present mood.

'It's just amazing how *accurate* you are,' she said, referring to our visit to Nerina's. 'Of course, none of us *believes* in any of it.'

'No,' I said, agreeing with her.

'Yet it's uncanny, strange.'

And *that's* why they bothered with me.

*Faith in one's
own talent
increases*

♡♣◇♤ **Chapter 2** ♡♣◇♤
Nine of Clubs

Although all that I have written so far is accurate, it is inaccurate because of what I have missed out.

We swerved round a corner. As usual I had taken my shoes off to drive. I have always done that. In that way you maintain at least minimal contact with the lethal machine you are controlling. My shoes, or in this case, sandals, shifted back from the passenger's side of the car floor, the hard wooden sole and heel cut warningly under my clutch foot, and I kicked sharply sideways, sending the sandal back to Vincenza's feet.

I looked in the mirror. My handbag was still safely jammed on the back window-ledge, the highest storage place in the car. I looked away, at the road, where the village was coming into sight. I had surprised myself, for I had been concerned, as we swept round that corner, about a pack of playing-cards.

I had instinctively been observing the custom, no, I must call it superstition, that these cards should be kept as high as possible, above mundane earthly things. Inside the darkness of my handbag, they sat safe in their silk bag secured with a silken cord.

Silk? Silk? I had used the remnants of fabric from an Indian silk shirt I'd made Edwin; a cartomancer's cards should be respected and cherished.

That was why I was in the car with Vincenza; that was why we had visited Nerina. I had been telling their fortunes. It had never been my privilege to meet such people. Now it was, and for that I had to thank the cards.

I decelerated at Vincenza's house in the main street. Another wave of dismay had swept over me. What was I doing? And for what? What sort of a life had I concocted for myself, where reality slipped further and further from me – and what 'me' was it slipping from? Most of the time I enjoyed my life. But these thoughts did come creeping into my mind from time to time.

'. . . really fancy Ferg,' Vincenza was saying. 'He fascinates me. He's impotent, I'm nearly sure, but that's a challenge.'

I slowed the car down by stone troughs of marigold and lobelia that Vincenza had arranged on the pavement outside her house.

Her only child, Martin, who I guessed was about ten years old, was looking out of the window, very still and pale, with fine blond curls. His face showed no expression.

'. . . he'll be in the Friars' Arms by now,' Vincenza was saying. 'He's always first in at opening-time.'

'Charming.'

'Ah, well, he *is* as a matter of fact. He'd love to meet you.'

'You mean he'd love to have his fortune told?'

I wondered if they'd get such a buzz from my cartomancy if I made them pay for it.

'Come on!' said Vincenza.

And here was the temptation. Even as I saw the doubt come into Martin's eyes, his fingers tighten, so little, on the curtain lining, I knew that, yes, I was going to go with Vincenza to the Friars' to meet this Ferg about whom she

16

was enthusing. I had to. For if he existed, as likely as not he would become one of the characters in my novel, which would clearly benefit from the addition of an impotent alcoholic.

I let out the clutch, and we began to move away. Vincenza didn't look at her house. The curtain fell back into place, and Martin's face faded, bodiless, back into the darkness of the room behind him.

There are a few parts of this book that I don't enjoy writing. The pain and disappointment of children hurts me.

We drove down the street to the Friars'. Its door stood open, even though it was only five o'clock, for the Friars' Arms was a hotel rather than a pub, so that it was harder to judge its infringement of licensing laws.

Across the road great iron gates were wide open, in the process of being re-painted. Black. Beyond them, a drive stretched away behind dumpy wooded hills covered now in bluebells. The blackened stone of the Friary rose behind them.

Recently, in the past five years, I believe, the Friary had been bought in a state of disrepair by a computer magnate from Clacton, who converted it into luxury flats. That was before Edwin and I came to live in the village. Above the brand-new turrets of the roof a conservatory rose, the anachronistic lid on the whole building. Below, cut into the hill, a row of eight garages with white up-and-over doors had been constructed.

In another age these might have been monks, these executives who drove their cars up the drive to these garages, and deposited wives laden with packages and children at the shallow steps that led to the studded door of the Friary.

Vincenza nodded across to it. 'Ferg lives there,' she said. 'A tiny little flat somewhere round the back. Costs him the earth.'

We pushed open the inner door of the hotel on our way to meet him, Ferg.

Or, as I had known him till now, Ferguson Baverstock,

17

Assistant Registrar at the seat of learning that succoured us all.

Everybody looked pale today, possibly because of the sunlight. I cannot speak for Vincenza, for any pallor she might have had was well concealed behind her make-up. Nerina had been pale and shallot-like. Martin was pale and unhappy.

Ferg was pale and ill.

He was far younger than I had expected. Perhaps he was thirty, possibly a little older. Or perhaps he was still in his twenties. It is not people's chronological age that I am good at judging. When people spoke of him, somehow they implied he was older than this.

I knew he was profligate, everybody had told me that. So I had expected him to be fat, or at least thickened. But he was slim and elegant, with a narrow face and fair hair. His hair surprised me most, I think. It was long, well onto his shoulders. It was fine, mouse-coloured hair, curled gracefully at the tips. It was not, consulting my list of stereotypes, the hair of an administrator, or a registrar. And his eyes were the colour of his hair, pale and hazel.

He was drinking beer out of a tankard, and talking to Armitage, our local butcher, who sat with him quite at ease. Both looked up momentarily as we came in. But so did everybody else, we expected it.

Then Ferg went on talking to Mr Armitage, and suddenly I realized that our entry, or rather Vincenza's entry, had meant nothing to him. He didn't recognize her, had perhaps never seen her before.

Vincenza went to the bar. 'What'll you have?' she asked me, hardly looking at Ferg, and we had the usual no-I'll-pay contretemps that men never seem to get involved in at bars.

Finally we came away with our drinks, and Vincenza moved towards Ferg's table.

'Hel*lo*!' she called, long before she reached it, so that she caused a lull in the attention of these early drinkers, still sober, with their desultory conversation not yet oiled.

Ferg, when he realized the booming man-like voice was

addressing him, paused in mid-sentence, his hand round his tankard. His face stayed politely blank, and he watched us cross the Axminster towards him.

'I'm Vincenza Corylan, we met at the VC's reception last Tuesday,' she said.

'Psychology,' said Ferg.

Vincenza's husband was Professor of Psychology.

She sighed. 'One is known by the sins of one's husband,' she said.

She sat down at the table, while Ferg and Mr Armitage watched, almost, it seemed to me, disbelieving this onslaught on their male fastness.

Vincenza turned to me.

'This is May,' she said. She got hold of my sleeve hard, so that I felt the give of the material, and to avoid its splitting I had little choice but to sit down.

'May who?' Ferg asked me, turning away from Vincenza.

I said nothing.

'May Knott,' said Vincenza, glad to poach the ball. 'And we don't talk about it, if you don't mind. May's heard all the cracks already.'

Armitage missed the point of her remark. A slow smile of malice lit his face.

'May Knott. Well, there's always a chance, then!'

No one laughed. They were too sophisticated for that. That's how it was. Vincenza and Nerina had changed their names, and I stuck with mine.

'May tells fortunes,' said Vincenza.

And immediately their faces changed. They smiled, of course, taking it all with a pinch of salt. But they had changed. It was nearly the same as telling them you were a doctor; they wanted your attention the same as that. They want you to tell them what to do about things. Doctors, fortune-tellers, they engender the same sort of feelings in most people, though we pretend that they don't.

Ferg said, 'What are you drinking?' And he was asking me, even though I still had a Martini in my hand.

I said I was going soon and didn't want anything else, and so, almost reluctantly, he turned and asked Vincenza, who asked for another whisky.

'Where's your crystal ball, May Knott?' asked Armitage.

Vincenza answered for me.

'She tells cards. She's very good. It's amazing.'

It certainly was.

'Just ordinary playing-cards,' said Vincenza.

But the cards are not ordinary. The cards were there before Tarot. They are the year, the seasons, life and death, the whole feel of nature is there in the cards, male, female, light and darkness, it is all there.

'It's a hobby,' I said. 'It's nothing.'

Ferg looked at me, half-smiling.

'Magic,' he said. 'Witch doctors. It's all *something*. Even if you were to lie through your teeth every time you told your cards, you would still have power to alter events. Do you realize that?'

'It's not really serious. I learnt it from a book.'

'You may have learnt it,' said Vincenza, who wasn't going to be left out of this. 'But it goes deeper than that. You've got the gift.'

I wanted to go. The talk of gifts made me feel uncomfortable. Learning to read the cards was a simple matter, not very different from learning by rote. And interrelating a few things.

'Anybody can do it,' I said.

'Not like you, they can't,' said Vincenza.

Ferg wasn't listening to her. He smiled into his drink. Then he smiled at Armitage.

'What method do you use?' he asked me.

Of course he would know all about cards. He knew all about everything. He was the darling of the Establishment, the after-dinner speaker, the Double First in Classics at Oxford. He could talk about anything, anything at all. I thought that he would even beat the housewives and taxi-drivers at *Mastermind*.

'It depends what you want,' I said, answering his

question. 'I generally prefer the Mystic Cross. Sometimes I use the Horseshoe.'

'The Horseshoe,' said Ferg. 'The gipsies' layout.'

'Do you play the mouth-organ?' I asked him, and at last he looked, just for a moment, impressed.

'Extraordinary!' said Vincenza. How did you know?'

But I hadn't known. It had been a joke with myself that here I was with one of those people who could turn their hand to anything, who knew a lot about everything. The question had been ironic; there must be something, I had thought, that he can't do.

But there didn't seem to be.

'Anybody,' said Ferg, 'can play the mouth-organ.'

'And anybody,' I replied, 'can read the cards.'

We were back where we started.

I went then, leaving Vincenza to walk home down the street on her own, I have no idea how much later.

I wonder if Martin was still awake when she got back.

*Below contentment
runs an undercurrent
of unease*

♡♣◇♤ **Chapter 3** ♡♣◇♤
Ten of Diamonds

Our house was not in the centre of the village. It was tacked on in its enclave of closes, crescents and views; new bungalows, new semis. But we lived in a more expensive detached house with a large garden all round it. It was petite but stylish, and all our immediate neighbours looked up to Edwin because of it, and called him the Professor.

Inside, the house had parquet flooring that was coming unstuck in little bits that we had become tired of sticking down again.

Mostly we were surrounded by retired people, or schoolteachers, though a few of our neighbours were in business. One managed a Lunch-o-fax warehouse and had a motor-boat that he took on the Mere every week-end.

'What do you *do* on a motor-boat?' I had asked his wife once. Even though the Mere is very large, I couldn't see the enjoyment in going round and round it for a whole week-end.

'We get drunk,' she'd said, as if it was a silly question.

A crowd of drunk Lunch-o-fax managers careening round a lake in motor-boats seemed a strange method of enjoyment to me. But it is probably entertaining to watch, and I mean to go down there some time and observe – from the shore.

Edwin's car was in the driveway. I swung round and pulled up behind him with panache. My handbag fell onto the back seat, and I reached back to pick it up almost before it had landed.

I walked past the kitchen window. Edwin, beating egg for the predictable Edwin-omelette, saw me, and came to the door to open it. He didn't open the door gallantly. He opened it because he was glad to see me, I think.

We kissed. I like it when Edwin gets home first. Even if it means chewing his omelette for supper.

I told him where I'd been, and his face opened up, because it pleased him that I was mixing with some of the interesting wives.

But when I told him I'd been reading the cards for them, he frowned.

'I wish you wouldn't,' he said.

'It's only in fun,' I said. 'It's not serious.'

'It could get you into an awkward situation.'

He turned back to the stove and the smell of burning egg, and I rummaged about under the sink, looking for the air freshener.

I told him how I had met Ferg at the Friars' Arms. I told him about everything except Nerina's vagina. Of all the things I told him, the colour of Nerina's bathroom seemed to amuse him the most.

We ate our supper that was delicately tinted with air freshener.

'How much did you write today?' he asked me, referring to my novel, which had reached page twenty-three.

'Not much. I was garnering material,' I said, and he looked uncomfortable, clearly worried that I had libellous intent. Then he cheered up, possibly because he remembered there was little chance of publication.

23

'You're very good to me,' I said.

Edwin is my patron. He keeps me and encourages me in my art. If I didn't live with him, I should starve.

Some of my friends have told me I am no better than a whore, living off Edwin. That's because I am a woman artist patronized by a man, and because I sleep with him. In fact Edwin gets rather a better deal in return for his patronage than, say, Verrio's patrons did. For he drank their cellars dry and finished up with such a state of DTs that he could only paint pictures of Hell.

I have not painted our palace walls with devils or demons, and I am doing my utmost to achieve a good verbal portrait of Edwin, my patron. However, there is the unsatisfactory detail that nothing I have written so far has been published, which no one mentions, though I suspect they are all thinking about it.

If I could prove myself successful, they would all forgive me for living with Edwin. But there again, if I was successful, it wouldn't be necessary to live with him.

After our meal I did the washing-up, and watched from the window above the sink as Edwin cut the hedge. He did this with infuriating little jabs with the shears, rather than a smooth sweeping movement. The blades of the shears snapped open and closed, making a sound like an irritable jackdaw with no sense of rhythm, and the skin of the hedge looked as lumpy as if it had suffered a recent attack of smallpox.

But I shall not complain to Edwin about his habits, as in a way I am his guest, and to complain would be discourteous. In any case he would tell me to cut the damned hedge myself, and this would be a nuisance, as my hands blister very readily nowadays.

Presently the phone rang, and I went into Edwin's study to answer it.

'Hullo,' I said.

And a voice said, 'Professor Harley?'

Now most callers would know that Professor Harley, Edwin, is a man, so for the first time ever I got some idea of how it would feel to be able to say yes, I was a

24

professor, and I thought what a satisfying sensation if I could.

I was so occupied thinking about this that I didn't ask who was speaking. I went to fetch Edwin from the garden, and took over the shearing of the pockmarked hedge, trying my hand at a skin-graft.

Edwin came back very soon. He took the shears from me.

'It was for you, really,' he said.

No one ever rang me up, except my mother, who worked some sort of fiddle on the switchboard at the Queen's Hotel in Leeds, where she was a chambermaid.

'For me? Who was it?'

'Ferguson bloody Baverstock. You left your scarf at the Friars' Arms.'

'Oh.'

I hadn't been wearing a scarf.

'Why on earth do you go round telling everyone you're called May Knott?'

This was a sore topic with Edwin.

'Because that's my name.'

He would have liked me to call myself Harley, to save embarrassment.

Edwin is not an argumentative person, so he didn't answer. If he had, he would have said that I should accept at least that I was called May Thompson, rather than May Knott, which he thought of as a touch of melodrama on my part.

Knott was the name I was born with. It was my mother's surname. May was the name she gave me. My adoptive parents kept this name in deference to my natural mother, and because they liked it. I found out about Knott when I was sixteen, and have assumed the name ever since.

Before we came here, two years ago, Edwin was pleased that I kept my name. He was, after all, only my patron.

Night fell, and we left the garden and went inside. Edwin went to his study, where he was writing a paper for a university conference that was being held in Dresden next June.

I went upstairs to the boxroom that I privately thought of as a garret, though it was centrally heated and close-carpeted, and there wasn't an orange-box in sight.

I didn't turn on the light. I sat at the desk and looked out of the window into the dusk. I could see the dark outline of the tors, and below them the lights of a few hill farms. In the distance a steam train blew its whistle. I got up and opened the window. Next door the lights were on in the billiard-room extension, as I had expected. The train drew nearer, until its sound crashed through the hedge at the end of our garden and rushed across our lawn and out of sight.

That would be the Flying Scotsman on its record-breaking run between King's Cross and York in 1938, I supposed.

My neighbour's son appeared at the double-glazed open doors of the billard room, and I ducked out of sight. I didn't want him to imagine that I had been deceived by his stereo and his silly recording, as I had been the first time I heard it.

I settled down to write, in the cosy pink light of my table-lamp.

I wrote about this farm-girl who lived with a professor, and formed a nearly platonic relationship with an impotent alcoholic.

Downstairs, Edwin had stopped working, and had turned on the television.

26

*This is a
time for giving*

♡♣◇♤ **Chapter 4** ♡♣◇♤
Ten of Hearts

I had first met Vincenza Corylan about fifteen months
ago, at a keep-fit class in the village Memorial Hall.

'You're a wife, aren't you?' she'd asked me, during a
short hiatus while a strip-light was swept in shards from
the floor after an over-exuberant toss of the Indian clubs.

It was a reasonable, though irritating, assumption.
She was asking if I was a university wife, of course. Our
village clung by its fingernails to its status. A few more
wives like her, and it would be entirely composed of
converted buildings and commuters and turn into a
suburb. At the moment it just managed to balance nicely,
for us incomers at least, between the original inhabitants,
most of whom had been born here and worked near by,
and Us.

I said I wasn't exactly a wife, but was living with Edwin,
and she smiled and apologized, saying that 'wife' was an
outmoded word, when you thought about it.

Vincenza apologized a lot, and readily took the blame
for things. Consequently it was necessary to spend a great

deal of time reassuring her that things weren't her fault. Quite soon I shall stop reassuring her, and see what happens.

When I went to have coffee with her the next day, she told me that she was a Principal Child Care Officer.

Which is why I stood, fifteen months later, outside a terrace-house whose flaked door bore the marks of many kickings. Vincenza had initiated me into what I privately considered to be my most obscene indulgence. She had persuaded me to become a member of the Child Care Support Team. Which, put more simply, meant that I was that most artificial of all beings, a Voluntary Social Worker. Which meant that I did the same work as she did, but didn't get paid for it. Which meant that I could make a botch-up of things and someone else would pick up the pieces.

I felt guilty about being a voluntary worker. I was quite sure my motives were suspect. And why was I playing Lady Bountiful when I could be earning money and supporting myself?

These things I pondered, standing on the pavement outside this nearly derelict house. At the partly boarded windows, the curtains were drawn. Not only was this Child Care caper time-consuming in my life as a novelist, but it didn't even add to the store of my experience, for I couldn't bring myself to incorporate it into my story for reasons that were almost professional. Worse, from time to time the cases I became involved with intruded so far into my consciousness that I couldn't get them out, and I blamed them for clogging the springs of my creativity.

I knocked again, or rather, I banged with the flat of my hand. I had been there about ten minutes. One or two doors down the street were open, and women stood there watching me. They knew as well as I did that Judy was at home.

I picked up a piece of broken glass from the gutter and slung it at the upstairs window.

'Judy!' I called. 'Come on down, you dozy bugger.'

I wasn't a particularly good voluntary worker, but I was

28

certainly an impatient one, and I had driven into town specially to see my wayward client.

It began to rain. I went back to my car and sounded the horn persistently. At doorways the women shifted their positions. It was not clear to me whose side they were on, mine or Judy's. More likely they were simply bored out of their minds and looking for entertainment.

I touched up my eye make-up in the car mirror.

The door of Number Ten opened. At first it shuddered like a fat man laughing, for it was damp and swollen. Then it burst wide and Judy stood there in a see-through nightie of pale blue nylon, well stained with tea, lager, or worse. Above her scuffed slippers her thin legs were marked with raised blobs in various stages, some recent, red and sore, others with purple scabs, some faded to pink shiny scars. Insect bites.

Judy peered at me with no enthusiasm.

'I was asleep,' she said, and it was a reprimand.

It was one-thirty p.m.

She ran her fingers through her hair, then she stepped back. Behind her, on the stairs, her two children clung to the banister.

'Well I really am sorry to disturb you and your hangover,' I said, and Judy laughed, because she never minded me knowing about her drinking habits, or about Arnie's, her husband's, either.

'Hey, Bella!' I called, and Bella, aged six, smiled, twisting herself to the banisters with shyness, then coming downstairs.

'Hello, Auntie May,' she said.

I picked her up, and she twisted her arms round my neck and put her cool soft cheek next to mine. Her knickers were damp and she smelt of sick and urine.

'Mind May's dress,' said Judy, and she flicked at my dress with her hand, smoothing it down.

'It's okay,' I said, which it was, because the dresses I chose to wear on these visits were enduring and washable. And, at the worst, disposable.

I held Bella away from me and looked at her.

29

'What did you do to your eye?' I asked. Which was tactful, because it was unlikely that Bella had inflicted a black eye on herself.

The bruising extended across her cheekbone. Her eyelid had the remains of sore puffiness that was now subsiding.

She saw me looking and hid her face in my shoulder.

'She fell off the bed,' said Judy, and she gave me a conspiratorial look. Don't tell on me, the look said.

I was all sympathy. 'Oh, dear. How did you do that? You tell me, Bella, how did you fall off the bed and bump your eye?'

There was a pause. I walked further into the house, and behind me Judy closed the front door.

Daren, aged eight, stood by the newel post, grinning, probably at his mother's slight discomfiture, or at the family conspiracy not to tell me who'd hit Bella. I ruffled his hair as I passed, in the true Voluntary Social Worker manner.

I went into the 'room', where an enormous fire was burning, even though outside was warm. A vast damp mark spread up the wall behind the sofa and under the window. Arnie got the coal from somewhere, I never knew where, and the fire burned all the time, big and warm and dangerous.

'Where's Arnie?' I asked, and Judy said he was 'helping' his friend with some window-cleaning.

I feared for Arnie, earning his casual money and collecting Welfare.

'Someone'll shop him, sooner or later,' I warned.

'He doesn't work near here,' said Judy, accepting that those who know you best are your worst enemies.

When I first started my visits to Judy, Arnie had been in prison and had been no concern of mine. My brief had been to support Judy, because it was feared she would never be able to keep the home together without him.

Arnie's original crime had been to break open the electric meter. This crime was easily detected by the meter-reader, and the electricity supply to the house had been cut off. Arnie didn't go to prison for this. The Electricity Board still at that time harboured the faint hope that he would pay them back, in slow instalments, what he owed them. But Arnie saw no justice in paying them money for electricity he had already used and which he was no longer receiving. He re-connected the supply, and was reported by a neighbour who saw his light on, and for this he was sent to prison, owing the Board well over a thousand pounds.

Judy was left to provide for the two children, in a damp house and with no electricity, for, despite the intervention of the social services, the Electricity Board still refused to re-connect her.

Now Arnie was out of prison and still the electricity was cut off. Arnie might have paid his debt to society but he hadn't paid the Electricity Board, so they tried to recoup by refusing to re-connect him unless he paid an exorbitant re-connection fee.

On the mantelpiece a candle bent forwards, softened by the heat of the fire. Drips of wax were building up on the broken tiles of the fireplace, and behind the mantelpiece spread a growing area of blackened wallpaper spattered with candle wax.

'Cuppa tea?' asked Judy, the blacking of Bella's eye now behind her. I tried to look pleased and said yes, that would be nice.

What was I doing here? I was a spy, that was all. I should have to report Bella's black eye. I despised myself.

Bella came and sat on my knee, and Daren sat beside me on the broken-down sofa.

What I was doing was Giving Support.

'Why aren't you at school?' I asked the children, though it was clear that no one would send their child to school with the sort of black eye that Bella had been landed.

'Looking after our mum,' said Daren, the practised little liar, and loyal member of this family group.

'What's wrong with you, Judy?' I called through to the kitchen, and there was a silent pause in the clattering, as

31

Judy unearthed a cup for me, no doubt from under piles of dirty newspapers and old chip pans.

'What d'you mean, what's wrong with me? Nothing's wrong with me. What's wrong with *you*?' Judy's voice was raucous with scorn.

I looked accusingly at Daren, who was watching me think. He grinned, undismayed as ever by the uncovering of his lie.

Vincenza had told me Judy's story, or I should say, she had given me Judy's case history, and here it is.

Judy's mother, soon after Judy was born, had become so mentally ill that she had spent the rest of her life in a Mental Hospital, leaving Judy to be looked after by her granny. But at the age of six, Judy was certified as sufficiently subnormal to become resident permanently in a Special Hospital, as it was known.

And there she stayed, for twelve years, until there was a change in the law, and many patients were released, including Judy, who, at the age of eighteen, went to live with her married sister in Stafford.

But married sisters have husbands, and Judy's sister's husband was out of work more than he was in it.

Judy herself wasn't expected to work until the social worker thought she was sufficiently integrated into society again. So, for a few months, she was at home alone with her sister's husband.

Wouldn't you have guessed what would happen next if you'd been the social worker?

Great was the furore when her sister discovered that Judy was pregnant. And it was even greater when she beat her to get the father's name, which Judy kept on insisting was her sister's husband. Her sister refused to believe this, and Judy was thrown out of the house. She had her baby, Daren, in a hostel. Presently she was pregnant again. This time she had no idea who the father was.

She met Arnie in a pub, and a relationship began, which had, when I first met her, lasted six years.

Constantly in trouble, loathed by the rest of the street, buttressed, within its limitations, by the DHSS, somehow or other the unit had survived till now, even through Arnie's prison stay.

When I'd first gone to visit she had been completely indifferent to me, though never really rude, for she had a crude code of survival that warned her I was part of the side that dealt in hand-outs.

She had tried to borrow money from me, often with stories of starvation, children in rags, freezing bedrooms, and so on. All these stories may well have been true, but early on I made the rule that I would never give her money, and I never did.

Now she called me her best friend, which saddened me, as well as making me uncomfortable, and I sometimes hoped that all the other probation officers, social workers, health visitors, and so on, who came to the house were also best friends, so that I didn't have to carry the responsibility on my own.

Once I asked Vincenza, who said no, she certainly hadn't been designated as a best friend, quite the opposite, and had I given Judy money?

I rocked Bella on my knee in front of the great extravagant fire, and Judy produced my tea proudly, in a filthy beaker. She was dressed now, in brown nylon trousers. Her stomach, devoid of all muscle, lurched out, straining the waistband. She wore one of Arnie's – I supposed – shirts. I didn't think Judy ever washed her clothes. She appeared to wear them till they dropped off, then she went to the DHSS for a complete re-fit.

So I thought, but I was wrong, as I found out when she handed me my tea.

'Oops, I'm in trouble again,' she said, and laughed, not caring.

'What's up, then?'

'Daft cow at the Laundrette got me for putting silver foil in the machine.'

'What did you do that for?'

Judy looked at me, impressed by my ignorance.

'You know. Instead of a coin. Well, I'd run out of fifty pees. And anyway, it's a racket at that place. She never has the water hot enough.'

'What's she going to do to you?'

Judy shrugged.

'Don't care what she bloody does. Says I've not to go there any more.'

'What'll you do?' I asked, thinking this deprivation wouldn't make much difference.

'I'll go to the one up the hill,' said Judy. She laughed again. 'It's nearer the pub anyway.'

There was a tapping at the window, and Arnie stood there, laughing at us, and I knew he was pleased to see me.

Both children rushed out of the room to tell him.

'Look what Auntie May's brought!'

Because I forgot to mention that I carried this do-gooding to extremes, and had made Daren a birthday cake, which was why I'd come here today, to give it to him.

Now I wished I'd pushed it under the door, if such a thing was possible, and driven silently away, for I felt – as I often did at this house – more damagingly fraudulent than usual.

'Oh, May, you are lovely!' said Judy impulsively, and once again I marvelled that anyone could ever have consigned her for all those years to a mental hospital. Not, I hope, because she thought I was lovely, but because her behaviour was often quite normal, and if Judy was mentally retarded, then so must a significant proportion of the population be.

'Had to come home,' said Arnie. 'That Mrs Corylan was visiting down the street we were working, so I bunked off.'

This told me something I had wondered about – that I was privileged to know that Arnie cleaned windows while receiving social security payments, and Vincenza was not.

I touched Bella's eye lightly with my fingers, and Arnie saw me and grinned.

'She fell downstairs,' he said, and as Judy contradicted him, I gave my warning,

'She'd better not. She'd better not fall downstairs,' I said, and I felt for the first time that I had become a thin membrane of protection for Judy's children, even for Judy, possibly the only person they still wanted to impress with friendliness.

Well, I was a good cook, and they liked my cake.

I'd brought Daren a birthday card too.

'Isn't that nice of Auntie May?' said Judy, and she asked me to read all the writing on it out loud, for she couldn't read at all herself, not even her own name.

After a reasonable – judged by me – time had elapsed, I thought I had earned the right to go.

I stood up, and the family accepted immediately that this was my right. I was the one who decided the terms of my 'support', and its boundaries.

'See you next Wednesday,' I said. The idea was that I always came on Wednesdays, no matter what, unless I was away on holiday.

Judy and Arnie never went away, not much further than the other end of town, except once when Judy got a job at a motorway service station and had to be bussed there and back. But that hadn't lasted long.

'Give Auntie May a goodbye kiss,' said Judy.

They all waited on the pavement as I drove away, because I always sounded my horn for them when I got to the end of the road and drove out of sight.

I did this as usual, and as usual, looking in my driving mirror, I saw them all double over with laughter.

All part of the cuddly routine, though I could never see why it was so funny, myself.

*Early summer heralds
a burgeoning
romance*

♡♣◇♤ **Chapter 5** ♡♣◇♤

Jack of Hearts

But I had more serious things on my mind, and matters which interested me far more than Judy and her family.

Ferguson Baverstock had occupied my mind ever since Vincenza and I had met him at the Friars'. And he owed me a non-existent scarf which I had every intention of collecting.

I had phoned him once at work, but his secretary had answered and told me he was at a meeting. She hadn't asked who I was. I guessed that she was used to women phoning him on personal matters.

'Can I take a message?' she'd asked, and this is what I'd said: no thank you, it's a personal matter.

It wasn't often that I went onto the campus. If I was in the town, I usually had lunch at the pub on the riverside where they served vegetarian meals. But I knew I wouldn't find Ferg there, and it was Ferg that I was looking for.

I was going through that romantic foreplay in the unrolling of a relationship where you begin to frequent the places where the object of your affection may, even on an extreme outside chance, be encountered.

At this stage I had to give myself a reason for my mooning about. I would not admit, even to myself, that bumping into Ferg was my ultimate goal.

Therefore I discovered this imperative need to delve into the sociology of futurism. This meant I had to visit the university library. I knew that nothing would be lost if I didn't find Ferg, which I hardly expected to, and face would be saved.

I crossed the river. A Swedish ship was unloading wood at the quay. The pilot boat was moored by the harbour light, waiting for the tide to flow. All was peaceful and summery, and for a moment I was tempted away from my goal. It seemed too good a day to spend on the draughty cement campus, picking my way between gollups of vomit, chasing some ineffectual male drunk.

Then I steeled myself. What was this faint-heartedness, this apathetic attitude to the titillation of an asexual relationship? And what about my novel?

I parked in the underground car park, and I was running up the steps to the main concourse, Guinevere Oval, when I met Edwin coming in the other direction.

'May!' He seemed pleased to see me, and quite surprised. He said it was lucky he'd bumped into me, as he was just coming home, and we'd have missed each other.

He assumed, but modestly, that I had come to see him. Or at least that, if I had come for some other purpose, I would have finished up by coming to see him.

That seemed like the end of my first attempt to meet Ferg. I told Edwin that I had come to look at the exhibition of Fascist Art that was being held in the Green Knight Gallery. Edwin was pleased about this. He liked me to have cultural pursuits. He said he'd come with me.

Ferg was coming out of the entrance as we went in.

'What a coincidence!' I said. 'I've been trying to phone you to get my scarf back.'

37

'I know,' said Ferg. Presumably his secretary had mentioned that I'd rung.

Someone buttonholed Edwin, who excused himself and moved to one side to talk to them.

'What colour was the scarf?' I asked Ferg.

His eyes closed slightly. He looked serious.

'What colour would you like it to be?' he asked.

He'd been drinking. I could smell whisky in a small aura around him.

'Orange is a nice colour,' I said, and he laughed.

'Right.'

Edwin came back, and Ferg waved to us both politely and went out into the quadrangle.

'It's coming along, I suppose,' said Edwin, who had read to page thirty-eight. 'Though I'm not sure where it's leading.'

Nor was I.

'Am I in it?' he asked.

I said no one in particular was in it. That's how novelists work, I said, they take a bit from here and a bit from there, and weave it into a completely different pattern.

'I suppose you put the Ferg character in for sex interest?'

'Well, for non-sex interest so far, you might say.'

'But she's interested in him sexually, isn't she?'

'Do you think so?'

It struck me that he was afraid everyone would think he'd been cuckolded. I was surprised, and foresaw difficulties.

'It's just a novel,' I said.

Edwin's face still looked set and worried. Patronage must be hitting him rather harder than he'd expected, I thought.

'Avalon's an inappropriate name for a university,' he said.

I had been pleased with it.

'I don't think I'll change that. It was the centre of the

activity of the knights of the Round Table. After all, Academia is a sort of Quest, don't you think so?'

'Not that sort. All Romance and Chivalry.'

I didn't answer. I thought it was a good angle to see a university from, and I didn't want Edwin to talk me out of it.

'If you'd worked for British Leyland, I could have written about motor cars,' I said.

'I didn't know your writing was so dependent on what I did.'

He had scored a point.

'Well, I'm inevitably in the university milieu if I live with you, aren't I?' I said. 'It draws me in.' Weak.

In fact it did not draw me in very much. I didn't go there very often. This afternoon had been my first visit to the hessian-faced walls of the Green Knight Gallery.

Sir Gawain killed the Green Knight, didn't he? I mustn't take this too far.

I sat in my garret re-drafting the first part of my novel. Outside, the fussy toots and puffs of the Bluebell Line were re-enacted for me. The train paused for the signal at the plastic-lined fish pond next door, then moved gently away in the direction of the village and towards the finish of the recording.

The Green Knight Gallery was vandalized during the night. It appeared that someone broke in and laid about themselves with a broom, ripping the hessian, knocking the pictures off the walls. The burglar alarm was activated and the vandal was chased into the woods that bordered the grounds of Camelot College by security guards with guard dogs.

But the intruder got away.

'It was a very young boy,' Edwin said, telling me about it. 'Very fair-haired.'

It just crossed my mind that Daren might be involved,

though this would be some coincidence. However, it was more likely than the resurrection of Sir Gawain.

When I had written a few pages of novel, I made out a short report on my visit to the House of Judy. With reluctance I recorded Bella's black eye. Otherwise, I reported, the family seemed to be in a stable situation, given that they had no electricity, and that the husband was out of work, and a few other variables, most of which the Social Services were already aware of.

Edwin brought me a cup of cocoa and a glass of Drambuie, and we sat in the half-light, not mentioning my novel.

'I have to go to Portsmouth Poly next week,' said Edwin, who earned extra pounds and prestige as External Examiner at various institutions around the country.

It was not usual for him to give me much notice of his actions. This was our understanding.

'Will you do anything in particular while I'm away?' he asked, and this broke all the rules. Patrons have limited territory, I feel.

'I shall try to get to page fifty, at the least,' I said. 'And I promised to read the Alsatian's hand for her at Vincenza's. And Judy's invited me to a knees-up at her local. I might go while you're away.'

Edwin smiled indulgently at the fulfilled life I was arranging round myself, though, of course, he had frowned at the mention of the cards.

*Beware of the woman
who arranges the
lives of others*

♡♣◇♠ **Chapter 6** ♣♦♠
Queen of Spades

It was a hot afternoon, and I felt sleepy. Most of the morning I had been sitting in the garden writing. It was good having Edwin out of the house. Portsmouth was a long way away, and I felt free and uninhibited.

I knew I owed this freedom to Edwin, and I was grateful to him, especially when he wasn't there.

Except for country noises – birds and things – my wooden shoes were the only sound, clopping along the cobblestones. No one else was in the street. It seemed too fine a day to spend inside. I wondered if the Alsatian would let me read her cards sitting in Vincenza's garden, or if she would expect the whole ritualistic caboodle.

I came to Vincenza's house. It had a door like a stable, painted white, with long black hinges. The top half was open. I looked into the lounge. Afghan rugs lay on the floor. Other rugs hung on the walls, among rows of pictures. Vincenza and Bertholdt were collectors, in a small way. Along the whole of one wall was a massive stone fireplace with a three-panelled oil painting in front

41

of it, masking the grate. The room stretched the length of the house, to wide french windows that opened onto a patio and the long narrow garden.

I could see Vincenza and the Alsatian, bathed in sunlight, beyond the cool shadow of the room. They sat on candy-striped patio furniture that I had last seen for sale in the local garden centre. They had long glasses in their hands and they were talking animatedly, so that I felt free to stand watching them, and to peer with curiosity round Vincenza's room.

Then I saw that someone was watching me. Lying full-length on the apparently mandatory Victorian chaise-longue, Ferg had been observing my prying with his amused detached smile which, if I didn't feel a certain amount of bias, I should call a sneer.

'Hullo,' I said. I opened the sneck and stepped into the room, while he lay, his chin slightly doubled as he looked at me, still not moving.

'I've come to see Hilde,' I said.

He sat up.

'It's the cartomancer,' he said, which was a greeting.

He put his hand into his pocket and brought out a crumpled silk bundle. He shook it and it spread from his hand like an orange flame.

'Your scarf.' He held it towards me.

I took it from him and drew it across my wrist, enjoying its sensuous softness, and the muted glow of colour.

I laughed, but not loudly, for I was thinking it was a gift fitting for a whore. I held it by one corner and pulled it round my neck. The soft fabric flowed at the command of my fingers.

'It suits you, Gipsy Woman.'

Vincenza stood at the other end of the room, leaning against the side of the window frame. 'Aren't you pleased with me, arranging this romantic encounter for you?'

Well, I was, though it would have been more romantic if she'd stayed on the patio, instead of barging in as soon as she heard my voice. Also, it suddenly felt uncomfortable. Vincenza's collusion with Ferg made me feel that I

42

had swum into a fish-net. I welcomed involvement with Ferg, but Vincenza's part in this was suspect, for I knew she had wanted Ferg herself.

Then I thought that she had probably got him anyway, and that she enjoyed manipulating me so that she could sit back on a little god-like cloud and say to him, 'You see what I can do for you.' I imagined that she would watch through a peephole if ever Ferg and I went to bed together, and that he would know this.

'It's very nice,' I said, handing the scarf back to him, 'but I don't accept gifts from strange men.'

The phone rang then, in the kitchen, and Vincenza went to answer it.

'What's strange about me?' Ferg dodged my hand, and I could see he wasn't going to take the scarf back. I draped it over the chaise-longue.

'I don't like being used to further anyone's mania for manipulation.'

'Look, I'm sorry if you're offended. We had to meet somewhere, and when Vincenza suggested her house, it seemed like a good idea.'

I thought of them scheming about me, and I didn't like it.

Ferg was looking at me in his appealing little-boy way.

'Maybe, if you'd like to, we could go to my flat next time.'

Maybe. I didn't answer.

'It was all I could think of. You're very difficult to get in touch with.'

On the patio, I saw that Hilde had risen, pulling herself up by holding lightly onto the table, and I realized she was slightly tipsy.

'Darling, so *nice*!' she said. I think she must have got this bar-fly idiom through watching very old British films.

'We are having such a lovely time. Vera's been feeding me on Pimm's Number One. Perfect for the time of year, don't you think? All these leaves and things floating on the top. It's so refreshing, all this generosity.'

Vincenza came back into the room.

'You just have as many as you like, my love,' she said to Hilde, putting her arm round the old lady's shoulder.

I saw that she had decided to take Hilde over, as it were to seduce her away from the parsimonious Nerina.

Vincenza poured me a drink from a stoneware jug. I sipped gratefully, while leaves of mint and slices of orange bumped lightly against my upper lip.

Ferg lay watching me. He had refused a Pimm's.

'I like to be able to taste my alcohol,' he said, and Vincenza poured him a very large gin.

'It's either gin or dry sherry,' she said. 'That's all we have in the house at the moment, apart from crême de menthe.'

Hilde sidled up to me and held my arm.

'I'm so excited you are going to tell my fortune,' she said.

It was like being able to play the piano. I got invited round in the same way. What she was saying was just get on with it.

But I had known to expect this when I took up reading cards, so I put down my glass and prepared for business. I got the cards, in their silken bag, out of my handbag.

Hilde reached out and felt the material between finger and thumb.

'So pretty,' she said.

Vincenza had set up a card table in the garden, to my relief. There was some talk and amusement about where exactly north was, for I had to sit with my back to the north, facing the 'questioner'.

'It's because of the influence of the magnetic pole,' I said, and they all laughed.

Vincenza and Ferg tried to hang around but I shooed them away, aided by Hilde.

'This is my show, darlings,' she said. 'May belongs to me, for this time, don't you?' she asked me.

No. You belong to me, I thought, but I smiled, saying nothing.

The other two retreated as far as the patio, where they

sat on the swinging sofa, quite close together, and talked to each other in low voices which unnerved me with their intimacy.

'Is there anything special you ·vould like to ask the cards?' I asked Hilde, as we settled down.

'No, darling. Just tell me *everything*.'

This was the usual sort of answer.

'Well,' I said, 'we'll see what is determined, and we'll see how you can influence that. There's nothing that can't be changed or developed for the better.'

I always said that to start with, to cover myself in case the questioner selected a heap of bad cards. No-one had done that so far, but there's always a first time.

'We'll use the Mystic Cross,' I said.

I usually dropped a few terms like that into the reading. If I had been a doctor, I should have been the kind who tells the patient just enough to impress them with my expertise but not enough to help them to understand the full nature of the condition.

'The Mystic Cross. Oh!' Hilde smiled, pretending to pretend to be impressed.

'Now,' I said, 'you must make all the choices, for we are looking at your life.' Make sure the questioner takes all the blame for her or his own life. I certainly didn't want to take any of it.

'. . . so first you have to choose a court card to represent yourself.'

I know now that it is at this point that the questioner begins to take this all seriously. I am not saying that he or she necessarily believes in it. Some probably think, well, since I'm here, I'd better see what goes on. And they resign themselves to some participation. Others begin, at this point, to take it all very seriously indeed.

Hilde belonged to the second group.

We discussed what sort of person she thought she was, as related to the traditional symbolism of the cards. Fair-haired and domesticated? Ruled by the heart?

'No, darling, not for a long time. And who is to say about the colour of my hair? When I was a child, my hair was blonde. Now it is as you see, but alas it comes from a bottle.'

Hilde's hair was black, greying at the roots.

'You see yourself as a dark person,' I suggested. 'Otherwise you would have chosen a fair colour for your hair.' I changed the angle. 'Do you see yourself as a young person, as a woman with feminine characteristics? Or do you think your qualities lie over towards the masculine?'

But Hilde was too old to make anything of this.

'I am a woman, of course,' she said reprovingly.

'And are you a practical person? A businesswoman?'

I wasn't going to pile up trouble for myself by suggesting any of the qualities that might have made her select a spade for her court card. There are problems enough relying on chance, without going to look for them.

Hilde pondered for some time what sort of woman she considered herself to be, and I was happy to lead her along in this discussion. I felt cocooned in the warm greenness of Vincenza's garden, leaning my arm against the copper trunk of the cherry tree that overhung our table of fate.

'Do you think, for instance, that you are a strong-willed person? A good organizer?' And so on.

Reading the cards reveals this sad fact, which I suppose those who first foretold the future knew instinctively before they started. It reveals the pathetic pleasure that a cartomancer's questioners take in discussing themselves with a detached stranger.

But I was not a detached stranger. I had met Hilde recently, and I knew a lot about her. Hilde chose for herself the queen of clubs. She would probably have chosen it anyway, without all the palaver.

I spread the cards face down across the table, using my left hand, because that is the hand nearest to your heart, as I explained to Hilde.

'Now,' I said, 'using your left hand, pick out any twelve cards, but don't look at them yet.'

'Darling, I am left-handed. Shall I therefore use my right hand?' asked Hilde. Her eyes were wide open, and she looked at me in utter trust, assuming I should have all the answers.

I pointed out that the left hand was nearest to the heart whether or not you were left-handed, and that the only difficulty would be if she was one of those rare people whose heart lies on the right side of their body.

'Oh, of course,' said Hilde meekly.

She began very carefully to select her twelve cards, laying them face down, one on the other, as I had instructed her.

I picked her cards up and inserted the queen of clubs where she directed me. There was silence as I turned them over and laid out the cross.

I sat looking at the cross for a few moments. As I laid them out I saw that Hilde had not chosen a fortunate hand, and my heart sank, for bad hands are harder work than good hands, and require creative efforts on the part of the cartomancer which would not mix well with this hot still afternoon.

I turned up the last card. The ace of spades. Death. But we cartomancers seldom mention that word. You can say that someone *has* died. But it is in bad taste to foretell a death.

I sat looking at the cards and Hilde waited almost without breathing. On the sofa, Ferg and Vincenza stopped talking and peered across the lawn, trying to see what was going on.

Then Hilde began to wail melodramatically.

'Death, death. The death card,' she moaned.

The ace of spades, coming at the end of the row, seemed to me to be in a remarkably logical position. What else could one expect at the end of one's life if not death, after all?

Vincenza stood up. 'Time for another drinky,' she called. She didn't wait for Hilde to answer, but went inside, and we could hear the clink of ice in glasses.

I began to reassure Hilde that all was well. The ace of spades was simply the end of one phase and the beginning of another.

47

'You see,' I said, relieved to focus elsewhere, 'here's the nine and ten of diamonds next to each other. You're going on a long journey.'

Tactless. Of course, Hilde began to howl again, and Vincenza brought her Pimm's to the table and made her drink it down as if it was medicine.

I tried again. 'You have the nine of diamonds, the card of courage. You will be able to cope with any difficulties that lie ahead.'

Hilde began to look less upset and more interested. She put her glass down on the table and I removed it with no fuss, setting it down on the grass by her feet.

As I did this, I glanced at Ferg. He was looking at me, and his look said that he understood exactly how I felt. Which was impatience with Hilde for taking this whole reading so seriously and a mild panic as I tried to extricate myself from the vagaries of the cards. I knew that the panic amused Ferg, and that he had the gossip's interest in seeing how I was going to get out of this whole situation.

Vincenza came back onto the patio and Ferg stood up. I turned back to the cards.

'I'll just phone my bets through, if you don't mind,' I heard him say. He went into the house.

'A fair woman plays a large part in your life,' I said to Hilde.

'That will be Nancy.' Hilde sat back on her chair with satisfaction.

'You have a strong emotional tie with her.'

'I certainly have, darling. She drives me mad, I can tell you.'

That wasn't the sort of tie I'd meant, but Hilde seemed viciously pleased about it, so I kept quiet.

No one was sitting on the patio now. Hilde and I were alone in the garden. We moved among the mute messages, while above us the leaves of the cherry tree stirred gently. My voice seemed dulled in the open space.

'Your strong sense of justice leads people, particularly young people, to seek your advice with their problems. . . .'

48

A card flipped past me and landed on the table by my hand. I looked at the Mystic Cross, but it was intact. For a moment I was nonplussed, for Hilde hadn't noticed what had happened, she was still looking at me expectantly.

I had just realized that the card had blown off the top of the remainder of the pack, when a warm gust lifted most of the cards, scattering them over the lawn, or onto my lap.

Hilde rushed round, picking them up, protesting, trying to re-form the cross. But I had no wish to help her with this, and pretended I couldn't remember the value of some of the cards, or their order. I also hinted that once the pattern was disarranged, the atmosphere had dissipated.

Reluctantly she agreed, and we collected up the rest of the cards in silence. We strolled back across the little lawn and Hilde drank the remains of her Pimm's as we walked. Clouds had covered the sun and the sky was losing its blueness, becoming mottled with black.

Inside the house, the television was on. Ferg lay on a sheepskin on the floor, watching the racing and drinking gin. He hardly looked up as we came in.

Vincenza was in the kitchen, I stood at the door watching her. She was wearing a pink silk kimono, slit up the sides to her bronze thighs, and it was obvious she had no other clothes on. She was slicing cucumber and its bland clean smell was all around her.

'God blew with his winds and they were scattered,' I said, as she looked up enquiringly.

'The cards,' I explained, 'they started blowing about.'

She turned back to the cucumber. 'Yes. I knew what you meant.'

I couldn't impress these wives with erudition, and it was silly to try. Of course Vincenza wasn't impressed by what god blew with his silly winds, because she was a graduate and had gone beyond such classroom quotes. Vincenza was more impressed if I came up with something to do with tractors, or the quantities of molasses in silage.

'Here's May. She's our agricultural expert,' she'd say. I was their token farm labourer.

'That was the office phoning,' she said.

She looked at my puzzlement.

'When you arrived.'

'Oh.' That seemed a long time ago.

'About the Trods. Arnie's hurt himself and had to go to hospital. Judy phoned the office. She'd tried to get in touch with you, but you were out.'

I stared at her, masking surprise and my irritation that she had not told me before. Why hadn't she?

She began to cut hard-boiled eggs into halves, calmly aware of my annoyance, and certain I would not give vent to it. I wondered whether she would have told me if Judy had died. Not until her afternoon's entertainment had run its course, I guessed.

'Would you like me to go into town to see how they're getting on?' I tried not to sound sarcastic.

Vincenza put down the eggs and smiled at me, giving me her full attention.

'Oh, if you would. It *is* my day off. You are a love.'

'It's nothing.' I went back into the lounge to collect my things, and Vincenza came to the door with me.

Hilde lay on the chaise-longue, her mouth open, snoring.

'Goodbye, Gipsy Woman.' Ferg hardly looked round, and on the television horses lumbered past the winning-post.

'I've won!' He slapped the floor with his hand.

I hoped there'd be a steward's enquiry, and his horse would be disqualified.

*Secret trysts may
tantalize rather
than delight*

♡♣◊♧ Chapter 7 ♡♣◊♧
Four of Spades

Daren was doing wheelies in the street, ignoring any possibility of traffic. His bike reared then landed with an inexpert thud on the tarmac, and he wobbled dangerously in front of my car.

I parked in front of Judy's door, and climbed out onto the pavement. It seemed pointless to rebuke him, as he cycled towards me, jumping off at the last minute, leaving his bike to crash onto the cobblestones. He looked at me, half-smiling, and I thought again how thin and pale he looked, how scanty his blond hair was, and once again it was a shock to realize that he was probably seriously undernourished, in this small town, in this modern age.

He peered into my car, looking for goodies. But I hadn't brought any, I had driven almost straight here after Vincenza gave me the message.

'Where's your mum?' I asked, and Daren turned away from the car, looking at me with no malice or blame because I had come here empty-handed.

'She's at the hospital with my dad,' he said. 'He had this

51

great big piece of skin hanging off his leg. He were bleeding everywhere. Ambulance had to come.'

'What happened? How did he do it?'

Daren looked straight at me. 'He were at the tip. Looking. He cut it on an old tin.'

I shuddered at the possibility of infection.

'He's not supposed to go there,' said Daren.

It was a compliment, and a warning. Don't tell anyone, Daren was saying. And he was saying that he trusted me. I hugged him.

'We'll go and fetch your mum in a minute,' I said.

We went into the house. I was looking for Bella, and I found her lying on the battered settee, fast asleep, with her thumb in her mouth. The fire had died down to red embers, I was relieved to notice.

I went into the kitchen and Daren followed me, monitoring my movements in his house, his chin raised as if he was watching my face for clues to what I was thinking.

Judy's kitchen was black-walled with damp, and with the black fat of smoking candles. There was a camping gas stove, also black. Even the canister that held the gas was blackened and smeared. Pots, all ill-assorted, all unwashed, were everywhere. I peered through the grimy window into a small yard, at the far end of which was the outdoor toilet that was the only one the house possessed.

In the other room Bella, hearing movement, woke up and began to cry. 'Mam, mam!'

I went back and stood by the door, not wanting to frighten her by my unexpected arrival.

'We'll go and get your mum from hospital. She's gone with your dad. She'll come home soon.'

Daren had followed me.

'Will we go in your car?'

'Of course,' I said, and there was a satisfied silence.

I sat on the edge of the settee and stroked Bella's forehead, which was warm and slightly damp. She pressed her head against my hand, waking slowly.

Daren came and stood by my knee. 'Can I go in the front?' he asked.

I felt maternal and uneasily responsible.

Later I sent him to get milk from the corner shop.

'What do you want for tea?' I asked him. I sent him for beans and burgers too, for that was his unhesitating choice.

I wondered about cleaning Bella up. Inevitably her knickers were wet. Her face was smeared and sticky. At first I thought Judy might be offended at my interference, at the implied criticism. Then, wiping away the grubbiness on Bella's face with a damp paper hankie, I realized that even if Judy noticed anything different, she would only be relieved to have any task taken off her shoulders.

I also wondered why she had forsaken the children and gone off with Arnie, who was clearly in more competent hands than hers once the ambulance arrived.

'Me mam wrapped the curtain round our dad's leg,' said Daren, and that explained the unusual amount of light in the room, even allowing for the grime of the window. He picked up the grey bundle of nylon voile that lay by the side of the fireplace.

'Blood,' he said, looking at my face, waiting for me to be impressed.

And so I was, for the curtain was well soaked with Arnie's blood, turning dark brown now, sticking in masses to the folds of the fabric. I tried not to think of the filth of the curtain, comforting myself that it hardly mattered, compared with the infected rubbish tip where Arnie and his colleagues roved with the gulls, scavenging for other people's throw-outs, old rugs, cracked pots and, rarely, a few real bargains.

Daren's complexion, as he held the curtain up for me, became paler than ever, and Bella turned away, burying her face in my knee.

'A lot of blood's good,' I promised. 'It washes the cut, keeps it clean. It always looks more than it really is,' I said, and so on.

The stricken remains of the little family digested this in

silence, possibly believing me because I was Auntie May, and Doing Good. Or possibly not.

'The ambulance man took the curtain off,' said Daren. 'He put a big bandage on it instead. He told our mam to stay here, but she wouldn't.' He sounded proud about this, his mum standing up to authority, for it wouldn't cross his mind that Judy had abandoned him and Bella.

I made tea, assuming there had been no lunch. I boiled the minimum of water for washing-up, before the meal, for I was afraid that the gas would run out – it was a relief that there was sufficient to cook with.

I felt mildly ashamed that I hadn't realized before that Judy had to use such a fuel for cooking. I should have known, I thought, for there was no electricity since it had been cut off, and the town was only now having gas installed.

We drove the car up the hill to the hospital. Arnie wasn't in Casualty. The sister on duty told me they were keeping him in overnight, as the surgeon had had to operate on him.

She looked at me professionally.

'Are you a social worker?' she asked.

The implication of the question irritated me.

'No,' I said. 'I'm a friend.'

'Mr Trod was in a very poor state,' she said. She looked absently at Bella and Daren, who stood on either side of me, overcome by the hospital aura.

'It's a serious cut, right into the tendon. It may be necessary to do a skin-graft.'

We trailed up long corridors, through plastic doors that slapped behind us, and we came to Arnie's ward. Everyone watched us walk down it, because Judy shrieked in her hoarse smoker's voice when she saw us, and came rushing to meet us. I felt strangely pleased, proud almost, coming to see Arnie, even though it was a waste of time, really, as I couldn't put it into my novel.

The children left me and went to cling to Judy, but she ignored them, looking at me eagerly, gabbling the blood-soaked details, while Arnie looked on, watching us hazily through the after-effects of his anaesthetic, waiting for us to arrive at his bedside.

'They're keeping me in,' he told me when I arrived, which Judy had told me already, for all to hear. But he wanted to tell me himself.

'They're frightened it might get septic, see. I had to tell them. I was pulling this chair from out under a fridge, and it came all of a sudden. I fell backwards, right onto this rusty sardine tin.'

I wanted to ask Arnie why he did it, the slow movement of scavengers across the tip, nothing wasted, the re-processing of society's waste.

'You've got enough chairs,' I said. 'Any more and you won't be able to get in at your door.'

That was what I said, putting blame behind me, for who could blame Arnie for going to the tip, any more than I could be blamed for throwing away old chairs?

But Arnie looked at me with a meaning look, then jerked his head towards his bedside locker.

'Show her,' he said to Judy, and he said it quietly, understood by Judy, who got up off the edge of the bed, where she had been sitting, and opened the top drawer. She put in her hand, then brought it out, her fist clenched.

'Open your hand,' she said to me in what passed for a stage whisper. 'Don't let anyone see.'

I opened my hand, and she dropped something into it. She and Arnie waited for my reaction.

It was a gold chain, half-way along which was a shiny red stone set in a crude golden circle. Already some of the gold on the links was wearing away, and with my good eyesight I could see tiny patches of green where the base metal showed through.

They were both watching me.

Arnie motioned with his head to the cradle that lifted the bedclothes off his injured leg.

'It were worth getting that,' he said, meaning his injury.

'Arnie reckons it's real,' said Judy. 'Real gold, real stone. It's a ruby, isn't it, Arnie?'

'Might be,' said Arnie.

'We want you to have it,' said Judy, and Arnie nodded, agreeing.

'Who, me? Oh no, I can't.'

''Course you can. We want you to.'

They really did want me to. They were my friends, who could give me things, just like ordinary friends did. I thought of the elegant silk scarf, and Ferg watching me. How different his look had been.

'It's very nice,' I said. 'Pretty.'

I held it up, and they looked round shiftily, to see if anyone was watching.

I put it round my neck, mentally swallowing my disgust, imagining that I could smell rotting sardines.

'Auntie May,' said Bella, and she stretched out her hand to touch the necklace.

We shall all get typhoid or worse, I thought.

Later we drove home in my car, leaving Arnie behind. Judy was very pleased with herself for going to hospital with him.

'I told them,' she said. 'I wasn't going to let them take Arnie off on his own, was I?'

And I said no, she wasn't.

'Auntie May made us some tea,' said Bella.

'I'm hungry,' said Judy, piqued.

'We saved some for you,' I said, but Judy said she couldn't be bothered to cook a meal, she was too tired.

She didn't offer to pay for the food, and why should she? For one thing she probably didn't have the money.

So I thought, kissing Bella on the cheek before I went.

But at the end of the street, sounding the horn as usual, I looked to see them waving, and saw that already Judy was shooing the children inside. I knew with a certainty that needed no proof that she was going to put them to bed and get off down to the Dragon. Judy didn't waste her money on boring things like food, and she was too sociable to sit at home on her own, thinking her thoughts by candlelight.

A car came out of the next side road, stopping right in front of me. I braked hard enough to activate my seat-belt.

'For god's sake!' I was furious.

Then I saw that the driver of the car was grinning at me, as if pleased with himself.

I wound down my window. 'You might have killed us both.'

He laughed. 'No chance. You're too cautious a driver for that. Besides,' said Ferg, 'I've been waiting for you for hours, and I wanted to be damned certain you didn't get away.'

Ferg gave a new dimension to the phrase 'urban jungle'. He was hunting me as if I was a wild animal he was determined to track down.

Yet although I knew this, some infuriating part of me couldn't help being flattered. I liked being hunted. It made a change from Edwin's rational approach, for one thing. And for another, I had an almost uncomfortable feeling of affinity with Ferg. Did the tiger feel this about his tracker?

Or perhaps I was the tracker, and Ferg was the tiger who was doing the hunting.

'Come and have a drink with me,' said Ferg, and it seemed an attractive offer. If Judy could have a drink, why not me?

Which is how I came to spend the rest of the evening at the Trout's Head. Once, I remembered that Vincenza must have set this up, for how else would Ferg have known where to find me? But I decided not to care. Pride should have no place in this relationship on which I seemed to be embarking.

We sat in an oaken corner, away from the svelte bar that was enclosed in a genuine four-poster bed. There were polished paving-stones and old wool rugs on the floor. The room wasn't full. Often during the evening we were alone, while the barmaid sat on a low stool behind the bar, the top of her head just visible, and it was so quiet that we could hear the clack of her knitting-needles. Then we would start to talk again.

What did we talk about? Does it matter? Who remembers the first evening's conversation of a love affair?

We talked, of course, about ourselves. Ferg told me about his Double First at Oxford, which seems to be an absolute must for most of the university folk I know. I told him about my eight CSEs, and how I had worked as a farm labourer when I left school, till Cissy Henshaw threw me out because she thought I was vamping Hens, which I was not.

I'd gone to London then, getting a job as a waitress at the BMA restaurant in Southampton Row. I'd met Edwin at evening classes. Other waitresses kept 'borrowing' my silver, and I knew I'd have to leave before my shortage of covers was discovered. So I was learning to touch-type, and so was Edwin, who had decided to type his own thesis. He was useless at typing, so I offered to do it for him, just to get some practice. Our 'arrangement' began at that time. We shared a flat in Cricklewood.

'I'm writing this novel,' I told Ferg. 'Edwin's my patron.'

He laughed, and said, as we all know, that you can't call it that, not if you go to bed with someone.

'We don't very often,' I told him. 'We've got single beds. It isn't like you think.'

I didn't tell him that there was a double-bed squeezed into the spare room, and that we sometimes ended up there, as sharing a single bed is just too sweaty.

'Where are your parents?' asked Ferg.

I looked away. 'I'm a Barnardo's baby.'

He apologized.

'Oh it's all right. I've got a mother, you know. She rings me up sometimes. Quite often, really.'

Please, *please* can I come and stay with you, I would beg her, and no you can't, she used to say. Now she would ask me please can't I stay with you, and that is what I would reply: no, I'm sorry. It's not possible.

Which is why I kept going to Judy's, I think. Because Arnie was a Barnardo's baby, though I never told him that I was too. I hardly ever told anyone. It wasn't wise to tell Ferg, I knew that, yet I still did it.

He let me tell him about Nerina's bathroom, and he laughed when I described it. Then he said he'd seen it when he went to the house, and I remember being slightly nonplussed, because he'd let me go on about it when he'd been there all the time.

Most of the time we looked and looked at each other straight in the eyes, and under the table our knees touched.

Ferg's father was an underwriter, and his sister worked at the Stock Exchange. It seems she had a Double First, too. Surprise me.

'What's your novel about?' asked Ferg.

But I couldn't tell him.

'It's unlucky to tell you,' I tried to explain. 'Once I've told it, I sort of lose interest in writing it down. Silly really.'

It might be silly, but I still wouldn't ever tell him, not till it was finished.

'Is anyone in it that I know?' he asked.

'It doesn't work like that. You pick things up from here and there and re-work them in a different pattern.'

Ferg looked at me for a long time.

'When are we going to bed together?' he asked.

'Soon. Tonight if you like.'

'What about the egregious Edwin?'

'We live our own lives. I told you.'

I wondered whether Edwin was sitting in a dark cinema in Portsmouth watching one of those symbolic films made before 1960. I wondered why I didn't want to make love with Ferg in Edwin's house. I wondered what 'egregious' meant.

For a few moments Ferg said nothing. He stopped looking into my eyes. He drank the rest of his pint in one

59

go, and I began to think back, how many had he put away since we'd been here?

It didn't look as if I was going to be his antidote to alcoholism.

I was relieved we'd driven out here in our own cars, and that I would have to drive myself back.

'I could meet you back at your flat,' I offered.

But Ferg seemed to have gone off the boil.

'That would be very nice,' he said in the way that meant it would not. 'Except that I have a friend staying with me.'

What are friends *for*? I wanted to ask. You've got two rooms, haven't you? It seemed prudish and not at all what I'd expected of the top set at Avalon. Surely he wasn't trying to whet my appetite by playing this game?

'Well,' I said. 'What about the bushes?'

'The bushes?'

'We could do it in the bushes. It's been done before.'

Now this is the weird fact. I am almost indifferent to the act of love, if such it be, which seems a silly arrangement to me. So while Ferg said, 'Oh,' in a disillusioned kind of way, I was sitting there making out how hot my pants were, whereas I would have been happy to talk to him all night with no tumbling and groaning at the end of it.

Was it possible that he felt the same?

But I already knew the answer. Vincenza had told me he was reputed to be impotent. I had been goading him, teasing him almost, with my offers.

'It seems,' I said, 'that we both suffer from the same problem.'

'What problem?' asked Ferg and his face had gone remote with distaste. He wasn't going to bare his soul to me, not tonight anyway.

'I'd better go home,' I said. And now it was the word 'home' that seemed distant and unlikely. I had better go to Edwin's home.

I followed the lights of Ferg's car between the high dark hedges, where cow parsley rushed towards us, and I thought how it would settle itself in silence behind us, after we'd passed by.

We came to the main street of Cornfield, and I flashed him before I turned off to Edwin's house in Edwin's crescent. His brake lights winked redly back in acknowledgement. I thought of him driving between the trees to the stage-set of his friary and the welcome of his friend. Was there really a friend, and if so, was the friend male or female?

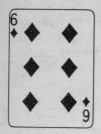

*A gift is
misconstrued*

♡♣◇♧ **Chapter 8** ♡♣◇♧

Six of Diamonds

I drove my car into Edwin's more modest front drive. We had never discussed the matter, but it was assumed without question that Edwin's car should go in the garage and that mine should be parked in the drive – sometimes we had to go to quite complicated manœuvres to achieve this.

So I was surprised to see a gaping black hole facing me as I switched off my headlights.

The garage doors were open, though I had left them closed and locked. But Edwin's car was not inside. Nor did I expect it to be, for he had driven it to Portsmouth.

My car clock told me it was just after eleven-thirty. There were no downstairs lights on in the other houses in the crescent. I hesitated, uneasy about getting out of my car, which seemed for the moment a tender shell of protection.

A shadow crossed my driving mirror.

Without moving my head, I swivelled my eyes and watched the silhouette of a man slide down the drive

62

towards my car. I felt the hush of clothing along its side.

I wound the window down as suddenly as I could.

'Hullo, Edwin,' I said.

He leapt back, and I heard the indrawn breath of his surprise.

'What on earth are you doing in there?' he asked.

He hadn't realized that I had only just arrived back.

'What on earth are you doing out there?' I parried, wondering how to answer his question.

We went into the house.

'My car broke down,' said Edwin. 'On the motorway, fast lane. It was pretty hairy.'

He had come back by AA Relay, leaving his car in the forecourt of Wren's, our local garage.

'But what about the exams?' I asked. He'd spent quite a few evenings working out assessments, while he watched TV.

'Oh it's all right. Today wasn't anything special. I'll go down by train tomorrow. It can all be done by phone if necessary.'

'You could borrow my car.' Too generous. I regretted it as soon as I'd made the offer.

But it worked out well.

'That's really nice of you,' said Edwin, touched, 'but it's no trouble going by train. Might as well have done that in the first place.'

It was easy after that to tell him about the Trods. I didn't have to lie, either. I let him assume that I'd spent the whole afternoon and evening with them, which is what I probably ought to have done.

We talked about cars' electrics on the way to bed. About which Edwin knew almost as much as I did. Nothing.

So I eased out of my uncomfortable position quite neatly, though it may well be thought that there are limits to the accountability to patrons, and that I should not have put myself under the strain of dissembling. Right. But I was pretty certain that this particular patron would not take kindly to any sexual gallivanting on my part.

63

Yet something was wrong about Edwin. He was talking far more than usual, explaining his actions, apologizing for them, almost.

I listened, undressing slowly, diagnosing faulty alternators, cracked rotor heads, or anything else that I'd heard could go wrong with cars.

But I wasn't thinking about these things. I was remembering that Edwin had approached my car empty-handed, as I had sat watching him in the car mirror. He should have been carrying his expensive fire-proof Samsonite briefcase, rarer than rubies, since it contained his precious examination assessments.

Surely he hadn't left such a valuable item in his car? And where was his suitcase?

'I'm thirsty,' I said, and I went downstairs.

Edwin's suitcase was in his study; his briefcase was on his desk. Moonlight shone onto the sharp shapes of both, for I didn't switch on the light.

So Edwin had been home before I saw him in the drive. I filled a glass of water and carried it upstairs.

Edwin had switched off his bedside light. He looked across at me.

'Tired?' he asked. His eyes were fixed on my neck.

'A bit.'

'Yes,' he said, 'I am too.'

He peered harder at me.

'What's that you've got round your neck?'

I put my hands up to my throat and felt the ruby and gold necklet.

'It's a present,' I said, 'from Judy and Arnie.' I laughed. 'Solid gold and ruby!'

Edwin turned away from me.

'Really,' he said, as if he wasn't interested.

Maybe he didn't like the necklet. Aesthetically it had nothing to recommend it. It looked like, and probably was, something out of a Christmas cracker.

Its value was sentimental. I swallowed, remembering how I'd come by it.

'I'm going to wear it always,' I said.

64

'Yes,' said Edwin. 'You probably are.'

His voice was full of innuendo, but I was thinking too hard about the briefcase to work this out as well.

'Edwin,' I asked, 'isn't it a bit unusual, examining students so early in the year? Don't they usually do their Finals later than this?'

'Yes,' said Edwin, 'that's quite right. This was a bit unusual, a Ph.D. thesis.'

How could I argue about that? I wasn't even sure what a thesis was. It sounded like an illness to me.

At least my question silenced Edwin. When I came back from the bathroom he was fast asleep.

In the morning he was up late, oversleeping after his exertion on the motorway yesterday. There was no time to discuss anything. I took him to the station in my car, and we spoke very little.

I waited on the platform, and he stood looking out of the carriage door. Still neither of us said anything that we were thinking. We talked instead about things we were not thinking about – repairs to his car, and so on.

At first I thought he was avoiding looking me in the eyes. Then I realized he was staring at the necklet again.

It was a joke, I told him. The necklet wasn't anything more than a cheap bauble.

Edwin looked at it as if for the first time. You would have thought he was bored with the whole subject.

The train began to move.

'Beware the Greeks,' said Edwin.

The train began to pick up speed, and he drew his head back inside.

Well, that was a funny interlude, and I could make nothing of it, nor was I trying to, for other things were far too interesting.

I called at Judy's house, since I was in town. I banged hard on the door, but there was no answer. A neighbour, watching me, told me that the children had gone off to school.

'She'll be back in bed, lazy cow,' she said, nodding her head towards the upstairs window.

This time I decided to leave Judy to nurse her hangover. I wanted to get back to the house, just in case Ferg phoned.

In fact the phone was ringing as I parked the car.

I rushed inside.

'Hullo,' I said, in my interesting-type voice.

It was Vincenza.

'Is everything all right?' she asked.

I supposed her conscience must be giving her some trouble and that she was referring to the House of Trod. I changed to my efficient voice.

'It seems to be,' I said. 'Judy's asleep and the children have gone to school.' I hoped she'd be impressed that I'd visited them this morning.

'Oh. Judy.'

Then I realized she wasn't very interested in Judy. She wanted to know about my meeting with Ferguson Baverstock. I decided at that moment that I was not going to discuss him with her.

'You're on your own, aren't you?' Vincenza asked with certainty, because Edwin had recently written a diary for *The Round Tablet*, our university journal, so everyone knew he was away in Portsmouth.

So I had to say yes, I was on my own, even though I hated to do this, because it is unpleasing when everyone knows your business, however unimportant or uneventful it is. Or possibly because it *is* unimportant and uneventful, and it is humiliating when everyone knows this.

'. . . well then,' said Vincenza. 'Why don't you come up to Nerina's with me? Maybe you could read the cards for Derek Thackray.'

Now it may be a fact that my writing has had very little success, but it is exasperating, nevertheless, when people assume you are sitting around at home doing nothing as soon as your partner is absent.

I pointed out to Vincenza that after yesterday's events at her house, and with Judy, my work had fallen behind.

Vincenza apologized immediately.

66

'Of course,' she said. 'And one doesn't want to do that sort of creative work in the evenings, I suppose.'

'No,' I said, as if I had missed the point, which was that she knew I had spent the evening with Ferg.

'Derek's hoping to get the boat out of the barn this evening. It's going to be all hands on deck. And Nerina's having a little ceremony for the occasion. Do come. I'm sure you'd enjoy it.'

Why was she so anxious for my company? What little scheme was she setting up? And how had Derek Thackray finished his boat with such dispatch?

There were endless possibilities, and though I could have sat in Edwin's garden and made them all up, it was far more stimulating to go and see for myself, so I accepted Vincenza's invitation at the third offer. It was, after all, a bright sunny day that would be wasted in this garden, for the hedge had grown straggly again, and I was saddled with the task of clipping it, ever since my ill-judged comments about Edwin's lack of prowess at topiary. It is true I did it better than he did, but I didn't do it as often, so the result was roughly the same.

I found that I was preparing for this outing with more care than usual, and this was fortunate, for after my bath I glanced in the mirror, where I saw a dark line round my neck, so that I looked as if my head had been cut off then stuck back onto my body. It was the mark left by the Trod jewels, and it was very hard to get off. In the end I used methylated spirit, thinking that its penetrating smell would no doubt lead to comments about meths-drinking cartomancers.

I cleaned the necklet with hair shampoo and a tooth-brush that I happened to find lying round the bathroom. Edwin's. But since he'd left it behind, he'd certainly have to buy another one in Portsmouth, so this one, blackened and smelling of shampoo, would be a spare, and it was just as well I had put it to good use.

The phone rang. It was Vincenza again.

'This kid's been brought in by the police. He was found last night messing about near the Friary lake. Poaching.

He says he goes up there quite a bit. He mentioned Daren Trod. Says he goes with him.'

'How do you mean?' I found myself being guarded, and I surprised myself. For what was Daren to me? Yet here I was, suspecting – knowing almost – that he was likely to be implicated. And wanting him not to be; wanting to get him off the hook.

'It looks as if they might be involved in the vandalism at the gallery. Is there any likelihood that he could get out at night without Judy and Arnie knowing?'

'I've never been there at night.'

'Can you find out if she leaves them alone in the house? We may have to slap on a care and protection order.'

'I can't do that,' I said.

'Why not?'

'Because that isn't what I visit them for. I never intended to be an infiltrator. You know that, Vincenza.'

'Yes,' she said, suddenly capitulating, as was her way.

There was a pause, and I thought that I had undone in one short phrase all my efforts to break into the Avalon jet set.

'Shall I see you tonight?' she asked, and it was a child's question, can we still go to the circus.

'I'm looking forward to it very much.' I said this with warmth, to compensate for my previous rejection, and because I wanted to show Vincenza that I was grateful she wasn't angry with me.

She laughed as if she was delighted with my extravagant anticipation.

'Good,' she said, and everything was all right again.

Which was the gift she had, however learned, of getting round people, of making them want to be liked by her.

You are selfish and manipulative, Vincenza, I thought as I put the phone down.

But I was glad she still liked me, and that I could still go to the party.

*An uneasy partnership
rallies against an
outsider*

♡♣◇♤ Chapter 9 ♡♣◇♤
Two of Diamonds

The sun was far from setting, even though it was in the
west. For the days were lengthening, and in the main
street of Cornfield there was a crescendo of window-
boxes, their flowers unseasonably in full bloom, favoured
till now in greenhouses.

Because next week was the judging for the Best-Kept
Village competition, which Cornfield had once won. As I
walked down the main street my head brushed against the
underside of hanging baskets, and twice I dodged the
drips from well-watered first-floor window-boxes.

The dons of Avalon, cloaking their desire to win with
amusement, entered wholeheartedly into the competition. And if they didn't, their wives did. To spur us all on
the Parish Council offered a prize for the best display, and
when I reached Vincenza's door I saw that she would
probably win it. I picked my way to her door between a
riot of lobelia, fuchsia, petunia, and so on, and I
wondered why our only fuchsia had scarcely pushed this
year's shoots through the earth, when here were magni-

ficent scarlet caps with white and purple flounces, their elegant stamens putting the finishing touch. They looked so experienced, so practised, as well they might, unfolding their genetic code in these pavement tubs.

I was thinking high-minded thoughts about them when Bertholdt opened the door for me, and for a moment I let my face show the surprise that I knew I should hide. For although I have referred to this house as Vincenza's, it belonged to Bertholdt Corylan as well, since he was her husband and lived there with her. In a way this is artist's licence. It would be tedious to refer all the time to 'Bertholdt and Vincenza's house', particularly as they both have such long names. Perhaps I should have given the house a name. All right. It was called The Barn, to distinguish it from all the other converted barns round about.

So Bertholdt opened the door of The Barn, and masking my surprise at seeing him there at all, I said hullo, and how clever it was of him and Vincenza to produce such a massive display of flowers for the competition.

He looked at me as if he was trying to tell whether I was serious.

'Oh,' he said, 'she got them all from the Garden Centre last week. She'll probably be disqualified.'

He had been sitting on the floor with Martin, poring over a book with him. He closed it as he got up, as if finalizing their discussion, and I saw its title. *The Young Idealist's Guide to Politics*. As we talked, Martin opened the book again, turning its pages slowly. He was one of those sophisticated intellectual children who are so vulnerable in the real world. I saw that he had begun a new chapter, entitled 'Anarchy'. And all the time Bertholdt and I talked, he kept glancing up, eyeing his father as if he was trying to remind him that it was his turn for some attention.

But Bertholdt was busy being a host, although a very natural and unaffected one. It was almost the first time I'd met him, and I was impressed.

He fetched a drink, a dry sherry. He held the bottle up to the light and pulled a face, as if he was surprised how little was left. I wondered whether Ferg had been drinking it. Then I thought that if he had there wouldn't have been any left in the bottle at all.

'I wanted to meet you,' said Bertholdt. He put his arm round my shoulder and hugged me. Upstairs the toilet flushed, then there was the sound of carpeted footsteps as Vincenza crossed a room above our heads.

The hug was pure friendliness.

'You and I,' said Bertholdt, 'are in the same line of business.'

I looked at him, unsure.

'Psychology,' said Bertholdt. His eyes smiled at the corners. 'You tell fortunes, don't you?'

'Well. That's just for fun.'

'Some time you must tell mine.'

But I would never dare to. I know the Bertholdt syndrome. He would be pulling me apart, analysing everything I said and looked, to the last comma.

'No,' I said. 'You're too clever for me. A professor.'

'Oh yes, of course,' said Bertholdt. 'To tell the truth I can't come to terms with being a professor. A professor!' He began to laugh. 'I can't believe it!'

He picked up a cushion from the chaise-longue and buried his face in it.

'Professor Bertholdt Corylan.' His voice came muffled from the Turkish tapestry.

I stood back against the wall, uncertain how to react. Bertholdt had begun to move around the room, still with the cushion over his face. He came back to the chaise, and its sloping end bumped against his thighs.

'Bertholdt Corylan, professor,' he shouted into the cushion. Then he tipped himself forward in a somersault, finishing up on his back on the chaise-longue, with his legs in the air. He threw the cushion at Martin. It bumped off his son's head onto the book, creasing the pages.

'Oh!' Martin began to look tearful, but then he picked up the cushion and threw it back at Bertholdt, and we all laughed, for my part at least with relief, because the antics had come to an end.

Vincenza came into the room looking bright and enquiring. 'What's going on?'

And when Martin told her, she said, fastening a gold bracelet like a snake over her bare brown wrist, that Bertie really didn't have any dignity. I saw that she was looking sideways at me, and I knew that what she meant was that he should behave in front of people of my sort, who were her inferiors.

Bertholdt understood what she meant, too.

'This May Knott,' he said, 'is a very important person.'

'Of course she is,' agreed Vincenza. 'Everybody's important.'

'May Knott,' said Bertholdt, 'is following one of the oldest callings in the world.'

I wondered what he was going to say next.

'Reading the signs,' said Bertholdt. 'The Oracle of Delphi, the soothsayer. Quite indispensable to the human psyche, however we may protest.'

Was he serious?

I decided to say nothing, and I stared at a table whose soft pattern of veneer I thought might be walnut. There was an ashtray on the table, crudely moulded in pink glass, in the shape of a face. The corneas of the eyes were convex, with a hole in the middle to represent the pupils, in one of which someone had stubbed out a butt-end.

'Mum, you're not going out again?' Martin's voice was querulous.

Vincenza laughed. 'Oh, heavens. If you had your way I'd be imprisoned in here and never get out at all.'

Martin looked at Bertholdt. 'Are you going out, Dad?'

Bertholdt held his hand sympathetically. 'Yes, old chap. Some stuffy committee meeting.'

'I liked it best at Nottingham. You didn't go to so many meetings then. You were at home more often.' He suddenly cheered up. 'Is Betty baby-sitting?'

'She certainly is not.' Vincenza turned to me. 'Last time she came we got home to find she and Marty had drunk the sherry between them and were making me a birthday cake. It took me about a week to get the kitchen to rights.'

'Was it your birthday?'

She looked at me sharply. 'Yes. That was the whole point. That's why Bertie was taking me out to dinner.'

Her skin was brown and freckled by the sun. She wore a yellow dress, a calyx that her head and shoulders rose from like a lily.

But Bertholdt's was a different perception.

'Where did you get that dress?'

She pirouetted. 'Do you like it?'

'You look like a banana split,' said Bertholdt, and on the floor Martin blushed almost as though he saw the comment as a slur on himself.

'No she doesn't,' he said.

Vincenza lit a cigarette and glanced at me.

'Daddy's jealous,' she said. 'He'd like to wear pretty clothes too, wouldn't you, Bertie darling?'

'Yes, I would rather,' said Bertholdt. 'Though personally I'd go for the knickerbocker glory.'

'The knickerbocker glory,' said Vincenza. She looked him up and down, and I wondered if they hated each other. 'Isn't that a little ambitious? Possibly a spotted Dick ensemble would be better suited to your personality.'

'Not worthy of you,' said Bertholdt.

'Mummy, I don't want you to go out,' said Martin. His face beseeched, and Vincenza turned to me, smiling.

'You see how it is, May Knott. The tyranny of the young. The hedging about of personal freedom. How wise of you to have no children.'

Then she turned to her son, to Martin, who sat close to tears, hugging his book. She put her hand gently on the top of his head.

'Derek's going to get his boat ready to sail. You don't want to make me miss the celebrations, do you?'

'Can't I come?'

'No. Too late. You've got school in the morning.'

Over his head she looked at me, mouthing an expression that I interpreted as meaning how awful, what a bore if Martin was to come, to cling to her, to spoil the fun.

Martin turned to me with sudden impulse as I stood watching this scene, an uncomfortable bystander. 'Can I come with you, May Knott?'

'Yes,' I said. 'You can come with me.'

In the room there was stillness. Vincenza stubbed her cigarette out in the centre of the other pink eye.

'Well, Marty,' she said, 'you've come up with a winner this time.'

One quick glance she gave me, but I was smiling, showing only a willingness to help.

Why did I do such a thing? Children got on my nerves. I nearly hated them.

Now Vincenza and Bertholdt joined forces against the outsider.

'What about Iain, who's coming to baby-sit? Are you going to abandon him? He wanted to play you at table football, don't you remember?'

Between them they mollified him, pointing out what jolly boys' games were his for the asking.

'There won't be much for you to do at Nerina's. It's a grown-ups' party. And May will be busy, I expect, reading the cards.'

'It would be very boring,' said Vincenza definitely.

'I don't mind,' I said, and I sounded weak-willed and mousey.

'No, May. We can't impose him on you. You have other irons in the fire.'

So they made it clear to their child what a nuisance he was to them and to me.

'Well, I don't mind,' I repeated. But I made the mistake of saying this to his parents, not to Martin himself. Martin, I should have said, I would like to take you to this party, and you and I can play hide-and-seek in the attic beyond the lime-green bathroom, even though to tell the truth I cannot stand children for more than three minutes at a time.

Also, I never know what to say to them, not having had much practice, since I was the only child in the household of my adoptive mother. Sometimes I wish I had never been adopted. Sometimes I wish I had stayed at Barnardo's, which I left when I was so young that all I can remember of it is wide windows overlooking a snow-covered lawn with a fox running over it.

If I had stayed at Barnardo's I should have had a better idea how to talk to Martin. For an instant I envied Arnie.

'No, May. It really was a nice offer, but he'd be better off staying here.'

They were annoyed with me for interfering.

Vincenza and I left. I didn't look at Martin, and he didn't say goodbye to me.

In the car Vincenza, looking straight ahead, told me how worried they were about him.

'He's so solitary,' she said. 'I have to be careful he doesn't become fixated on me, whilst at the same time not rejecting him. Having a job helps. He appreciates me, doesn't take me for granted. He's often home for several hours before either of us gets back. Teaches him self-reliance.'

I shall not agree with you, Vincenza. You may be right, who is to say? It is the perennial problem facing a career woman.

'He could always pop round to see me if he needs anything,' I said.

'Oh no.' Vincenza dismissed this. 'You have your own life to lead.'

And so, as we made our way to my old workplace, we swapped clichés on this subject, and I offered support which I did not expect Vincenza to accept, and she rejected it whilst expecting me to insist. Stalemate, thank goodness, for what should I have done if Martin rolled up at Edwin's house every afternoon?

I can't understand why I keep putting myself forward for these do-gooding ventures, when the first person I should be doing good to is myself, and the second person is Edwin. Somewhere further down the line is my mother.

And I am going to make sure she stays there, further down the line.

The important thing in my life is my novel, for that will liberate both Edwin and myself.

Yet I must not think in these terms. What is my novel, after all? Merely a story, a few hours' entertainment at the most, since I am not Tolstoy, or Márquez, or someone like that. For me, writing can only ever be a precarious way of earning a living, and I should be deluding myself if I thought of writing in grand, sacrificial terms. So Judy and Arnie, and Martin and, I fear, my mother, should take precedence over my writing.

Unfortunately, however mediocre my novel may turn out to be, it cannot proceed unless I put all these people behind me.

But we had arrived at Nerina's, and I was going to a party, and Edwin was away in Portsmouth, and so I put these thoughts in another part of my mind, where they could roost and fester, but where they wouldn't bother me for the moment.

*This home-lover leaves
the washing-up
to others*

♡♣◇♤ Chapter 10 ♡♣◇♤
Queen of Clubs

Nerina was standing at the top of the steps to her front door. She was holding on to the jamb on either side, for support, and as we drove into the yard she kicked one leg up with a very high kick that brought her ankle up somewhere near her left ear. She was bare-footed, with roseate nail varnish that glinted in the evening light. Her toes were neat and straight, and there was no sign of the plaster cast.

Everyone was congratulating her on its removal.

'But where is it?' asked Vincenza. 'I haven't signed it yet.'

'No good, darling. It smelt horrid. Really embarrassing. It's a shame, really, as I'd have liked to keep it. Some of the drawings were almost professional.'

She was bewailing that one leg was far thinner than the other. So we all looked at her legs, and we noted what neat ankles she had, and what good taste in nail varnish.

There must be women somewhere who I have something in common with, I thought. But I didn't expect to meet them at this party. I looked around this loud array of women, and for once I was glad that I was just ordinary, so that I could sit about and no one would notice me.

The women were drinking sangria made, Nerina told us, with cheap champagne. Which is better than lemonade. The men were in the cowshed, where the women presently drifted to join them, being, it seemed, quite unable to manage without them.

Only Phyllis Thackray stayed, sitting on the front steps, not even bothering to smile enigmatically.

I hovered uncertainly, wondering whether I should talk to her, and if so, what I should say. I guessed that she would be quick to snub me.

'It seems very large for the cowshed,' I offered.

She looked at me blankly, daring me to repeat myself.

'The boat. I hope they can get it out. That door's not very wide.'

'Oh, they'll get it out all right. Derek's too fly to make a howler like that.' Then, after a pause, she added, 'I'm sorry to say.'

There was nothing to reply to this that I could think of. I stood looking at her, wondering if I could edge past her and go to the loo.

Phyllis Thackray looked at me defiantly, and I guessed that she was thinking about Nerina and her husband, and how I probably knew more about their relationship than she did.

Her eyes filled with tears.

'Stuff the bloody boat,' she said.

I thought of telling her that really Nerina had been quite discreet; that no one had told me anything. But I remembered Nerina lying on the couch with Derek at her side, and I remembered him standing in the bath, unabashed by Vincenza's arrival at the top of the stairs. And so he should be.

Yet he wouldn't have stood there laughing at us if Phyllis had been around. Nor would Nerina's hair have trailed gently across his hand as he sat looking at her.

I wanted to comfort Phyllis as she sat there on the steps, a middle-aged magistrate in her dungarees, knees angrily apart. She was probably as able as Derek, and she no doubt knew his weaknesses well enough to give him hell.

In any case these affairs strengthen a marriage, we are told.

This didn't seem the right moment to assure her of this. It crossed my mind that she would have been more comforted, savagely amused, even, if I could have told her about Nerina's vagina.

Someone once called me the master of the *non sequitur*. When I found out what it meant – for the classics didn't figure in my impressive collection of CSEs – when I found out what it meant, I was flattered, inasmuch as I am flattered to be the master of anything you can be mistress of. Now was a good opportunity to use my skill, I thought, for I needn't worry about my profile where Phyllis was concerned.

'Have you any children?' I asked her.

'Yes. But if you're thinking they're going to support me about this, forget it. We believed in permissiveness for one thing, and for another they're both away from home and we never see them.'

'Oh,' I said, thinking that I certainly would very soon lock myself into the loo or, last resort, drag myself across to the cowshed and the awed women who thronged it, even though this action would demoralize Phyllis still further. I had, after all, come here to celebrate the boat's departure.

'They really believe it'll convince me, that they'll stop seeing each other if the boat goes,' said Phyllis. 'It's a mystery to me why they think it's so important, the role I play in their adolescent little affair. I think deception must be part of the fun, the frisson.'

'Yes,' I said. 'I think it must be.'

I was following the principle that it is more comforting when people believe you than when they protest you have nothing to worry about. I could have said oh no, Phyllis, I'm sure any attraction there may have been will come to an end now the boat's going from the cowshed. That would have been like a doctor telling you your boils are nothing to worry about, now that just one of them has been lanced.

Phyllis looked at me for a few moments. She looked at me in a way that is considered insolent, letting her eyes travel over my body as I stood there thinking how to get away.

I tried to imagine what she thought about me, how she summed me up.

She'd know my background. I guessed that because I knew how every wife was pulled apart over the coffee and mints after dinner parties. She would think that I had no class, no background.

I let her look at me, and I thought about this. Was it possible that I was without these, and was this an advantage?

I decided to think about this later.

'What do you see, Phyllis Thackray?' I asked her. And her eyes stayed then, stopping roughly at the level of my waist, a nondescript feature that I had obliterated by tying a rope girdle round my hips.

She was equal to this approach.

'I see a woman of twenty-seven or thereabouts who relishes our suffering,' she said. 'Nature has endowed you with useful assets, May Knott. Because your face is so pale that you never blush, never give yourself away. Only the freckles round your nose give a hint of the open-air, or I should believe that you have lived all your life in some north-facing room in a flat below street level.'

Flattering stuff.

'I'm twenty-nine, to get the record straight,' I said.

'Well, I dare say you'll look twenty-seven for the next ten years at least. You have that type of skin. Doesn't wrinkle. A quirk of the hormones, over-active pituitary, something like that.'

I noticed that Phyllis herself had no worries on this score, for her skin was showing promise of lines and wrinkles in several directions.

But Phyllis went on to show that she didn't believe that looks are everything.

80

'What you have,' she said, 'is a quality I myself find aggravating. You don't get involved, you don't express opinions, you're never part of anything. That's why men find you attractive. You absorb their personalities like blotting paper, if you're not too young to know what that is.'

'You aren't a very kind person, are you, Phyllis?' I asked, expressing an opinion, just to show I knew how.

'You're watching us all, using us, and I don't see why I should be kind about that.'

This is how people are. You try to be considerate and they turn on you. I was a safe target, distracting her from sniping at Nerina and her husband. I was fulfilling a useful social purpose.

The conversation would no doubt have gone from bad to worse, but Nerina came round the corner of the house.

'Phyllis! There you are. We're all waiting for you. The ceremony wouldn't be the same without you.'

Phyllis stood up.

'Coming?' she asked me, as if I was a friend she couldn't manage without.

We started to walk across the yard, and Nerina waited for us at the corner of the house, to save wear and tear on her newly mended toe. She smiled at us, and Phyllis muttered to me, 'You see. This is my big moment. There wouldn't *be* a ceremony if I wasn't there. Such power.'

When we caught up with Nerina, Phyllis went on ahead, to avoid making small talk with her.

Nerina grimaced at me. 'So embarrassing!' she mouthed.

'For everybody,' I agreed, and she stopped smiling.

Her face changed. I knew this even though we were looking eye to eye at each other. I sensed the drop of her cheeks and mouth, the droop of her shoulders.

'Oh, my god,' she said. 'How am I going to do without him?' She sniffed. 'One day he's besotted with me, the next, Phyllis puts the screws on and it's all over. I know I'm expected to let it all finish with a good grace,' her eyes filled with tears, 'but I can't. I don't suppose it means a

81

thing to him. He'll just move on to some other sucker.'

'Put it down to testosterone. He must be pretty strong on male hormone.' I was trying to be sympathetic, and she looked at me sourly, understanding.

'Yes, well maybe I could slip a couple of oestrogen tablets into his cocoa and redress the balance,' she said.

And on top of all this, Louis hadn't yet turned up, though he was due back from Avalon ages ago. 'I can't understand it,' said Nerina, 'punctuality's one of his strong points.'

'I'm sure he'll be all right,' I said. 'Unless he's had an accident or something.'

This remark was in bad taste, and Nerina knew it. She looked at me sharply, then shivered. We walked the rest of the way in silence that went unnoticed, for so much noise was coming from the doors of the cowshed, mingling with the uncow-like smell of paint and tar. There were metallic clanks and hammerings, as a section of scaffolding was removed.

Derek was standing on an old table, touching-up the boat's name, 'Philander'. When I saw the name, I was taken aback. Now there was a real breach of taste, in the circumstances. Had Derek chosen it with black humour? Had Phyllis chosen it ironically?

Vincenza saw me looking at it. She came up to me with a dark blue glass in her hand. The glass looked like something to do with alchemy, and I half-expected smoke to lip over the top of it and ooze down the outside. I noticed other people drinking from the same sort of glasses. Nerina must have bought a job lot at Boots, I thought.

'Good name, isn't it?' asked Vincenza.

'I don't quite. . . .'

'*Phyl*lis *and De*rek,' said Vincenza. 'Phil-and-der. Get it?'

'Yes. Good.'

'It's a joke,' said Vincenza.

'So are glass eyes,' I said, but at that moment the last of the scaffolding was lifted away, and a cheer went up, so no one heard me, which was lucky for me because, as Phyllis rightly said, I like to avoid hassle, and already I wished I hadn't made any comment, even though there wasn't much likelihood of Vincenza realizing that I was referring to her glass ashtray.

'Ferg's here somewhere,' said Vincenza, standing on tiptoe to look round.

But Ferg and I had already seen each other, which was enough, for the moment. As long as we each knew the other was there, and that each of us knew that the other one knew, that was quite exhilarating enough for a few minutes. For hours, if necessary. No, not for hours. We hadn't reached that stage, for our last meeting, as you know, had ended on a somewhat unsure footing, and reassurance was needed that all was well between us.

However, I was quite content to be introduced to Maurice Ford and his wife meantime.

'Do you enjoy auctions?' his wife asked.

I told her I could take them or leave them, and I saw that she was disappointed with this answer.

'You're not trying to recruit May, are you, Evelyn?' Phyllis asked loudly, from behind me, and Evelyn Ford laughed.

Recruit me for what?

'The Holy Grailers,' said Phyllis.

It sounded religious; spiritual at the least. In fact, it turned out to be an organization worthy of *Moneycare*, and showed me just how on the button these university wives were. The Holy Grailers were a bunch of wives who combed the regional auctions for portable antiques or near-antiques and then had a beano in London about twice a year, when they went down to re-sell their bargains at immense profits.

'The trouble is, the market's drying up,' said Evelyn. 'The demand's the same as ever, greater, if anything. But everybody's climbing onto the bandwagon.'

She needed more recruits to cover more auctions. But I knew I couldn't help her. I can recognize a Victorian chaise-longue through sheer familiarity, having seen so many. Even then I wouldn't recognize a fake. And who wants to cart a chaise-longue down to London, in any case? The Holy Grailers were looking for salt cellars and tortoiseshell hair tidies, that sort of thing.

'You could just bid for pretty things,' said Evelyn, trying to encourage me, though I could see she wished she'd never mentioned it. Her eyes were on my neck.

'That necklet, for example. It's not exactly new, is it?'

Everyone looked at my neck, and I put my hand up, touching the red stone with my fingers.

'Oh, I don't think it's valuable. Someone gave it to me.'

'Art Nouveau costume jewellery,' said Evelyn. 'It's not *real*, but it is authentic. It would fetch quite a bit at the right place.'

Good old Arnie.

'Oh well. I don't think I want to part with it.'

'I'll give you £40 for it,' said Evelyn, as if she hadn't heard me.

People were beginning to crowd round, peering at my neck, reaching out to touch the red stone. Someone rolled the chain between finger and thumb, as if it was a bit of fabric. The fine hairs at the back of my neck caught in the links, and I ducked forward with a squeal. Ferg had disappeared. I seemed to be surrounded by hard faces that smiled, indifferent to my suffering.

'I don't want to sell it.' This came out too loud, and there was a pause. Everyone backed away, and I thought I was going to be left alone.

But a voice close behind me said, 'Tell my fortune with the cards. After this farce.'

I swung round in relief, recognizing the voice I most wanted to hear.

Ferg was there, so close that his face was almost out of focus.

'Yes,' I said. 'I'd like to tell your fortune.' People moved apart for us as we walked over to the bar, improvised from the old drinking trough, well-scrubbed, I guessed, by Hilde.

I had been a passing interest. Already talk was beginning again about other things. Like the UGC and the SSRC, and other initials that blew a cold chill under the doors of various departments in Avalon.

Meantime, Derek Thackray had backed his Range Rover up to the cowshed door.

Nerina looked flustered. She raised her voice, and everybody told everybody else to shush. There was a sort of silence. Nerina smiled.

'Louis was supposed to be giving a little speech at this point, but he hasn't turned up,' she said. 'So I'd just like to wish Phyllis and Derek every happiness with their boat that we all know Derek's put so much work into, and to hope it floats when he puts it on the water.'

Out of her pocket she produced some rose leaves, and she threw them up at the boat. Everyone clapped, and they floated back down, landing on her hair, and on Derek's shoulders, which we all ignored, since it was an unfortunate touch of symbolism. Phyllis stepped forward and brushed them off Derek's shirt.

There was champagne, still cheap, but without the sangria, as Vincenza hissed to me. We toasted the boat, and Phyllis, and Derek. Then Derek toasted Nerina and Louis for lending him the barn, and mentioning how delighted he was to hear this very day that Louis had been given tenure in the department.

Everyone except Ferg and me became very involved in lowering the boat onto its trolley and manhandling its tow-bar. The boat tipped forward slightly, its first movement. Then it began to move out through the door like a beheaded swan. We stood in near-darkness as it blocked the daylight till someone thought of switching on the light. By that time the back of the boat PHILANDER – its name picked out in yellow on a swirling white ribbon of paint – was nearly through the doorway, and outside there were shouts and warnings, till the tow-bar fitted into place on the Range Rover, and suddenly daylight returned, the end of the eclipse, and Ferg and I stood alone in the cowshed. In one hand he held a bottle of champagne, and in the other a glass. Whenever I meet Ferg, I thought, I shall first wonder whether or not he's sober. That is what I wondered now, till I remembered I had drunk several glasses of sangria and two glasses of champagne, and my judgment was unreliable.

Ferg raised the bottle slightly and looked at me, offering me a drink. I held out my glass, and he was refilling it when Nerina came back with Derek.

'Oh, you're still here,' she said.

Neither she nor Derek looked pleased to see us, and it was clear that they had hoped to have the cowshed to themselves.

Ferg held out the champagne bottle.

'Have a drink,' he offered.

But Nerina pushed his hand to one side. Then, as an afterthought, she took the bottle from him.

'We've come for the drinks, as a matter of fact,' she said. 'Nothing more embarrassing than running out of booze at a party.'

There was a pause while we all thought of far more embarrassing things than that.

Nerina picked up a tray of champagne bottles, and Derek rushed forward to help her as she staggered a little.

'*Oops!*' she laughed, like a tinkle of cymbals. 'It's hard getting used to this leg. Anyone'd think I was a bit woozled.'

'Not at all,' said Derek. 'It's too heavy for you, that's all.'

Nerina lifted the big glass jug, now empty, from the trough.

'I'll send Hilde for the rest of the things,' she said.

I had the feeling that as she looked round she was making sure that there was nothing of value that Ferg or I might take a fancy to.

We stood apart, politely waiting for them to go.

They had just gone through the doorway when there was the sound of hurrying footsteps.

Nerina was the first of us to recognize their owner.

'Oh, my god!' she said. 'Where have you been? We waited and waited.'

Louis came into view, looking red-faced and sweaty.

'Terrible,' he said. 'There's been a terrible accident on the motorway. Traffic's completely blocked on the north-bound carriageway. I waited for ages. Then I drove off the hard shoulder and just left the car on the grass.'

'What!'

'It's all right. The police said I could go back for it later. There's total mayhem down there. I hitched a lift in Armitage's van to Cornfield and walked the rest of the way.'

'It'll be on television,' said Nerina, handing him the sangria jug, which he took without seeming to notice.

'We'll be on the News. I hope it's no one we know.'

'Two Royal Mail vans and about quarter of a mile of private cars all concertina'ed. The central reservation's crushed flat.'

'Nasty,' said Ferg.

'Just the same,' we heard Nerina say as they began to walk back to the house, 'you could have phoned from somewhere. Derek's given you tenure.'

'Well, not *me* exactly.' Derek's voice became less distinct as they moved away across the yard. But I saw Ferg smile as we both recognized grovelling thank-you tones coming from Louis.

'What, after all, could be more important than tenure?' asked Ferg. 'The accident signifies the disorderliness of nature, the uncertainty of life. But tenure is stability, recognition for one's work, one's value to the group, the whole purpose of one's life.'

'And,' I said, 'the indispensable services of one's partner in achieving that purpose and recognition.'

'Right,' agreed Ferg.

'Hilde will be here in a minute.'

'Then,' said Ferg, 'we must go somewhere quiet where we won't be disturbed, and you can read my cards.'

*Perseverance will
bring plans to
fruition*

♡♣◇♧ Chapter 11 ♡♣◇♧
Three of Diamonds

We crossed over to the house, meeting Hilde on her way
to the cowshed with a big black tray.

'May, darling! If I'd known you were still there you
could have carried some things for me.'

But I had other things to do. I smiled and didn't take
the hint.

Ferg and I sat in a small room off the lounge that Nerina
called the parlour. It had diamond-paned windows, and
the evening sun shone across its floorboards, though the
lounge was as usual in shadow. There was no furniture in
this parlour yet, only an old black beam, that we sat on.

'I'll have to put the cards on the floor,' I said.

I felt reluctant to do this.

Then Ferg put his hand into his pocket and pulled out
my scarf, my orange flame.

He laid it on the floor, as if he was Sir Walter Raleigh,
and it has only just struck me that it seemed more
important to both of us to protect the cards rather than
the delicate silk scarf.

The parlour had no door, it was an alcove off the lounge, with its own stone fireplace and what would presently be an ingle-nook. People came and stood at the opening gawping at us but not quite having the nerve to come right into the room.

Later I realized that they were conniving at our affair. At the time I thought they were curious about my prowess as a cartomancer.

I laid out the cards. I still wasn't sure whether Ferg seriously wanted me to tell his fortune, or whether it was simply an excuse for us to indulge in this intimacy.

I had smiled, talking to him about his choice of court card (he chose the king of clubs). And for once I had no feeling of apprehension that he might have chosen bad cards, as I laid them out. I felt excited, suddenly seeing everything in its most positive light. No card that he could have chosen would present problems for me. I should be looking for relationships that would be meaningful to us both. In a way I was telling my own fortune as well as his. I looked for queens (me), for strangers, for a fuller life, and so on. I knew I should find them, and that I should link Ferg's life, for this time, with my own.

So as I turned each card over, and laid out Ferg's Mystic Cross, I didn't at first feel concern at their lack of promise. I knew I only needed one or two positive cards in order to give a reading that would fan our attraction for each other.

Thirteen cards I laid out, altogether. Seven down, supposed to represent the present situation, and the line across, which is the influence on this situation, what Ferg would make of the given features of his life.

When this was done, I looked, in a champagne haze, at the cross he and I had made together. Thirteen cards, and not a red one among them, not one heart, not one diamond.

Ferg had sat back on his heels and was looking at me in touching expectation. Seven spades, including the ace, and five clubs, including the king, of course, because he'd chosen it as his court card.

It crossed my mind that he had somehow engineered his choice in order to put me on the spot. Cards were second nature to him, I knew, for he was a heavy gambler, a poker player.

Yet at this moment he wasn't looking at me knowingly. His look was almost childlike, almost trusting.

'How did you manage that?' he asked, and I knew he assumed that in some way I was responsible for his choice. I was surprised that he seemed to have no idea what a doomed set of cards he'd selected.

He smiled and pointed at the ace of spades, the first card I'd turned over.

'You'll have a job getting out of that,' he said.

Silently I blamed Hilde. She'd made the ace of spades notorious, so that it was hard to talk your way out of it.

'Yours,' I said, 'is a life of two seasons, of summer and winter. Symbolically, your life by-passes the nuance of spring, of autumn. It's a life of sun or darkness.'

At the alcove one or two people paused, listening.

'You are fortunate that you have it in your power to control your own life, for it is a life of struggle and problems, where much is given to you, and where there is much to lose.'

Now this is the strange thing, that I speak like this, almost in a different language, when I am reading the cards.

A few more people gathered round, keeping at the entrance, not coming into the room. I was only half-aware of them, for reading the cards is like writing my novel, I become absorbed in it. Sometimes I feel as if I am using a part of my brain that usually remains dormant – I seem to feel it stretching like a piece of dried chamois leather. But I knew about the people because they began to form a barrier of silence between the parlour and the large white room where the party was in progress.

I had expected Ferg to make light of this seance, to tease me, to be scornful. But he sat quietly, looking at me in a fixed manner that made me wonder again how drunk he was.

Ferg had selected some dire cards. That shouldn't have mattered. I should have been able to tell him anything. I should have been able to snatch meanings for these cards out of the air. I could have said that the eight of spades represented strength and security when considered together with the ten of clubs, or that it meant a long journey of discovery. I could have said anything at all. What did it matter? Because after all the cards were an expediency for me, that was all. Yet I never did this. I had learnt the significance of each card to cartomancy as once, years ago, I had learnt my two–times table from my adoptive mother, Emmy Thompson.

'The pivotal card,' I said, pointing to the central card in Ferg's Mystical Cross, 'is the eight of clubs, the gamblers' card. Your whole life revolves around taking risks. With your personality you can ignore red tape. There are no rules that cannot be broken. You by-pass the usual channels. For you, inspired guesses will bear fruit. Nor should you spend time in analysing motives or hunches, for this leads, with your personality, to confusion and complication.'

'The Death Card.' I heard the stage whisper, and I guessed it came from Hilde, who had pushed herself to the front of the onlookers.

'Things are not easy in your life,' I said, ignoring the stir in the group at the alcove. 'There is duality, a change of circumstance. If we look at your life till the present, we can see there have been stresses within the family, times when you have felt it wiser to go it alone.'

'Extraordinary,' said Ferg.

The party was becoming silent. More and more people had drifted over to the alcove. I heard someone, Hilde perhaps, shush them.

'I see a young boy,' I said. 'Emotionally immature, self-indulgent. It's not clear whether he has played a part in your life, or whether it's you yourself. A young brother, a friend, possibly. It could even be a younger sister.'

Ferg didn't help me. He still stared at me, as if mesmerized.

'Whoever he or she is, they must not be relied on.'

Someone sniggered. Nerina came loudly into the lounge.

'Sandwiches anyone?' She walked across the room, and a plate clattered onto the table. Then she saw the crowd, and I heard her tiptoe over to join them.

'There is curiosity surrounding your life, gossip possibly. And there are endless discussions.'

'Committee meetings,' said Ferg, agreeing with me, while our audience sniggered, and I saw that he was treating this reading seriously, anxious to believe in it. So much for the Double First.

'I see another warning, that you mustn't trust a colleague or confide in him or her,' I said.

'What about my sex life?' asked Ferg, and everyone laughed.

'I see two women, one good, one bad,' I said. It had become very quiet. 'One is attractive, full of vitality and good works, a woman that other women are jealous of. A good home-maker, yet impatient of her home.'

'What of the other woman?' asked Ferg, as if such a paragon was not for him.

'Beware of the other woman,' I said, and the audience laughed appreciatively. The cards are sexist, and there are no really good women in them, but the queen of spades is the worst. 'In other ages,' I said, 'this woman would have been a witch.'

'Ah!' said Hilde's voice.

'She is ambitious and ruthless in the pursuit of power.'

'Well, Gipsy Woman, I hope it's you, because I'm not afraid of such a woman,' Ferg said, and he leant across the table and touched my hand. No one heard him speak except me, for they were all laughing and applauding, 'Rough luck, Ferg!' in the way they do when any man is threatened with a tough woman.

I found myself wondering whether to identify with the queen of clubs, the dark, vital and successful woman I had provided for him. Or should I identify with the queen of spades, who flanked his other side? At this moment I didn't feel particularly ruthless or ambitious. But what of my attempts to break into this circle? Wasn't that ambition? What of cartomancy? Wasn't that ruthless?

'And how will this relationship end?' asked Ferg. 'What will come of it?'

'That isn't on the cards,' I hedged. 'Only those involved can finally determine what will come of it. I can only give warnings, show predispositions, and suggest courses of action.'

I looked for a few moments at the bad cards that finished Ferg's ill-fated cross. 'Whatever course you take, there will be risks. But you must be determined in your actions, and take them decisively. I see wealth, a large sum of money. Yet you must guard this carefully, for there is a warning here, that a valuable article will be stolen or lost.'

'What's the three of spades?' asked Ferg, for that was the last card on the limb of the cross.

'The eternal triangle,' I said, and everybody laughed again. This was becoming a comedy act. 'That doesn't necessarily mean a stumbling-block in love. It could be a rival in business, or some other relationship. It could be matriarchal interference.'

'Oh,' said Ferg, and he put his hands to his head in mock despair, playing to our audience. 'Not mummy again!'

I changed the subject.

'Well,' I said, 'everything is in flux in your life at the moment, and there are opportunities ahead. It looks as if the problems will come to a head and then be resolved. It's true that there are obstacles, but once encountered, they will be overcome if you take firm action, and then the way ahead will present no impediments.'

Impediments! I'd never used the word before. I was dubious about my interpretation, because in order to end on a positive note I had mentally swapped the order of some of Ferg's cards. This was the first time I had doctored my interpretations, and it made me feel uncomfortable, as I leaned forward, smiling confidently at him,

93

and began to collect up the cards. Under my fingers the silk scarf ruckled in small waves. I put the cards away in my bag, even though Nerina and Phyllis were both calling to me, for once in accord, asking me to read Derek's hand. But I had no wish to involve myself in their tug-of-war over that undeserving, under-sized academic, a description that Ferg whispered to me as we bent over together, folding the scarf with exaggerated care, so that our fingers touched.

'Now you must take the scarf, Gipsy Woman,' said Ferg, offering it to me. 'For it has held my fate, and some of yours as well.'

So I took the soft flame and put it into my pocket.

We went out into the lounge together, and people, still gathered round the mouth of the alcove, moved away from us, letting us pass easily. They stared at us in the manner of spectators who have a right to do so because they have found out something secret about us – as the crowd stares invasively at newspaper subjects whose private lives have been laid bare in one of the Sundays.

We agreed that we were entitled to more champagne, in payment for our entertainment value. We had lost our glasses, and only tumblers remained unused on the long window-sill where the drinks were now lined up. The tumblers were arranged round an almost full jug of orange juice, for Nerina's guests had no tendency to teetotalism. Ferg grabbed two tumblers and filled them with champagne, handing one to me.

'We shall leave this rabble, Gipsy Woman,' he said, no doubt taking the decisive action he'd been advised upon. 'Therefore it is only prudent to stock up with adequate provisions.'

He took a lump of cheese and an olive on a stick out of a cocktail hedgehog, and motioned with his head for me to leave the room with him.

But I didn't leave at once, that would have been too obvious. Across the room I could see him waiting for me. He was in shadow in the hall, where the light filtered down from the staircase, picking out the angles of his face

94

in pale greenish shades. Slightly stooping, in the manner of tall people in old houses even when it is not necessary, he leant over to listen to Hilde. I saw her lift her hand and feed him, a petit-four I supposed. She put it to his lips, and I saw him open his mouth, pulling his lips back from his teeth to clench it, while she laughed in pleasure, as you might when feeding a horse a carrot.

An arm went round my waist, colour swirled in front of me. Perfume that I thought too sweet could not be avoided, unless I gave up breathing. Vincenza's face came close to mine, and she was smiling. How bright her eyes were, and her cheeks were the colour of strawberries. Banana split. Fruit salad.

'May,' she said. 'We're all talking about Edwin. He's going to become famous, like Asa Briggs, or Basil Bernstein. Did you know that?'

Her question sounded genuinely interested.

'He's a natural scholar,' I said, not admitting anything, or denying it.

Vincenza shook her head. 'Natural scholars don't often become famous,' she said. 'Think of G. E. M. de Sainte Croix. You couldn't be more of a natural scholar than he is. But who's ever heard of him?'

Not me, for sure. So I just waited, not answering her question.

'No,' said Vincenza. 'You've got to have other qualities if you want to make a name for yourself.'

'What are those?' I asked, sipping my champagne and trying not to show my impatience. But Ferg seemed to have settled into a chin-wag with Hilde, smiling, listening courteously, making the occasional comment so that her flattered laughter boomed across to us where we stood by the door into the kitchen.

I tried to think about Edwin's qualities, but all I could think of was his burnt omelettes and how his principal hobby seemed to be watching television, now that he had given up cutting hedges.

'Oh, May!'

Vincenza looked at me, and her look surprised me, for

it wasn't a worldly, impatient look, it had kindness in it.

'Nobody outside academe ever heard of the Breton Lays till Edwin put them on the map.'

'The Breton Lays. A deadly combination,' said Derek, and I saw that Vincenza was, as she had said, part of a group, that now surrounded us both. 'Love and the supernatural. You can't go wrong with a combination of the two.'

'It won't be long before our Edwin's a television pundit, our Expert on Medieval Affairs, something like that.'

'*And* every housewife's heart-throb.'

The comments came from all around me, and I tried to tell myself that they were not aimed at me, I had dropped into the midst of a conversation that would have taken place in any case. Vincenza was looking at me; they all were. I sipped my champagne, thinking of the unlikely combination, Edwin and the supernatural.

Under my feet the floor felt soft and spongy. I was standing in a clearing on soft damp grass, surrounded by trees. From time to time a face appeared from behind one or other of the trees.

Vincenza's face said, 'You are a perfectly medieval partner for Edwin, May darling. A pale, mysterious seer.'

Phyllis' face looked from behind another tree.

'Public image has become integral on the campus . . . the importance of attracting Overseas Students to one's department. . . .'

Derek's face said, 'We are reduced to ingenuity in order to achieve viability, to survive, in fact, in the Humanities.'

Nerina said, 'Really Hilde is a liability. There isn't a clean glass in the house. She was supposed to be doing the washing-up. Where is she, for god's sake?'

The trees faded away. I was standing on the Afghan rug, and its wetness seeped between my toes, through the thin soles of my sandals. Someone had spilt their drink at my feet, where Nerina was grovelling around on her knees with a cloth.

'If you could just move a little to the. . . .'

'Oh, I'm sorry,' I said. My glass was empty.

'No harm done,' said Nerina, standing up very carefully.

Surely she didn't think it was me who had made that mess on her rug?

'Here,' said Derek, taking my glass. 'Let me get you another drink.'

'Are you driving?' asked Phyllis in a magisterial manner, and I said no, I wasn't, not at the moment, which made me laugh.

'Mummy darling, do come and give a hand,' Nerina called to Hilde, and now Ferg was standing beside me, holding my arm.

'Come and get some fresh air,' he said, and as he led me away, I heard Nerina complaining to Hilde.

'Darling, at this rate I shall be sober at the end of the party. I'm having to do everything myself. Where's Louis got to?'

And Hilde's reply: 'I may be your mother, but I am not your skivvy.'

Heart's desire.
The 'wish' card

♡♣◇♠ Chapter 12 ♣◇♠
Nine of Hearts

It seemed we were not to get fresh air after all, for Ferg was helping me up the narrow stairs where I had once been before, to the lime-green bathroom.

At this moment lime-green seemed a particularly vicious colour, and I backed away. But he had his hand under my elbow.

'You aren't afraid of me, are you?'

Which seemed a strange question, having nothing to do with green and baths.

Then we were at the top of the stairs.

'A door!' I said in surprise. And it was true that the bathroom now sported a stripped oak board door. It was closed.

We waited, saying nothing to each other. Ferg now had his arm right round me. His hand moved up to my breast, and I knew he was looking down at me, waiting for me to show some sort of reaction. But I couldn't think of any, except that I wanted the door to open.

Which it did. Louis opened it from inside. When he saw

us waiting there, he turned back and said something.

'Pardon?' I asked, assuming he must be talking to us. But then his dark-haired research student, the one with the 'I Ran the World' T-shirt, appeared, and slipped past us down the stairs, not looking at us. Louis smiled brightly and followed her.

We went into the bathroom.

'I Ran the Bath,' said Ferg, turning the taps on, and I giggled.

'Lock the door,' I said.

But Ferg had thought this scheme out beforehand. No use locking the door. If there is one need everyone has in common, it is a lavatory, and they would soon be clamouring to be let in if we locked the door against them.

He turned off the bath-taps and looked down to the other end of the attic, where there was still no partition, or any light, except that which came from the bathroom end.

'Come with me,' he said.

He helped me over some of the joists, onto an area of hardboard.

'Down here.'

Among other discarded furniture there was a white dresser, the laminated chipboard type that Nerina no doubt bought in her harder-up days, but which had no place in her present life-style. Beyond the dresser was more hardboard floor on which was a pile of old curtains.

Ferg began to spread these over the floor as someone came into the bathroom, and we ducked down behind the dresser, completely hidden from view, in dark shadow.

The person presently went out, flushing the loo, but not, I remember noticing, washing their hands. I shall never know who it was.

'You see,' said Ferg. 'No one will have any idea we're here. Well, no one except Louis and "I Ran the World", possibly.'

He knelt on the curtains, which gave the least possible softness to the floor, for I heard his knees making grating sounds on the hardboard. He pulled me down beside him.

I had a moment's doubt. It seemed squalid, making love to the rhythm of the flushing loo and other related noises.

'You and I,' said Ferg, 'are archetypal flies on the wall.'

'We can't see anything,' I said.

But Ferg opened one of the dresser doors very gently, so that he made no sound.

'Look,' he said.

I looked.

The dresser, constructed to minimum standards for maximum profit, had no back. Through the crack in the partly open door we were gazing straight into the bathroom.

The bathroom door opened. Nerina appeared. As one, we both began to close the door. Then, an afterthought, we both opened it again, as one.

We watched Nerina, who, I can tell you, weed the same as anybody else. After that she touched up the nail varnish on her toenails, balancing each foot in turn on the front ledge of the shower. Then she sat on the edge of the bath waiting for the varnish to dry.

Someone tried the door.

'Coming in a minute,' she called.

She waved her feet about, to encourage them to dry. Then she stood up and checked her hair and washed her hands.

Someone tried the door again.

'Coming!' she called brightly. And in a lower voice, she muttered, 'Sod off.'

But what was all this about Ferg being impotent?

His hand was inside my knicker elastic. Nerina left the bathroom and we closed the dresser door.

The bathroom was in almost constant demand, but hidden behind the dresser we made what must count as fairly satisfactory love, although the floor was so hard, and I refused to take my clothes off. We both assured each other that we didn't have high expectations for our first attempt, which, as everybody knows, though they don't seem to know that they know it, is a surefire way of reducing doubt and tension. Ferg told me this afterwards.

I did think of Edwin. I thought I would redouble my efforts to finish my novel so that I could start another one that might be more successful. After all, I thought, if he's becoming so famous – which made no sense to me at all – he presently won't be bothered about being a patron, so I'd better get on before I get thrown out.

Ferg was lying on his back telling me about his homosexual experiences at Oxford in quiet moments between the loo visits of party-goers, and he had got to the bit where he says what he likes about me is that he can tell me anything, when Hilde came into the bathroom singing 'The Red Flag'.

She closed the door with a bang that made our dresser door open of its own accord. Then she fumbled for a few moments with the door lock.

We had no wish to peep at her performance, and were just closing our door, when Hilde kicked off her shoes, one of which came flying to our end of the attic and landed close to the edge of our curtains. We saw that she was clambering into the bath. She unhitched the pink lace cushions that were provided as headrests, and turning onto her side, she snuggled them under her cheek. In half a minute she was asleep, snoring in a way that couldn't be ignored.

We looked at each other in some consternation. It seemed as though this unusual episode in our lives had come to an end.

'I could have stayed here for hours,' we both agreed.

Usually I would have left decisive action to someone else. But Ferg showed signs of capitulation, so I decided it was up to me to hold this act together.

It was easy. I simply tiptoed over to the door and unlocked it. I put Hilde's shoes neatly together by the side of the bath. Then I slipped back to our hiding-place.

Like two children we waited in delicious anticipation, laced with a hint of danger, to see what would happen.

The bathroom door opened and Derek Thackray appeared. He saw Hilde immediately. Undoing his flies, he walked over to her and took a closer look. Then he went to the lavatory and relieved himself. He left the room without looking again at the body snoring in the bath.

Well, that didn't work. Of course, if all the visitors to the bathroom took the same evasive action as Derek, the only inconvenience to us would be the sound of her snoring.

'I wouldn't mind if only she could snore in tune,' said Ferg. He insisted that she was doing a rendition of 'Colonel Bogey'.

However, Vincenza appeared next, and presently a whole gang invaded the bathroom, and Hilde was hefted, protesting in German, out of the bath and, from what we could gather, into Louis and Nerina's bedroom.

I sneaked out and borrowed the lace-edged cushions, and we lay with our heads in herbal fragrance, close to each other, while Ferg stroked my face, looking at me from time to time, though most of the time his eyes were closed. I put my arm across him, and he sighed, 'May Knott.' We dozed, though I remained alert even in sleep, for I didn't feel as secure as Ferg seemed to. People came and went in the bathroom. I half-heard them, but the dresser door stayed closed, I had no interest in spying on anyone. Ferg was asleep now, breathing gently against my face.

There is comfort in lying close to another person, though from time to time, as I surfaced into consciousness, I knew I should go, and leave Ferg to sleep off his sex and champagne. But I kept delaying, and presently I too fell into real sleep.

Inconstancy

♡♣♢♠ Chapter 13 ♡♣♢♠
Two Eights

For moments the two voices only disturbed me enough to
float into my sleep and hover there so that, if I had been
able to think about them, I should have believed I was
dreaming.

'I can't. I can't tell her anything.'

Around me there was the smell of potpourri. And there
was pine oil and lavender. Pine oil and lavender didn't
come from the cushions. Ferg's breath still touched my
face. I heard the soft splash of water; the atmosphere felt
different, warm and damp.

Two people were having a bath in the green circular
bath.

I disengaged my arm and rolled over onto my stomach.
Ferg drew an audible breath, almost like a snore. But
he didn't disturb the bathers. The splashes continued,
as desultory as the conversation. Then they became
more purposeful. I opened the dresser door a small
crack.

Vincenza had a loofah in her hand. She was rubbing it

over a man's back, which showed through the white foam bubbles, brown and satiny.

Vincenza was in the bath with Edwin. Vincenza was talking about me to Edwin. Vincenza was scrubbing Edwin's back. Edwin was at Nerina's house, he wasn't at Portsmouth. Possibly he never had been. Vincenza and Edwin. Vincenza and Ferg. What was she trying to do to me? I opened the door further.

'You should tell her,' said Vincenza, and in the bath Edwin shifted his buttocks.

'You can't tell her anything. She puts it all in her damned novel.'

'What a shame,' said Vincenza, and she slowed her efforts with the loofah, using longer, soothing strokes. She had skinny shoulder-blades, I noticed. I imagined her as a skeleton.

'It's just the sort of thing that's meat and drink to her,' said Edwin in a poor-me voice. 'Finding a papal dispensation in the foot of a lectern, royal incest. Can't you imagine what she'd do with that? She'd have it all down on paper the moment I left the room.'

'I thought she let you read everything she writes.'

'Yes, she does. But she's so uncommunicative, for all I know she's got two novels on the go, the one she shows me, and another, different version.'

'That's a bit paranoid, isn't it? She's not up to that sort of scheming, is she? I mean, even if she could work such a plan out, she's not really up to covering more than the basic, personal relationship sort of plot, is she?'

Thank you, Vincenza.

But Edwin demurred, as they say in very boring books.

'Don't underestimate her. She's deeper than you might think. Look at the cartomancy business. And she's suspicious about me coming back the other night. She's not entirely naïve.'

Ah. So he'd read to page sixty-four. I'd often wondered whether he read my ms. when I wasn't there. I tried to imagine him coming into my study, turning the pages, reading what I'd written. I wasn't disgusted, for, as my patron, Edwin was entitled, I felt, to read my work at any time he wished, unlike Ferg, or anyone else. That was his privilege, but it was a privilege that I didn't know he took advantage of.

I was flattered that he took my novel seriously enough to read in my absence. I had noticed he had to steel himself to settle down and read each section as I wrote it. Now I knew why. Because he had already read it. Poor Edwin.

'Does it in fact matter if she gets hold of it and shoves it into her novel?' asked the hateful Vincenza, rinsing the soap off Edwin's two-timing back.

'Yes, it does. I want to get the facts authenticated and all the work complete before I get any publicity. She's written the first sixty pages. She'll never sustain a novel of more than two hundred pages, so she'll get it finished, on present form, before I can get all my background work done. She'll be published before me.'

'Oh, I doubt it,' said the thoroughly skeletal Vincenza of the shrunken brain-box. 'There's very little chance of publication, surely, going on past form?'

'I wouldn't say that, exactly,' said Edwin. He had to show a modicum of faith in me, being my patron. His voice became plaintive. 'I have to live a life of deception, pretending to watch television every evening while she's upstairs working. She can't stand TV, so it's the only way I can get away from her. It's not easy, working in the same room as all that American rubbish, I can tell you.'

'Poor Edwin,' said Vincenza, while I was wondering if he'd been infected by all the trash he'd been watching, or trying not to watch, which might be why he was sitting here in the bath with a tatty Child Care Officer who was showing all the signs of illiteracy.

'I shouldn't worry,' soothed this bony matriarch, 'I think we've got our May fixed now. Ferg'll take care of her.'

Oh no. Oh no. I was tensed, ready to spring up, to rush into their bathroom, to face them.

And so I would have, but the sleeping Ferg stirred at

my side, and I saw that if I confronted them I should reveal myself as the dupe they thought that I was. Vincenza had primed Ferg, who had taken me on. They were all laughing at me, using me, as I had been laughing at them and using them.

Turning away from the cupboard door, I peered closer at Ferg. The voices hadn't the same significance for him that they had for me. He still slept soundly, unaware that he had been revealed as a play-acting, fraudulent stick insect.

I dug my finger hard into his ribs. Life was hateful. But at the same time I cupped my other hand over his mouth so that any sound he made would be muffled and unheard by the conger eels who writhed in the bath.

But Ferg made no sound at all. My vicious dig had no effect on him, for he was sleeping off his drunken debauch, as I now saw it.

'I'm not sure that Ferg's such a good idea,' Edwin was saying. 'There's this fellow she goes bird-watching with. I've no idea who he is. Never seen her with him. It seems to me there are quite enough men in her life.'

Bird-watching! Me, May Knott?

'I can't imagine May bird-watching,' said Vincenza thoughtfully.

Nor could I.

'This Hugo person,' said Edwin. 'Kingfishers.'

Oh dear, oh my! Oh merciful queen mother of hearts! Hugo! *Hugo*! I'd forgotten all about him. And there he was, at the very beginning of my novel. What was I going to do with him? Could he perhaps be deleted altogether?

Hugo was a figment of my imagination. There had never been Hugo. There had never been a kingfisher at the bridge, as far as I knew. I had put Hugo into the story at the very beginning and then forgotten all about him.

And silly Edwin believed in his existence, though if there were half a dozen Hugos it shouldn't matter in the slightest to him.

None of this explained why Edwin was in the bath with Vincenza.

106

But perhaps it did.

'She's so deep, so devious. To tell you the truth I shall be relieved if her book becomes a best-seller, or someone buys the film rights, or something. Then I shan't feel so obligated to her.'

Oh, Edwin. It distressed me to hear him put into words my own feelings exactly, and I felt hurt.

'She's had a terrible life, you know.'

'So have a lot of other people,' said Vincenza, hard as a petrified loofah. 'You can't take them all on, dear Edwin.'

There was a wet noise like two melons knocking together in the dark. Edwin was kissing Vincenza. I wondered if I was going to be sick into the cupboard.

'That's why it's such a relief to be with you, Vincenza. You're so strong, so practical. I can lean on you.'

Don't lean on her, Edwin, don't. We can do without her. We were, in fact, doing very well without her.

There were more melon noises.

'I always fancied a bath in here,' said Vincenza. 'But, of course, there's no pleasure in having it on one's own. Not in a double bath. Nothing voluptuous about that. It was delicious of you to accept my invitation, dear Edwin.'

It was weak and duplicitous, as a matter of fact. Everyone was hateful. There was no one to trust.

The water was gurgling out of the plughole, and the two lovers – no, possibly they weren't, yet – were standing up in the bath drying each other with pink fluffy towels.

'You must come and see me some Wednesday afternoon,' Vincenza was saying, 'I'm usually free on Wednesdays.'

Yes, why don't you, Edwin?

'Well,' said Edwin, 'it would be a bit difficult. . . .'

You're surely not backing out now, are you?

But then there was banging at the bathroom door, and Phyllis Thackray's voice called, 'Vincenza, are you in there? I think you should come quickly.'

'Oh, no!' groaned Vincenza. 'Not another tedious inadequate!' Then, louder, she called, 'What's the matter?'

Phyllis rattled the door irritably. 'It's Martin. He's here in his pyjamas. It's really rather sad.'

'God!' said Vincenza to Edwin. 'Is there no freedom whatever?'

She wrapped the towel round herself and gave Edwin a quick hug.

'I've got to go,' she said. Bare-footed, she padded to the door, turning as she unlocked it. She pulled a face: 'Call of nature, I suppose you could say!'

She left the room and I heard her tripping down the stairs. 'Marty, love, whatever's the matter?'

All tolerant and humorous.

The door of the bathroom opened, and Phyllis' face appeared round it. She saw Edwin as he balanced on one foot, putting on his underpants. Her face went blank with comprehension.

'Will you be long in here?' she asked.

She was not the sort of magistrate who gives a naughty boy a violin if he says he wants to take up a hobby, despite her earlier protestations of permissiveness.

It was a pity that she appeared at that juncture, because it would have been an ideal time for me to confront Edwin; to step out from behind the dresser, coolly. 'Oh, Edwin! Hullo!'

He was throwing his clothes on, I thought I could hear him panting. I decided to step out anyway, even though the timing wouldn't be quite right.

'Wait for me, Edwin.'

He swung round.

'May!'

What else could he say?

I smiled at Phyllis, who was staring at us both.

Edwin was standing gaping at me numbly.

'Well, go on,' I encouraged. 'Down the stairs, Edwin.'

He went zombie-like downwards, and I followed behind him. At the bottom, I looked back. Phyllis was still watching, as if bemused.

Edwin got hold of my arm.

'Where have you been? I've been looking everywhere

108

for you. I thought you'd gone off somewhere with Ferg Baverstock.'

Oh, I see. Bathing with Vincenza was retaliation, I suppose.

'Where have *you* been Edwin? I thought you were in Portsmouth.'

I would have said, 'Take me home, please,' but it wasn't my home, and I didn't want to go there.

*Selfishness
holds sway*

♡♣◇♤ **Chapter 14** ♡♣◇♤

Seven of Spades

A little dervish came whirling towards me, pyjama coat flying.

'May Knott asked me to the party. You did, didn't you?'

Martin had hold of my other arm. Tears were running down his cheeks. Behind him I saw Vincenza shrugging as if helplessly, as she hitched up her pink towel toga.

I knelt down, pulling away from Edwin.

'Yes,' I said. 'I did ask you to the party. And I'm very glad to see you.'

I put my arms round his cool little body, for it was dark now, and a cold mist lay in lakes round the farmyard.

'You want me, don't you, May Knott?'

'Yes. I want you very much.'

We clung together, while the women watched, curious. I had thought that in that entire gathering I had no friends. Yet here was Martin, who had stumbled to this wild place and arrived precisely when I needed him.

He rubbed his snotty face along the shoulder of my tie-

110

and-dye track suit. I took off the jacket and wrapped it round him.

Vincenza moved forward, but I swung round and scowled at her, and she stepped back, sensing retreat was wisest. Sensing perhaps that I knew about the antics in the bath.

'Come and have a drink,' I said to Marty. 'You can have anything. Anything you like.'

He brightened. 'Can I have a shandy?'

'You can have anything.'

Edwin said, 'May....' But I brushed him away, and Marty and I went inside.

We looked round. The room was dishevelled, with glasses everywhere now that the chief glass-washer had been put to bed.

Louis appeared from the kitchen. He looked abstracted.

'Hullo, Marty, old chap.' He turned to me. 'Nerina's dashed off in the car. She's behaving rather hysterically. She developed a sudden morbid interest in accidents and insisted on driving down to the motorway bridge to see the remains of the pile-up. Derek's following her in the Range Rover.'

'He's gone in the Range Rover? I thought the boat was hitched to it,' I said.

'Yes. There wasn't time to unhitch it. He just took off, boat and all. We were worried, but quite honestly I thought it would be better to give them both a chance to sort out their problem.'

He peered round as he spoke, as if he was looking for someone, and I saw 'I Ran the World' making her way across the room towards him.

'In any case,' he said, 'my car's already down there, and it would have meant borrowing one. It's really rather a shame Phyllis delivered her ultimatum and Derek's got to take the damned boat away. Nerina will be hell for at least a week. That's why she's driven off, of course. Making a statement in her usual dramatic way. And Sir Galahad's speeding to her rescue, dragging his trusty steed behind

111

him. Ah me, the urgency of the Quest. It's all in vain, of course. She's put away a lot of booze very quickly. She'll throw up if he starts any of his passion stuff.'

'Would you like Marty and me to go and look for them?'

'It's a good offer,' said Louis. He put his arm round 'I Ran the World', who was gazing at him with her protuberant eyes. 'But it's too silly. We can't all disappear into the mist like Abominable Snowmen.'

'Abominable Snowmen go into the snow,' said Marty.

But Louis wasn't amused. 'Haven't you heard,' he said, 'of mist on mountains? Anyway it's not important. A figure of speech.'

Marty looked round. 'Where's Christian?' he asked, expecting to see Louis and Nerina's son.

Louis emptied ice into a plastic ice-bucket, still programmed to be the party host, even though his wife had disappeared into the mist followed by her lover and his boat.

'Christian's staying the night at his friend's house in Avalon,' he said, with a hint of reproof.

Martin sensed the reproach. Colour welled into his face, and he looked down at his drink as if his relish in it was no longer enjoyable. How easy it is to spoil such things for children.

What made it worse was that he and I had nothing to say to each other.

'Where's your baby-sitter?' I asked, casting around.

'He's playing table football.'

'On his own?'

'No. He brought his girlfriend. They didn't want me. I snuck out of the back door. They think I'm in bed.'

'They'll get a bit of a shock when they find you aren't.'

We both laughed, thinking about this. Then we stopped laughing, thinking about Vincenza and Bertie thinking about it.

'Marty, darling.' Vincenza was coming down the stairs, and I knew that she would be fully dressed and in command of herself now. And in command of Marty, and me.

Marty turned to me. 'I don't want to go. Not yet. She'll take me home.'

Usually this would have been a relief to me, an opportunity to rid myself of a tedious appendage. The shyness between Marty and me didn't mean that we wanted to escape from each other, though. I could have said you've had your fun now and your mother's upset and worried about you. Shouldn't you go back to her?

But the more Vincenza was upset and worried, the more I should be pleased, and I didn't feel that I owed her any of the conventional favours.

Nevertheless, revenge on Vincenza was not my first thought, I was surprised to find. Now Marty and I had joined forces, however tenuously, I didn't want to lose him, and I felt a need in myself to support him and to try to provide him with something that would please him.

'Let's go down to the motorway bridge,' I said. 'Let's see if we can find Nerina and bring her home, possibly.'

'But Professor Thackray's gone to look for her.'

'Well then, we'll hunt them both, stalk them to the motorway.'

'Has anyone seen . . .?' Vincenza's voice was nearer now.

I steered Marty into the kitchen and closed the door.

'Climb into the sink,' I hissed at him, remembering Hilde.

I opened the window. 'Now. Out you go. I'll follow.'

He became as absorbed as if he was seeing himself as a cadet on an obstacle course. Except that he was awkward and clumsy, not used to such manœuvres. He fell over the drainage tiles outside the window, and for a moment I thought he was going to cry. I clambered down beside him, and he straightened up.

'I've got mud on your jacket.'

'It's not important.' I closed the window and we dodged across the yard to my car.

'Keep in the shadows,' I whispered, and we ducked and steered dramatically till we were beside my car.

I heard Vincenza's voice, impatient now, with a more concerned edge to it.

We set off in fine Superman style, the wheels spinning in the muddy yard before we raced away to the lane and bumped from one pothole to the next.

Then we were on the road, roaring across the desolate moor with the mist closing in around us, as I remarked in a running commentary to Marty.

'To the rescue!' I cried, putting my foot on the accelerator, and Marty beside me egged me on:

'Faster, Catwoman, faster!'

'. . . And so they hurtled fearlessly into the. . . .'

'Into the black depths of unknowingness,' supplied Marty, 'wrapped around by billowing clouds of argon, perilously protected by the thin red enamel of their oxygen capsule.'

I glanced sideways at him. He was grinning, laughing at me, waiting for me to take my turn. We swung round at a blue motorway sign.

'"North two points," directed the navigator, removing the front of the glove compartment to check the hidden computer.'

Marty opened the glove compartment. He examined its contents.

'Extra strong mints,' he noticed. 'Emergency rations. Can I have . . .?'

But he never did have, because a blue heart began to beat in the mist ahead of us.

Her red nail varnish glinting suggestively under the fine net of her black tights, Catwoman jammed her foot on the protesting. . . .

I braked hard under the teetering shadow that reared above us, and immediately ahead a darker silhouette leapt to one side of the car. I stopped. A face came into focus at Marty's side of the car. I reached past him and wound down the window.

Accident, accident, mouthed the face, and I thought, this is too much for Marty. He mustn't see.

'Switch on your hazard lights,' said Marty beside me.

'Pull back, reverse,' the cop was saying. He glowed in the dark. Lights, orange and blue, seemed to be flashing everywhere. And towering over all was a blue clinker-built wall that reflected the lights off its newly glazed surface.

We reversed, pulling into the side of the road. I switched off the engine. There was a second's silence, then the police two-way radio crackled into the mist around us. My hazard lights made comfortable clicking noises. I thought I heard someone crying.

'You'd better stay here,' I said to Marty.

I began to get out of the car. So did he.

'I'm coming,' he said, and as cold dampness swirled round me, I thought that was a good decision, for if a car came quickly round the corner, my car would be a sitting duck, and so would Marty.

We got out, slamming the doors in the dripping silence.

The *Philander* was slewed across the narrow road, completely blocking it. On the left, the Range Rover was canted over the cutting that fell away from the road.

I gawped. For it was as if the boat had decided to take part in the fantasy that Marty and I had been concocting as we drove along. It was the ghost of a boat.

The Range Rover's lights were still on, part-way down the cutting, beaming over the wild flowers that grew there, and I remember thinking really summer's only just begun, for cowslips were there, still in flower, though with some of the calyxes shrinking and blackened, at the end of their season. But other flowers looked bright and pretty, while above them the boat straddled the road, tipped partly on its side, at a broken and unnatural angle to the tow-bar.

I walked towards it in the wet silence. The driver's door hung open from the Range Rover, and there were parallel lines of bent grasses leading from it. So Derek had left the car.

'Derek!' I called, and I thought he'll never answer, he'll never recognize my voice, for I had never called him by his name before, and it seemed too familiar, impertinent, almost.

I heard kitten wails coming from somewhere on the other side of the boat, and my first thought was that he had sustained head injuries, that he would be wandering around with half his brain dripping down his back, and that Marty must be protected from such a sight.

My second thought was that I wanted to be protected from it myself. Surely I could stay here with Marty? He was my first responsibility. What were the police for, anyway? And they wouldn't appreciate amateurs floating around, getting in their way.

'Can you just give me a hand?' asked the cop.

Policemen weren't supposed to ask you to help them, surely?

He was standing at the other end of the boat, waiting to lead me round, and the way he waited there I knew he wanted me with him, that he had the same reluctance as I did, the same dread of twisted flesh at the moment of discovery.

'You must stay there,' I insisted to Marty. 'It's important that you warn oncoming traffic about the obstruction. Stay at the side of the road and wave them down.'

In the dusky blue and orange light that flitted round us, his face looked serious and adult.

'Come if you hear me call,' I said.

He nodded and began to walk slowly back down the side of the road, away from me.

The kitten noises were becoming more muffled. I hurried towards the boat, and I saw that its side was grazed, with some of the slats of wood snapped and jagged.

We went round to its other side, into darkness.

But it was an orange-glowed darkness, an inferno, where we balanced on a black plane and below us was brilliant chemical light and shouts and ant-like activity, as though we were looking down on another planet, or into hell.

We were on the motorway bridge, and below us twisted cars, caravans on their sides, the evidence of human frailty and its consequence on consumer durables, were being hauled about and towed away, so that tomorrow we could forget all about it.

And above all this, Nerina's car, which I saw as my eyes adjusted to the light, was jammed against the railings of the bridge, and the kitten noises crept from inside, where a blackness was humped over the steering wheel.

Another blackness flopped towards us, and I stepped back, catching my breath as I would have done if a bird had taken off suddenly at my feet.

Derek Thackray's face came into focus.

'The door's jammed,' he said. 'She's trapped in there.'

Another teeny wail came from the car.

My face was very close to Nerina's as I bent down to peer at her. Her window seemed to be open, which surprised me until I felt glass crunching under my feet. I walked gingerly, feeling the threat of splinters against my bare big toes, for her window was sprayed across the ground I was walking on.

She was looking at me. I saw black shadows, the holes of her skull where her eyes must be.

'Nerina,' I said, trying to sound calm, 'it's me, May Knott.'

She began to sob in a slow clumsy sort of way.

'My front teeth are loose,' she said. 'I've lost my top lip. There's blood everywhere.'

She went on crying, while I tried the door. But it wouldn't open.

The black bulk of Derek Thackray bulged behind me.

'She just stopped slam in the middle of the road,' he muttered to me.

'Help's coming, darling,' he said. But he can't have meant us, because we were very little help indeed.

Nerina was holding her hand over her mouth. I fumbled in my pocket, and my fingers clutched the scarf Ferg had given me. I handed it to her, and she pressed it to her mouth, while I remembered Arnie and the sodden curtain by the fireside at Number Ten. We waited.

Below us, on the motorway, the floodlights were doused suddenly, and traffic began to flow again, at first

117

slowly in one lane, then with more confidence, until the familiar Doppler swoosh resumed, and we saw an ambulance flash beneath us, then a fire engine.

'They're coming here,' said Marty.

Minutes later they arrived.

They broke into the car with a metal lever, and I thought that if the car hadn't been a write-off before, it certainly would be now, one side stoved in against the bridge, the other forced open. Nerina was helped out, while Marty and I stepped back, watching from a distance. She was wheeled to the ambulance in a little folding chair that made me think she looked like Minnie Mouse.

'Are you her friend?' the police asked me. 'Are you going with her in the ambulance?'

I said I was a distant friend, but that I had a child with me who I had to take back to his mother.

'You could follow in the car,' they suggested. They seemed to want me to come.

'Would you like me to come with you?'

I stood at the back of the ambulance looking into its bright interior. Nerina was sitting on one of the beds with Derek next to her. She was holding a white pad to her mouth, and her blood was very red.

Derek spoke to me. 'I'd go, but I have to stay here to see to the boat.'

Then Nerina took her hand from her mouth and said some rude things about boats and Derek's relationship to them.

Derek stood up and began to climb out of the ambulance.

'I suppose you blame me for this,' said Nerina sharply.

'Darling, you have to admit you stopped with no warning, slap in the middle of the road.'

We all looked at the mushy top lip, and the welling of blood round Nerina's upper teeth.

'You'd probably be unscathed if you'd put your safety belt on,' said Derek, right there, in front of all us witnesses, and the police.

118

'I didn't know you were colour-blind,' said Nerina. 'What are brake lights for?'

But her mouth was swelling fearfully, and repartee was too painful for her. She began to cry as I picked up my scarf and she saw the blood on it.

'Don't you think it was a bitty thoughtless, going to watch an accident and forgetting to do up your safety belt?' Derek persisted, and I thought what a sanctimonious prig he was, how already he was trying to dodge responsibility for ramming his lover's car.

On the other hand, I felt some sympathy for him as I pictured Phyllis' fury when she heard they'd lose their no-claims bonus, all because of Nerina.

'Can you see to my car?' Nerina mumbled to me, her mouth swelling up by the minute, and I promised I would. So I stayed behind to see to her car, and Derek stayed behind to see to his boat, and Nerina went off, friendless, to the Royal Avalon General.

'She's in good hands,' Derek said to me, the creep, as the ambulancemen slammed the doors of the ambulance. He said it to me, but he smiled in the headlights at the men, who said nothing, being used, I suppose, to such sycophants.

*Assistance comes
from an unlikely
quarter*

♡♣◇♤ **Chapter 15** ♡♣◇♤
Six of Clubs

Time had passed, though I had no idea how much. Marty
and I were in my car, returning to the farm.

We had stayed at the bridge till the ill-fated *Philander*
was winched onto a truck, with Derek muttering about
breaking her back and so on. The Range Rover was still
working, and with a little help from the winch he managed
to reverse it up the steep slope. Presently the boat went
past beneath us. It would have looked alien and ghostly,
except that one of its sides was stove in, and somehow this
demolished its image. Who ever heard of a broken ghost?
It looked ashamed and, as Nerina might have said,
embarrassed. I found myself wondering whether it would
make an undignified re-entry into the cowshed, or
whether the actors in that little drama had had enough of
it and Derek would have to find somewhere else to repair
it. Perhaps Phyllis would make him sell it. If Ferg were
here he would be betting on whether it would ever sail, I
thought.

Nerina's car had been taken away too. Its back was

crushed in, and the whole of one side. Thinking about it on the way back to her house, Marty and I decided that the chassis had been twisted, which might explain why her door was jammed.

'It's a good thing she hurt her mouth so badly,' said Marty.

'Why?'

'Because the police couldn't really breathalyse her.'

I had to return to the farm because Vincenza was there. I no longer felt any responsibility for driving her back to Cornfield. Edwin could do that if he liked. But I supposed I had to return Marty to her.

I also felt some responsibility to report to Louis about Nerina, even though I knew the police were likely to have been in touch with him.

And so they had been. When we arrived back at the farm, I found that Louis had already left, in a car belonging to 'I Ran the World'. I needn't have come back at all. I could have taken Marty back to his home in Cornfield and gone on my way, possibly never again returning to this place.

Where I stood in the hall, surrounded by people who stared at me with hostile curiosity as Vincenza came up the steps and entered the hall behind me.

As I had driven into the yard she had dashed across and run to the car, and almost before it stopped she had opened Marty's door.

She had looked coldly at me.

'Get out, Martin,' she'd said, getting hold of his arm, almost pulling him out of the car.

He had half-turned towards me. He had been about to say something, I know he had, and afterwards I remembered this small half-gesture and comforted myself that we had parted as friends.

I never spoke to him again.

'Go to your father,' said Vincenza.

I got out of the car and looked across the yard, to where she was pushing Marty.

Bertholdt was sitting in his car watching us.

'Here, Marty old chap,' he called.

He saw me looking at him, and he shrugged minutely, as Pontius Pilate might have done. Don't expect me to put myself on the line in this matter, his shrug said to me.

But what the matter was, I still had to find out.

I had decided to ignore Vincenza and her righteous anger, and I had gone back to the house to find Louis. Behind me I heard her footsteps following me.

And now I stood in the hall, having been told that Louis had gone, and I thought how much wiser if I'd followed my own inclination and gone straight back to Cornfield. And I thought that conscience and a sense of duty were luxuries that were best left unindulged.

Hilde was standing on the stairs.

'Witch!' she hissed at me.

I was off-guard. But I saw, by the way the guests all turned their faces in my direction, that something had been discussed already.

'Pardon?'

'You did this to my daughter, you did.'

'Did what?'

'You knew about the accident. Before Louis came home tonight, you knew about it. Evil witch.'

'Of course I didn't know.'

'You are irresponsible, May, and not fit to be in any relationship whatsoever where young children are involved.' This was Vincenza, behind me.

They were all there, Edwin, Ferg, Hilde, Vincenza, and other faces that stared blankly at me, people who I'd just begun to know, who I have not yet had time to write about.

'You told Nancy that Louis had been in an accident. I heard you. Before he arrived this evening you knew about the bad *Stimmung* that was around us. Yet you let my little girl, my Nancy, drive to her destruction.'

'That's crazy.'

'You read the cards. You bring us death and illness. You are an evil woman.'

'No I'm not. The cards aren't serious. It's a hobby, that's all.'

'Listen, darling, we know enough psychology to know what harm you can do with your nasty little suggestions and innuendoes.'

'What do you mean? You asked me to read the cards. I never read them unless I'm asked.'

'But you make damned sure that you *are* asked, don't you?'

Edwin, my patron, my partner, why are you just standing there, why aren't you de-escalating this situation?

I looked at him, and he looked straight back. Don't expect me to help you, his look said. I warned of this, his look said.

His look didn't say what about Hugo and the kingfisher, what about Ferg who you disappeared with? Nor did it say now that you know about the bathroom orgy this is a good way for me to project my guilt onto you.

I shifted my glance to Ferg, in whose arms I had so recently been lying.

Ferg lifted his glass to his lips. He was smiling. As I looked, he moved his hand very slightly towards me, as if he was wishing me well in this predicament, drinking a wry toast to me. Thank you and goodbye, rather moderate lover, I thought.

'Leave us alone, with your evil eye, your wicked magic,' said Hilde, and she began to come down the stairs towards me.

'You've done this sort of thing before, haven't you, May Knott?'

I spun round to face Vincenza, and all around me were the people of Avalon, of Camelot, of Academe, who hated me.

Inside me a tide welled. An endocrine tide that I couldn't control was surging through me. I wanted to turn and run away. But Vincenza was there. And I wanted to protest, no, no, there's nothing, nothing.

'What do you mean? What have I done?'

123

'With Hens and Cissy Henshaw. You seduced him. You used your arts to good effect, didn't you? You're a byword in the village. We gave you a second chance, and you abused it.'

They were closing round, I was in a court and they were sitting in judgment on me.

'How can you believe that? There was nothing, nothing. Never. Cissy was obsessed. Hens was good to me. . . .'

Someone sniggered, oh yes. Anything I said would make things worse. Yet I went on.

'Cissy wouldn't listen, she wouldn't believe me.'

'Why not, I wonder?'

Vincenza's dress was suddenly an evil bile, its gloss out of place. She was a character out of a bad play, dressed in the wrong costume.

'You can't believe all this. It's village gossip. It's ignorance. You're all from the university, you understand these things, clever people, intelligent.'

You are my last resort, the people I respect, who I have admired at first from a distance, and then pined to be accepted by.

'You're a meddler, you play with things you know nothing about. You're a manipulator, unfit to be around children.'

They had pinned me against a wall, though there was no wall in that place that I could physically reach, and I would have welcomed the feel of it against my back if there had been.

Now I hated them. They laughed scornfully at my plea: 'But you're clever, you must understand because you're clever.' They weren't clever and they didn't understand. They were a mob, no different from the village crowd who Cissy had mobilized to jeer at me when I'd left ten years before.

There was a fierce rasping against my neck. Vincenza had grabbed my necklet and snapped it away. She held it in her hand, the two ends of its broken chain dangling from her fingers.

124

'I'll have this,' she said. 'It must seem a very minor offence to you, receiving stolen property.'

But it wasn't stolen. My hands were reaching out, grabbing at her dress.

'Give me that back!'

The proof of friendship, of generosity, of kindness.

I was tearing her dress, stripping it away from her, and she was screaming.

Then Edwin was dragging me off. 'For god's sake! What a scene. What's got into you?'

And Ferg was holding Vincenza, laughing. 'Calm down now, my love. Nothing's worth that much hassle.'

'She stole my child. She seduced Martin.'

My arm stung where Vincenza had scratched me. Someone slung a waterproof round her shoulders, oh they were so decent, so respectable. There was a diagonal scratch down her neck where I had dug in my fingernails. Her hair stuck out at bizarre angles.

And so did mine, I expect.

'Let her go.' And here was Phyllis, coming through the door like Solomon, and by her side was Bertholdt.

Since that night I have thought about Phyllis often. Her head ruled her heart. She was, I think, an interesting combination of the queen of diamonds, but with a touch of spades, for she was consciously just.

Edwin let go of me. I would have gone then; I was going, I had reached the door, when Bertholdt took hold of my arm. I began to struggle, assuming he was about to harangue or insult me.

But he looked at me kindly.

'Calm down. You won't be able to handle this if you don't.'

'I'm getting out.'

'Yes, I know.'

He led me down the steps into the dark, and I saw Vincenza watching us, watching him, as though he was a father who she knew she'd displeased.

'I hate them. They're so cruel.'

Bertholdt turned to face me.

'Why do you think they're so angry?'

'Because they're stupid. They're ignorant and superstitious. I'm not a witch.'

'No, of course you aren't.' His voice was comfortable, a hand on ruffled hair. 'But you are a psychologist, however untrained. And you must have noticed how the last thing people tell you they're angry about is the thing that really bugs them. They look around for other, often quite convincing reasons, while the real cause may remain unknown to them and to everybody else.'

'What is the real cause?'

Then Bertholdt seemed to go off on another track.

'What you have to say may or may not be true. It's how you say it that's important. If you want to convince, if you want to get your point across, then you must use guile, diplomacy.'

But I do. That's exactly what I do.

We had reached my car. Bertholdt opened the door, and the interior light went on. He reached in and picked something up from the driver's seat.

'I've got this back for you,' he said.

He handed me the ms. of my novel, in its red spring-backed folder.

My novel, here on this farm.

'I found it fascinating, speaking for myself,' he said. 'Unfortunately the others were solely concerned with identifying themselves within its pages, so they missed some of the more subtle plotting and nuance.'

'But how did it get here?'

'Edwin apparently showed it to Vincenza recently. She got him to bring it here for the others to have a look at. We all had a good browse through it while you were at the accident. Lucky for you, you showed old Phyllis up in quite a good light, which I expect is why she took pity on you just now.'

'But that's not how novels are written. The people aren't real people. They're amalgams, mostly invented.'

Bertholdt laughed.

'Try telling that to Hilde or Vincenza,' he said.

126

I was relieved that I hadn't yet written the next twenty or so pages.

I began to get into my car.

'I'm leaving Edwin,' I said.

'Ah.' Bertholdt closed my door for me. 'Then I suppose Vincenza will leave Martin and me and move in with him.' He sounded as though he was planning next week's meals, which perhaps he was.

I held the folder close against me, imagining how their eyes had bored into it, and I felt as if I was standing in a room that I knew well, which had been burgled, but where I couldn't see what had been taken.

I knew Bertholdt was watching me.

'Is that your only copy?' he asked.

'Yes.'

'You should always keep a spare,' he said automatically.

I have thought of that. But it seems pointless to me. If the house burnt down, so would both copies. And if anyone wanted to destroy it, they'd destroy both copies, wouldn't they? Surely he didn't expect me to keep a spare in the bank?

But I wasn't in the mood to discuss this. I slid into my seat, and sat staring straight ahead. I was trembling.

Bertholdt leaned against the door.

'Where are you going now?' he asked.

Home, home, home.

But the garret didn't seem like home, and I had no wish to confront its landlord.

I didn't reply.

Bertholdt opened the door, and held it open.

'Don't drive off till you know where you're going,' he said.

I thought for a moment.

'I do know,' I said.

'That's all right, then.'

He began to close the door, and I was grateful to him for not asking me where.

I switched on the car lights. I could see the blur of

Marty's face peering at us from his father's car. I waved, and the angle of his face changed. His hand seemed to rise darkly, just once.

The farm door was shut. No one in the house seemed to care about my going. Last time, Cissy had driven me down to the station on the tractor, and Hens had stood at the door, watching. She hadn't said one word to me the whole way.

'I can drive now, Hens,' I said out loud, though he couldn't hear, being dead of a heart attack five years ago. Hens had taught me to drive the tractor. I wanted him to know I could do things.

Accomplishments
flower where they
were not expected

♡♣♢♠ Chapter 16 ♡♣♢♠
Queen of Hearts

I drove away, intending to go to Edwin's house first, to collect my belongings. On the moor by the roadside a pylon swam upwards out of the mist. Through my open window I heard the sound of static rippling through the insulators, and saw the pale blue light that hovered round them in the dampness. I accelerated, thinking how afraid I should be if the car broke down, thinking how afraid Marty must have been as he trekked along here, dressed only in his pyjamas.

I thought about my belongings. What were they? A few items of costume jewellery my mother had given me as Christmas presents; a walking stick Hens had made me, with a head carved in the shape of Sheba, his cow-dog. My typewriter. Ah, that was essential. Then there were my passport, driving licence, and other papers. I wasn't concerned about clothes, much as I enjoyed them; all mine were cheap and easily replaceable.

Then I thought that the only thing I possessed that truly belonged to me was here in the car with me: the first hundred pages of my novel. I needn't go back to Edwin's, not for days, if I didn't want to.

I drove across the bridge where I had never seen a kingfisher with Hugo, who didn't exist, and up out of the valley. There was a sudden crash of light and noise. The railway shuttle that connected Avalon with Gilford rushed past along the embankment above the road, and my hand tightened on the steering wheel. Beside a farm someone was cutting logs in a corrugated iron shed whose metal sides whined and reverberated with the sound of the circular saw. Inside, the shed was orange with light. It seemed strange to be sawing logs so late at night.

But perhaps it wasn't so late after all. I tried to guess the time. Such a lot had happened since we had arrived at Louis and Nerina's. I thought it might be about eleven.

I thought of my alarm clock that Edwin had bought me at the market. At this moment it would be lying on its illuminated face, pushed under my bed. I thought of the garret in darkness and the trains chuffing over the garden that I should almost certainly never hear again.

Edwin had never been at Portsmouth. 'I came home early,' he'd said, when I was so shocked to see him at Nerina's.

So where had he been? Why was he bothering to deceive me? That was supposed to be the strength of our relationship, that we needn't concern ourselves with deception, for it was supposed to be a working, practical relationship.

He was deceiving me because he'd made some sort of discovery and he was afraid I'd defuse it by using it in my novel. How ridiculous! I laughed out loud, thinking of the contrast between Edwin's learned paper and my story-telling.

Then I slowed down, thinking that after all there might be some mileage for learned discoveries in my book.

I came to the roundabout at the end of Cornfield's main street. I should have turned left after this, to get to Edwin's house. Instead I went straight on, past Vincenza's barn, where the windows were in darkness, past the

Friars' Arms and the dark opening that was the entrance to the grounds of the Friary itself.

I was on my way to Avalon. As I passed the square in the centre of the village, I saw that the clock above the drinking trough showed the time as twenty minutes to twelve.

I found Judy, as I had expected I would, in the Dragon. I pulled up outside, seeing the light still cascading over the pavement, and when I switched off my engine I heard the sounds of revelry, singing, and somewhat boozy cheering.

There were no curtains at the windows, but it wasn't possible to look into the bar because the glass was heavily frosted to deter you. I crossed the pavement, dodging a couple who spilled out of the door, parted from each other as they hit the cool night air, then connected themselves up again and moved away.

Judy was standing on a table singing 'Paper Roses'. I stood just inside the door watching her, while other customers turned round to look at me as I entered. She knew all the words, belting them out with enormous gusto. It was the first time I'd seen her wearing a dress, an orange synthetic fibre one with a flounce at the bottom that reached way above her knees. Her legs were bare, and I could still see the bites on them, but she wore very high-heeled black court shoes, and she balanced there on the table, unconsciously twisting her body into a sexually suggestive pose. Her teeth gleamed white in their pink gums. It was the first time I'd seen her wearing those too.

'We're closed.' The barman was washing glasses. He shouted across to me as Judy took a breath.

I pointed at her, mouthing that I wanted to speak to her. She'd begun to dance a few steps, orchestrating her audience to sing along with her, and a surge of affection and drunken sadness swilled over me. Judy was a maimed moth that carries on trying to fly after you've swatted it and broken its wings.

But Judy didn't care anything about this. She stood on a

131

table and sang and learnt the words to tunes, while I agonized away and introspected and thought how awful everything was.

The singing came to an end, and Judy began to cough. 'Somebody give us a fag.' But nobody did, and after she'd stood there waiting for a few moments, while they turned away, she yelled, 'Well, somebody give me a hand off this bloody table, then.'

I pushed through the crowd and stood by her. I dragged a chair over with one hand, and held my other hand up for her.

She screamed in delight and began to laugh in her gasping cackle.

'May Knott!' She got hold of my hand and tried to drag me up onto the table.

'Everybody! This is my friend, May Knott.'

I resisted her pull.

'Come on, May. Come on up and give them a song.'

'I can't,' I said. 'I don't know any songs.'

''Course you do.' She began, 'My grandfather's clock was too big for the shelf. . . .'

'I don't know it. Only the first line.'

The lights flashed on and off, and I stood back, reprieved. 'They're closing.'

'Take no notice,' said Judy.

But she climbed down, with many a wobble, onto the floor.

We hugged.

'You got a ciggie?' she asked me, and I felt guilty admitting to being a non-smoker.

'I'll buy you some,' I offered, and she put her arms round me again.

'Meet my best friend, May Knott,' she introduced me to the barman, and he handed over the ciggies, giving me an amused, knowing look.

'Oh, yes?' he said.

'Yes,' I said, not entering into his conspiracy.

I counted out the money and saw that after I'd bought Judy's fags I should be left with about four pounds.

'Get my friend a drink,' Judy ordered the barman.

But he refused. 'Who's paying?' he asked.

'On the slate,' said Judy, with a great bellowing laugh, and she turned to me, unabashed.

'I was broke when I came in here tonight, and I've been bought three Guinnesses. Not bad, eh?'

I congratulated her.

'Why did you come this late?' she reproached me. 'We could have had some fun, you and me.' She looked around. 'They're all looking at you. They all fancy you, you know.'

'I was at a party. I couldn't come before.'

Judy looked me up and down.

'You're drunk, aren't you?' she asked.

I said I didn't think I was any longer. 'I've been in the fresh air, sobering up,' I said.

People were beginning to leave. A few men came up to Judy, putting their arms round her shoulders, pinching her bottom.

'Goodnight, my darling,' they said, mostly, and on the whole Judy brushed them away.

'Get off, randy devil,' she'd say. But then she'd turn and laugh, showing she didn't mean it as anything but a compliment.

We stood outside on the pavement.

'Can I come with you?' I asked my best friend.

'You want a cuppa to sober up?' she suggested.

'No. I mean can I stay the night? I could sleep on your settee.'

It took a moment for her to take this in. Then she grabbed hold of my arm.

''Course you can stay the night. You can stay every night for all I care. Arnie'd like that. He fancies you.' She laughed. 'Wait till I tell him!'

We drove down the street in my car.

'What's happened, then?' Judy asked. 'Your old man thrown you out, has he?'

'Yes, in a way.'

'Arnie'd best not try that on me,' said Judy. 'I'd cut

133

everything off him if he did that.'

'He won't try it,' I said.

'Mind you, it wouldn't make much difference if I *did* cut everything off, come to that.'

She laughed heartily again, and settled herself beside me more comfortably.

'He don't mind, though. He don't mind me having other fellers. Saves him the trouble, he says.'

As we turned into her street, a shadow slipped across the road in and out of my headlights, a flicker of a shape, caught in mid-run, and I recognized the fair straight hair and the pale profile of Daren. I turned to see Judy's reaction, but she hadn't noticed, and I remembered she was short-sighted but never wore glasses. I saw the door of Number Ten pushed open and then closed, and by the time I pulled into the side of the road there was no sign that anyone had entered the house.

Judy didn't ask about luggage when I got out of the car. She pushed open the front door, which wasn't even shut.

'The door's open,' I said.

'I always leave it like that,' she said. 'That way, if anything happens to my kids they can get out easy, see.'

'What if anyone tries to get in?'

She laughed. 'Are you kidding? Who'd want to get into this hole?'

'Someone might want to hurt the children.'

I felt her turn to me, in the dark hall.

'Who'd want to do that? They'd better not try. I'd kill 'em.'

She appeared to be fumbling on the stairs.

'Where's the flaming matches?'

She found one and struck it. It flared up, and she grunted with satisfaction, picking up a small stub of candle which she had left ready on the stairs. She lit this with the match, and at last we could see the hallway, the peeling paper and the black growths of damp.

'Fancy a cuppa?' she asked.

A cuppa was exactly what I did not fancy, but I accepted. We sat on the sofa, staring into the dying fire.

'Do you still love him?' she asked. She had never met Edwin, and I had never told her much about him.

'Not really. I've just sort of got used to him.'

There was no romance in Judy's life, yet she seemed to expect it in mine.

'Why did you live with him if you didn't love him?'

'Because he paid the bills,' I said, and she slapped my hand.

'Oh, you're naughty.'

'He didn't mind.' Somehow it seemed necessary to defend myself. 'I looked after him, and he looked after me. He wanted me to write a book.'

'A book! Oh, May Knott! I didn't know you were clever.'

She sounded disappointed.

'I'm not,' I promised her.

'What was the book about?'

'It was a story.'

She was impatient. 'I know it was a story. What was it *about*?'

To Judy, all books were stories.

'It was about this girl who worked on a farm.'

'Is it about you?'

'Bits of it are.'

She changed the subject, perhaps thinking of reading.

'Bella's got to go to one of them backward schools.'

She said it with resignation. 'They've all been shouting things at her in the street.'

'Are Bella and Daren in bed?'

'Of course they are.'

She saw me looking at her in the silence that followed. She got up and lit a cigarette.

'It's all right,' she said. 'Everyone knows where I am. They'd come and get me if anything happened. It's only round the corner.'

'Supposing Daren went out at night after you'd gone to the pub?'

I wasn't pleased with myself having this conversation. It seemed ungrateful, a rejection of Judy's hospitality. And it was hypocritical. Hadn't I only recently driven a child round the countryside whilst I was drunk?

'He don't go out at night.' Judy took a long drag on her cigarette.

'Well, supposing?'

'I'd bloody-well belt him, that's what.'

She gestured with her hand, and the cigarette slipped through her fingers. She stood up, swearing, trying to catch it, and I watched the glow-worm dance of it as she knocked it first onto her dress, then onto the couch, and finally onto the floor.

She let out a wail and snatched the candle off the mantelpiece, holding it close to the dress. She turned to me.

'Is it all right?' she asked, unable to see it herself.

'There's two burn holes, right in the front.'

She put the candle back in disgust.

'My friend'll make me pay for it. Fat chance.'

'Did she lend it to you?'

It turned out the dress was on appro. from a mail order catalogue.

'She'll just have to send it back,' said Judy, picking up the cigarette and taking another pull at it. She laughed. 'She can tell them it don't fit. Tell them it's disgusting sending it out like that, burn marks an' all.'

Well, that was settled.

No more was said about Daren and Bella.

When the candle had burnt right down, Judy left me and went to bed. I heard the soft rasp of her fingers as she felt her way up the stairs, and the creak of a bed as she threw herself onto it.

I lay on the couch and pulled her fake fur coat over myself. It was warm in the room, and lumpy on the couch, where grey brains of cotton waste poked through slits in the black vinyl upholstery.

I slept.

*Tomorrow will
come sooner
than you think*

♡♣◇♤ **Chapter 17** ♡♣◇♤
Five of Hearts

Something was touching my face, a light touch with sticky undertones. It moved caterpillar-like down my forehead, along the side of my nose. It entered my left nostril.

I opened my eyes.

'Hullo, Bella,' I said.

She drew her hand back.

'Hullo, Auntie May.'

Rain was running down the window-pane, and light filtered into the room as if we were at the bottom of the sea.

'Come here, little sea-horse,' I said to Bella, and I sat up to hug her.

As I lifted my head, I thought for an instant that something was clamped round my forehead, pinning me to the pile of beaten-up teddy bears that had been my pillow during the night. A bad case of hangover had moved into my skull, and even the thin light threatened to blind me.

Both children looked at me in silence as if I was a rare

species of fish that had fetched up in this underwater parlour.

Then Bella came closer, and I put my arm round her. 'What's the time?' I asked.

Daren crossed to the transistor on the window-sill, and lifted something off it. Then I remembered that through the night I had been half-aware of the hollow ticking of an alarm clock.

He held the clock up for me to see.

'Too late for school,' he said.

It appeared to be half-past one.

'It goes backwards,' said Daren.

I sat there, blearily trying to work it out.

'What time is it, Mr Wolf?' I asked, giving up.

'Half-past ten.' He grinned, pleased with himself, and I smiled too, just about.

'Clever, aren't you?' I said, feeling the weakness of this remark.

I began to rub my midriff above the elastic of my tracksuit bottoms. Presently I noticed my fingertips were travelling over hot itchy bumps.

'I have to do it for me mam as well,' said Daren. He was watching me scratch myself, but he was referring to time-telling.

'She can't read,' said Bella. They both watched to see what I thought about this.

'She can sing,' I said. 'She knows all the words to lots of songs.'

There was a tiny lessening of tension.

'I know "Grandad we love you",' said Bella.

She began to sing, in her little-girl voice, watching me to make sure I was listening. I put on my rapt look with fixed smile.

Today, I thought, I must go down to Social Security and sign on. I must find somewhere to live. I must after all get my belongings from Edwin's, especially my typewriter.

There was a sharp knock on the front door. Bella stopped singing and she and Daren darted, well trained, behind the sofa.

Daren put his head up over the back of it.

'Hide, quick,' he hissed to me.

The net curtain had never been replaced since Arnie's accident, so unless the other curtains were drawn across the window anyone could stand on the pavement and stare into the room. Hiding seemed like good advice.

I leapt off the couch, stifling a yelp as my brain lurched against the underside of my scalp. The door into the parlour stood open, so I nipped behind it and was screened from view, though I could peep through the crack on the hinge side and see the window clearly.

'Who is it?' I whispered to Daren and Bella. 'What do they want?'

Although there was no risk of anyone outside hearing our whispers, Daren and Bella were too experienced to take a chance on it. My question met with silence.

I looked through the crack. At first I thought someone was looking straight back at me, leaning the outside edge of their hand against the glass to cut out reflections. It was Edwin. I stared back, and it was as if our eyes locked, though I knew that in fact there was no chance that I could be seen.

'May!' he called. 'May, are you there?'

Inside the House of Trod we held our breath. Above us, I thought I heard the faint creaking of springs as Judy turned over, irritable at this disturbance of her lie-in.

Outside, Edwin, my patron, stood in the rain plotting how to get me back.

'Oh, my god,' he said out loud, which seemed to be a comment on the state of the room. Then he disappeared.

He had discovered that the front door wasn't locked. I was still peering through the crack in the door, when I felt a hand on my arm.

'Oh!' I jumped back in horror. Edwin, standing in the darkness of the hall, bent his face towards me.

'Why are you here, of all places?' he asked me in a voice that disparaged this place I had regarded as a haven. 'We've been worried about you all night.'

I pushed him as hard as I could, away from the door.

The shock of seeing him so unexpectedly close must have given me added strength, because he fell back off-balance against the stair wall. I dashed round the door and into the parlour, slamming the door behind me, leaning as hard against it as I was able.

Outside in the hall I heard the sound of plaster flopping off the wall onto the floor, then the soft sound of Edwin's curses as he crunched across it. The door handle turned.

'Don't be silly, May,' he said, feeling my resistance. The door gave inwards a little, and I had to push with a jerking movement to keep it shut. Suddenly it became easier to hold off the attack, because Daren had put his back against the door beside me, jamming his feet against the skirting. Then Bella put her hands below mine.

'Go away, you nasty man!' she shouted. My sentiments exactly.

There was such a banging and a shouting going on that I was only vaguely aware that footsteps had crossed the floor above me. Afterwards I remembered that I'd heard Judy shouting, telling everyone to shut up.

Then she must have heard Bella's yells and my protests.

Above us, her window shuddered open, though we hardly noticed. Edwin heard it, though, and it made him pause in his attack. We heard him retreat down the passage. Then, from the street, he gave a howl of rage, at which Daren relaxed, head cocked sideways, listening. He pushed Bella away from the door.

'Get out now!' he hissed to me. 'Through the back door and over the wall.'

I got the impression that scenes like this were probably quite frequent at Number Ten.

Judy, looking out of her window and hearing the turmoil downstairs, had clearly taken some sort of outrageous action on my behalf, and it was up to me to take advantage of her efforts.

I could hear anger now, words hurled from Edwin, and, from the window above, Judy's wild laughter and repartee.

I didn't stop to find out what had happened. We opened

the door a crack, and I could see down the hallway and into the street, where Edwin seemed to be standing in the gutter, well away from the house, looking upwards.

I slipped out into the shadow, through the open kitchen door. The back door was unlocked, and as I stepped out onto the green, algae-covered gloom of the back yard, I heard a rush of feet down the hall, and a massive slam, as Daren closed and locked the door against intruders.

But escaping from Edwin was no more than a gesture. As I scrambled onto the coal bunker, and from there onto the treacherous tiles of the lavvy roof, I was thinking that escape was pointless, because my car was unapproachable, overlooked by the enemy. And without it I felt like a snail with no shell.

I lifted one foot over the cement that clutched spears of broken glass to the top of the wall. Everything was wet, and the soles of my shoes slid uneasily over damp surfaces. My spine jarred right up to the top of my skull with the impact of my landing when I jumped down into the alley that ran along the back of Judy's terrace. I ran dispiritedly, dodging between dustbins and puddles, thinking of the mud that must be splattering the backs of my trousers.

The alley turned at a right angle, and I slowed down. At its mouth I could see a slice of Judy's street. I could hear Edwin's voice, raised and angry, and Judy still shrieking at him.

I crept to the end of the alley and put my head round the corner of the last house, so that I was looking down the road. At the end of it, a wall topped with barbed wire cut the street off as if it was a piece of grey ribbon. Steam flopped in gentle clouds over the wall, and over everything was the faintly fishy smell of boiling crabs and lobsters.

In one of these clouds stood Edwin. My patron looked wetter than the drizzling rain would have led me to expect, until I glanced upwards just as Judy tipped the blue plastic bucket she was balancing on the window-sill, and the last of her night's slops – and other previous

141

nights, most likely – went splashing over the pavement.

Edwin, well warned by now, dashed into the street, dodging the amber waterfall.

I slipped tactfully in the other direction, round the offy on the corner and into the main road, silently congratulating Judy on her positive approach to deprivation. As I trotted past the Maritime Museum, I had time to wonder how many other households in England were still able to summon this organic resource to their aid in order to repel unwelcome guests, an advantage of having no inside toilet that I hadn't thought of till now.

It had also given me a possibly related idea. I was making my way to the Avalon General Hospital, for where better to spend the next hour or so than in the warmth and dryness of the Orthopaedic Ward, in the company of my second-best friend, Arnie? It was certain that Edwin would leave Number Ten when he realized I'd gone, and then I would be able to go back for my car.

*A shaft of light
at the end of
the tunnel*

♡♣◇♤ Chapter 18 ♡♣◇♤
Ten of Spades

Outside the Charge Nurse's office I waited to get permission to visit Arnie. The office was a makeshift cubbyhole cut off from the entrance to the ward by panels of glass set into a wooden framework. The glass had been covered with a plastic film resembling the crackling on Ming glaze, to give some sort of privacy. But one section had come unstuck, and I could see inside.

'You realize, Nurse, that your screaming could have had serious consequences to the patients on this ward? Some of them have heart conditions.'

'I'll have a heart condition myself, Sister, if I find another cockroach crawling over my uniform. It's not hygienic. They're all over the drinks trolley!'

I peered into the office with interest. A hospital drinks trolley seemed like a controversial introduction into the Health Service.

But the offending trolley stood in the middle of the office, innocently laden with Ovaltine, Horlicks and other health-giving beverages.

The dressing-down went on and on, while in the ward the patients wasted away with dehydration. The sister in charge was sallow-faced, enjoying herself, even though the nurse she was reprimanding showed no signs of being humbled.

I knocked on the glass, and both of them looked up sharply. The ticked-off nurse came to the door.

'You're not supposed to wait there,' she said, disapproving, showing no sign of gratitude for the respite I'd provided her with. I thought how these rebukes were an essential part of the hospital routine, the confirmation of the hierarchy.

The nurse was shooing me away, out of the corridor, when the sister called, 'What is it, Nurse?' And she had to go back into the office to explain who I was and how I'd wanted to see Mr Trod out of visiting hours. Through the glass I could see and hear them consulting. I knocked on the window, and they both looked round, affronted.

'I'm going away,' I mouthed. 'It's the last time I'll be able to see him.'

The sister got up and came to the door. Sister M. Sankey, I saw that she was called.

'Yes, you can see him for a few minutes, till the new shift comes on,' she said.

'How is he?' I asked.

She looked closer at me, trying to place me.

'Are you a social worker?' she asked.

Why do all nurses think this?

'No, I am not,' I said.

'You're a relative of his?'

Wrong again. 'I'm a family friend,' I said.

But she knew everything.

'You're a voluntary worker?' she guessed. She smiled, satisfied, when I didn't answer.

She walked down the ward with me.

'Mr Trod's wound has unfortunately become infected. There's very little natural resistance there. He's having a course of vitamins and he's on a specially nutritious diet to build him up.'

Arnie saw me.

'Hullo, my darling,' he called to me, and the greyish yellow of Sister Sankey's complexion deepened.

I hugged him, smelling all around him the sick-sweet smell of antibiotics.

'Here,' I said, handing him a packet of Players and a bar of fruit and nut.

'That's smashing.' He stroked the packet of chocolate. 'I don't want to open it,' he said, and laughed. 'I'll keep it for ever.'

On the shelf of the locker beside his bed his urine bottle was full to the brim. He saw me looking at it.

'Handy things, those,' he said.

Sister Sankey began to go back up the ward.

'Only a few minutes, mind,' she had to say over her shoulder.

We both watched her as she bustled away.

'Get lost,' Arnie advised her, under his breath. But we soon forgot about her.

'I came to see you because I'm going away,' I said.

'Too bad,' said Arnie. 'I thought you was coming tonight. I was going to give you a surprise. They're playing a request for you on the hospital radio. You'll miss it now.'

I apologized. 'What's the tune?' I asked.

'"Paper Roses",' said Arnie. 'They don't have that many to choose from, see. Judy chose it for you.'

'That's nice,' I said, 'I like that, "Paper Roses".'

Then I told him about Judy singing last night in the Dragon.

'She can't half belt it out,' said Arnie. 'Deafens you, she does.'

He wanted to know where I was going.

I lied to him. I told him I was going to another town to stay with my mother.

He looked at me and shook his head.

'Funny thing,' he said. 'Don't know why but I always thought you was Barnardo's like me. Isn't that funny, 'cos you never said?'

Then I told him how I'd never lived with my mum, how I'd been at Barnardo's and then with this adoptive mother. He slapped the sheet with the flat of his hand.

'I knew it! Isn't it funny how we can tell?'

He asked me about my adoptive mother, what she'd been like, whether I still saw her.

'She took this fertility drug,' I told him. 'She couldn't have kids, so they gave her this drug.'

'Did it work?'

'She had triplets.'

He laughed. 'You had plenty of company, then. Kept you busy, I shouldn't wonder.'

'No. She didn't want me round once she'd got her own kids.'

I didn't want to talk about it, especially not now. I didn't want to think about it either.

'Give me back to my mother!' I'd begged the social workers. They interviewed me, one by one. First one would ask the questions. Then she'd be on her day off, and another would take over and ask me the same questions. Then one of them would leave or get promotion and a new face would appear, 'I'm Edna,' or Barry or whatever, all ever so pally, 'I want you to think of me as your friend.' But you don't pay your friends.

'We'd like to send you to live with your mother, of course, but it just isn't suitable,' said Barry, or Edna, who remembers?

It was like now. It was so like now, this minute, that as I looked down the ward I thought this must be how it's going to be all the time, no home, no people.

'They sent me to live on a farm near here,' I said to Arnie. 'They wouldn't let me stay with my mum.'

'Why not?'

Because she didn't want me.

'They said she drank too much.'

But I knew what it was. Whenever they told her I was coming back, she got drunk and got herself arrested.

My mum didn't want me back.

'You've done well,' said Barry, or Edna, because I was

146

sixteen and had got these eight CSEs.

'It's a pity,' they said, 'that they weren't "O"-levels, because then you could have gone on with your education.'

But at the school I went to, no one did 'O'-levels. Even the teachers would have had a job to get 'O'-levels at that school, if you ask me.

So that's how I ended up at Henshaw's farm.

Arnie said, 'You look too posh to be Barnardo's. 'Course you aren't really, not if you've got your mum.'

'It still counts,' I said, and he agreed. But I could see he was thinking of something else.

'Skin graft hasn't taken,' he said. He motioned to the inside of his thigh. 'They took the skin off there,' he said. 'How many d'you think you can have?'

He described how the nurse had lifted the dead graft away with forceps, earlier in the morning.

I had no idea how many he could have, but I tried to reassure him.

'There's plenty of skin on you for hundreds of grafts,' I said. 'They can just go on trying till they get it right.'

But neither of us really believed this. It wasn't the sort of luck that Arnie had.

At the entrance to the ward I could see a figure making towards the plastic flaps of the doors from the corridor. The face wasn't visible, but there was something about the walk, the way the head was held, that made me frown.

Arnie saw my grimace and looked towards the doors, just as Vincenza burst through them.

She must have seen me immediately, but she gave no sign. She kept her eyes on Arnie as she came down the ward, and she was smiling her most impersonal smile. We watched in silence as she approached the bed.

'Hello, Arnie,' she said, not hullo. Smile, smile.

She nodded in my direction.

'I didn't expect to see you here, May,' she said.

We were conspiring, me and Arnie, even though we had never discussed Vincenza. We said nothing unless we were spoken to.

It crossed my mind that Edwin had sent Vincenza to look for me. But I discounted this. Edwin would never have guessed I was here. Perhaps Vincenza's visit was simply coincidence.

'May and I have some rather sad news for you.' Vincenza said it brightly, indicating that after all it wasn't so sad, that the inconvenience would soon wear off.

'What sad news is that?' I couldn't think of any information Vincenza and I shared that would affect Arnie.

'Well, May,' said Vincenza, as one worker to another. 'As it happens there's another case that requires exactly your touch, so I'm afraid I'll have to move you from the Trod, er, involvement. I'll speak to you afterwards about it. Perhaps we could have a cup of tea at Merlin's.'

'No, we can't,' I said. 'And I'm not doing any more case-work. I've finished with Child Care.'

I said it so firmly that conversation round the ward ceased. Everyone pretended to be engrossed in work, but they were all listening. I didn't care.

'Well, that's very sad,' said Vincenza. 'It won't be easy to replace you. I'm sure Arnie'll miss you.'

'What's going on?' asked Arnie. He looked at me, shifting his weight, glancing at the cradle that humped the bedclothes over his feet to protect them from weight.

'Nothing's going on at all,' I said.

'Won't you be coming any more?' asked Arnie.

Arnie and Judy aren't tomato plants that I water while you're away on holiday, I thought. I had opened my mouth to say this, but I didn't want to squabble about them. Not in front of Arnie.

'Well,' I said to Vincenza, 'it won't make any difference to Judy and Arnie and me, because we're friends. They're nothing to do with work. I come to see them because I want to.'

Arnie looked from me to Vincenza.

'That's very nice,' said Vincenza. 'Of course, we'd have to advise against your involvement. Sadly it seems you haven't had enough experience with children. Not having

148

any of your own might have something to do with it. And, of course, your background isn't too stable.'

'What's she on about?' Arnie asked me.

Vincenza ignored him.

'Edwin and I had a talk with your mother last night,' she told me. 'The poor lady had been phoning all evening, but you were out.'

She turned to Arnie, a stylized gesture, for she was not addressing her barbs to him.

'She's never been to see May in all these years, imagine! She's never seen Edwin – didn't recognize his voice when he spoke to her. She didn't even know his name.'

She turned back to me. 'And she thought *I* was *you*!' She laughed. 'Isn't that funny?'

It was so funny that I picked up Arnie's water-jug and tipped it right over her sneaky head, noticing, as my eyes slid sideways, that the righteous figure of Sister M. Sankey was speeding, poker-stiff, towards me.

I was on my travels again, and Arnie was laughing, cheering me on.

I ran down the ward, into the sluice, where a nurse stood at a sink, jabbing at a heap of bed-pans with a dish mop.

'You can't come . . .' but I didn't hear the rest.

I ran across the steamy wetness of the tiles to the window that opened onto the car park.

Then I was away, speeding over the drying tarmac, while behind me the window was slammed shut, in case, I suppose, I changed my mind and tried to clamber back in again.

As I ran, I saw a car begin to move out from the ranks of parked cars. I paid no attention to it, all my effort was concentrated round my own body. My lungs wheezed in painful gasps, my legs were weak and shaky. I had begun to count each breath, every step. Athletics had never played a major part in my life.

The car swung round, and I heard it come down the line behind me. I moved to one side, lumbering on, but trying to look as if I did this sort of thing all the time, as if it was perfectly normal.

But as the car came abreast of me, it slowed down to my pace. Impatient, I glanced sideways, waiting for it to pass. Ferg's face was peering back at me.

'Get in,' he said.

I told him to go away, crudely, in a couple of brusque words that cost me two paces of effort.

But Ferg wasn't going to go away. The car began to crawl along beside me. I dodged between the parked cars into another lane. He speeded up, and in a few moments was there beside me again.

He wasn't laughing. His face looked drawn, and there were pouches under his eyes. He looked as if he had drunk a lot of champagne the previous night, which he had, as we know.

The car park was immense. Its extension seemed to be made out of a demolished terrace block. I leapt gracelessly over the puddles, stumbled over halves of brick. Presently, not allowing enough lift over a puddle, my foot caught on a brick that stuck up like a stepping-stone. I fell.

The car stopped and Ferg got out. He stood looking at me as I got to my feet. I felt muddy water trickling off my bottom, down the backs of my legs. This was the last blow to my tracksuit. I looked accusingly at Ferg. How unfair that he should be standing there unblemished and dry while practically everybody else dripped soggily in various fluids.

Saying nothing, I got into his car and sat down hard on the upholstered seat, getting some satisfaction at the thought of how wet and grubby I was making it.

Ferg drove slowly out of the car park, past my escape route. The window had been opened again.

'They're watching me.' Two heads seemed to be standing in the dimness. But their dreadlocks were made of string: two mopheads sent to spy on me.

Ferg glanced up at them, saw they were mops and looked back at me. We began to laugh.

'How did you find me?' I asked.

'Chance. I gave Vincenza a lift down here. I went to the kiosk to get some Aspro, and when I turned round I saw you leap from the window. Impressive. Naturally I assumed you were trying to discharge yourself, so I thought I'd give you a bit of help. You shouldn't have run away from me.'

'You didn't help me much last night.' I still smarted from his indifference when I had needed support at Nerina's party.

'It wouldn't have done any good. It would have made Edwin more hostile towards you if he'd known for certain anything had been going on between you and me. As it is, you're in a pretty strong position, catching him and Vincenza *in flagrante*, and he hasn't anything but suspicion to hit back with.'

'I'm leaving him,' I said.

'Yes,' said Ferg, 'I suppose you are.'

'He's following me around.'

'Anyone would think,' said Ferg, 'that he was fond of you.' He frowned at a sudden thought. 'He's not in hospital, is he?'

It was too tedious to explain. 'No,' I said.

'You weren't discharging yourself, were you?'

No again. 'Please will you take me back to my car?' I asked. But I didn't expect him to.

'If I take you back to your car, what then?' he asked. No, that meant. And what then, indeed?

'What is required, Gipsy Woman, is a change of environment, an atmosphere of tranquillity, where things can be worked out dispassionately.'

Discussions

♡♣◇♤ **Chapter 19** ♡♣◇♤
Two Jacks

We worked these things out on a crown bowling green at a park in Wigan, where the thick lush turf nestled cosily in the shadow below a railway embankment. It took a long time to drive there, even on the motorway, and we must have passed other bowling greens in other cities, of equal quality. But Ferg knew about this one, and kept saying how special it was. His uncle had lived in Wigan, he said, as if this justified our outing, even though his uncle had moved to Wales years ago. The bowling green was still there, surrounded on three sides by rhododendron bushes and cypresses that absorbed sound and breeze, so that we moved around on the grass in a bowl of warmth and silence, while above us in another world trains hurtled past on the main line to London, or the North.

Presently I noticed that our pace, walking to and fro, was no quicker than that of the two other players, two very old men with caps on. Bowls was ageing me.

'Tonight,' said Ferg, 'you must come home with me. No one will look for you there. Only Vincenza, possibly, but I can handle her.'

This pleased me, to have some conspiracy with Ferg against Vincenza.

'What about your friend?' I asked, and Ferg paused in mid-stoop, his hand curved across the shiny wood.

'Friend?' You would have thought he didn't have any.

'The one who's staying with you,' I reminded him.

He swung his arm back, his eyes narrowed on the jack. The wood ran smoothly over the turf. But he had misjudged the speed, and it rolled over the edge into the gutter that surrounded the green. He stood up.

'My sister,' he said. 'She's staying with me. She's not too keen on people she doesn't know. But we'll get over that. She's not too bad at the moment.'

'Not too bad?'

He shifted, lifting his little rubber mat impatiently.

'She's a schizophrenic, you know. She's staying with me for a week or two.'

'I'm sorry.'

'Yes,' said Ferg. 'We're all sorry.'

Behind the hedge rose a tall green shoe with a red shiny roof. We bought sandwiches at its window, from a lad who was dressed like the Old Woman, and who blushed with shame as he served us. We turned our backs on him for pity, and went back to the greens, where there was a shelter. Sitting here, we watched the two old men. No one else came to play. It was as soothing as peering into an aquarium.

Ferg put his arm round me. 'How you have calmed down, my Black Queen,' he said, nibbling my ear. He smelt of tuna and cucumber.

'I've never met a schizophrenic person,' I said.

He moved his head away.

'New experiences, however morbid, will enrich your writing,' he said. He broke the crusts off his sandwiches and threw them onto the path for the sparrows. 'Always remember that,' he said. 'Then you can be an observer, not a participator.'

'I like participating.'

153

He looked at me and smiled slyly. 'And you're very good at it. But observing's less painful.' He sighed, perhaps because he wanted only to observe, yet he kept being dragged into participation.

After Ferg had taught me the rules of crown bowling, we stopped scoring. But if we had scored, I should have lost. Ferg played for Camelot College.

The woods punctuated our conversation like fat full-stops. We threw, then, as we walked towards the jack, we talked. We reached the jack, still talking, discarded the losing bowls, occasionally measured distances. We seldom remarked on the winner. It was nearly always Ferg, of course. I was lucky if I shared the honours with him.

But the scores didn't matter. As the woods travelled over the grass, it was if someone stroked me from my neck right down my spine, a long, soothing stroke. And this was Ferg's intention, to soothe me. Sometimes I saw him looking at me. He wasn't laughing at me. And because I expected him to, this made his concern all the more important to me, and all the more surprising.

'What am I going to do, Ferg? Where am I going to stay? And how shall I ever finish my novel now?'

'Finishing your novel is the least of your problems,' said Ferg, taking aim. 'Getting it published is another matter. But if you want to be a participator, you had better stop writing and get on with participating. You could probably make a good living telling the cards. You're good at it.'

'That's just another aspect of storytelling.'

But Ferg wouldn't have this. No, he said, there was more to it than that. And I didn't argue, though to myself I thought he had it the wrong way round. A story had to resolve itself, but the story in the cards can be left hanging in mid-air; it is all the questioner expects, and makes it far more intriguing – and safer for the cartomancer.

I thought wry thoughts. Did Ferg's Double First qualify

him in this way, to know how to comfort me? And why did he want to bother?

'Won't they be missing you at work?' I asked him, which will give the reader some idea of how little I knew about universities.

Ferg laughed. 'I shan't miss *them*,' he said. 'And I'd sooner be playing bowls with you than playing table tennis with Ashley Bainbridge.'

Playing table tennis with Ashley, Dean of Admissions, said Ferg, was a matter of wits that had nothing to do with skill defined in its more conventional sense. For Ashley cheated, given the opportunity. He'd never been the same, Ferg told me, since he'd been knocked unconscious while defending Student Records at a somewhat heated demo.

'That's how he got his nickname, Horatius Bainbridge,' said Ferg.

'You mean he started cheating after that?' I asked. To which Ferg replied that he'd probably always cheated, but now you could catch him at it, that was the difference.

'Finding you somewhere to stay shouldn't be too difficult. A lot of the staff have got holiday cottages round Avalon that they let out during the summer. Someone will be only too glad to have you staying at their place, to stop it getting damp. They prefer long lets.'

'How shall I pay the rent?'

And Ferg put his arm round me. 'With your body, Gipsy Woman.'

I pulled away from him, the only time during the afternoon that he offended me. He watched me as I stood scowling at him.

'I'm only examining possibilities,' he said.

He calmed me down by letting me win the next set two—nought, though I have only realized this as I come to write about it.

'Why, why, Ferg, are you taking so much trouble for me?'

Ferg drew me close to him, and laughed softly, perhaps at himself.

'Because I like you, Gipsy Woman.'

'Do I give you a feeling of power?' I asked him.

'I don't need any more power,' said Ferg.

The embankment's shadow had zigged over the surrounding shrubs before the Old Woman sauntered onto the path and stood, pointedly watching us, with his arms folded. We took the hint, and left the green, handing the bowls in to a flap in the toe of his shoe, and Ferg pocketed our deposit in registrar-like fashion.

The next thing, said Ferg, was to get something to eat.

We ate fish and chips, driving the car off the motorway at Horley. The best fish and chips in the world, said Ferg, although he only ate half a fish and no chips. He handed me the other half, saying he'd be eating at home later.

Back on the motorway, keeping his eyes straight ahead, he began, 'Now look, Gipsy Woman, there is a complication.'

Only one?

'The problem is, where are you going to sleep tonight?'

It's true about the sensation of sinking innards. Mine did this now. For hadn't Ferg already promised me that I could stay at the Friary with him and his sister?

'Yes,' I said, not reminding him of this.

He glanced quickly at me, and put his hand on my knee.

'Don't worry,' he said. 'It's just that I've been thinking about this. It might be too fraught if you stayed at the flat. The last thing I want to do is trigger off one of Lavinia's attacks.'

'It's the last thing I want, too,' I agreed.

'After tomorrow it should be possible to find you somewhere more permanent to stay. But tonight I have something more romantic in mind.'

Now he was looking ahead, smiling, but not much. He's slithering out of something, I thought. And I thought: He doesn't want to have to make love to me.

156

'I can sleep anywhere.' You see how tactful I can be, though I was disappointed, because to be honest, I hadn't wanted to sleep at all.

Quarrels

♡♣◇♤ **Chapter 20** ♣♠◇♤
Three Jacks

We had arrived back at Cornfield, though this was a gated
lane unfamiliar to me possibly because it finished with
what seemed to be little purpose, in the middle of a field.
When we reached the end of it, Ferg didn't stop. He
drove on across the tussocky grass, cursing the black and
white cows who seemed to think some sort of bonanza
had arrived and began to rush towards us from every
direction. We swerved round them and pulled up at a red
stone stile.

'Come on,' said Ferg. 'I want to show you something.'

We climbed the stile. Tall bamboo-like grasses whispered close to one side of a path, bringing a sudden
change in the air, as if everything else had stopped
breathing. Yet behind this whispering I could hear
another sound, a raucous mewing and crying that seemed
out of place in these meadows, till, in a break in the grass
wall, I was looking onto a pond, and the raucous sound
flooded round me. The pond was alive with hundreds of
seagulls, who jostled for position on a small island in its

158

centre, settling for a moment or two, then rising into the air, swirling round, then back again to the island or the water, so that the pond seemed to move restlessly, like a sleeping hedgehog covered with fleas.

I shivered. To come upon a river at dusk makes me fearful: the dark snake that threatens my path. I had not been expecting the pond. It was quite extensive, and on its other shore, which I now looked across to, the reeds had been cleared. I saw that we were in the parkland of the Friary, the fields stretching away up a slope to its lawns and the walls of its gardens, and the woods beyond. The whole back of the building, which I had never seen before, had come into view.

'Which bit do you live in?' I asked Ferg.

He pointed vaguely, and afterwards I wondered at this; perhaps he didn't want me to know.

'This is where I thought you could spend the night,' he said, and he nodded to the side of the little lake.

In the thickest of the reeds a house reared up on stilts. In the darkness of the shed below, a rowing-boat rocked and tugged at its painter. There was a balcony above and a muslin curtain billowed from an open window.

Ferg was looking at it.

'Lavinia's been here this afternoon,' he said. We watched the curtain for a moment or two.

'Isn't that a good sign?' I asked. I didn't think disturbed people opened windows, quite the opposite, they wanted to shut themselves in. Then I remembered that quite often they opened windows so that they could throw themselves out. I think Ferg was thinking this too, but neither of us spoke of it.

'The boat-house is her pouting-place,' he said indulgently.

'Does she pout often?' I asked, but Ferg closed up as if my question had been intrusive, and I saw at last that this Lavinia, with her Double First, her stockbroking, and her schizophrenia, was a barrier between me and Ferg, between Ferg and more or less everyone else. And I saw that it was unlikely that any of us would surmount this

159

barrier.

Ferg looked back at the Friary.

'She'll have gone back. She doesn't like it when it's getting dark.'

He turned to me with sudden decision.

'Look, I'll show you round, then I'd better go. She's probably cooked me a meal, and she gets upset if I don't come back. I'll slip down here later and bring you a sleeping bag or something.'

So this boat-house episode was to be a surreptitious affair. Those were the sort that Ferg would always enjoy the most, I thought.

We climbed steps made of logs slippery with a damp I guessed they never lost. At the top was a narrow platform with a rustic porch round the door, beside which was a concrete garden gnome speckled with lichen. Ferg tipped him over sideways, holding on to his pointed hat. On the boards underneath was a key, which opened the door to the space above the boat-house.

'Come in,' said Ferg.

Inside was warm and woody, and surprisingly dry. We walked on bare boards, but the room was comfortably furnished, with a table, and chairs. On the table was a jam-jar filled with buttercups.

Ferg crossed the room and closed the window. Then he crossed back again and kissed me. It was a long kiss, but abstracted. He's thinking about Lavinia, I thought, and what she's got for his supper. I was glad I'd had the extra half-portion of his fish at Horley, for it looked as if it was going to be a hungry night for me.

'This is going to be a long night,' I said as we disengaged. I hoped he'd bring me something in a thermos, but realized this was too optimistic, for how could such comforts be prepared under the eyes of Lavinia?

'It was uncanny, how you saw Lavinia in my cards,' said Ferg, as if he guessed I was thinking of her.

Did I? Telling the cards is disconcerting. I wouldn't say it puts me into a trance-like state, but nevertheless it is

160

hard for me to remember what I've said afterwards, unless I jot things down in my notebook right away.

It didn't seem either tactful or professional to admit this, so I kept quiet.

'It was an eery sensation,' said Ferg, 'seeing her face there in the cards.'

Then I remembered how Ferg had selected the two black queens; how a younger brother or, as I now perceived, a sister, was a strong influence in his life. The sister and the queen were the same person, I thought now. And I eased myself out of any identification with the queen of spades. No, I was the queen of clubs, in Ferg's hand. I would doom Lavinia to be queen of spades. And I saw, jealously now, that Ferg had tried last night to cast me as a spade because he wanted Lavinia, so to speak, as a club.

'You must beware of someone close to you who you can't trust,' I reminded him.

'I know.' He hugged me. 'That's why I'm leaving you here,' he said ambiguously.

I suppose he thought I would be flattered.

He showed me how to work the butane fire, telling me how warm and cosy I'd be.

I had thought at one time, ages ago, it seemed, that I had prospects of being warm and cosy with *him*, not on my own, marooned in someone else's boat-house.

But prospects change, and I knew I should be grateful to be anywhere warm and dry where I could hide from Edwin.

'Thank you, Ferg,' I said.

He stroked one of the buttercups tenderly, while I wondered which bit of Lavinia he was fantasizing about.

'You've even got flowers,' he said.

I thanked him again, as he didn't seem to have heard the first time, and in any case now there were the flowers to be taken into consideration.

Ferg was a disappointment to me, especially after the buttercup incident, for I am a great believer in symbolism. So after all I was relieved when he finally slithered down

161

the steps. From the window in the door I could have watched his entire progress back to the Friary. I began to do this, but it got boring after a minute or two, and I turned away and took my notebook out of my handbag.

In the life of a novelist, I wrote, there is no need ever to be at a loose end, because the novel is always there waiting to be written. And when it is finished, there is the next one to embark upon.

This did not cheer me, the thought of novels stretching on and on in this altruistic way, giving me something to do. I sat on the edge of the sofa writing these pompous statements, trying to console myself for the loss of Ferg, who had never been there to lose in the first place, though I didn't admit this to myself.

Presently he came back. He'd brought a sleeping-bag and a winceyette nightie that he told me was all he could find in the way of nightgear. I held it up and we both looked at it. It was pale blue, printed with roses and violets.

'She doesn't usually wear things in bed,' said Ferg, excusing her taste in old-lady clothes.

'It'll be nice and warm,' I said. More important, it would be something to wear while I rinsed and dried the muddy trousers of my tracksuit.

Ferg seemed to be listening all the time, till he unsettled me too, and I began to wish he'd go. I expected a wild-eyed fiend to come flying across the park to find him.

He kissed me and fumbled around my clothes in a half-hearted sort of way, but the spirit had gone out of us both. Already I was wondering about tomorrow, when I should have to leave this place, which felt so insecure.

'Can I put on the light, later?' I asked him.

'Of course you can. We rent the pond and the boat-house. You needn't feel uncomfortable about being here.'

So Ferg went away, promising to come back early in the morning, and I wrote my novel, as far as page 162. Or that is what I hope. Perhaps it will all have to be re-written, who knows?

The wild-eyed fiend arrived in the small hours. She

came into my dreams first, as I lay asleep on the sofa huddled into the sleeping-bag.

My ears signalled to my resting brain, which scrambled the message. I dreamed that my mother had come to fetch me. 'Come home now,' she said. I knelt on the grass. 'Come on,' I said. I was holding my hand a couple of inches from the ground, trying to make a small brown toad jump over my fingers.

Come on, come on, said a voice that wasn't mine, and the floorboards shook under the sofa as someone banged on the door. Come on, come on.

The voice was sad and waif-like, and I should have thought of that, how it contrasted with the shuddering of the door.

'Yes,' I said, and I soothed, knowing that Lavinia was waiting for me, and that I had to handle this right, for Ferg's sake.

I slid out of the sleeping-bag and crossed the room in bare feet. My trousers, reflected in the weak moonlight, hung like an amputated torso over a chair I had placed in front of the gas-fire.

I switched on the light and unlocked the door.

Lavinia stood there and straight away I thought of Ophelia, and Christina Rossetti, and all the sad beautiful pale people in the world, while we hovered in the mist over this pond where, in darkness, no birds sang.

Lavinia's hair was of finest gold. It crept in soft tendrils from under her silk shawl, and I couldn't help noticing the Christian Dior label embroidered in gold thread on a rose of pale ivory.

'Fergy! Fergy,' cried Lavinia piteously, and a pearl rolled from her eye and dropped onto her silk slippers of palest aquamarine.

'Ferg isn't here,' I said in a forthright tone of triumphant innocence.

But Lavinia pushed me aside and rushed into the boat-house. She began to wail in utter distress, 'Fergy, Fergy.'

'Look,' I said, as naturally as I was able. 'He really isn't here.'

Idiotically I opened a cupboard, in which hung cups on hooks, and a very old fishing-jacket. I sniffed. The cupboard smelt of sugar, which was a smell I hadn't thought of since my childhood, and which it seemed irreverent to notice at this tense moment.

I turned, and saw that Lavinia was staring at me in horror.

'My nightie!' she exclaimed. 'I got it in the Sales at Dickens and Jones.'

'That explains everything,' was my reply, which I regretted very soon afterwards, because Lavinia hurled herself at me and ripped it from neck to somewhere-round-my-knees in one tearing wrench.

'Get it off,' she said.

It wasn't much use to me any longer, so I stepped out of it with what dignity I could, which was quite a lot, because the huge tear made graceful movement possible.

But now I stood naked before Lavinia, and nakedness is a disadvantage when you are confronting a furious wraith.

Lavinia seized a cup from the cupboard, grabbing it with such violence that she tore off its handle. Then she hurled it at my defenceless body as I stood about six feet away from her.

It hurt.

'Lavinia,' I said, trying to bear in mind that she was a very sick person, whilst at the same time thinking that she was behaving like an ordinary jealous lover. 'Lavinia, I didn't mean to offend you in any way. Please forgive me.'

I wondered if I should have recognized her illness if Ferg hadn't told me about it. For Lavinia's irrationality could have been interpreted as the insecurity of any threatened or dispossessed hysterical person, and I wouldn't have known the difference between that and some more sinister psychological syndrome. I didn't regard Lavinia as a rival. A rival is someone you compete with, and if Ferg was so obsessed with his sister despite her illness, there was no point in my pursuing a sexual relationship with him.

164

Then I said the magic words, by instinct. 'You have the prime place in Ferg's life. It says so in his cards.'

Lavinia put her hand down. I am a doctor, or a priest, and I can lay my hands on you and heal you, I might as well have said.

'What else did it say?' she asked meekly.

And so I told her, through chattering teeth because the door was still open and mist streamed in from the reeds below us. I emphasized a few items and made a few more up, I am ashamed to say, but this was in the interests of survival.

Then Lavinia, calm as a boiled egg, crossed to a shelf and took down a box. She threw it onto the table.

'Tell my cards,' she ordered.

'Only if I can put my clothes on.'

But she began another tantrum and I gave in.

We sat at the table and she selected her cards and I laid them out.

I didn't care what I told her, all my scruples had disappeared with my clothes. I was only concerned with keeping her calm. Shall we be here all night? I wondered. Will I die of exposure?

'You have been very ill,' I prevaricated, 'but recovery is within your grasp. . . .' Well, so it may have been.

Lavinia listened to me, enthralled as a child.

But help was at hand. There was the sound of footsteps, and then of grumbling and thumping.

Lavinia jumped up and rushed to the door.

'No, no!' she cried, just as Ferg appeared. 'No, Fergy, you mustn't see her.'

Ferg peered across the room at me. He was very drunk.

'What are you two up to?' he asked the room.

I made a dash for my trousers, but Lavinia was there before me. She snatched them off the chair, and shielded me with them before I was half-way across the room. Then she stood in front of me, wafting her shawls and things around, all to protect me from the lascivious eyes of her brother, who in fact was still stumbling about demanding to know what was happening, and had clearly not appreciated that he was losing his only opportunity ever to see me with nothing on.

I had hoped for warmth; modesty was a poor second indeed. My trousers were still very damp, and stuck to my legs coldly. I had better luck with the top half.

'Oh, you poor thing,' said Lavinia, looking at me with total sympathy. 'You must stay the night, we won't hear any argument about it.'

I pretended gratitude, to the Ferg *obbligato* of what's going on, and Lavinia guided him with great solicitude down the treacherous steps. Presently I heard their voices as they staggered back across the park.

'. . . will come home from a long journey to rescue me from an awkward situation,' Lavinia was saying, quoting our cartomancy session.

'What journey?' Ferg was asking. 'What's going on?'

Their voices faded into the thin mist and the sleepy nod of buttercups.

To pastures new

♡♣◇♤ Chapter 21 ♡♣◇♤
Two Clubs

The lapping of water became more persistent during the night. Soft uneven bumps told me the boat moored beneath me was jostling against its landing-stage. In sleep I half-noticed these sounds, and they comforted rather than disturbed me. As the breeze freshened, rain began to patter onto the corrugated iron roof. The late start to yesterday's sunny finish hadn't been a good omen.

With the dawn, a new sound, that of the gulls awaking, began to make sleep impossible.

I sat up. The butane must have run out during the night. The stove no longer flickered, and still my trousers weren't dry.

I shall end up with either piles or rheumatics, I thought as I dressed yet again, and once again sat on the sofa thumbing through my notebook. After seeing the state he was in last night, I didn't expect Ferg to arrive till much later.

I picked up my pen.

Sandra had always wanted to play the drums. Instead,

167

she joined the Salvation Army and learned to play the cornet.

There was no Sandra in my story. I bracketed the sentences, thinking they might come in handy in some later novel, and I heard someone coming up the steps.

A pale grey face peered through the window. Ferg's.

'Look, I'm sorry about last night,' said Ferg. 'I went out for a couple of drinks, and she'd gone when I got back. I'm afraid I made the mistake of telling her you were here before I left, in case she saw your light. I didn't want her to be frightened.'

To myself I thought that it would take more than a light in a distant boat-house to frighten Lavinia. It occurred to me that Ferg had told her about me out of sheer mischief.

'Where is she now?' I pretended not to sound apprehensive.

'Asleep. She took a couple of Moggies when we got back to the flat last night. She won't be awake for hours.'

He looked at his watch and frowned. His hair was wet, slicked back from his face in the manner of heavy drinkers who have to persuade themselves that they are smart and capable, in the sick ache of the morning after.

'I've phoned Phyllis Thackray. She can probably help you with somewhere to stay.'

I forgave his hair.

He was going to take me back to my car, by which time we guessed Edwin would have left Cornfield to go to work. The idea was for me to pick up my belongings from Edwin's, then drive round to see Phyllis some time later in the morning.

Ferg almost seemed to brush his hands. 'There, that's that, and I was a fool to get involved in the first place, but at least I have discharged my duties with honour,' his hands said.

'I couldn't have managed without you,' I said.

The trouble with letting people help you out is that you have to be so grateful all the time.

He'd left the car in the field, and we lurched away almost shamefacedly. We had both failed. I had failed in my dream of gaining him as a lover. There had been too much to do, and I hadn't made enough effort. And I never stood a chance against Lavinia. Blood, in this case, was thicker than semen. Mixed, the two were positively glutinous.

As for Ferg, he had failed in his half-hearted attempt to free himself from his sister. You'll have to drink more, Ferg, I thought, feeling the lump on my hip where the cup had struck me last night during Lavinia's rage. We had all made sacrifices for each other, but they hadn't been enough, and once I was away from here we should all be back where we started.

Except that I was leaving Edwin.

We picked up a student who was hitching into Avalon. She sat in the back, and her presence was some relief, making intimate conversation impossible.

When we reached the end of Judy's road, Ferg stopped and I got out.

'I'll see you,' said Ferg.

And, 'Thanks for everything,' I said.

Half-way to my car, I looked back over my shoulder. The student was clambering out of the back. The car drew away, and there they were, sitting comfortably, next to each other. I saw that Ferg was laughing.

Judy's curtains were closed. I unlocked my car and started the engine. I didn't feel like persuading her to talk to me this morning.

I drove into Edwin's drive as if I belonged there, in that house. At the front door was a woven basket, with a wicker lid. I lifted this and looked inside. At first I thought it was some sort of joke, or witchcraft. The basket was full of dandelion heads.

The Lunch-o-fax manager's wife came out of her front door. She wore black, and heavy make-up that she bought from the Avon Lady as a sort of exchange for her own plastic goodies.

She saw me peering into the basket.

169

'I thought you might like them, dear,' she said. 'Saint George's Day, that's when we should have picked them, supposed to be at their best then. We were a bit late, I'm afraid.'

The dandelion heads were closing up in exhaustion and despair.

'What are they for?' I asked. I imagined you were supposed to feed them to frogs at midnight. Or swing them three times round your head for a thousand pounds and a handsome husband.

'Wine, dear. They're to make wine with. We thought you might like to have a go. We picked too many. Two quarts, it said. Well, we didn't have an idea what two quarts was . . .'

'Thank you,' I said. 'Good idea.'

I went into the house, setting the basket down in the hall. I heard the Lunch-o-faxes drive away to work in their TR7. The dandelions were a nuisance, but I was touched. The Lunch-o-faxes had done their best to be friendly while I was living with Edwin. They had been a useful butt and I should miss them.

In the kitchen was a note from Edwin.

May.
    We are mature enough to work this out together. Call me at work, or we could meet somewhere for lunch. In any case we could discuss it tonight when I get home.

He hadn't quite reduced it to the level of a problem with the central heating, but it was near enough. There was a postscript.

Your mother called. She isn't well.

Edwin was always reproachful about my attitude to my mother. The tiny fact that she had abandoned me when I was a child didn't seem to register with him. 'She regrets it now,' he'd say. 'You can't hold things against people for ever, surely.'

170

Saint-like.

It didn't take me long to pack. I shoved things into the car and tried to look as if I was making up a load to take to Oxfam, in case any curious neighbours were watching, even though they would find out soon enough what was going on.

I stood in the hall.

'Goodbye, Edwin,' I had written on his note.

There was a faintly bitter smell, coming from the dandelions. I picked them up and took them into the back garden. I dug a trench at the bottom of the hedge and tipped them in, covering them carefully with earth. This seemed kinder than dumping them in the dustbin.

Friendship

♡♣◇♤ **Chapter 22** ♡♣◇♤
Two Sevens

Phyllis Thackray had no truck with converted watermills or antique barges or telephone sub-exchanges. She lived on a private estate of large new houses, where everyone owned a Great Dane or an Irish wolfhound. Sometimes on Phyllis' estate there would be nine burglaries in a single night. That's why, Vincenza had once told me, Phyllis had decided to be a magistrate; so that she could take the law into her own hands.

I pressed her bell. Chimes which reminded me of an ice-cream van (forbidden on this estate) echoed through the house. Phyllis swam towards me. I could see her coming, through the reinforced glass of the front door.

'May, dear,' said Phyllis, 'I've been expecting you. I'm so sorry to hear about you and Edwin. I hope it's only temporary.'

I told her it certainly was not.

She looked down the path to my car.

'Yes, well,' she said. 'You can borrow the cottage for the winter, for as long as you like, dear. We don't start bookings till next May.'

She ushered me into the kitchen for coffee, and she must have felt uneasy about owning a second house, because she began to justify it.

'The cottage is my little pied-à-terre,' she said. 'It took me a long time to save up for it. It gives me a sense of security to know it's there if ever I want it. I don't seem to have a very easy life.'

Her eyes filled with tears as she looked at me. And so did mine. Now I thought of it, I didn't seem to have an easy life either. There was no security in my life, no sense of belonging with any of the people or situations I found myself with. As each stage of my life ended, it is true that I found security in the next one. But it was only ever temporary, and I never knew when I should be thrown into the next struggle.

So, because I felt sorry for myself, I sympathized with Phyllis and couldn't speak, or I should have burst into tears. We held hands over the table. Poor Phyllis, I thought. You are so plain. If you were pretty it would be a different story. Also, Phyllis was too capable for her own good. No man is likely to let himself in for a torrid affair with a woman magistrate, especially, so it was rumoured, one who was likely to be elected as Chairperson of the Bench next October.

A torrid affair, I felt, would be the remedy for Phyllis at this point in her life. (Now I think differently.) Phyllis' best hope, I thought, was that the Mafia would move into Avalon and one of their handsome henchmen would be detailed to seduce her.

'Phyllis,' I managed to say, 'I'm very sorry, I really am.' Because I couldn't think of anything at Avalon that would attract even the least ambitious *mafioso*.

We both had a large gin and hugged each other. Phyllis didn't *bend* when I hugged her. Although she was big, she had no spare flesh or softness, and I felt hugely warm towards her.

'You are a very *good* person, Phyllis,' I said. 'And that surely is the most precious thing of all.'

173

But precious though it may be, it didn't make Phyllis happy or elated; as his fleeting affairs made Derek.

We drove to the cottage. It was a perfect holiday cottage, one of a row set back in a bank that overlooked the estuary.

'It faces south,' Phyllis told me, and she pointed out that this made it warmer, so there would be a saving on fuel.

Then she insisted on lighting the fire, while I made some tea, which we drank as we watched the fire die out slowly. Practical people are often bad at fires. Phyllis said she had never got her Second Class at Guides because she hadn't been able to light a campfire with two matches.

Almost everyone I know says that. It is surprising Girl Guides has survived so long, with all these failures around.

Phyllis stirred milk-powder into her tea.

'I'm not sure if I should tell you this,' she began.

'Tell me and get it over with,' I advised, for I knew she'd tell me anyway now.

'You see,' said Phyllis, 'you and Edwin were very fortunate, really.'

I stiffened. Not a magisterial lecture, surely?

'How's that?' I asked.

'Well, you had what might be called a symbiotic relationship. You depended on him for encouragement in your writing. . . .'

'. . . and for my keep,' I helped her. 'And he depended on me to keep him and his rotten house clean, is that it?'

'Not exactly. It's to do with the work he's doing on Marie de France.'

'Who's she?' I'd never heard of her.

'Marie de France was half-sister to a king, and arguably the first novelist. She wrote about love and the supernatural. Like you do.'

I'd heard *this* before.

'There isn't much love in what I write,' I said. 'And there's nothing at all about the supernatural.'

Phyllis smiled, because she knew more about all this

than I did.

'You're a cartomancer, aren't you?' she asked. 'And you write about love more than you realize.'

Then Phyllis told me, what everyone else at Avalon already knew, that Edwin was researching the work of this de France person using detail he was obtaining from observing how I went about my writing.

'Of course, he couldn't have let you know, that would have undermined the whole project,' said Phyllis. 'It was going to be a surprise for you. When he'd finished the work there was a plan to televise the whole project for *Arena*. You were going to be one of the "stars".'

I didn't believe her at first.

'That's not possible. If Edwin had been planning such things, I should have known about it. Letters from the BBC, they always have the logo on the envelope, and there'd have been phone calls, visits from producers, that sort of thing.'

Phyllis was tolerant about my naïveté.

'There were such things. All the time. Everyone but you knew about them. Nothing would be sent to the house, silly. Everything would be done through his office. It stands to reason.'

Ah, yes. It did indeed stand to reason. The office at work; the *poste restante* of the restless husband, the itchy wife. Edwin had had access to my garret, to everything that was mine. But half his life, his office life, had been closed to me.

Phyllis touched my hand. 'You see how it was. He was going to make you famous.'

'I'm going to make me famous,' I said, trying to sound convincing.

I sat back, thinking of those hard-nosed camp-followers of Academe conspiring with Edwin, all in the interests of widening the boundaries of knowledge, of course.

'What a bunch of creeps,' I said.

'Well, dear, you may be right. But I just thought that if you knew, you might want to reconsider your position.'

I said nothing, and she got up to go.

175

I know it was all done out of kindness.

When Phyllis had gone, I could have phoned my mother, Shirley Knott. I could have, but I didn't. I stood at the window and looked at the river. The tide was out, and rain drifted over the dull sandbanks.

Shirley had told Edwin she wasn't well.

'I don't care about you, Shirley Knott,' I said out loud.

For when had Shirley Knott ever cared about me?

What did I do? I asked myself. What terrible thing did I do, that made my own mother give me away?

Shirley Knott had made me pay for that bad thing all my life. Yet now she was asking me to help her.

Too bad. If love was reciprocal, so too was indifference. Now it was my turn to reciprocate.

*A hard time lies
ahead*

♡♣◇♤ **Chapter 23** ♡♣◇♤
Six of Spades

From time to time the papers tell us that there are millions
of pounds stashed away at the DHSS, all waiting to be
claimed by people that the department must know about –
or how would they compile these figures?

Perhaps a modest fraction of that money belongs to me,
though most of the time I try not to think about it. A
feeling of post-flu depression comes over me when I think
of the DHSS and my relationship to it, for I have a blind
spot for claims and money, and in any case I can never get
past the first hurdle whenever I grit my teeth and go and
queue in their offices. I like to think that somewhere,
hidden away on some floppy disk, I have rights there. But
what are they? I don't know. Sometimes I think I am the
least-entitled citizen in the British Isles, though I am sure
plenty of others would compete with me for this title.

But until I stayed at Phyllis' cottage, there had always
been someone to keep me. In other words, to give me
food and shelter, in return for various services, the nature
of which, according to Phyllis, I had sometimes not

understood. First, I had performed the service of being a child to childless parents. When I became redundant, I had been sent to the Henshaws' farm as a skivvy, or, as they called it, a 'trainee'. After the short time spent as a waitress at the BMA in Southampton Row, I'd bettered myself by going to live with Edwin.

I was twenty-nine. Apart from the waitress stint, I had never earned any wage other than pocket money. My possessions had all been given to me, and there weren't many of them, as we have seen. Only my car, a gift from Edwin, was of any value, and it was doubtful whether I should be able to afford it now.

And still my shelter was provided, because Phyllis refused to accept any rent.

I was the last of the serfs. But perhaps not. And I had to eat.

I cried at the Job Centre, and they were sorry for me. They offered me a good job as a clerk in their own office and they were hurt and offended when I turned it down.

'I don't want anything that I have to think about or concentrate on,' I tried to explain.

The novel had to be finished. It was, it seemed to me, the only goal in my life, just to finish it. Real people had betrayed me, but I hoped that my novel couldn't do this, for I believed at that time that I could control its plot, and also its characters.

In the end I walked into a cut-price clothes shop and asked for a job, and they gave me one. I sold nighties with holes in them, and jumpers that came apart under the arms, where they couldn't be mended: all the garments that I had bought for myself over the years because they had seemed at the time to be bargains.

There were some real bargains at the shop. By and large they were snapped up by the assistants themselves, most of whom seemed to spend a large proportion of their wages on buying the goods they were there to sell.

Independence frightened me at first. I dreaded going home at night to my cottage, knowing that all the other houses in the row would become unoccupied as autumn drew on. Twice a day the tide came to the foot of the rocky bank that was divided into tiny sections so that all the cottages had a small garden. I came to know the times of the tides, and to hear them approaching or withdrawing beyond the mouth of the estuary. Even at work I would suddenly remember how the tide would be flowing in front of my house.

At night the sound of the rising water would percolate into my dreams, and I would open my eyes to see the draught blowing the curtains at the windows, as though the tide was breathing against the glass. Then I would switch on the electric blanket and let the heat seep underneath me till I fell asleep again.

Usually the thin curtains hung limply at the windows, damp from the salt that crept all around the cottages. For I only dared afford a fire at weekends. The rest of the time I rationed my coins for the electric meter, and each night, when they were all used except one, I went to bed, whilst across the room the other bed stayed bare and neat under its pink candlewick covering.

I never sat at the table to eat. The table had become my desk, my altar, with the typewriter rising amongst the complicated heaps of pages into which I had arranged my novel.

Ferg didn't get in touch with me. I would think of him often, and was tempted to phone him or to call in to the Friars' Arms after work, to see if he was there. I resisted. Instead I would ask Phyllis about him when she came to see me.

She told me the whole of Cornfield and most of the university were discussing the revelation that his sister was living with him. It was regarded as suspicious in itself, as he had kept it such a secret till now. The night after I'd been at the boat-house, Lavinia appeared in the bar at the Friars' and screamed at him to come home, saying she couldn't trust him ever again. Worse, said Phyllis, she'd been wearing nothing except a nightie, torn right down the front. People had drawn their own conclusions, right or wrong, and Armitage had told everyone that he'd never drink with Ferg again. Even Ferg's typist had given in her notice, Phyllis told me.

'Lavinia will have to go,' she said. 'It's surprising how small this place is, when any rumour like that gets out. You can see why he drinks so heavily, can't you? It's one of those dreadful situations of utter dependency between two people who can't break away from each other and who end up destroying each other, if you ask me. It's just as well,' said Phyllis, 'that you didn't get involved.'

'I did,' I pointed out. And I yearned for poor lonely Ferg who drank alone and went home every night to his doomed relationship.

Yearning is a sort of illness, Phyllis told me. Each time you are strong enough not to give in to it you make it easier to resist. Like slimming. 'It may seem hard,' she said, 'but these infatuations pass, believe me.'

I supposed she was referring to Derek's involvements, so she was speaking from a sort of vicarious experience.

'Deeper, less flamboyant relationships are more meaningful and endure great hardship,' she said.

For her sake, I hoped she was right.

If yearning is an illness, then my work at the shop was a drug that helped to dull the pain. But I dreaded the moment when a customer would recognize me.

Hilde came to the shop first. She bought a jumper, and only noticed me when she got to the till. She seemed delighted to see me.

'Darling, we all wondered what had happened to you.'

She looked at the jumper that I was pushing into a paper bag.

'You see how we are influenced by your fortune-telling. Now I spend as little money as possible to save for a rainy day.' She leant across the cash-desk. 'The ace of spades. When it comes I shall be ready for it.'

'It's only entertainment,' I told her, she mustn't take it seriously.

But Hilde smiled knowingly. 'It is not for you to say,

my darling.'

'You read fortunes in the cards?' Kathy, on the till with me, had been following this conversation.

Then the girls looked at me differently.

'May, tell our fortunes, go on.'

And during our twenty-minute breaks, while we huddled in the cupboard half-full of coat-hangers that was our rest-room, I would read their cards. And they listened, very serious, giving each other advice how to avoid some of the threats that I had already softened for them in the telling.

One by one they all found their way to the shop, those women who had been at Nerina's party. Mostly they just nodded at me politely, and the girls would say afterwards, teasing:

'That was another of your friends, May, come slumming to have a peek at you.'

It was strange. I didn't go to visit Judy and Arnie, even though I was lonely at times and could have done with the company. I was too close to them with my needs. I had never felt mighty when I visited them, but, fallen, I felt humiliated.

'I can't be any help to them at the moment,' I told myself.

Phyllis came round to the cottage one night, looking bleary. We drank coffee, during long silences.

She told me people were refusing to serve Ferg in the local shops.

'Lavinia will have to go,' she said.

Was incest legal among consenting adults, was the next thing we discussed. Phyllis said she hadn't got round to looking it up yet, she hadn't the spirit at the moment, but she would certainly go into the matter.

She sighed. 'No taboo is sacrosanct any longer.'

She looked even more miserable, and refused a glass of

my Boots home-made wine.
   'Everyone misses you,' she said.
   I didn't believe her.

Usually ruled by reason, he lays bare his heart

♡♣♢♤ **Chapter 24** ♡♣♢♤
King of Diamonds

One morning, at the shop, I was gazing at the split in the crutch of a pair of long-johns, when I saw Edwin coming towards me. I folded the dreary garment and slipped it under a pile of more perfect items.

'Good morning,' I said. 'Can I help you?'

'May,' said Edwin, and for some moments neither of us said anything. You could say he was looking at me longingly, though I was not sure what he was longing for. The missing pages of my novel, probably.

'It's your mother,' he said.

This was unexpected. 'What about her?' I asked.

'She's not well. I think you should come and see her.'

'I can't afford the time to go all that way,' I said, assuming my mother was far away in Yorkshire.

'She's not in Leeds. She's here, staying with me. She's my housekeeper,' said Edwin.

Such cunning. 'Honestly, Edwin, you've got some nerve, interfering in my life like this.'

'Please come and see her,' Edwin said.

183

But it was a trap, and I wasn't going to fall into it.

'You'd do anything to get me back,' I said with disgust.

'Yes,' said Edwin meekly, 'I think I would.'

He pleaded. 'She so wants to see you.'

To which I replied if she wasn't well she'd be better off seeing a doctor.

'That's just it,' said Edwin. 'She won't go to one.'

'Go away, Edwin,' I said heartlessly. 'My mother is of no more concern to me than I was to her. You have brought her on yourself, which I'm very angry about.'

'May,' said Edwin, using a different ploy. 'Come back, please. I miss you so much.'

Of course a silence happened just as he said these words, I miss you so much, and the girls began to giggle to each other.

'You've been spying on me, using me in a horrible underhand way,' I said. 'How can I ever trust you again? You have deceived me in every possible way.'

At the till, Kathy mimed applause behind Edwin's back.

'Oh, May,' said Edwin. 'How can either of us trust the other?'

He picked up a pair of long-johns and pretended to examine them.

'Edwin,' I said, taking them out of his hands, 'please don't handle those if you aren't going to buy them. You'll make even more of the stitching come undone.'

He surrendered the wretched things.

'It wouldn't have worked if I'd told you about it,' he said. 'I was only trying to analyse how you write. Surely there's nothing wrong in that? I wanted to relate modern creativity to the first tentative steps taken by the narrative.'

'You could have told me. It's the slyness that upsets me.'

'It wouldn't have worked if you'd started to think about how you were doing it. You'd have lost your spontaneity, become self-conscious about your methods, probably even have changed them.'

'A human experiment,' I said. 'I feel like a pig that's been forced to smoke cigarettes.'

It was a poor comparison, and Edwin frowned.

'I'll tell you all about it any time you like,' he said, and I thought, Right, so now I know the experiment's finished.

'Even though the research can't be completed until you've finished your novel, I'm quite prepared to abandon it at this stage, if you're so upset about it,' said Edwin, guessing my thoughts. 'The house isn't the same without you.'

'What about Vincenza?' I asked, for if Bertholdt had so confidently expected her to leave him I had assumed he must be right in his prediction, since he was a professor of psychology.

But he'd reckoned without Edwin, who now looked at the cigarette burns and the trodden-in tar on the shop carpet and blushed.

'I knew about you and Ferg, she told me about you,' he said. 'I was just trying to be independent, like we'd agreed. It's the first time I've ever got involved with any woman except you, and that's the truth. The truth is, May, that I was a virgin when I met you.'

He looked round fearfully for eavesdroppers, but now crates of flood-damaged woollies were being delivered by the gross, and no one could have overheard him even if they'd wanted to. There was a faint smell of mildewed cardboard. Some of the crates were splitting open as they hit the floor, disgorging metallic green cardigans with faulty zipped fronts.

'It wouldn't have been any good living with Vincenza. She's far too sophisticated for me, for one thing. And she's left Bertholdt loads of times and then gone back to him. She'd have done the same to me, and how would I have faced him in the SCR after that?'

'I'm sophisticated,' I said, feeling slighted.

Edwin looked at me, and the word tender came into my mind. He looked at me tenderly.

'You aren't,' he said. 'You are like a hurt child. You are the baby in the hollow of the ash tree, one of the oldest myths in literature, Le Lai La Freine, and Moses, and long before that even. And I would like you to marry me, though . . .' as I started back in distaste '. . . there's no need if you'd rather not. But ours is a good relationship. All this could have a happy ending. Your mother likes it at Cornfield. She'd love you to come back. She's had a hard life, and we could help her now.'

'Why should we help my mother?' I asked. I had the feeling that he had to do so in order to strengthen the parallel with the Lai La Freine.

'That way,' said Edwin, 'you would be inside the warmth of a family group. You'd be re-united with your mother, which would slowly heal the scar that you have to live with.'

'Neither of us would be happy living with a selfish alcoholic,' I said, and when I had said it I felt as if I had let my mother down most dreadfully, that things could never now be right between us.

'She could have treatment,' said Edwin, but he didn't sound convinced about this.

Someone called me across the shop, for the chaos of split cardboard boxes and mildewed garments was becoming a customer hazard. Edwin was asked to leave by the manageress who had overheard us. She told him not to bring his personal problems into her shop again.

Reunion

♡♣◇♤ Chapter 25 ♡♣◇♤
Two Aces

Why didn't my mother come to see me? Why did she send Edwin on her errands of reconciliation? Was she really ill? Did Edwin really want me home, and if so, why?

All these questions I pondered between my efforts for survival and the slow progress of my writing.

I knew Shirley Knott was at Edwin's house, of course. But Cornfield was some miles from the estuary and Phyllis' cottage. I knew that some time I would go and see her. There was no hurry.

There was more urgency than I realized.

One night in mid-September I was sitting later at the typewriter than I had meant to. With the now-familiar 'click' the light snapped off. My electricity ration had run out.

I sat for a few moments watching the slow fade of red as the element in the electric fire cooled. I was thinking that my frugal routine was becoming reassuring, that at last I was beginning to settle here.

The phone rang.

I fumbled for the receiver.

'May?' It was Edwin.

'Edwin. I asked you not to ring me. And why are you phoning so late? It must be past eleven.'

Then Edwin apologized. He said he never would have bothered me, but he'd had a phone call from the Morgana Club in town. 'It seems your mother's been taken ill,' he said.

'The Morgana Club?' I'd never heard of it. And why wasn't Edwin helping Shirley?

'It's a sort of drinking club,' Edwin said. He sounded uncomfortable.

'You let my mother go to a drinking club on her own?'

'I didn't know that's where she was. She told me she was going to see some friends. And so she was, I suppose.'

He sounded very mature and reasonable.

'Well, why don't you go and see to her,' I asked, 'since you're the one who asked her to stay here in the first place?'

'Of course I would,' said Edwin. 'But they said she asked for you. And in any case I'm catching the night train to Edinburgh. I'm giving a paper there first session tomorrow morning.' He began to plead, 'Look, May, I do understand how you feel. And I'd go and bring her home if I could. We can't just leave her there.'

'*We* can't!'

'She's your mother, you know.'

Edwin is so tribal.

'I'll go,' I agreed, in the end, and he thanked me, with much gratitude, then began to give me directions for finding the wretched place.

The Morgana Club was in a square near to the town centre. I was surprised to know of its existence here, for I had thought of this square as the stronghold of dentists and solicitors, the Georgian terraced houses divided into respectable offices smelling faintly of glycerine of thymol.

But such places have basements, and it was from one of these that disco music flared up the stone steps, only to be stifled among the laurels that pushed their branches through the railings as if they were trying to get away from this grimy refuge.

I climbed down the steps. A mock-Spanish door confronted me, with mock-Spanish bolts driven into it in a neat pattern, and a mock-Spanish grille that I could peer into as easily as those inside could peer out.

I peered in.

Dim orange lights made to look like torches lit up an entrance across which I could see the toilets, the ladies' denoted by a high-heeled shoe, the men's by a macho-style riding boot.

The door of the women's room was propped open by two feet, whose legs disappeared behind an orange chenille curtain. A shoe hung from the toes of one foot, its high heel forcing the foot sideways at a bizarre angle, giving it the appearance of a broken limb. The other foot was shoeless.

I knew that the tired veins encased in their brave crimson nylon belonged to my mother, Shirley Knott.

The bouncer was too bright to stop me as I pushed past him, for I must have made my purpose plain. I had one aim, and that was to see my mother. Yet also I didn't want to see her. A small part of me still hoped that when the curtain was drawn back I should see another face, the face of a stranger.

I pulled back the curtain, and for a fraction of a second I thought that I was indeed looking at someone I had never seen before. It was her colour that so changed my mother's face. This face had the purple-white mottling of someone whose blood has retreated to its marrow in a last effort at preservation, leaving the skin and muscle to shrink and flag in numbness far away from the thinning current.

If there had only been this, the colour of deadness, to

disguise my mother, I might still have recognized her in that first instant. But this body that lay half in and half out of the ladies' retiring room, as if it had made instinctive attempts at the last to retire with decency, breathed inwards deeply and slowly with the deliberation of a tide sucking the ocean out of a cave, then just as slowly inundating it again.

It was not my mother's breathing. It was not the breathing of any being that looks out at the world and expects to be a part of it, whose lungs inflate unthinkingly yet in time with mood and physical need. Some other part of this body that was still – but only just – a *being* had taken it over, directing its survival. *Breathe!* said the medulla.

As I knelt and lowered my face to hers, my mother sighed, her lungs emptied themselves in sadness for us both, and in this exhalation I heard something of her voice, as if she knew I was there and was expressing her sorrow that we should find ourselves at last together in such circumstances.

'Mummy, Mummy,' I said while the bouncer held back the curtain, and someone on their way to the toilet (for life and the emptying of bladders must go on) stepped clumsily over her feet.

Mummy, I am yours, part of you, and we belong together. We are the same flesh.

This was my feeling, of completeness and love reciprocated, for there could be no rejection now.

'Ah-h,' sighed my mother, and the sigh came from the very centre of her mind.

'I'm with you, me, May Knott,' I told her. Even then, in this reunion of our bloods, I had to say all my name, as if I feared that she would never know me simply as May.

Vomit began to overflow from her mouth, and the breathing lost its deep rhythm, becoming choked and confused.

'Turn her on her side,' said the bouncer. 'You'd never believe it; give her a couple of gins and she's ka'lied. We'll have to get rid of her. She can't hang around here.'

'Call an ambulance,' I said.

The bouncer paused in the act of re-arranging my mother's legs. He looked at me with scorn and disbelief.

'Are you some kind of a nut or what? She's your mother, isn't she? She's drunk, my love, it's as simple as that. Are you teetotal or something? She'll likely be booked if you call an ambulance. And it's more than my job's worth anyway, ambulances at the club.'

'My mother is very ill,' I said. 'She's not drunk, she's dying.'

This knowledge was inside me with certainty, even though it was my first encounter with a very sick person, and I had never seen anyone who was dying.

'Well,' said the bouncer, 'she's not going to die in here.'

He bent down as if to lift her. What would he have done? Hefted her in a fireman's lift up the stone steps, while her head thumped against his leg, her scalp a dinner-plate decorated with its stiff curls, her skirt hanging down over her shoulders like the frill round the body of some prehistoric fish?

He would have left her, my mother, Shirley Knott, on the pavement, and stepped back behind the door to his phony orange life.

I stood astride her body.

'Leave my mother alone.' My voice was loud and aggressive, I was making a scene. Faces began to appear at the darkness of archways.

'An ambulance. An ambulance. My mother's dying.'

I was shouting in hate and fear, though the fear was a low note that underpinned the hate and was overpowered by it. At this reunion, this birth of love after twenty-nine years of indifference, the bouncer was the obstacle, the last evil wizard to fight, and then I should be there, in the heart of my mother.

I was not afraid of the bouncer. I was afraid of death, that after all I should never be loved; that the last chance of such a possibility was beating slower and fainter, ebbing away into plush acrylic torchlight.

'Call an ambulance for the lady.'

Here came the owner, or manager; whatever there is in such places. He never spoke to me, never looked at me. But he bent over and looked at Shirley, just one glance he gave her.

'Call an ambulance,' he said.

He knew about dying. He inclined his head at the bouncer.

'Leave it off.'

The faces disappeared from the archways. The bouncer went back into the office with the manager. Clients crossed their legs and waited to use the toilets. Shirley Knott and I were alone.

But not quite, for the hospital was close by, and almost immediately I heard the klaxon of an ambulance, its brusque comfort coming nearer. I heard it as it entered the square, as it stopped in the street above us. Still Shirley and I were alone. It was me that opened the door to the ambulance-men.

'She's in a coma,' they told me. One of them looked around, sniffing. There was a hint of chemicals, almost a disinfectant odour of cleanness, yet displeasing, in the club. I had already noticed it, associating it with the synthetic quality of everything around us.

My mother's face disappeared behind a crumpled oxygen mask.

As I climbed into the ambulance to be with her, I heard a thunk of dismissal from the club below us.

Someone had closed the door.

Health difficulties

Chapter 26 ♡♣◇♤
Eight and Nine of Spades Adjacent

All kinds of tubes led in and out of my mother.

'She'll pull through, we think,' is what the doctor told me when I was allowed into the ward to see her.

'This type of coma is rare in people of her age. However, it's not unknown, and when it happens, it's very dramatic. It must have been a shock for you. All the signs were there, of course, long before this. But it needs someone experienced to recognize them. People simply think she's had too much to drink.'

'Your mother is a diabetic.'

He smiled. 'We'll try and get her sorted out,' and he said again, 'She should pull through all right.'

Behind him a nurse strapped black cotton round my mother's arm, hiss, hiss, hiss, and mercury rose on the blood-pressure gauge till the nurse stopped pumping, and in the silence the mercury slipped backwards till it was pinned by my mother's life.

Sitting by her bed, I held her hand. I gazed so hard at her that presently she seemed to be framed in a mist into which everything else melted away, till a green circle surrounded her as it might have done in a very old photograph.

Her eyes flickered and her hand tightened in mine. It was as though she was being pulled gently through the circle, insinuating herself carefully, so as not to touch its edges, which began to have a medical look that I suppose I associated with operating theatres and surgeons' gowns. Her head turned wearily on the pillow, but she smiled at me.

'Blurred,' she said.

Floating, still in the circle, she turned her wrist, dragging me towards herself. With no sense of movement I left the chair. She pulled me through the circle with great care. It closed behind us, and Mr Knott (to whom my mother had never been married), Edwin, the doctor, all were forgotten.

We were in a high-ceilinged room, and we sat on the floor, for there was nowhere else to rest. We leaned against each other.

'I gave you away because I loved you,' said my mother. 'It seemed right to punish myself; I was worthless.'

'It was me you punished,' I told her. 'All my life I have believed that you didn't want me because of some wrong I did. Because I am bad, no matter how I try to be otherwise.'

'All your life I have wanted you,' said my mother.

She breathed gently and evenly. 'I am afraid to do things for you,' she said. 'I'm not good enough for you.'

The mist melted. In the ward, voices and movement surfaced again. I got up from my chair and pulled the mask away from her face. She opened her eyes fully. Oxygen hissed faintly, making a small draught on my hand.

'We've been away a long time,' she said. She shifted her body, as if to make it more comfortable on a hard floor.

'Come nearer to me,' she said.

I bent over till my face nearly touched hers.

Pressing her weight onto her elbows, she raised her

head and kissed me.

'You've had a hard time,' she said.

She had become sleepy, and her eyes closed.

'Stay with me as long as you like. I'll look after you now,' she said.

'She's talking rather a lot,' said the nurse, readjusting the mask. 'I think you'd better wait outside.'

I went outside and sat in the corridor.

The floor was hard and I was cold in the high room. I hardly heard my mother's footsteps. Her feet were bare, and only a faintly tacky sound told me she was coming, for the floor was polished and her feet stuck slightly with every step.

She sat beside me, not wanting me to wait for her all on my own.

When at last I went back to her bedside, she seemed to be asleep. But as I sat down, she said something to me without opening her eyes.

'The keys.' She lifted one hand a few inches off the counterpane.

Hurt, I foraged round in her locker.

I found the keys and put them in her hand.

'They're safe,' I said, trying to soothe, to cover the bitterness I heard in my voice.

She shook her head very slowly from side to side.

'No,' she said, and she lifted her hand again, holding the keys away from herself.

'For you. I want you to have them. It's time for you to go home now.'

They were the keys to her attic hotel-room high above the railway station in Leeds.

A change in direction

♡♣◇♠ Chapter 27 ♡♣◇♠
Three Twos

There was no avoiding Edwin at the hospital.

My mother was fond of him, that was clear. And since I could hardly forbid him to visit her, it was natural that from time to time our visits to her bedside should overlap. At first he would apologize if he arrived while I was there, and he would go and wait outside in the corridor. I tried to forget he was there, yet I felt pushed, crowded by his mute contrite presence, knowing he was patiently waiting his turn to come into the ward.

After about a week it seemed to me that our visits coincided more and more, which I resented because Edwin's hours of work were far more flexible than mine, and he could have visited during the afternoon, when I was at work.

'Why does he always turn up just after I get here?' I said crossly to Shirley Knott.

'He doesn't come to see me,' she said. 'He comes to see you.'

This was an exaggeration, and, of course, I denied it

hotly.

Then my mother and I would talk scrappily to each other until one of us, glancing all the time at the ward doors, saw Edwin's hesitant face appear round the flappy plastic. 'Oh!' Great surprise. 'It's all right, I'll wait outside.' Then we would relax.

It began to happen, I feel almost ashamed to admit, that on the few occasions when Edwin didn't turn up, I would miss him, wondering where he was, and whether he would be here next evening, even though it was nothing to do with me. Once he missed three evenings in a row. 'Where can he be?' we asked each other, my mother and I, although I suspect she knew very well. His absence became our main topic of conversation.

The fourth day was Saturday, when I worked till late. 'Edwin came this afternoon,' said my mother when I visited her in the evening. 'He's been away in London.' She watched me. Yes, she knew what I was thinking. Why did he come in the afternoon? Didn't he want to see me any more, was that it?

'That's good,' I said. 'It's better to spread your visitors out, isn't it?' Like Marmite or raspberry jam.

He wasn't there on Sunday afternoon. My mother was cheerful. She'd been for a walk in the hospital grounds.

'They're going to let me go for a little spree round the town tomorrow,' she told me. She showed me the cache of barley sugars she had to keep in her handbag, for if she felt faint.

'They're sending me to convalesce soon. At a nunnery.' She pulled a face.

On Sunday evening Edwin's car pulled up next to mine as I parked in the hospital car park.

'I thought you'd gone away for ever,' I said, very jokingly, though I found that I was pleased and relieved to see him.

'Look,' I said, as we walked down the corridor together. 'It's rather silly you waiting outside. Why don't we go in together?'

And so we did, much to Shirley Knott's unconcealed

197

delight. Afterwards he asked me if I'd like to have a coffee with him, and I accepted as grudgingly as I was able in the circumstances, which were that I wanted to see him quite a lot.

On Sunday nights the choice of coffee bars in Avalon is limited. We made our way to Casualty and sipped coffee from the vending machine.

'You've lost weight,' I told him.

'I'm lost without you,' he answered, and I shook my head in disbelief at this new melodramatic Edwin.

I remembered that I'd missed him.

'How's Vincenza?' I asked.

'She won second prize at the Onion Show last Sunday at the Friars',' said Edwin. 'Armitage got the First. Rumour has it that she's moved in with him.'

I thought of Bertholdt and Martin resigning themselves again to her absence.

'It turns out it was Martin who vandalized the Green Knight Gallery,' said Edwin, as if I had spoken. 'Apparently it was a gesture against Fascism. He was objecting to the Fascist Art Exhibition.'

'Well, it won't be much good putting him into Child Care, will it?' I asked with some malice.

I was sorry about him, remembering our escapade at Nerina's party, and what a good friend he'd been to me. I remembered his miserable little body clutching at me, dressed in pyjamas: 'You asked me to come, didn't you, May Knott?'

'How's the novel?' asked Edwin, and I told him I'd got as far as page 197.

'It's going rather slowly,' I admitted.

This was a mistake.

'Then you should come back to live with me. You see how it is, your novel needs me as much as my work needs you.'

'My novel does very well without you, since you mention it, Edwin.'

But as I said this, I realized it had not been progressing as smoothly since I left him.

'It can only improve your novel, eliminating so much stress in your own life. Your mother can keep her independence, we'll convert the garage into a granny flat. Both cars can stand outside in the drive. That's equality.'

He must have been stung by my remark, so long ago, about having to leave my car outside in the drive.

'Oh, Edwin, you are a good friend to me. Novels are not, I suspect, improved by eliminating stress, but perhaps you are right, we should live together. And you've been very good and thoughtful about my mother.'

I was very tired, and Edwin's suggestion seemed attractive, like an offer of sleeping on a soft mattress when you had expected to lie on the floor.

My mother would have to live with me, in any case, and I knew she liked Edwin. Next spring I should be homeless, I didn't earn enough money, and often I was lonely.

'Are my emotions shallow?' I asked Edwin.

He considered, frowning.

'No, I don't think so.'

'I always wanted my mother to love me. That's why I didn't want her to live with us at Cornfield, because I thought she was just taking advantage of me. But that's not right, is it? You shouldn't want love in return?'

Edwin wasn't sure about love, he said. You have to separate it from its romantic image, he said, and there couldn't be balance without a certain degree of reciprocity.

I tried to tell him about the experience I'd had with Shirley the first night she was in hospital, but it sounded woolly and unconvincing.

He hugged me.

'Come back soon,' he said.

'Yes.'

It wasn't that in accepting Edwin's offer I was settling for second-best. No. I was adapting to society.

'It'll be an exciting life,' Edwin promised me. 'Trips to

France, Canada, possibly. Meeting people. It's a whole new scene since the lectern. We're doing a TV programme on that, by the way. I'd like you to appear. After all, you've played your part in all this.'

Ah, so Phyllis had been right.

He began to tell me about his dramatic discovery. . . .

'I never wanted to deceive you,' said Edwin, which is what people always say, I have noticed, when they finally come clean, even though they have usually enjoyed the deception, as long as it wasn't known about.

It was because he held my writing in such high esteem, Edwin said, that he had not been able to take the risk of telling me about his most fortunate find. He was afraid, as he had told Vincenza, that I would incorporate it into my novel. 'It was so exciting,' he told me, and his eyes were shining. 'I so longed to share the discovery of the parchment with you, the day I found it in the foot of the lectern.'

'Poor Edwin,' I sympathized. 'Never mind, you had all the rest of the University and its wife to discuss it with.'

He looked at me suspiciously, but I stroked his hand.

'It's not the same as you,' he said. 'You know, of course,' he said (which I did not, of course), 'that one of the reasons the study of Marie de France fascinated me was that she may well have been the Abbess of Shaftesbury, and that gives her local interest in Avalon, naturally. It's always a good thing for the local university to concern itself with the immediate area.'

'But Shaftesbury's miles away,' I said.

Edwin dismissed this. 'Its estates were tremendously extensive, encompassing this whole area, as far as Gilford.' He shook his head. 'Strangely enough, it was Ferg who gave me the tip-off about the lectern after it was dredged up from his lake by some kids and left on its side half-way across a field, as if they had been meaning to take it away but had lost interest, or it was too heavy. It wouldn't look anything special to anyone who wasn't an

200

expert. That's why it's to Ferg's credit that he saw it was interesting and mentioned it to me. He's really been very good, just handed the thing over with no fuss. He's even allowing us to film at the lake for the *Arena* programme. For a fee, of course. We're doing a reconstruction of how it was found. And it would be so right if you were there helping to find it, May dear.'

He reached over and touched my hand. I don't like being called 'dear'. I much prefer the northern 'love', which Edwin never uses, having spent his early life in Canterbury.

'But it's *been* discovered, and anyway I wasn't there.'

'It's a reconstruction,' Edwin said, 'and that gives opportunity for artistic licence. It's more interesting for the viewers if we discover it as a team, you and me. And that's what I'd like to do most of all, share everything with you.'

This was a bargaining situation. 'You won't mind if it finds its way into my novel?' I asked.

He looked doubtful.

'After you've released the news,' I conceded.

He agreed to that.

And I agreed to appear on his programme. Which I would have agreed to in any case. How could I miss such an opportunity to widen my experience? And Edwin was well and truly about to become my partner. Wasn't he?

One evening later that week the phone rang, twice. But when I picked up the receiver there was no reply. I could hear talking and music. 'Hullo, who's there?' I kept repeating, and then there was a click as the line went dead.

It was late. As usual I had come home from visiting my mother, discouraged Edwin from coming back with me, eaten my baked beans on toast, then rolled into bed, exhausted as much by the stress of organizing my life round visiting times as I was by the extra physical effort I was having to make. I was asleep the third time the phone rang, and waking, I nearly didn't answer. Although it wasn't much later than ten o'clock, I was mildly incensed that someone could intrude on me at such an hour, during what seemed to me the brief time of rest before I set off again on my round of work, visiting, home, bed.

This time, after a pause, Ferg's voice said, 'Have you deserted me, Gipsy Woman?' His words hesitated, as if he had to search for each one, and I knew that he had been drinking. Have *you* deserted *me*? I might have replied, for since the day he drove away from Judy's road with his hitch-hiker, I hadn't seen him.

If I had not been so tired, I might have felt some excitement when I heard his voice. But I was, and I didn't. Besides, during these weeks I had been schooling myself to do without Ferg, and I had begun to succeed. And it isn't fashionable to tolerate a man who shares his favours with other women, as Phyllis had advised me.

So I was cool with this once-only lover, who I had so recently sighed and yearned over. I asked him if there was something he wanted to speak to me about.

'I miss you, Gipsy Woman,' he said. The words came out sadly but blurred.

I didn't answer.

'How is your mother?' he asked.

Really, there is no privacy in Avalon, or for miles around it.

'My mother is improving, thank you,' I said. 'She's being transferred to a convalescent home some time next week. How is your sister?'

It was beginning to sound like a conversation in a French textbook. There was a long pause at the other end of the phone while Ferg did his translation.

'Ferg,' I said. 'What's a lectern?' I hadn't wanted to confess ignorance about this to Edwin, I suddenly realized, yet I didn't hesitate to ask Ferg.

'You've been talking to Edwin, haven't you?' he asked.

And when I didn't answer, 'It's a reading-desk with a sloping top that they use in churches to read the Bible from,' he said with no scorn. 'From the Greek, *lektron*, meaning a couch.'

Did this mean the Greeks read lying down? I pondered. And was the *lektron* the forerunner of the chaise-longue?

'Thank you, Ferg,' I said.

'Can I come round and see you?' he asked.

'No,' I said, 'it's late,' though it was not. 'I have to be up early. I must go now.'

'You can be very cruel sometimes,' he said. The words came out jerkily, and I knew that he was crying. Crying into his cups, I thought. I put the phone down.

You would have thought I would spend the rest of the night tossing round restlessly. But I didn't. I fell into dreamless sleep and only awoke when the alarm clock buzzed me in the morning.

Gulping my breakfast, late as usual, I looked for precious seconds at my desk calendar. The seventeenth of the month. Thirty days have ... I worked it out on my fingers. Fourteen days till the end of October. Fourteen days of freedom, then my notice expired on the cottage and I would leave my independence, such as it had been, for ever.

I pulled back the curtains. Fine blue sky reflected on the water. The sand dunes gleamed clean and yellow. Uncertainty and insecurity were almost at an end in my life. I assured myself this was an enormous relief.

And yet, and yet....

The gambler's card.
Everything to win

♡♣♢♤ Chapter 28 ♡♣♢♤
Eight of Clubs

Edwin was not up to date with his account of Vincenza's adventures with Armitage. She'd had second thoughts about that liaison sooner than usual. Later I heard that during her brief and no doubt passionate stay with him he had suffered a heart attack, which although only mild had been a danger signal, and she had returned unusually speedily to the Corylan residence, The Barn. A wise move, for the Armitage relationship would hardly have thrived with the threat of mouth-to-mouth resuscitation hanging over it.

It was clear to me that something of the sort had happened when I returned on a sunny autumn afternoon to the warm sandstone of Cornfield's main street.

Through her window I saw three onions sitting proudly, arranged with elegance on a green chiffon scarf on the window-sill. A blue notice beside them informed me they'd won a second prize. It is immodest and unduly competitive to display a First Prize, but a Second Prize denotes other merits of which Vincenza was clearly well aware.

I stopped at the Mace to buy groceries. Vincenza was in the shop with a large armful of orange toilet rolls that were on offer.

She greeted me as if we had never clashed.

'How nice to see you,' she said. 'We've been wondering when you'd come back.'

She stacked the toilet rolls on the cash desk.

'On account, Vera, please.'

I congratulated her on the onions.

She smiled. 'I borrowed them from Alan Armitage. Just as well they didn't win a First.'

She took my arm and lowered her voice.

'Do you know that slob skewered them all through the bottom with a darning-needle in case I grew them on from seed? You can't be more calculated than that.'

I refused her offer to drop in for a cup of tea, saying I was expecting a phone-call from my mother.

'Ah yes. Your mother,' said Vincenza. She seemed to remember the water-jug, and her voice became distant. Then she pulled herself together.

'I suppose we owe you some sort of apology,' she said. 'We rather overdid the censure bit, especially from what I've heard since.'

She edged me to the pet-food shelves where she could whisper in some sort of privacy.

'It seems there was more than we realized in your card-telling caper. Ferg's been a naughty boy.'

'What's different?' I didn't want to hear about Lavinia, but, backed up against the Pedigree Chum, I couldn't get away without pushing Vincenza over.

'. . . so he wasn't impotent at all, my dear. We never stood a chance against his own sister. Goodness knows how many years it's been going on. It explains the stress, all that drinking. . . . Guilt manifestations. None of the local shops will serve him now.'

'Look,' I said, 'I've got to go.'

'You know what I think?' she persisted. 'He was trying to get away from her by being involved with you.'

Anyway, Vincenza said, it had come to an end. Lavinia, she said, had gone back to Oxford to live with her parents.

'She's gone?' Now I was interested.

'She went yesterday. Ferg's desolated. Didn't turn in for work today, so I hear.'

She left the shop, balancing a lighthouse of toilet rolls.

'I'll tell Nerina and Hilde I've seen you,' she said, and I was not sure whether I was meant to be pleased by this or to regard it as a threat.

Shirley Knott, my mother, was out of hospital, and convalescing, complete with diet sheets, syringes and urine-testing kit.

Soon she would be coming to live with us. Worse still, I was shortly to be married to Edwin, though only for reasons concerning National Insurance and the Inland Revenue.

But both these events would have their bright side, and from time to time I was surprised to find myself looking forward to them.

'I'll look after you, little May,' my mother kept saying. But she didn't touch me, or hold my hand. Instead she stroked her budgie, who was called Reggie, and promised him she'd never leave him, wherever she went, he'd go too. I think Reggie promised her the same. At any rate he let her kiss the top of his head, which showed how much he trusted her.

'We'll make a good team,' said Edwin, and I think I agreed with him.

'You just leave everything to me,' my mother said, 'all you have to do is get on with your writing. I can't understand what you're on about myself, but that's what education's done for you.'

I parked my car in the road outside Edwin's – my – house. The garage had been demolished, and a high-quality stone-faced extension was rising in its place. It would presently become a well-planned self-contained flat.

I said hullo to the builders, then went into the house.

Edwin was away in London, as he quite often was at the moment, with his media work, as he referred to it. I could have waited till he returned before I came back. Yet I preferred to be here on my own. How many more times would it be possible?

In the kitchen he'd left a note pinned to the fridge with magnetic butterflies.

'Welcome home, May dearest.'

On the table was a tray of eggs and a paper bag containing wizened mushrooms. No surprises in Edwin's diet.

The 'dearest' made me uncomfortable. I am my mother's daughter, I sighed to myself. I liked to be welcomed home, but I toyed with the idea of deleting 'dearest' with Tipp-Ex.

Thank you, Edwin, I printed in red felt-tip at the bottom of his note. My message looked formal. I added a kiss. It looked silly. The ink soaked through the paper and marked the fridge.

A great sense of something about to be lost overcame me. There was no need to marry Edwin. Perhaps I would die before I reached pensionable age, then the marriage would be a wasted exercise.

I began to sift flour into a basin. I would visit Judy, and I would take her nourishing soup – or more exactly, cinnamon cookies.

Afterwards, with the spiced smell of cooking creeping round the house, I walked from room to room, and a perverse nostalgia nagged me. I had never felt this to be my home, and therefore it hadn't been. Now I understood that this had conferred a freedom; that perhaps I had not wanted it to be home. But soon I would be unable to deny it any longer.

I ran my hand down a ready-made curtain bought for the least expense at the Co-op. Everything in the house was like that. Cheap and serviceable. You get what you pay for. Poor Edwin was about to get me. And my mother. And we were about to get him. Perhaps Shirley had been right all along. Why did we have to saddle ourselves with each other?

But everything had changed. She was coming here because she wanted to. And I wanted her to come. And I wanted to marry Edwin.

Mrs Edwin Harley. Rubbish. I would always be May Knott.

Ferg came into my mind, an ill-fated excursion into independence; neither of us wanting to copulate, but doing it just the same, while Vincenza pulled our strings up, down, up, down.

'What did you really feel, Ferg?' I asked out loud, my voice sounding still and deadened by the adequate curtains, the British Home Stores cushions.

Then I knew something clearly and without doubt. Ferg had liked me, had genuinely been attracted to me.

Ferg, you drunken, corrupt bastard, we are a partnership, I am sure of it. How could we have whispered such confidences to each other, made love in such squalor, understood each other, unless there was some bond between us? You are a rake, Ferg. Yet I empathize with you in a way that will never be possible with Edwin. And you look at me and know all my weaknesses and faults, and they amuse you. If Edwin knew of them, they would shock and disgust him.

Our partnership would be disastrous, Ferg. Yet that is the way of things, for there can be no progress within the mothballs of security.

No one can argue with that, because how can there be progress inside a mothball? I was carried away by my own rhetoric.

I knew where I must go. I must go to Ferg. Vincenza had no power after all. She had merely managed a situation which would have arisen whether she had been there or not.

In the late afternoon I picked my way between heaps of

stone and the cement-mixer in the driveway, laid the cake-tin on the floor behind the driving-seat of my car, and set off to see Judy. In my pocket was a pair of earrings I'd bought her for twenty-five pence at the market near the cut-price shop.

From the pit of my stomach, as far as I can be anatomically certain, anticipation swilled till it heightened sensation in the minutest capillaries. I could feel it behind my fingernails.

Certainly I was looking forward to seeing Judy. And I hoped Arnie would be at home by now. But the pleasure of going to see them was coloured by another: *eros*, the drive, as we are told, that gives height and depths to the whole meaning of existence. I knew that after I had been to Number Ten I was going to search for Ferg.

And there is this about *eros*: I did not doubt that I should find him, if not today, then tomorrow, or some other day. Some time or other we were going to be united, and as long as I felt that this was so, every experience – arranging breeze-block stepping-stones over the mud-sunk drive, the care with which I placed the cookies in the cake-tin between layers of doyleys, the expression on my face if I caught sight of myself in the reflection in the car window – all were as if Ferg was watching me, or as if I was performing these minimal acts for him, even though I knew with some other part of myself that he would deride some and regard the rest with, at the most, indifference.

The gates of the Friary were open as usual when I drove past. The street lamps – special rural design to respect our village status – were just coming on, glowing a dark orange, and the Friary drive wound into darkness between the trees. I peered along it as the car passed, hoping that some lovers' coincidence would at this very second cause Ferg's figure to be there, in those few hundred feet. But the drive was empty of everything except fallen leaves that had been swept into heaps at intervals along it.

Across the road at the Friars' Arms, where, tradition

had it, the friars had kept their mistresses, there was a light in the porchway, and the door was open as usual.

Alongside a wall blood-stained with Virginia creeper there was already a large number of cars. They had been there when I passed at lunchtime, and now I remembered that the races were on today and that pubs would have been granted licence extensions.

As I drove up to Number Ten, I was startled to see light blaring from both upstairs and downstairs. I could see light bulbs, unshaded, where none had been before.

The Trod house had gone electric.

I peered in at the window, and there was the whole family. They sat in silence, watching the tele, where tonight's weatherman, Michael Fish, was apparently describing eclipses, with suitable diagrams.

I tapped on the glass, and Judy looked round. Then she leapt up.

'Oh, May Knott! I never thought we'd see you again.'

She laughed her great pleasure laugh and ran to the door to open it for me. Then Daren and Bella came too, 'Hullo, Auntie May,' though they were preoccupied, wanting to get back to their television. 'There's going to be a total ellipse starting in an hour's time,' Daren informed me.

Only Arnie didn't come to greet me, and this was because his foot was still not strong, though the second skin graft had taken.

'It's still delicate,' he said, and he told Judy to fetch me a drink of sherry to celebrate my return, and Judy's win this afternoon at the Races.

'What happened?' I asked. 'How did you get your power re-connected?'

'Social Services,' said Judy. 'The conditions weren't suitable to have him back home, see?'

'It's an ill wind,' said Arnie.

When he got up to look for the sherry that Judy couldn't find because he'd hidden it from her, I saw that he was limping very badly. He saw me looking, even though I turned my eyes away almost in one blink.

He smiled with a sour satisfaction.

'Bad, isn't it?' He tapped his foot.

'It'll improve,' I said.

There was other news.

'We're moving, Auntie May,' said Bella.

'You've got a house?' I was glad for them, of course.

'It's a grand house,' said Judy. Yet she looked uncomfortable, her glance shifting to Arnie as if she was waiting for him to say something.

'Arnie's been to see it,' she said.

'Yes. Better than this old dog kennel,' said Arnie.

'Haven't you seen it yet?' I asked Judy.

'Well, no. There's the kids, see.'

She seemed to be making difficulties.

'That's nothing. I'll take you in the car,' I offered.

Then Judy laughed, but not her usual laugh.

'You'll have a long way to drive then,' she said. 'It's at Stoke, our new house. Near to my sister's.'

She got up suddenly, as if she was going to hug me. But instead she stood by my chair and drank her sherry in one gulp.

'I shall miss you, May,' she said. 'You're my best friend.' She was truly sorry, I knew. Yet there was excitement in her voice, the thrill of things changing.

'You won't miss me as much as I'll miss you,' I said. For the house of Trod had become an essential part of my repertoire, an escape route that I enjoyed taking, and one where I had always been made welcome.

'I'll miss you more than you'll miss me,' insisted Judy and we began to laugh and shout at each other, with the children joining in. I'll miss you most. No, I'll miss you the most.

I wondered about the husband of Judy's sister.

'He's Inside, see,' said Judy. 'Four years. Child abuse.' She lowered her voice. 'His own daughter. She's only seven. Our Edie's divorcing him. So she's on her own. That's why she wants me to go there. And Arnie likes it there.'

'It's all right,' conceded Arnie, who had half-listened while he watched television.

'We'd wait forever for another house in Avalon.' Then she began to cry. 'I'm sorry, May. I'm sorry we're going.'

'I'll come and see you,' I promised, and I thought that perhaps I really would. Once, twice perhaps. In the rest of my life I might see Judy two more times after she left Avalon.

'We've got something for you,' said Arnie, trying to lift the doleful atmosphere.

He fumbled in his pocket, and brought out the necklet he'd given me, that Vincenza had snatched from my neck, claiming he'd stolen it.

'Mrs Corylan brought it round. What a surprise, it wasn't stolen after all. Serve her right, she had to apologize.'

'Horrible cow, she is,' said Judy.

He held it out to me, and as I took it I saw that it had been mended. Arnie didn't mention this. I assumed Vincenza had had it repaired before she handed it over to him. Although she was always saying how sorry she was, she did not usually do so when she was actually at fault. So I wondered whether Bertholdt was behind this, whether he had insisted on the necklet being restored. Giving it back to Arnie and not to me would be a sort of compromise.

I put it on with that feeling of relief when something that has been lost is found. It reunited me with the Trods. Whenever I wore it, I should be reminded of Bella's arms as she clasped them round my neck.

I gave Judy the earrings. They swung from side to side, dangling below her pudding-cropped hair, making Daren and Bella laugh. One of them stuck so that it pointed outwards away from her ear.

'Are you turning right?' asked Arnie.

It was twenty-five pence well spent. Was it gratification of power that made me visit the Trods? Surely not. Yet whenever I visited them I felt uncomfortable unless I had something to give them.

'Would you like . . .' I asked, pausing to increase the drama of the favour, 'to see a real Television programme being filmed?'

And I told them about the discovery of the lectern in the Friary lake and how we were going to 'rediscover' it for a TV film.

The excitement I had expected from them didn't happen. Arnie looked at Judy, Daren looked at Arnie. There was silence.

'I want to come, Auntie May,' said Bella, as if she knew by instinct that this would please me.

'Is it one of those wood things like they have in churches?' Daren asked, after a pause.

'Yes,' I answered.

'Well, me and Robin who lives next door found it,' said Daren.

'He did,' said Judy, as if she thought I wouldn't believe this.

'How much is it worth?' asked Arnie, who was obviously thinking of the Antiques Roadshow.

'It isn't the thing itself,' I explained. 'There was a document hidden in its foot. They're still deciphering it – there are letters missing, and it's difficult to read. It's been taken to the British Museum in London.'

They were impressed, all looking at Daren.

'You see, Daren,' said Judy, 'you could have been famous.'

'If he hadn't been poaching,' said Arnie. 'If he hadn't been breaking his probation.'

'If he hadn't damned-well sneaked out of bed leaving our Bella all on her own in the house,' said Judy crossly.

So Daren could never lay claim to his historic find. Because if he did, Judy and Arnie would be done for neglecting their children, and Daren would come before the Court again for committing the offence of poaching whilst still on probation.

The unlucky family of Trod.

But they wanted to come, even though I kept protesting

213

no, no, it's not going to be like it really happened, not at all.

'That's all right,' Judy promised me. 'We don't mind May discovering it, do we?'

And they all agreed. If someone was going to take the credit, it might as well be me 'and your Edwin,' said Judy generously.

Later I asked her, 'What's this about you winning at the Races?'

'It was Arnie. He saw it on television yesterday on the local news. Twenty to one. It said on the tele it was the town favourite.'

'Town favourite!' Arnie scoffed. 'None of us had ever heard of it till then.'

'So I went to the Races with Arnie's friend, the one you met at the Dragon. Put ten pounds on.'

She looked at me triumphantly, settling back in her chair, waiting for me to work out how much they'd won.

'You mean you won two hundred pounds?'

For answer, Judy fished behind the radio, now pushed to the back of the sideboard out of the way. She brought out a bundle of notes, holding them by their waist and flapping them. They made a small metallic breeze in my face.

I was impressed. 'You're rich.'

'We'll have a blow-out at the pub tonight,' said Judy. 'We'll treat everyone, spend the lot.'

She watched me to see if I was shocked.

'You want to save some,' said Arnie, possibly to please me.

'Two hundred pounds is nothing,' said Judy, indifferent to her poverty. 'There was this posh bloke queuing up in front of me. He won over a thousand.'

'Over a thousand pounds?'

'What else?' asked Arnie, poking the fire. 'Them with the most money wins the most money. We could've won two thousand if we'd had it to put on in the first place.'

'You'll come with us tonight, to celebrate, won't you, May?'

214

I should have gone, I should have.

'No. I'd really like to, but I have to be home for Edwin. He's coming back from London tonight.'

But not until two a.m. Afterwards I thought that perhaps it wasn't only my wish to find Ferg that made me refuse. It was pique too. A paying-back because they were leaving me.

'I'm glad you and Edwin are friends again,' said Judy. And she told me once more how nice Edwin was, and how sorry she was that she'd thrown slops all over him.

'I've got to go now,' I said.

They were moving house at the end of the month.

'I'll help you with the move,' I promised, and they both laughed.

'What move?' asked Arnie. 'There's nothing worth moving. We'll sell it all before we go. Or give it away.'

They came with me into the street. The moon was full, and we looked for the eclipse that the weatherman had been telling us about on television.

It was there, a fat bite out of the bottom left. Arnie was fascinated.

'That's us,' he told Daren, while Bella clung to Judy and sucked the hem of her skirt.

I left them there, and in the sky we began to inch ourselves across the face of the moon, that still glowed, but dimmed, beneath our stretching shadow skin.

*A mystical episode
clears the vision*

♡♣◇♤ **Chapter 29** ♡♣◇♤

Seven of Hearts

Why don't I begin at the beginning? What time is it, to
start with?

This is my own quest. I am the maiden plunging into the
forest to search for her knight. Why should knights have
all the fun of the Quest, after all? They often get lost, and
when they do, it is up to us maidens to go and look for
them. After all, Ferg is a pretty erratic knight, and if I
waited for him to come and find me I would probably be
hanging around in forests suffering from severe exposure
for the rest of my life.

The time is after midnight. It has taken me over an hour
to don my courtly armour, if you count the first essential,
a scented bath.

And now I am going forth into the dark wood where
irony is no defence, and I am armed only with the shield
of fantasy. For I am sharp enough to know my quest will
not succeed if I appear before my Heart's Desire dressed
in my Swaledale thornproof sweater with the leather
elbow patches, and my serviceable green wellies. Read

216

on. . . .

Sound changed, in the way it must for blind people. The gates stretched high above me, and I passed through their cage into the dark silence of the Friary grounds. I walked down the middle of the drive, into a world of uncertain affluence where the leaves of the beech trees had shrivelled too early, burnt last spring by rain from which they had never recovered. A few of the leaves ran ahead of me, scuttering birds with broken wings, prisoned within the corridor of tree trunks.

Silk glided over my nipples. It rippled in folds against my calves, reassuring me of my potency. The fabric caressed the inside of my thighs as I moved. I was an offering, wrapped to whet a god's appetite. His temple rose in front of me, and only moonlight shone from its windows, reflecting from the dull copper of the moon, now completely eclipsed. Tenants of this temple had thick-lined drapes, and if any of them were still awake this midnight, their lights stayed well obscured.

I walked on the tarmac with no sound, but small sounds were close to me: the snapping of twigs, the hush of dried leaves. Further away, I thought I heard splashes, the suck of water, from the lake. My headband tightened across my forehead, taut as skin. It seemed to me that if I had looked down into water I should have seen antlers and the soft eyes of a beast.

I stood at the foot of the steps that curved up to the main entrance. A pillared portico was stuck, lean-to fashion, onto an arch far more ancient, from which a face looked down at me, wiped of expression by erosion. We have seen you before, May Knott, said the gargoyle. It had no nose, and it spoke without a mouth. Yet its tongue survived, hanging dog-like down its chin.

So many May Knotts have been here, in search of so many Fergs.

I denied the gargoyle. I gave it no satisfaction by running up its steps, through the door it guarded. Though I had never been here before, I knew that Ferg lived at the back of the building. I crept round the side, past

217

windows whose bars touched my arms with coldness. There must have been some other path, because this one was overgrown, with rhododendrons tearing at my shins and catching in my hair, while to the other side of me the house was damp–walled, as if I was walking by the side of its cellars.

Then I was in the open again. Gravel crunched under my feet. In front of me a lawn stretched to the black line of a ha-ha beyond which cows grazed in a metal meadow.

A few steps led to a door near me. And the door was open, though there was no light inside. Ferg's flat.

He's drunk, I thought. He's in there somewhere, on his back, too smashed to close his own front door. I wanted to see him. Shake him, wake him. Ferg, you are my lover. Only in you can I find the things I have been looking for.

I leaned against the wall, in the shadow of a chimney breast, relishing the thought of my next actions, how I was going to enter the flat, find him, lay myself next·to him. For one hour only, yet how timeless that hour would be.

I changed my balance, moving away from the wall, about to climb the steps.

Something changed, there was the faintest sound, the smallest movement.

Above me the door was closing, very slowly, as though in some distant part of the building another door had opened. I hesitated, and the door gained speed, closing with a definite click.

Ferg, let me in. But I knew he would not.

I climbed the steps, pushed at the door, but with no hope. For some moments I stood there.

It's not important, I thought. I have been to your house, I have climbed your steps, touched your door. I can wait. We both can. I shall come back and back, till one day you will be here, and you will let me in.

Still the moon was in total eclipse. This time I walked round the other side of the friary, where there was a gravel path that ran down to the drive and joined it.

Leaves were burning. I could sense the drift of bonfire smoke. I stood still, lifting my head to savour the smell.

218

Away through the trees I heard pensive crackling as the breeze persuaded the fire into flame again. It must have been smouldering for hours, I thought. In front of me neat piles of leaves were planted along the drive in pyramids, as I had noticed them earlier this evening, and I remembered that it flicked in and out of my mind that they shouldn't be here; that it should be these leaves that were burning. But in these grounds, among so many trees, the leaves could have been swept from anywhere.

That was the first unease.

And the second was that I could smell something else. I could smell fossil fuel. Paraffin or petrol. Fossil fuel and leaves. How could there be anything sinister about a bonfire in autumn? Leaves smoulder, then catch alight with no warning, the damp ones burning the fuel that has been patiently waiting for this critical moment.

Under the branches that now sprang into silhouette, sparks lifted, escaping from a sheet of flame that seemed to ignite in mid-air, lighting up one side of the tree trunks as if they had been painted for a stage-set.

There were other sounds, and it was these that made me feel exposed, as I stood in pale silk that shimmered against the steps. The moon began to slough off the earth's skin, flooding the friary with its cold light.

I scuttled on tiptoe to a beech tree, flattening myself against the shadowed side of its trunk.

I was still. But someone else was not. I heard other steps that shuffled on in the trees after mine had stopped.

Someone else was here. Someone had set fire to the leaves, which crackled and spat, and which I could see burning under a black arch of branches some distance away.

I began to dodge from tree to tree, each one nearer to the fire; and then nearer.

It is the stalk of a tree. A stump, but tall as a person, and the leaves have been arranged around it. A black trunk with this heaped garland of flames.

I am standing in the clearing. So near that I can feel the heat of the fire.

The tree trunk is walking out of the garland. It is alight. Its bark is alight, but still the pith of it is black. It walks with dignity, even though it staggers a little.

It is walking towards me, a tree trunk bursting into flame. Its feet hit something, there is a hollow metal clank as it kicks a petrol can.

Then Ferg's eyes are looking at me from the tree trunk, from the flames. He is coming towards me. His tie is alight, a ribbon of flame. He can't see me. His eyes look. He walks. But he is dead. He feels no pain. His flesh is burnt far below the level of pain.

His eyes say, You see what happened to me, May Knott? Well then, he did see me; he knew who I was. I wore this silken skin for you, Ferg. I tore it off the moon and now. . . .

Oh I stepped away. I let him go past me, bumping through the trees. Because of the silk, you see. I would have burned too. When he came close to me I felt the heat on my clothes. My skirt was hot under my hand.

Pieces of his clothing fell off him, glowing like charred newspaper. He smelt of petrol, and I was glad I even had time, watching him, to be glad about this, because I could pretend not to notice the other smell, the smell of burning flesh. Of blood.

He fell and lay face down. He never screamed, he never groaned.

I ran away. I left him. So that wasn't love.

People were coming. The main door of the Friary was open. People were calling, coming down the steps carrying torches. The gargoyle shook his head at me. Ah, May Knott, you will have to live without romance.

I dodged through the trees, scratching my arms, tearing my hair on twigs. My headband was ripped off, but oh I was cunning and I stopped and untangled it from a holly bush. I would leave no trace. I had never been here.

Then I seemed to be standing still, even though my limbs were moving. My mind was still. The scenery jerked by; the gates passed me and I stood breathless on the pavement in the main street. Voices came in drunken 'jollity from the Friars' Arms, where the extension on Race days was an excuse for no closing-time at all. I began to walk along the road, and there was no thought in my mind, nothing. From the other side of the high wall I could hear distant shouts in the Friary grounds. I walked faster.

A car came along the road behind me. I heard its brakes go on, felt it slow down. I started to run, and for a few yards I could hear it following me. From the corner of my eye I saw its wing, heard the nearside window wound down.

'May. Are you running away from me?' It was Edwin. His face was laughing at me. He opened the passenger door.

'Oh, Edwin, Edwin.' And I leapt into the passenger seat, closing the door with as little noise as I could.

'Whatever are you up to at this time of night?' He was smiling at me, touched that I had been so glad to see him.

Blue light flashed in the driver's mirror. But accidents were no longer remarkable, and neither of us referred to it. Edwin was too curious about me. The lights disappeared, turning into the Friary grounds.

He was waiting for me to answer.

'I've been jogging. I wanted some exercise.'

Edwin is an unworldly person. But even he could not accept this. He looked at my dress. It was damp now, with dew and perspiration, and it clung to me like wet wallpaper.

'No,' said Edwin. 'You haven't been jogging. Now tell me what you've really been up to.'

'Oh, Edwin, Edwin. I've killed Ferg off.'

We turned into the drive, and Edwin patted my hand.

'That wasn't really necessary, was it?' he asked. 'I'd become rather fond of him. Couldn't you have sent him away, found him another job, something like that?'

I was crying, clinging onto him, and he began to stroke me in his awkward Edwin way, being somewhat out of practice.

'It's not so serious, May. I'm sure you'll manage

without him.'

How can I manage without Ferg, and how can I expect sympathy from unromantic Edwin?

Romance is a nuisance, and the only person who knew that till tonight seems to have been Edwin.

He was looking at my neck.

'You're wearing that neck-thing again.'

I felt the ruby stone in it.

'It reminds me of Judy and Arnie, because they gave it to me. Now they're going away.'

Then Edwin laughed. 'Well, that's all right. I always thought Ferg gave it to you.'

We went into the house.

Long ago Edwin and I had exploded the myth of orthopaedic beds. They are not good for your joints; they are bad for them, showing them no mercy, hard as an artificial hip replacement. In one way only are they satisfactory; they are good to make love on.

'Come,' said Edwin. 'You've given yourself a terrible shock.'

And he led me upstairs to the spare room, and onto the bed which we had bought because we had believed it was good for us and would alleviate pain which we didn't have when we bought it, but which we acquired soon afterwards.

The room was small, its walls loomed close around us. It was all bed, was that room, and I was glad of it, for I had had enough of open spaces, and here, admitting the pulsing body of Edwin, crushed under his torso, I was safe from any other attack; his body above me, the orthopaedic bed below, and the walls all around. Except for the window; but you can't have everything. Flickers of light came from the window. I think the railway buff was burning old tapes.

I closed my eyes and made comforting love with my future husband.

222

♡♣♢♤ Chapter 30 ♣♢♤
The Dreaded Ace of Spades

At Ferg's lake, in the shadow of his boat-house, we were filming the discovery of 'Edwin's' lectern.

Water was coming over the tops of my wellies. Beside me, Edwin was making a great show of prodding a pole into the mud at the bottom of the lake.

'Remember to turn towards the shore,' he muttered to me.

Then, louder, he called, 'Here's something, I think. Can you give me a hand?'

I turned towards him as we'd arranged. But then I remembered I had to face the shore. I swung round too quickly, trying to ignore the backdrop Friary in whose windows I was hoping to catch a glimpse of Ferg.

I lost my balance. I saw streaks of colour, a black eye dancing on the water, and then I was gulping in the gritty lake, while the boat rocked wildly to the side of me.

'Rather too realistic, ducky,' said the cameraman, mopping up with a handkerchief.

We began again.

223

'Here's something, I think. Could you give me a hand?'

This time, turned to the shore, I allowed myself to glance at the park, which swept up to the Friary. I saw the gravel driveway, the chimney-breast where I'd crouched the night before. Ferg's door, I noticed, had a light above it, and even from here, in daylight, I could see its unhealthy colour, the look that lights have when they are switched on in bright sunshine. Last night there had been no light there, only the moon.

A police car was parked at the foot of the steps that led to the door.

Nearer, at the lake's shore, a small crowd had gathered to watch us filming. Someone waved to me, but, of course, I didn't wave back.

I waded towards Edwin, who was tugging at something below the surface.

'Just hold on here, can you?'

I bent down obediently, and we began to pull, with a great show of effort.

'Not too quick,' said Edwin, through closed lips.

Slowly the object moved nearer the surface, as the boat and the camera shifted gently. Even in the muddy water I could see it from where I stood. It was an old school desk of the type that is no longer in use, except possibly at Eton. I had my finger in the round hole where the inkwell had once been.

The desk rose and broke the surface of the water.

'Cut!'

We both let go.

Edwin began to wade ashore.

'What about the desk?' I asked. I could see it settling back into the mud.

'Leave it,' said Edwin. 'Someone'll pick it up later.'

The real lectern had been in a shower cubicle at Camelot College for more than a fortnight, where water cascaded over it twenty-four hours a day. Securicor were contracted to protect it, much to the dudgeon of college security personnel, and until further notice the showers in the women's changing-rooms were closed, which had already given rise to charges of sexism.

But it was only the small-minded who were cavilling about such details. Avalon was national news, and it was the lectern, and Edwin, who were responsible for this.

The discovery of the lectern, of course, was Daren's responsibility. But I had to admit Edwin's own discovery outshone it.

'I just had a hunch,' said Edwin. 'They found a similar lectern in a lake near Newstead Priory during the last century. It was probably thrown there for the same reason – to hide it from the King's Commissioners at the Dissolution of the Monasteries. They found the charters of the Priory in one of the lectern's ball feet, in quite good condition.'

He had prised open the feet of the Cornfield Friary lectern. The parchment was inserted, rolled up, inside the right front foot.

It had been taken for dating and deciphering to the British Museum.

'You knew all that time and you never told me. You told Vincenza, but you didn't tell me.'

No discovery, however important, could obliterate this deception from my mind.

Edwin had taken the parchment to London, rolled up in a damp towel.

That was the day he told me he'd gone to Portsmouth.

As we squelched from the water, the neighbourly Lunch-o-faxes approached with diffidence, offering the college the use of their boat, *Salad Daze III*. Edwin thanked them with absent-minded grace, as befits a professor who has his own TV programme, and whose applications from Overseas students have increased threefold over the last three months, thus moving our university ever nearer to solvency.

Rain before seven, fine by eleven. The sun shone down and began to heat the water in my wet-suit as I crunched over the shingle at the lake's edge. The small crowd parted for me, staring at me in what I think was gratified silence.

225

I tried not to look at the Friary. I tried to forget that I wanted to see Ferg again.

A little hand pulled at mine.

'Auntie May?'

Bella was looking at me in uncertainty, as if I might not remember who she was. I would have picked her up, but I was wet and rubbery.

'Hullo, Bella. Where's the great discoverer?'

Bella was tugging at my hand. The lake was behind me, forgotten. Ahead, the sun jagged off the ludicrous battlements of the Friary. It was autumn now, fine and warm, but damp, as if there was nowhere for the wet air to go. It hung about the bronze trees and in globules of split light on the grass.

The door of Ferg's flat opened. Two policemen came down the steps, turning slightly, as if to say goodbye to someone.

At the back of the crowd I could see Judy. She was looking at me, and I was surprised that she hadn't dashed forward to embrace me. Dismayed, I began to see that this silly prank ranked as fame to her.

'Hey, Judy!' I called, and she came towards me, but reluctantly, it seemed.

Then I saw Ferg. He was looking towards us, where the little crowd was dispersing now, the more curious of them ambling over to the boat-house to take a closer look.

Bella held my hand tighter and looked upset.

'What's that noise, Auntie May?'

Ferg was howling. He was standing looking towards the lake and seemed to be looking at me. Another long howl came from his direction.

People stopped talking and turned to stare. 'What . . .?'

Howls drifted one by one over the silence.

'That fellow's throwing a loop,' said the cameraman.

But I had heard something else. Ferg was calling something. 'May Knott!' he was calling between howls, 'May Knott, May Knott, May Knott.'

I let go of Bella's hand. To one side of me I saw Edwin turn to look at me as I began to run, in the heavy wellies

226

and wet-suit, up the grassy slope of the park.

My body begged me to breathe. I shall die, I thought, and I remembered that this was possible in such conditions, so as I ran I wrenched at the velcro and zip that imprisoned me. The zip burst open, its teeth scouring my breast. Still I could only run sluggishly, panting and gasping.

I was half-way across the grass now, and I could see his eyes fixed on me. I threw myself across the silly ha-ha, swearing, as usual, with my last energy.

He had his arms round my neck, and great sobs wrenched through him as he said my name.

I stroked the back of his head.

'There, there,' I said, though I had no idea what I was there-ing about.

For a moment or two I thought I'd done the right thing, for Ferg seemed to relax.

Then he wrenched violently away from me.

'Lavinia's hanged herself,' he said.

Dread showed in my face before I could mask it, and Ferg saw.

'Oh, Gipsy Woman, why didn't you leave us alone?' He began to weep.

This didn't seem very objective, but how could I defend myself in the midst of his distress?

'I'm very sorry,' was all I could say.

Then he rushed at me and began to pummel me, dangerous wicked person, screamed Ferg, lashing at me, while I turned away to protect myself.

'No, no, Ferg, you've got it wrong. It's only a game.'

And he screamed, 'You killed my sister.'

By now we were on a stage, with the audience grouped below us, on the other side of the ha-ha.

'Why *her*?' moaned Ferg. 'It was *my* ace of spades, why didn't you kill *me*?'

But somehow Phyllis had appeared, and she put her arm round him. 'Come along in, my love, you know differently, come along,' and slowly she persuaded him up the steps. 'May never meant any harm,' I heard her say.

Edwin was standing beside me.

'Yes, well,' was his only comment. 'Get your clothes on,' he said, 'and we'll go and have some lunch.'

This much I will say for him. He never said, 'I told you so,' even though he had warned me so often about the cards and the trouble they would bring me.

Later on, in the afternoon, Edwin presented the real lectern to the cameras, in the Indoor Recreation Centre.

In the shower-room the water had been turned off for a few minutes only. Edwin stood beside the lectern, and I watched, standing on a shoe locker.

'I'd always had an interest in Marie de France and the Breton lais,' Edwin was saying. He spoke easily and without self-consciousness.

'We know Marie spent some time at Cornfield Friary, in the small village lying to the north-east of Avalon. She dedicated her work to a king, and we have assumed this to be Henry the Second of England.

'But who was she, and why did she come to this country?' Edwin asked earnestly.

'One theory is that she was Henry's half-sister. She wrote down the lais, translating them from the French and Breton, though Piramus tells us – and this is significant – that she made verses of them that *are not in the least true*.

'But what,' asked my loving partner, 'do we mean by "true"? It is this aspect of the very earliest form of the narrative that I was examining when the exciting find of the lectern was made.

'And it seemed a good idea to examine the work of a novelist whose life I was very familiar with and to tease out what I knew to be facts from fiction and to see from this whether I could obtain any clues to how the novelist weaves her – or his – pattern out of the truth.

'Of course,' he smiled disarmingly, and for one flicker his eyes looked in my direction, 'it would not have done at all for the novelist to *know* that I was analysing her work in this way.

'Underlying the superficial structure of plot. . . .'

He went on to talk about sub-texts, while I busied myself staying awake in the steamy atmosphere of the shower-room. . . .

'. . . so there was something, a knowingness, about the early work of Marie de France, that puzzled me; something that we don't find in her later writing.'

'And then . . . the experts gave us their verdict about the parchment. . . .'

I had been in the house when the expert arrived.

He had shown us the findings, projecting slides onto the lounge wall.

'Without doubt,' he had said, 'this is one of the important finds of the century.'

The parchment had been old long before it sank with the lectern into the waters of the lake. It had almost certainly been hidden for very shame for the previous three centuries.

The parchment was a papal document, bearing the signature of Pope Adrian IV, annulling the marriage between Marie and Henry. Henceforward she was to be designated Marie de France, Abbess of Shaftesbury.

The grounds for the annulment were reasonable, given the acceptance of social taboo. Henry II had incestuously married his half-sister.

'. . . and the clues, if we know how to look for them, are there in her work.'

Edwin had almost finished.

I went outside, the unknown writer who had unwittingly assisted him with his fascinating detection. I wondered whether it was true – whether he would have gained some inkling of truth from Marie de France's work if the annulment had never been found.

Things are not always what they appear

♡♣◇♤ **Chapter 31** ♡♣◇♤
The Joker

Edwin came out of the changing room, carrying his squash kit. He took my arm.

'You're on shaky ground, you know,' he said. 'Henry the Second was only nineteen when he married Eleanor of Aquitaine. He didn't have much time to marry anyone before that. And you've got your annulment dated 1154, which is two years after he married Eleanor.'

'It's artist's licence,' I said. 'I wanted the marriage to be annulled by the only English pope in the history of the Church. It's more likely that influence could have been brought to bear on him. And there's no reason why Marie shouldn't have been a child bride. Everything happened earlier in those days, including death. You had to cram more into a shorter time. Henry was only fifty-six when he died, and that was pretty good going for those days.'

'Look, May,' Edwin held my arm tighter. 'You really can't juggle the facts like that. If I have to be in your novel, at least let me have my facts straight.'

Oh, Edwin. How vain you are.

230

'Don't you wish you'd found that lectern?' I teased him, but he didn't laugh.

'In any case,' he said, 'it's most likely that Marie de France's dedication is to Henry's *son*, who was also called Henry, and who was king during his father's lifetime. It may not have been meant for Henry the Second at all.'

I stopped short, and Edwin winced, pulling his arm away.

'Better and better,' I said. 'Henry's son was the illicit offspring of Marie and her half-brother. How's that for an ingenious idea?'

Edwin laughed.

'It's instructive how you garble things, May.'

But I had begun to think there might be something in this theory after all. It could even be extended to cover the murder of Becket in 1170.

'It's a good theory, Edwin,' I said. 'And I admire you for thinking of it.'

'Come and have a drink,' said this exasperated academic, searching for common ground.

At the Sword and Scabbard he treated himself to two double whiskys, while I sipped my sherry and bored him sideways examining the possibility that Henry the Second threatened allegiance to the anti-Popes between 1162 and 1170 because he was having a blackmail squeeze put on him by Pope Alexander III.

'Anything's possible,' said Edwin after his second drink.

You would have thought this would have inspired him, that anything was possible, but instead he looked dejected.

'Maybe you should study in greater depth,' he said. 'A degree in History, for example.' He brightened up. 'That'd put an end to your wild ideas, May.'

231

*A friendship
is severed*

♡♣◇♤ **Chapter 32** ♡♣◇♤
Two of Spades

Much later, when we returned home, I found that
Vincenza had slipped a note under the back door.

'Come and see me. Tonight,' it said.

I didn't want to see Vincenza, but now I was getting
married to Edwin I seemed to be losing freedoms in all
directions.

Edwin made it clear how important it was for us all to
rub along together. 'You've only got to observe the basic
niceties,' he said, urging me to go.

I drove the few hundred yards from our house to The
Barn.

Bertholdt opened the door. When he saw it was me, he
put his hand on my shoulder and pulled me gently into the
house. 'Come in, May.'

Vincenza wasn't in the room, being the sort of person
who dashes upstairs or into the garden when the bell
rings, so that she can make an entrance later on.

There was no sign of Martin.

'Now, May,' said Bertholdt. 'You mustn't feel guilty

about this. It isn't your fault in any way.'

'Why should I think that it was?' I asked.

'The sense of guilt, the belief that you are an evil person,' said Bertholdt, 'it all stems from your conviction that your mother would only have given you away – as you saw it when you were a child – if you had committed some unspeakable crime.'

'What crime?' I asked. I wasn't going to confess anything to Bertholdt.

'There's a mischievous side to Vincenza,' said Bertholdt. 'Don't let her suggest to you in any way that you had anything whatever to do with Ferg's breakdown.'

Vincenza appeared, bare-footed, at the bottom of the stairs.

'No, May, that's right. We aren't primitive savages, swayed by meaningless omens like the ace of spades.'

'Be careful what you say, my darling,' Bertholdt said to her, and he poured her a gin and Martini.

Vincenza took it, but she still looked at me.

'Do you want to know how Nerina got on after her accident?' she asked.

'Of course. I've thought about it often.'

'I expect you have,' said Vincenza. 'Well, she's been very fortunate. There's only the slightest mark on her upper lip now. She sat on that couch of hers for days with her cat, letting it lick the wound, which was all stitched up, of course. It licked and licked. Quite obscene. It's a middle-European custom that Hilde knew about. But it worked. It's a laugh, really; the only scars are where the stitches were.'

'I'm glad,' I said.

It crossed my mind to suggest Nerina might use the same treatment for her vagina, but I kept quiet.

'You've had a bad time,' said Bertholdt. He put his arm round my shoulders and hugged me.

'For god's sake stop pawing her,' said Vincenza.

I looked round for some way to change the subject.

'Where's Marty?' I asked.

This was not a good question.

Vincenza took a large gulp of her gin.

'He's gone away to school.'

'You mean boarding school?'

'Yes,' said Bertholdt, for Vincenza didn't answer. 'It's a very good school, with progressive ideas. Actually, it's a public school.'

'Well,' I said to Vincenza, 'that'll give you more time for your job.'

It pleased me to say this.

Vincenza crossed the room and opened a little drawer in her William-and-Mary chest-on-stand.

'I asked you over because I wanted to give you this,' she said.

She held it out to me. I backed away, not wanting to hold it, but she shook it at me, moving nearer, insisting.

It was the flame-coloured scarf that Ferg had given me. It was what was left of the flame-coloured scarf, for one side of it was charred and blackened.

'I found it in the Friary grounds,' said Vincenza, and she half-smiled at me.

But Bertholdt stretched out his hand and took the silk from her.

'Don't take it, May. It could be anything. It could be any scrap of material.'

He carried it across the room and threw it on the fire, where it crumpled and shrank and disappeared.

I stood almost in the centre of the room, expecting a grand tantrum from Vincenza. But there was nothing. It was as if the incident had never happened.

'Did you hear that Nerina attacked Hilde with an axe?' she asked me. 'She sliced a piece out of Hilde's calf, and Hilde had to escape through a window that happened to be closed.

'Nerina phoned me. I had to go up there in a thunderstorm. When I got to the house, there was blood everywhere. We trudged all over the moors looking for her. We found her in an old outbuilding. We were all soaked, it's a wonder we didn't get pneumonia. Nerina was terribly drunk. She was on her own, except for Hilde.

Louis had gone away for the weekend with his latest student, and Phyllis Thackray phoned her to say Derek had just proposed to a typist in his department who was on the rebound after an affair with a chemistry student.'

I stared, unable to take all this in.

'You're being bitchy, dear Vincenza,' said Bertholdt.

'Am I? All right then, it wasn't a chemistry student, it was the director of the Indoor Recreation Centre. That gives the story a healthier sort of flavour, don't you think?

'You see,' said Vincenza, looking at me. 'We can all do your sort of thing. I myself have always wanted to write a novel. But I wouldn't demean myself by writing the sort of trash you've stooped to.'

'If you say much more,' said Bertholdt, 'May can claim you're slandering her. And with some justification.'

'Is it slander?' asked Vincenza. 'That's what I call her novel.' She turned to me. 'You know what's happened?'

I waited.

'What's happened is that you've made poor Ferg so uncomfortable here that he's really got no choice but to leave. He's had to take any post that was available, which means he's ended up being appointed to Admin at Heriot-Watt of all places. And at a lower grade than he's got at Avalon. That rubbish you told him when you read his cards at Nerina's. Someone interpreted it as suggesting he was having some weird relationship with his sister. Libellous, I call it. He hasn't even *got* a sister.'

But how can I be blamed for that?

Then the door-bell chimed. When Bertholdt opened the door I saw my mother standing there, looking uncertain.

'May? It was miserable convalescing. All Florida Spring Vegetable soup and senile dementia. So I discharged myself. I caught the bus from Avalon. Then I saw your car here. You don't mind me coming, do you?'

No, no, I didn't mind at all. I grasped the sling she dangled me.

'I'm coming, Mummy. This very minute.'

And I went.

Eventual contentment

♡♣◇♤ Chapter 33 ♡♣◇♤
Two Nines

This is a new year. There was snow on the crocuses when I
went to buy a grapefruit at the Mace early this morning.
As I reached the narrowest part of the pavement, a
pantechnicon came out of the Friary grounds. It edged up
onto the kerb beside me to let the school bus pass on the
other side of the road. Salted muddy slush splashed my
wellingtons as the huge brown wall of the van passed
alongside me. Crawford's Removals, Edinburgh. I knew
that behind its aluminium sides were piled Ferg's belongings, on their way to Scotland and his new life at Heriot-
Watt.

I imagined his wry, knowing smile, and his voice.
'Goodbye, Gipsy Woman,' he was saying.

'Goodbye, Ferg,' I said out loud.

I have been in my office (which I no longer think of as
either a garret or a study) for over an hour. I shall not
think of Ferg again – not even when Edwin and I make
our annual pilgrimage to the Edinburgh Festival later this
year.

236

Instead I shall think about my new car, a wedding present from Edwin, my husband. It goes well, and there are still more than four months on its guarantee.

My mother is living with us now, in her delightful little flat, which she insists on showing all our guests. She is proud of its contents too. She is especially proud of the Victorian chaise-longue acquired at one of the auctions that she attended with the Holy Grailers, who have a growing respect for her sharp eye for antiques and the astuteness of her bidding. 'She's a quick learner,' they say.

Her flat is her retreat, she tells our visitors. It's lovely to have somewhere you can go that is just yours, your own space, she says.

Most of the days she spends in our space, particularly our kitchen. But what does it matter to me, because it isn't my space anyway. It never was.

My car is my space, a bubble that I can float about in. I know every place for many miles where you can park and be inside the view.

Which is why I am thinking about my car. I hope it will last for ever.

Downstairs my mother is calling me for coffee made on the new machine she's given us.

She looks at me indulgently as I come into the kitchen.

'Had a good morning?' she asks, though the time is only ten-thirty.

I thank her. 'Yes, thank you, quite good.' I never confess to a *good* morning.

The back door opens and Edwin comes in. He crosses to the sink to wash his hands, because he's been gardening.

'Dandelions!' he swears. 'Can't get the damned stuff off. It's extraordinary,' he says, 'a great patch of dandelions. Can't think how they got there.'

'Where?' I ask, and he points to the hedge, where I buried the Lunch-o-faxes' dandelion heads.

He sits down at the table, looking comfortable and at ease. He likes my mother's ministrations, he's glad she's come to stay.

'What page have you got to?' they both ask me, in unison.

'About 238,' I reply.

'Good, very good,' says Edwin.

'It must be nearly finished now,' my mother says.

And I agree. 'Yes,' I say. 'It is.'

Douglas Adams
The Hitch-hiker's Guide to the Galaxy £2.99

'People of Earth, your attention please . . . Plans for development of the
outlying regions of the Galaxy require the building of a Hyperspatial
Express Route through your Star System, and regrettably your planet is
scheduled for demolition.'

For Arthur Dent, earthling and homeowner, a severe case of planning blight
is the overture to a remarkable set of travels, guided en route by an equally
remarkable book, *The Hitch-hiker's Guide to the Galaxy*.

Life, the Universe and Everything £2.99

'One of the strangest events in the history of life, the universe and
everything occurred here on Earth shortly before it was demolished' . . . The
most careful consultation of *The Hitch-hiker's Guide to the Galaxy* and *The
Restaurant at the End of the Universe* has left millions unaware of why
Earth has always been shunned by the rest of the Galaxy. Now all – and
more – can be revealed . . .

'Why stop now, just when I'm hating it?'
MARVIN THE PARANOID ANDROID

So Long and Thanks for all the Fish £2.99

' . . . a girl sitting on her own somewhere in Rickmansworth suddenly
realised what it was that had been going wrong all this time, and she
finally knew how the world could be made a good and happy place . . .
Sadly, however, before she could get to a phone to tell anyone about it the
Earth was unexpectedly demolished to make way for a new hyperspace
bypass, and so the idea was lost for ever . . .'

In this, the fourth book in the hitch-hiker trilogy, Arthur Dent finds this girl
in the last place in the universe he would expect to find anything, but
which 3,976,000,000 people will find oddly familiar . . .

Douglas Adams
The Restaurant at the End of the Universe £2.99

'Good evening, ladies and gentlemen, I am your host for tonight, Max Quordlepleen, and I have just come straight from the other end of time where I have been hosting a show at the Big Bang Burger Bar . . .'

If you've done six impossible things this morning, why not round it off with breakfast, lunch or dinner at Milliway's, the Restaurant at the End of the Universe . . .

'Indispensable reading' DAILY MAIL

Douglas Adams and John Lloyd
The Meaning of Liff £2.99

At last! The definitive dictionary of words for all those previously wordless objects and meanings for all those previously meaningless words, where a 'harbottle' emerges 'as a particular kind of fly which lives inside double glazing' and 'quoyness' is 'the hatefulness of words like "relionus" and "easiephit"'.

Erma Bombeck
Family – The Ties That Bind and Gag £2.99

Erma Bombeck finds a mother lode of laughter, compassion, pathos, poignancy, and nostalgia in the small and large triumphs of family life in the '80s.

A grown family come home to spend the weekend . . . a group who share the same genes and last name. But they've never eaten the same breakfast cereal, watched the same TV shows, liked the same people, or even spoken the same language.

Theirs is the story of a strange little band of characters trudging through life, sharing diseases and toothpaste, coveting one another's desserts, inflicting pain and kissing to heal it better, and trying to figure out the common bond that binds them all together.

This is not the definitive work on the family. It only covers everything that will make you laugh . . . or cry.

Erma Bombeck writes a humour column which is read by over 30 million readers of 900 newspapers around the world. Well known to TV viewers in America, she has been repeatedly named in the annual World Almanac list of the 25 Most Influential Women in America.

Peter Mayle and Gray Jolliffe
Man's Best Friend £3.99

Over the years man has achieved many things. Yet he has never quite come to terms with the constant companion in his trousers. He humours it when it behaves badly, forgives it when it doesn't behave at all. It is lazy, demanding, socially unreliable and selfish. By rights it should be outlawed from polite society. Short of surgery there seems no hope of improvement – perhaps the worst is yet to come.

Wicked Willie's Guide to Women £3.99

We have had women's views on women. We have had men's views on women. But never before have we had the definitive insider's view on women – Wicked Willie.

From Freud's big slip to the language of love, from the eternal triangle to the passing fancy, these shameless revelations will confirm every woman's worst suspicions.

For our male readers, this comprehensive guide to many different types of women will provide some valuable insights which will make them no less baffling than they ever were.

This is undoubtedly a contribution towards better understanding between the sexes. A small contribution, perhaps, but who said size was important?

Peter Mayle and Gray Jolliffe
Wicked Willie's Guide to Masculine Misbehaviour £3.95

The Low Down on Men

Who knows what base desires lurk in the hearts and minds of men?
Women have suspected the worst for centuries, and here to confirm it all is
a fearless guide to the unfair sex.

No stone is left unturned, from the courtship tactics of three men in a pub
to the tired businessman's favourite excuses; from the significance of
designer underpants to the true reason for office parties. And, smirking his
way through this disgraceful series of revelations is Wicked Willie, living
down to his reputation as the world's most persistent mischief-maker,
secure in the knowledge that someone else will always get the blame.

Boys will be boys and girls should be warned. But it's probably too late.

All Pan books are available at your local bookshop or newsagent, or can be ordered direct from the publisher. Indicate the number of copies required and fill in the form below.

Send to: **CS Department, Pan Books Ltd., P.O. Box 40, Basingstoke, Hants. RG21 2YT.**

or phone: 0256 469551 (Ansaphone), quoting title, author and Credit Card number.

Please enclose a remittance* to the value of the cover price plus: 60p for the first book plus 30p per copy for each additional book ordered to a maximum charge of £2.40 to cover postage and packing.

*Payment may be made in sterling by UK personal cheque, postal order, sterling draft or international money order, made payable to Pan Books Ltd.

Alternatively by Barclaycard/Access:

Card No.

Signature:

Applicable only in the UK and Republic of Ireland.

While every effort is made to keep prices low, it is sometimes necessary to increase prices at short notice. Pan Books reserve the right to show on covers and charge new retail prices which may differ from those advertised in the text or elsewhere.

NAME AND ADDRESS IN BLOCK LETTERS PLEASE:

....

Name————————————————————————————

Address————————————————————————————

————————————————————————————

————————————————————————————

————————————————————————————

3/87

'Thank you for the excellent treatment, Nicole.'

She frowned, looking for mockery, but found none. Her gaze was held briefly by dark, heavily lashed eyes that seemed to weigh her up very precisely, in a personal rather than a professional way, but which gave away nothing of their owner's conclusions. When he had gone, Nicole slumped into her chair. She really must pull herself together, she thought. It was no use blaming Dr Sloan Reilly because he wasn't Bob!

Dear Reader

Practice Nurse Amy Kincaid finds that she is IN SAFE HANDS in Margaret O'Neill's latest GP story, while Canadian physiotherapist Jane Easter tries to convince Dirk that the unknown can exist in Sara Burton's BEYOND HEAVEN AND EARTH. A convalescent home is the unusual setting for Clare Lavenham's offering in SISTER AT HILLSIDE, and the beautiful Great Barrier Reef is the backdrop for Judith Worthy's STORM IN PARADISE.

Travel the world without leaving home!

The Editor

Judith Worthy lives in an outer suburb of Melbourne, Australia, with her husband. When not writing she can usually be found bird-watching or gardening. She also likes to listen to music, and the radio, paints a little, likes to travel and is concerned about conservation and animal cruelty. As well as romantic fiction, she also writes books for children.

Recent titles by the same author:

A HEART UNTAMED
CROSSROADS OF THE HEART

STORM IN PARADISE

BY

JUDITH WORTHY

MILLS & BOON LIMITED
ETON HOUSE   18–24 PARADISE ROAD
RICHMOND   SURREY   TW9 1SR

*First published in Great Britain 1992
by Mills & Boon Limited*

© Judith Worthy 1992

*Australian copyright 1992
Philippine copyright 1992
This edition 1992*

ISBN 0 263 77920 3

*Set in 10 on 12 pt Linotron Times
03-9211-53454*

*Typeset in Great Britain by Centracet, Cambridge
Made and printed in Great Britain*

CHAPTER ONE

'MORE flowers for you, Mrs Mason! Special delivery. They came on the mail boat this morning.'

Nicole Gardiner placed the huge vase of orchids on the patient's bedside cabinet. She looked down at the woman and smiled as she gave her the card which had come with the flowers. There was no response from the pale lips, and the deep blue eyes were expressionless. Her skin was almost as pale as the pillows on which she was propped. Her rich auburn hair had been combed that morning by a nurse and arranged about her head.

'Thank you, Sister,' she said, not even glancing at the flowers, or the card.

'Are you going to get up today?' Nicole asked.

A slight shake of the auburn head indicated no. 'I'm so tired,' the patient murmured, eyelashes weakly fluttering.

Even without make-up, and ill, she was still a beautiful woman, Nicole thought. All that was missing was the special sparkle and sensuality that millions had tuned in every week to see on their television screens. Coralie Mitchell had become a household name, an actress aiming for the top, and no one had been in any doubt she'd reach it.

Then, without warning, it seemed, she had vanished off the screens and no one knew where she was. Except a few close friends, apparently—those who sent flowers—and the staff at the Lodge, where she was registered as Mrs Carol Mason.

'She needs a psychiatrist,' Nicole said, a few minutes later, as she poured a cup of coffee for Jan Roberts, the senior sister. 'She's sinking deeper and deeper into depression instead of climbing out of it. She seems to have trouble concentrating and she tries to conceal that her hands are almost always shaking. She seems to have no control over her mouth sometimes too.' A deep frown appeared between her expressive green eyes, and she raked a hand anxiously through her short blonde hair.

Jan nodded. 'It worries me, the way she just lies there and stares at the wall for hours at a time. I've tried to persuade her to sit outside, or take a walk in the grounds, but she won't budge. What is it, do you think? I thought maybe Parkinson's disease, but surely her doctor would have diagnosed that.'

'Does she have one?' Nicole wondered. 'We've had no medical reports. Toff just told us she was coming for a rest and must have complete privacy. I think it's probably psychological.'

Jan agreed. 'Like a love affair gone wrong? Something to do with her career?'

'Whatever it is,' Nicole said, 'she isn't prepared to talk about it.' Her frown deepened even further. 'I'm worried about her too, Jan. But what can we do? She came here to rest and relax, and that's what we're all about. We can't force her to have medical treatment if she doesn't want it. And we're not a psychiatric clinic anyway.'

Jan tucked a few strands of wayward brown hair into her chignon. 'Maybe Dr Reilly will be able to get through to her.'

Nicole glanced at her watch. 'Which reminds me— he's supposed to be coming on today's flight.'

'Since he hasn't been on it twice already when he was expected,' remarked Jan with a sceptical twist of her mouth, 'I wouldn't bank on it.'

Nicole smoothed her hair back with both hands and smiled. 'You hate newcomers as much as I do, Jan, don't you?' Her eyes teased.

Jan grumbled, 'I hate having to get used to new ways.' She took her coffee-cup to the sink to rinse it. 'The devil you know is always better than the one you don't.' She laughed. 'And Bob Granger was a bit of a devil, you have to admit.' She gave Nicole a searching look. 'For a while I really thought you two. . .'

Nicole flinched. 'Well, you were wrong,' she said shortly. 'Bob was fun, that's all. I never imagined there'd be anything serious between us.' She stared out of the window across the translucent blue-green water of the Pacific Ocean and was angry with herself for feeling even the mildest stab of pain.

'Just as well,' Jan said bluntly. 'He's definitely one of the roving kind. There was never any possibility he'd stay here longer than a few months.'

Long enough for a stupid woman to fall in love, though, Nicole thought, castigating herself all over again. She ought to have known that Bob would never fall in love with her, and that she was just asking for a broken heart, but she had fallen under his spell in spite of herself, in spite of the shallowness she had known was in him, but which she had chosen to ignore. She'd been a fool. It was always foolish to fall in love with a colleague, and she certainly wasn't ever going to do it again.

'We'd better get the medications out of the way,' she said briskly. 'If Dr Reilly does come today, I dare say he'll expect to be shown around right away. Although

I suppose I'll have to take surgery again. I can't expect him to start work at once.'

The sound of a plane passing overhead made them both pause and exchange a glance.

'Well, we'll soon know if he was on it,' said Jan. 'Danny went down to meet him, I suppose?'

Nicole nodded. 'I hope he hasn't had another trip for nothing.' She opened the door. 'Come on, we've got time to see everyone before he does arrive—if he does.' She smoothed her crisp white uniform and straightened the mauve linen jacket she wore with it. Jan's uniform was pale pink, and both colours were reflected in the pastel-painted walls of the clinic, which in turn reflected the delicate hues of the bauhinia tree—the butterfly tree, so called because its flowers resembled butterflies. They grew profusely in the garden, along with a host of other tropical plants.

The Lodge was part of Bauhinia Sands Resort, an exclusive, expensive holiday resort on Bauhinia Island in the Whitsunday Passage, just off the Queensland coast, near the Great Barrier Reef. It catered for jaded executives, media personalities, business tycoons and anyone else who could afford its luxuries. The clinic attended to the day-to-day health problems of the resort guests, and also accommodated patients who needed rest and convalescence after surgery, or who wanted privacy and seclusion in which to recover from nervous breakdowns, stress and other traumas.

Nicole glanced out of the floor-to-ceiling windows in the first room they entered with the medications trolley. From the Lodge's high position on a headland there was a panoramic view across the long curve of the bay with its white sand and palm trees and the resort buildings framed against the small mountain which dominated the island. Bauhinia Island was thickly wooded everywhere except for the beaches and the golf course, and between the headland and the resort there was a stretch of rainforest. Nicole could hear the pied currawongs' bell-like calls ringing out from its canopy.

'Wonderful view, isn't it?' said the patient, dragging her attention back. 'I never get tired of it.' He was a man in his sixties, who had suffered several heart attacks and had high blood-pressure. He chuckled. 'It's almost enough to keep me here for good!'

'That might be better than keeping on coming back because you've overdone it again,' said Jan bluntly. Grant Maguire was a workaholic, and he came to Bauhinia to recuperate after each heart attack. 'You can't keep having these attacks, Mr Maguire.'

Nicole took the thermometer out of his mouth. 'Yes, you really ought to ease up. There's no point in being the richest man in the graveyard.' She gave him a stern look.

He wagged a finger at her. 'You're bullying me again, Sister, but because you're so attractive, both of you, I'll ignore it!' He laughed, then said seriously, 'You're right, of course. But I'd die of boredom if I couldn't work. It's in my blood. I built Maguire's Construction Corporation up from nothing; it's my lifeblood that's gone into it.'

Nicole did not argue; neither did Jan. There was a limit to how much advice they felt they could give. As they crossed the corridor to the next room, Jan remarked, 'Some people never know when to hand over the reins to someone else.'

'He's right, though,' Nicole said thoughtfully. 'He probably would die of boredom if he gave up working.

Or anxiety. He'd worry himself to death in case his son wrecked the business.'

'Which he probably will do,' predicted Jan cynically. 'There'll be a take-over, the son will make millions and squander it all on high living and women.'

'The son's married with five children!'

'Which makes it all the more likely!'

Still laughing together, they went into the next room, which was occupied by another heart patient, one who had had a triple bypass, but who had not recovered as rapidly as most. Alec Robinson was still having trouble adjusting, so his doctor had sent him to Bauhinia.

Among the rest of the patients there was a car-crash victim, a leukaemia sufferer, two nervous breakdowns, an anorexic, a case of severe arthritis and one of asthma. At the moment, there was only one admission from the resort, a young woman who had sprained her ankle rather badly.

Nicole and Jan finished their round, and Nicole tapped her watch. 'They ought to be here by now.'

'Bet he didn't make it,' said Jan. 'I reckon he's changed his mind. Probably a job he fancies more turned up.'

Nicole's brow furrowed. She said, 'I hope not. We can't go on too long without a medico. What if there's an emergency we can't cope with?' But some quirkiness in her half hoped he wouldn't come, didn't want him to come, hated the thought of a replacement for Bob. . .

Jan lifted her shoulders. 'If they need an operation, you ship them out, or call for an air ambulance.' She grinned. 'But you and I and the defibrillator can cope with most things, Nic!' She paused, and pointed out of the corridor window. 'There's Danny. Oh-oh, nobody's with him and he's not carrying any luggage. I think our man must have missed his plane again.'

Nicole, watching the porter approaching the building, was ashamed of her feeling of relief. That was selfish. The Lodge needed a doctor. What was the new one playing at? Did he really have a genuine excuse, or was he just messing them about? She felt a slow simmer of annoyance beginning. 'I'm going to phone Murray,' she said. 'He might know what's happened this time.'

'Darling!' said Murray Peterson, the resort manager, when Nicole greeted him. 'I know what you're fretting about.' He called everyone darling, including any man he fancied. Nicole liked him. He was easy to work for, a reliable friend, and, romantically, no problem.

'Well, what's the excuse this time?' She couldn't help the sceptical edge to her voice.

'He's coming, sweetheart,' Murray assured her placatingly. 'With the boss.'

'With the boss?' she queried.

'Yeah. Seems they're buddy-buddies. What do you know?'

Nicole pulled a face. 'I suppose that means he's one of those yuppie types.'

'Because he's a mate of Toff's? That's slander, darling.'

'Well, if he moves in the same circles as Toff. . .' Nicole said drily.

Murray gave a salacious laugh. 'He might be a good catch, darling!'

'For someone, no doubt. Not me.'

'I was only thinking—seeing you let Bob get away. . .' Murray liked to bait her.

'I didn't! I don't chase after men unless they're millionaires!'

'Oh, so that's it. It's Toff you really fancy.'

Nicole laughed, 'Don't tell him, Murray. He might give me the sack!' She called a halt to the banter and demanded briskly, 'When are they coming?'

'Toff phoned a while ago. They should be here any minute.'

'Toff's private plane, I suppose?'

'No, it's in for service, he said. They're taking the water-taxi!' Murray laughed as though it were an amazing idea. Which, Nicole thought, it probably was. The owner of Bauhinia Island, Toff Barrett, did not usually use water-taxis. He was a high-flying young entrepreneur in the hotel business who had bought Bauhinia Island three or four years ago and transformed it into the exclusive resort it now was. He was flamboyant, charming and self-assured, and Nicole was never quite sure whether she liked him or not.

'I suppose they'll have lunch before he comes up here,' she surmised.

Murray confirmed it. 'Expect him when you see him, darling,' he advised.

'Yes, I've been doing that,' Nicole replied drily. She added, 'I dare say it won't be until after surgery.' That was held every day at two-thirty.

Murray grasped the opportunity eagerly. 'I'm having a bit of back trouble, darling. If I come up later, could you take a look at it?'

Nicole gave a little sigh of impatience. Murray was an incurable hypochondriac. 'I've told you, Murray, I'm not a doctor. I can only treat what I'm qualified to, and authorised to do. Leave it till tomorrow and you can see the doctor then. I dare say he'll be ready to take surgery tomorrow.'

'Oh, all right,' he said reluctantly. 'I just thought maybe a nice massage. . .'

'See the physiotherapist.' There was a resident physio at the resort to deal with problems besetting participants in the various sports on offer, like golf, windsurfing, water-skiing and scuba-diving. He was also available for any Lodge patient who needed physiotherapy.

Murray snorted. 'He doesn't like me,' he said. 'Besides, he *hurts*!'

Nicole laughed. 'Come on, Murray, there's probably nothing a few brisk lengths of the pool won't cure. You need to take more exercise and eat less. You know you're just a teensy bit overweight.' He was rather more overweight than that, but she felt it was undiplomatic to harp on it.

'You are *cruel*,' he whined, then added with good-natured venom, 'I hope Dr Reilly *eats* you alive!'

As she put the phone down, still laughing, Sharon Rivers, the junior nurse, burst in.

'Nicole. . .quick! Mrs Waters has fallen and I can't get her up!'

'Not again!'

The young English nurse nodded. 'She was trying to take a bath by herself.'

Nicole ran down the corridor after Sharon. 'How many times have we told her not to without one of us?' she groaned.

Mrs Waters was arthritic and frail, but stubbornly independent as well as being almost neurotically hygienic and, like Murray, somewhat overweight. It took some minutes to restore her equilibrium, assuage her desire for cleanliness by supervising a shower, and dress her. By the time she was restored to her wheelchair, it was lunchtime.

'I'll take a look at your bruises later,' Nicole promised. 'I don't think you've done any real damage.'

'Of course I haven't!' Mrs Waters hated fuss. She waved a heavily beringed hand. 'I'm all right, Sister—quite all right. There's no need to make a big drama out of a little fall.'

It was strange, Nicole often reflected, how often one thing after another seemed to happen right on lunchtime, or knock-off time, or other inconvenient moments. When she idly remarked on this to Sharon as they took a late lunch together, having been delayed by two more calls after Mrs Waters, Sharon grinned.

'Somebody up there doesn't like us, Nicole,' she said in her breezy Lancashire tones. 'Doesn't think nurses work hard enough, so puts it on them when she can.'

'She?' Nicole raised an amused eyebrow.

'The Great White Nurse in the Sky,' said Sharon, deadpan.

Nicole pushed her plate away. 'Well, I'd better run along to the surgery or *She'll* be heaping fire and brimstones on me! We've got quite a few appointments today.'

'Probably the result of whatever gourmet garbage they got for dinner last night,' said Sharon wickedly.

There were, in fact, no stomach upsets that day. Sometimes there were, but none that could ever be blamed on the resort food, which was first-class. Rather they were as a result of an excess of it combined with alcohol. Nicole had nothing worse than a splinter to remove, a light sprain to bandage, a bruise caused by a head getting in the way of a golf ball, and a couple of cases of sunburn.

'I'll clear up here,' she told Sharon as the last patient went out.

Sharon left, and Nicole was just preparing to close up when a figure loomed in the doorway.

'This is the surgery?'

Startled by the deep male voice, she clattered a kidney dish on the bench and turned round. A large, rather scruffy man stood in the doorway, his head almost touching the lintel, his broad shoulders threatening to widen it. He had a day's growth of beard on his chin and a cut oozing blood on his forehead. He dabbed at it with a blood-stained handkerchief which was wrapped around his left hand as though he had injured that too. Dark, almost black eyes were fixed on her face. One eyebrow was raised queryingly. Nicole felt the oddest little tremor in her stomach.

'You've cut yourself,' she said, slightly alarmed at the weakness in her arms and legs as she moved across the room towards him.

'Very observant of you.' He moved from the support of the door-jamb and staggered slightly.

Nicole caught his arm. 'You'd better sit down.' She eased his considerable frame into a chair. 'You look as if you've been in a fight!'

He gave a dry chuckle. 'With an inanimate object!'

'Oh, yes,' said Nicole, with a look that was meant to convey that she did not believe everything patients told her. 'Well, let me take a look.'

Her hand brushed his as he removed the handkerchief pad. She was acutely aware of the warmth of his skin and the prickle of hairs on the backs of his fingers.

There was a deep cut in the groove between the middle and ring finger extending across his palm.

'I walked into the bathroom cabinet door,' he said shortly. 'I'd just stowed my toilet gear away and I forgot to close it. Knocked a glass off the shelf and tried unsuccessfully to catch it. It smashed in the basin and I managed to slice my hand on it.'

It sounded genuine and, picturing the accident, Nicole was tempted to laugh. Perhaps he'd had too good a lunch. She could not, however, smell any tell-tale alcohol. She said, 'You look a bit shaky. But you can't have lost much blood.'

He seemed to have read her thoughts. 'If you're thinking I was stumbling about drunk after too much to drink at lunch, you're wrong. I only drank mineral water.' His eyes reproached her.

'I wasn't. . .'

'I'm tired, that's all,' he muttered, and dragged his uninjured hand through the dark hair that fell in a thick wave across the other side of his forehead from the wound. 'Haven't had a lot of sleep recently.' His tone suggested the reason was personal and rather painful.

Nicole felt sympathy in spite of his rather abrasive manner. 'And you've just had an accident that's shaken you up a bit. But don't worry, your injuries aren't bad enough to spoil your holiday, or are you here for a conference?'

He stared at her for a moment, not answering. A suggestion of a smile played about his mouth, which she saw was wide and firm and tantalisingly sensuous. Without the stubble, he would be quite handsome. He seemed about to say something, then changed his mind. 'Well, get on with it,' he urged impatiently. 'You can clean and disinfect the wounds, can't you, and put a dressing on them?'

'That's precisely what I will do,' Nicole answered, resenting his imperious tone. She reached for a packet of sterile gauze and tore it open, handing him the pad. 'Just keep this against the cut on your hand for a moment. Your head's not bleeding much now.' Again their fingers touched, and Nicole drew hers away quickly. She caught his eye and for an instant was sure he was laughing at her.

She prepared a disinfectant bath and thoroughly cleansed the cuts. The one on his forehead proved to be quite small once the drying blood was washed away, but it was now showing signs of bruising around it, and was swollen. Usually Nicole would have chatted to a patient, but for some reason her usual small talk seemed to have dried up. The man was forbidding, and she felt unaccountably nervous as she attended to him. She could sense his impatience with her. It was as though he resented having to ask for her assistance. Probably he was a man who was never ill and even a slight injury was a blow to his masculine ego.

'I think steri-strips will be enough,' she decided, fetching the required dressings and applying one to each wound. She glanced at him. 'Do you play golf?'

'Yes.'

'Well, it might be as well not to for a few days, until your hand heals, or you might tear the edges of the wound apart.' She smiled. 'How long are you here for?'

He looked hesitant. 'I'm not sure. . .'

'Well, I suggest you look in the day after tomorrow, unless there's a problem in the meantime. Our new doctor will be here then, and he can take a look at it for you.' Without thinking she gently touched the swelling around the dressing on his forehead. 'Your head's going to be a bit sore, and colourful, I'm afraid.' Aware of his closeness, she stepped back. 'Now, if I could just take a few details. . .' She sat at the desk and, pen poised, looked across at him. 'Your name and cabin number, please.'

'Reilly. Sloan Reilly,' he said slowly, and when she looked up, waiting for him to finish, he stated calmly, 'Doctor's residence.'

Nicole felt as though the ceiling had fallen in, and her face must have shown it, because his mouth twitched with amusement at the effect of his deception.

'*Dr* Reilly,' she said, angry with herself for not tumbling to it.

'Sloan,' he submitted. 'And you're Sister Gardiner. I may call you Nicole?'

His thick dark lashes only partly concealed the smoulder in his eyes, and she felt her cheeks warming. 'Why didn't you say. . .?' Anger surged up briefly.

He shrugged. 'I thought I'd just see how well you coped with an emergency.'

'Hardly an emergency,' she retorted, outraged at his deception and disturbed by his suave masculinity. 'You weren't bleeding to death.'

The dark eyes chided her. 'There's no need to be defensive, Nicole. I have no fault to find with the attention I received. You acted promptly and efficiently.'

Nicole was still annoyed that he had seen fit to test her, as though he had automatically doubted her ability. She allowed irony to edge her voice. 'It's kind of you to say so, Dr Reilly.'

'Sloan,' he repeated. He let his eyes slide over her.

She wasn't quite what he'd expected. Younger, and he hadn't imagined beauty. With her short blonde hair, cut in a sleek but rather tomboyish style that fell in a fringe to just above unplucked eyebrows and wide-set green eyes, and her full mouth and deliciously shaped nose, she had a clean-cut outdoor-girl look. Slim, with slender calves and ankles, she was not, he suspected, without interesting contours under that concealing uniform and jacket. The squareness of her shoulders and a firmness around her mouth suggested she didn't suffer fools gladly and was on top of her job. A tough opponent, he assessed, but she'd be a loyal ally. If she was ever on your side, that was. She was angry with him now, and perhaps he deserved it, but he would surely make her laugh later. Or was that just male ego? He smiled inwardly at himself.

Nicole glanced down at the card in front of her. 'I'll still have to fill in the details, even though you are the new medico.'

'You don't sound very pleased to see me,' he remarked.

She lifted her gaze. 'I thought you were never coming. We've been expecting you for a couple of weeks.' She levelled her gaze, her green eyes sparking. 'I don't like deception. You could have told me at once who you were.'

'I had no ulterior motive, I assure you.'

Nicole had no intention of forgiving him too easily, nor any of making an issue of it. She wrote down the details of his treatment, then stood up. 'Would you like a couple of codeine or paracetamols? Your head must ache a bit.' New doctor or not, he was still her patient.

He got slowly to his feet. He still felt a bit groggy. And a bit sheepish. Fooling this woman hadn't been the most sensible thing to do, and he wasn't sure why he had. Perhaps his subconscious had sensed that she was antagonistic and he'd wanted to postpone confrontation as the new doctor for as long as possible. 'No, thanks,' he said. 'I'll be fine.' He glanced around the room, then his eyes settled back on her face. 'Well, I'm here now. Would you like to show me around?'

Nicole felt a strange kind of panic. It seemed that all at once her feelings for Bob had become all mixed up again. She knew that her antagonism towards Dr Reilly was partly because of it, that in some peculiar way he had aggravated her turmoil. She curbed a strong desire to run, and said, 'You said you were tired. You look worn out, as a matter of fact, and with that bump on your head I think you ought to rest today. Things are usually quiet mid-morning. Shall we say tomorrow about ten-thirty?'

'In view of the delays,' he said mildly, 'I feel I should get into harness as quickly as possible.'

Nicole smiled faintly. 'I think we can manage without you for another twenty-four hours,' she said. 'We've been without a doctor here for more than three weeks.'

His brow furrowed slightly. She was exerting her authority, letting him know that she ran the clinic, not him, even though officially he was in charge. Maybe his predecessor had encouraged her. According to Toff, he'd spent most of his time on the golf course or chasing women.

Sloan said, 'I'll take your advice and rest up until dinnertime, but I imagine things are pretty quiet in the evenings here. What about a quick tour this evening? Then I can start work tomorrow in earnest, without interrupting your routine.'

Nicole moistened her lips. This was a battle of wills,

she thought. A very small one, but a battle none the less which could set the terms for their future relationship. Bob had been so easy-going; this man promised to be authoritarian. 'I'm off duty in the evenings,' she said. 'We have a night nurse. Of course, I'm on call if I'm needed.' She added, 'As you will be.'

Watch your tactics, Sloan thought. Be diplomatic. You're not welcome yet. 'You have a date?' he enquired.

'With a good book,' she answered sweetly.

'It wouldn't take more than half an hour to show me round the place,' he suggested.

Nicole knew she was trapped. To refuse would be rude and bode ill for their future professional relationship. It was very churlish of her even to think of being uncooperative.

'All right,' she said. 'You'll be dining with Mr Barrett, of course?'

'While he's here,' Sloan said. 'He's staying for a few days, I gather.'

Nicole pointedly consulted her watch. 'If you'll excuse me—I've got a few urgent things to do.' She had paused mid-sentence because she had been going to call him 'Doctor', but even though she had stopped herself she hadn't been able to call him 'Sloan'. It was silly. She was going to have to use his name sooner or later. Sooner rather than later, in fact, like tonight. What was the matter with her, reacting like this? Why did she feel threatened?

'Of course,' he said. 'I'll leave you to it. Thank you for the excellent treatment, Nicole.'

She frowned, looking for mockery, but found none. Her gaze was held briefly by dark, heavily lashed eyes that seemed to weigh her up very precisely, in a personal rather than a professional way, but which gave away nothing of their owner's conclusions. All that Nicole could conclude from her own appraisal was confirmation that Dr Sloan Reilly was probably a very sensual man.

When he had gone, she slumped into her chair and rested her head on her arms on the desk. She really must pull herself together, she thought. It was no use blaming Sloan Reilly because he wasn't Bob!

CHAPTER TWO

OFF duty, the clinic staff had their meals in the resort restaurant; on duty their meals were brought up to the Lodge with those for the patients. Nicole had always enjoyed going down to the restaurant in the evenings. It made a nice break—especially when Bob had been there. . .

She sighed as she contemplated her wardrobe. During the day dress in the resort was casual, but at night guests dressed up. Nicole had always enjoyed that too, changing out of uniform into something a little more glamorous. She often thought how lucky she was being able to enjoy most of the luxury the resort offered without having to pay for it—and getting paid herself.

But tonight she felt edgy. Dr Reilly—Sloan—had shaken her composure and she was annoyed with herself for allowing it to happen. She reached into the wardrobe and unhooked a hanger on which was draped a sleeveless bottle-green taffeta dress with a short jacket. She held it up against her and surveyed her reflection in the wardrobe mirror. The colour enhanced her eyes and fair complexion. It was her favourite and one of the most flattering of her outfits. She swirled the skirt and looked at herself critically.

No, she decided, I'm not out to *impress* him. She shoved the hanger back on the rack. For crying out loud, it doesn't matter what I wear! Roughly she extracted a demure brown dress with a cream lacy collar and elbow-length sleeves.

Her hair, which she had pushed into waves as she came out of the shower, was now dry and she combed it, fluffing up the fringe a little and smoothing the rest behind her ears. Her make-up was simple—a touch of eyeshadow, a whisk with a brown mascara wand across her thick but light-coloured lashes, and a cool orange lipstick. Silky 'bare-leg' tights gave a sheen to her long shapely legs, and high-heeled cream sandals emphasised her slim ankles.

She sighed. It was nice dressing up, but nicer still if there *was* someone to dress up for. Since Bob had left she hadn't bothered to go to the dances in the evening, hadn't troubled to get to know any of the unattached males who came and went from the resort, and who might have invited her to have dinner with them, or while away an evening in the nightclub. Or even go snorkelling or sailing on her day off. She had curled up in the armchair in her unit most evenings after dinner with a thick paperback. Romance between the covers of a book was the only kind she wanted.

Ready, Nicole checked with Lindy, the night nurse, then called for Jan, who was eager to show off a new dress. She whirled in front of Nicole in gold and black polished cotton.

'I can't afford it, of course. It's a designer label,' she said with a grimace. 'But Terry's seen all my gear!' She sighed deeply. 'Oh, to have a wardrobe that would stretch for longer than a fortnight!'

'So you've mortgaged your next month's pay to the resort boutique,' laughed Nicole. 'Well, why not? What else is there to spend it on?' She inspected Jan from all angles. 'You look fab, Jan—really! It suits you perfectly. But. . .' She paused, her eyes narrowed anxiously. 'But are you sure you're not going a bit over the top with this Terry?'

Jan buckled on black patent sandals with heels twice as high as Nicole's. 'Yes,' she agreed with a grin. 'But I'm not kidding myself, Nic. When the crunch comes, if it does, I can take it. If I find he's married with seven kids, I'll be only mildly surprised.'

'You might get hurt, though,' Nicole warned. In her estimation, Terry Brannigan, the handsome American Jan was seeing almost every night, was definitely the playboy type.

Jan gave her a knowing glance as she coated her lips with gloss. 'Like you?'

Nicole shrugged. 'Come on, I'm hungry. And Terry's probably chatting up someone else while you dither!'

It was a little less than a quarter of a mile from the Lodge to the resort, along a track which traversed the rainforest and skirted the edge of the golf course. Motorised buggies were provided for staff and patients to go to and fro. Nicole and Jan slid into one and Nicole released the brake. She steered it expertly down the long slope into the rainforest, negotiating the narrow bridge over the creek carefully and then coasting around the perimeter of the golf links. It was not yet dark and several dedicated golfers were still straggling in. A brilliant sunset was just dying on the ocean and a few dark clouds were building up on the horizon.

'By the look of it, we might be in for a storm,' Jan remarked.

'So long as it isn't a cyclone,' said Nicole, crossing her fingers. 'They've had a couple of close encounters on the coast further north lately.'

'It's the season for it.' Jan pointed suddenly. 'Look,

Nic, over there—a sailing ship! Isn't it fabulous? It looks all ghostly, like the Flying Dutchman!'

Nicole smiled at her friend's fancy. 'I hope the skipper isn't so tortured a soul, and I bet the crew won't be invisible!' She let her eyes stray to the three-masted ship anchored in the bay. Its furled sails were still reflecting the last of the sunset and the water was as still as glass beneath its bow. The scene looked almost as though it was painted, like one of the big watercolours of island scenes that decorated the walls of the clinic.

'I wonder if Dr Reilly did arrive,' mused Jan. She glanced at Nicole. 'Didn't you say Murray told you he was coming over with Toff? But I haven't seen him yet, have you?'

Nicole bit her lip as she realised she hadn't mentioned the patient who had turned out to be the new doctor. Now she felt guilty, as though she had done it on purpose.

'As a matter of fact I have,' she said. 'He had a slight accident and came along to surgery this afternoon.'

Jan's eyes widened. 'Nicole! And you never said a word!' She was affronted.

'Sorry. It sort of slipped my mind that you hadn't met him too. I'm showing him over the clinic after dinner tonight.' Nicole gave Jan a sidelong look. 'He's dead keen to start work first thing tomorrow.'

Jan caught the look and groaned. 'What's he like?'

Nicole guided the buggy into the parking area behind the hotel. 'Tall, dark and handsome, Jan. Just your type!' She laughed at Jan's outraged expression. 'Actually, he had a day's beard on his chin when I saw him and he looked decidedly scruffy, as though he'd slept in his clothes and forgotten to bring a comb. I thought he'd been in a fight, but it seems he'd staggered about his quarters and cracked his head on the open door of the bathroom cabinet. Then he knocked a glass off the shelf and cut his hand when it smashed in the basin.'

Jan bubbled with mirth. 'Crikey! I hope he isn't accident-prone.' She asked seriously, 'He wasn't. . . drunk?'

'No, I don't think so. Just tired, maybe.'

'They had an alcoholic doctor here once,' Jan recalled. 'When the resort first opened. Danny told me. He used to have to take him home every night and put him to bed.'

'Somehow I don't think drink is Dr Reilly's problem,' said Nicole. 'But he did admit in an oblique way to *personal* problems.'

'A woman, no doubt,' decided Jan with her usual cynicism.

They strolled into the hotel via the staff entrance at the rear and made their way to the restaurant. There was a special area reserved for staff and some were already drifting in. Jan went off to meet Terry, and Nicole made her way to her usual table. She felt bleak, as she had every night since she no longer shared her evening meals with Bob. Someone else would probably join her, but there was no one who could fill the void that Bob's departure had left. Even in the midst of all these people she was lonely. But Bob Granger wasn't worth the heartache—she knew that. It was anger and disappointment she felt more than unrequited love. And humiliation. Well, it had been a learning experience, a mistake she wouldn't make again. She smiled grimly to herself as she consulted the menu. There was no chance anyway that she'd lose her heart to the new doctor, no chance at all. It made her laugh to even think of it.

'Private joke, or can you share it?'

The same deep tones which had startled her earlier in the day now made her jerk her head round. 'Oh, Dr Rei. . . Sloan! You gave me a start.'

'Something funny on the menu?' he enquired, looking over her shoulder and scanning the gold-printed list.

'No—no, I was just thinking. . .' She tilted her chin. 'Private joke, I'm afraid.'

Without meaning to, she stared at him. Clean-shaven now, he looked the same yet different—devastatingly different, in fact. His hair was smoothly brushed and he had altered the parting so that it covered the cut on his forehead. His eyes were totally black in the subdued light of the restaurant, and now, without the stubble, she could see his mouth more clearly, the firmness of his lips, the sharp jawline and slight cleft in the chin. It was a sensual face, but enigmatic. She wasn't sure if his smile meant he was laughing at her, or if the narrowing of his gaze concealed the same instinctive kind of antagonism she felt towards him. He seemed wary, as though she might be an adversary, which was precisely what she felt about him.

'Are you expecting someone, or may I join you?' Sloan asked, indicating the chair opposite hers.

Nicole was taken aback. 'I thought you were dining with Toff.'

'Some friends of his arrived late this afternoon, unexpectedly. On that sailing ship—you must have noticed it in the bay—so I did the decent thing and opted out.' He eyed her speculatively. 'I told Toff I wanted to have a chat to the clinic's charge sister, anyway.' He allowed a confiding grin. 'Besides, I want an early night. I only had a couple of hours' sleep this afternoon.'

'I'm not expecting anyone,' said Nicole, without putting too much enthusiasm into her voice. Dinner with the doctor was not a prospect she had prepared herself for, nor one she relished.

He sat down. His grey suit was immaculate, she noticed, as was his silver and maroon striped tie and crisp white shirt. She wondered idly why he had arrived like that, where he had been and why he hadn't slept. Somehow, Jan's explanation that the reason had to be a woman did not seem convincing.

He spent a few moments consulting the menu, then, when they had both ordered, looked directly across the table at Nicole. 'We don't have to talk shop, Nicole. My questions will keep until later.'

'I don't mind. . .'

'Off duty is off duty,' he insisted, and went straight on, 'How long have you been here?'

'Two years.'

'And where were you before that?'

'A private hospital in Brisbane, a geriatric home in Sydney, a children's hospital in Melbourne, and I went overseas for a year. . .' She laughed. 'I've been a bit of a rolling stone. This is the longest I've stayed anywhere.'

'Because you enjoy the glamorous lifestyle and luxurious surroundings, no doubt?' He sank his spoon into the avocado vinaigrette which had arrivd.

Nicole had ordered the same. She tasted hers and, sensing a note of sarcasm in his tone, answered, with a smile, 'Anything wrong with that?' What did she care if he thought her shallow? She certainly wasn't going to confess that she might not have stayed so long if it hadn't been for Bob Granger, and that she was in fact intending to leave soon. All that was stopping her was not being sure what she wanted to do next. Somehow, looking for another job had lost its excitement.

Sloan did not give an opinion. 'What made you come here in the first place?' he asked, filling her glass from the carafe of white wine he had ordered.

Nicole shrugged. 'It was accidental really. I was on holiday. I took a day trip to South Molle Island and I happened to get talking to someone there who knew there was a job going here. I'd left my previous job, so on the spur of the moment I rang up and applied for this one. I suppose I was captivated by the atmosphere here, the sea, the islands, the Reef, and I like sailing and scuba-diving. It seemed ideal. I wondered why I hadn't thought of getting a job up here before.' She didn't say that the person she had met on South Molle Island had been Dr Robert Granger, who had insisted she give him a call, and that his irresistible smile had ensured that she had.

Sloan made no comment, so she said, 'What made you come here? Did Toff talk you into it?'

'No—well, yes, in a way, I suppose.'

'You and he are old friends, I believe.'

'We went to school together in Sydney. We lost touch for years, until recently when, by coincidence, his father became a patient of mine.'

'Were you in private practice, or a hospital?' He'd grilled her, so Nicole had no compunction about doing the same to him.

'A hospital. The Southern Cross in Sydney. Know it?'

Her eyes widened. 'Do I? I trained there. It's a marvellous place.' She paused, looking intently at him. 'You'll find it very different here. What were you doing at the SX?'

'Surgical registrar.' He smiled flatteringly. 'Surely I must remember seeing you there.'

'It's a big hospital—hundreds of nurses. Maybe we weren't there at the same time, anyway.' They compared dates and found they had missed each other by a year.

Nicole ventured to say, 'You'll be bored out of your mind here, Sloan.' He won't last long, she was thinking. Any doctor worth his salt wouldn't enjoy the sinecure that this virtually was, permanently.

'Will I? From what I've seen so far, I don't think so.'

Nicole lowered her eyes. 'Well, if you're content with a job that isn't too onerous and allows plenty of time for other pursuits, you'll be OK. Do you sail, snorkel, any of those sorts of activities? Oh, yes, you did say you played golf. Well, you'll be able to indulge yourself here.'

'I hope to do some scuba-diving,' he told her. 'And yes, I do sail and water-ski. I also surf and windsail when I get the chance.'

'This'll be paradise for you, then,' said Nicole.

Sloan considered her for a moment. 'Don't you find looking after people who are already pampered is less satisfying than ordinary nursing?'

'They're all human beings,' she said. 'If they're sick, they need treatment.' She conceded, 'Sometimes I do feel I'd like to get back to a big busy hospital, and I dare say I will in due course.'

'Unless you catch a rich husband first!'

His teasing smile did not prevent her indignation.

She didn't mind that kind of teasing from Murray, but she resented it from the new doctor. He seemed determined to see her as trivial. 'That isn't what I came here for!'

The dark eyes were penetrating. 'But it would be a bonus.'

He evidently didn't believe her, so she thought, well, let him think what he likes. 'If it happened!' she answered flippantly.

He glanced around. 'From what Toff tells me, there are always quite a few eligible, well-heeled males and females without partners around the place. Especially when there's a conference on.'

'Is that why you took the job?' Nicole asked sharply in retaliation for his remark. 'Are you looking for a rich widow or divorcee?'

He looked at her steadily. 'I deserved that.'

She was smiling forgivingly before she knew it. 'Why *did* you take the job?' she asked.

He hesitated for a moment as though considering his answer carefully, then said, 'Partly as a favour to Toff, because it's not easy, apparently, to get doctors to come here, and partly because I have a daughter who's a bit of a problem. I want to get her away from the undesirable crowd she's mixing with and try and shake some sense into her. She'll be coming up for the school holidays. We've had a bit of conflict lately and I hope to make a fresh start.'

'And her mother?' she queried.

The shadow of pain which clouded his face was so intense Nicole could almost feel his anguish. 'Helen died three years ago.'

'I'm so sorry. . .' She bit her lip. 'I didn't mean to. . .'

'It's all right. I think I've come to terms with her death, but Lucy hasn't. She was just thirteen when it happened, on the brink of puberty, just when a girl needs her mother most, perhaps, and now she's a very difficult adolescent—a tendency to be wild, I'm afraid. It was because of her that my arrival was delayed, twice. And then, when I thought we'd reached a compromise, I had no end of trouble at the last minute getting her to go back to school. She'd run away, you see, not for the first time. They weren't keen on having her back, as you might imagine.' He paused, staring at his empty plate for a moment, then lifted his eyes to Nicole's, distraught for a moment as though discovering he was thinking aloud. 'Well, that's more than enough of my problems. They can't interest you. Are you going to have a dessert?'

She could not say that his problems did interest her. That she was experiencing a burning desire to know more about him. That would have surprised him as much as it surprised her, and he would think her merely idly curious. 'No—no, thank you. I'll just have coffee,' she said.

It was just after nine when they left the restaurant. Sloan had already been introduced to the buggies, and he made straight for the rank. A full moon was rising above the dark ocean as they set off and there was a slight breeze. The air was warm and heavy with the scent of frangipani, and the shrill calls of the flying foxes pierced the night eerily as the big fruit bats searched for food in the trees. Nicole was reminded of the many times Bob had driven her back to the Lodge, and a shiver ran through her as the memory of his arms around her, his lips on hers, drifted through her brain. The sudden pounding of her heart and swift surge of desire appalled her, and she closed her eyes tightly, desperately trying to make the images go away. How treacherous one's own body could be!

Sloan said nothing, just concentrated on keeping the buggy on the track, and, Nicole presumed, his own rather gloomy thoughts.

'There isn't really a lot to show you,' she said, as they crossed the yard in front of the staff units and went into the clinic. 'Shall we start with the surgery?'

'Yes, if you like.'

She led the way and unlocked the surgery door, switching on the light. Sloan followed her in. She said, 'There's no charge for treatment for guests, but the convalescent patients pay, of course, like the hotel guests.'

She showed him the small theatre cum treatment-room, and opened cupboards and drawers to reveal equipment. She showed him record cards and prescription pads, and explained how the clinic liaised with the resort's pharmacy for supplies of medications.

Sloan listened, nodded, and said little. He asked a few questions but rarely commented on Nicole's answers. She had the uneasy feeling that he was weighing it all up and finding the system wanting. Her antagonism surfaced again, more because she didn't know what he was thinking than because he said anything to offend. She had a strong feeling he was silently criticising, and that made her feel defensive.

He looked around the room and commented, 'It's a bit small.'

'It doesn't get a lot of use,' she said, straightening the cover on the examination table.

Sloan prowled, sizing the place up, and Nicole wondered nervously what was going on behind those heavily browed dark eyes that seemed to be absorbing everything like a sponge.

He muttered, 'I think we could make a few improvements.'

She was alarmed. 'Such as?'

Sloan smiled at her disarmingly. 'Rearranging. Reassessing needs, maybe. We'll see.' He looked at her expectantly. 'Now where?'

Apprehensive now, and annoyed because he would not be more specific, she showed him the staff-rooms and facilities for staff and patients, her own office and the nurses' room where the night nurse, Lindy Carter, was on duty. After a short chat with Lindy, they went on to the patients' lounge where there were still several convalescent patients watching television or chatting. Nicole introduced the new doctor to them and they spent several minutes exchanging pleasantries. Like Bob, Nicole thought, Sloan Reilly had plenty of charm. He would have the patients eating out of his hand in no time, especially the women. But if he was going to try and make sweeping changes. . . She groaned inwardly.

There was one notable absentee from the lounge— Mrs Mason. As they went out, Nicole mentioned her to Sloan and voiced her concern.

'I'm not sure she ought to be here,' she confessed. 'We can't provide the kind of care I'm sure she needs. I don't think rest is enough. I don't even know what's wrong with her. She wasn't referred by a doctor. She just came of her own accord, and insisted on complete privacy.' She added, 'Shall we see if she's awake? Would you like to meet her now?'

'Why not? But don't let's disturb her if she's asleep.'

In the corridor they met Lindy coming out of the

patient's room. Nicole asked, 'Is Mrs Mason still awake?'

Lindy nodded. 'She just rang for a warm drink. It's the same every night. She can't sleep, but she won't take a sedative. I gave her some Ovaltine, but I doubt if that'll put her to sleep. She says she lies awake mostly all night, and I believe it. The dark shadows under her eyes. . .' She shrugged helplessly and threw a look of appeal at Sloan that conveyed more or less what Nicole had said minutes ago.

Nicole tapped on the door and they entered Mrs Mason's room. The bedside lamp was on and the patient was clutching the mug of Ovaltine she had been given, sipping from it. She looked blankly at Nicole and then her eyes shifted to the figure behind her. An extraordinary expression transformed her face, and she gave a sharp intake of breath and slopped some of the drink she was holding on to the counterpane.

As Nicole automatically hurried to take the mug, Mrs Mason exclaimed, 'Sloan! Of all people. . .'

And behind her, he said, 'Coralie! What on earth. . .? You're the last person I expected to find here!'

Nicole took the mug from Mrs Mason's shaking fingers and placed it on the bedside cabinet, then mopped at the spillage on the counterpane.

She glanced from one to the other. 'You know each other? What a coincidence!'

Mrs Mason suddenly looked nervous and began fussing. 'That won't do,' she said sharply, as Nicole tried to mop up. 'You'd better get a clean counterpane. If you leave it, it will stain.'

Nicole knew it wouldn't, but she rolled back the coverlet and removed it from the bed. 'I'll leave you to talk,' she said tactfully. 'I'll bring you a clean counter-pane later, Mrs Mason.' She glanced at Sloan. 'I'll be in my office.'

He said, 'There's no need for you to wait, Nicole. I've seen all I need to see tonight.' He smiled ironically. 'Don't let me keep you from your book.'

She felt summarily dismissed. 'I'll get Lindy to bring the clean counterpane,' she said, and left them together.

'He knows her?' Lindy was flabbergasted. 'He knows who she is?'

'I got the impression he knows her very well,' Nicole said. 'The way they looked at each other was. . .'

'Like lovers?' Lindy, excited at the prospect of romance, was all agog.

'I don't know! Intimate, I suppose.' Nicole checked herself. 'It's none of our business, Lindy.'

'Of course not,' agreed the night nurse, with a twinkle in her eye. 'But it livens up a dull night.' She sighed, 'He's gorgeous, isn't he?'

'Is he?' countered Nicole, assuming a diffident look.

'Well, if Coralie Mitchell thinks he is, there won't be much hope for us poor drudges,' said Lindy. 'If that's the kind of company our new doctor keeps, we're outclassed, Nicole.'

'I think that goes without saying,' Nicole agreed. 'He's a friend of Toff's too, don't forget.' She showed Lindy the counterpane. 'She was so surprised to see him she spilt her drink. Will you take her a clean counterpane later when he's gone? She practically ordered me to take this one off. It was just an excuse to get rid of me.'

She dumped the soiled counterpane in the laundry basket and strolled towards her unit. She stood for a moment or two in the moonlight, watching the spark-ling path it made on the water, then instead of going inside she slipped off her shoes and padded across the grass to a seat under a palm tree. It was a warm night and the breeze fanned her face gently, but it did not calm the turmoil that had suddenly erupted inside her.

I need to get away from here, she thought. I need to make the move. I can't stay here brooding over Bob. The sailing ship was darkly silhouetted against the night sky, rocking gently on the ocean. A couple of lights flickered aboard her. Maybe I'll get a job on a cruise ship, she thought. That'd make a change. She was absorbed in her thoughts, unaware of time passing, when a sound made her jump.

'I thought you'd gone to bed.'

For the third time that day, Nicole was startled by now familiar deep masculine tones. She turned her head as Sloan slid on to the seat near her. 'I wish you wouldn't keep creeping up on me! You gave me a fright.'

'Sorry. I didn't realise there was anyone here until I was on top of you. You were in the shadow of the palm tree.'

'I was just going in,' said Nicole, wishing he didn't make her feel so flustered.

'It's a beautiful night. Balmy,' Sloan said. 'I couldn't resist the combination of tropical moonlight and the ocean either.'

'Aren't you tired?' she asked. 'And I'm surprised you haven't got a headache after that bump.'

'I'm tough,' he answered, and the moonlight glinted off his white teeth and gleamed in his eyes.

Disturbed by his scrutiny, Nicole remarked casually, 'What a coincidence your knowing Mrs Mason.'

'Yes.' There was a slight pause, then he said, 'You know who she really is?'

'Coralie Mitchell. We're used to people being incognito here. We respect their privacy, of course.'

There was a longer pause, then Sloan said, 'You were right to be worried about her. She's not in good shape at all.'

Nicole dared to ask, 'Do you know what the problem is? We were given no medical report.' Could Jan be right and it was a broken heart? she wondered. Was Sloan the culprit? If so, fate was evidently taking a hand.

His answer came as a shock. 'Overwork, personal problems and too many prescribed tranquillisers. She's come here to effect her own cold turkey.'

Nicole was aghast. 'But. . .'

'I've told her that giving up drugs isn't easy, that withdrawal ought to be properly controlled. Just chucking all the pills away isn't the best way to shake the addiction.'

'What was she taking?' she asked.

'Oh, the usual benzodiazepine tranquillisers. A regular cocktail at one stage, apparently, and of course alcohol as well didn't help.'

'Why didn't she seek proper medical help?'

'Because she's ashamed of what she sees as her weakness, and also she's afraid of people getting to know. She's scared she might not get work if it gets around she's been addicted. Drug problems can make people very unreliable.'

'Surely she knows a doctor doesn't talk about his patients?' queried Nicole.

'She was afraid of having to go to hospital. The Press get to know things however hard you try to cover. And when you're ill, people notice and talk and speculate. They're speculating enough now because she's "gone on a very private holiday", which is the story her agent has put about. She's pretty desperate, because she doesn't dare to be away too long.'

The path of moonlight across the water shimmered in the breeze that rippled the ocean surface. Nicole said, 'Can you help her?'

'I can try.'

She asked carefully, 'Do you know her well?'

Sloan sounded evasive when he answered, 'Fairly well. I haven't seen her for quite a while. She got married eighteen months ago, but they're separated. That's a significant part of the problem. I know now why Toff was so keen for me to take this job on. He's a friend of hers, and it was his idea that she hide away up here.'

'He didn't tell you?'

There was a moment's deep silence from the man at the other end of the bench. Then he said, 'No.' A burst of ironical laughter followed, then, 'He probably thought I'd accuse him of ulterior motives.' Sloan rose abruptly. 'I'm going in. What about you?'

'I might as well.' Nicole rose too and walked back with him.

'Barefoot!' he teased. 'You'll ruin your tights.'

'Not on the grass.'

He stole a sidelong glance at the woman beside him, carrying her spiky-heeled shoes. She wasn't very tall without them, even smaller than in her wedge-heeled nurse's shoes. She looked fragile and ethereal in the moonlight, tiptoeing lightly across the lawn, quite different from the slightly austere young woman in uniform he had first encountered, the Sister Gardiner

who was very definitely antagonistic towards him.
Why? he wondered.

As they skirted a hibiscus bush something flew out
of it and brushed their faces—a bird or a bat, Nicole
wasn't sure which. She gaved an involuntary little
scream and stumbled. Sloan caught her round the waist
and for a moment he was just a silhouette against the
moon, then his face was close to hers, his mouth
touching her lips, and she wasn't even trying to move
out of his way.

As his arms closed around her body, her own hung
limply at her sides, one hand holding her shoes, the
other her bag. Her pulses were racing, her heart
pounding, and as his lips covered hers and subtly
coaxed she found herself responding to a kiss so
passionate that it kindled desire with shameful speed.

Then, just as quickly as her passions had been fired,
so was her anger. She pulled away from him. 'What a
nerve!' she whispered hoarsely. 'Just who do you think
you are? What do you think I am?' She turned her
back and ran, her stockinged feet flying over the grass.
She fled into her unit without even glancing behind her
and locked the door, leaning breathless against it.

'Bob. . .' she whispered, and covered her face with
her hands. 'No. . .no. . .no. . .' She had let Sloan
Reilly kiss her because for a magical moment it had
been Bob returned to hold her in his arms. But she
didn't want Bob back. She wasn't in love with him.

She flung herself down on the bed and pummelled
the pillow with her fists. She was never, never, never
going to be some man's victim again. Nor was she
going to let her body betray her in some man's arms,
not ever again.

CHAPTER THREE

NEXT morning, as she showered, Nicole recalled her parting words to Sloan the night before with embarrassment. How prim and prudish she must have sounded! But clever retorts had never sprung easily to her tongue, especially when her composure had been shattered.

And Sloan Reilly had definitely done that with a vengeance. As she massaged shampoo into her hair, Nicole felt her whole body flush with heat at the memory of his kiss. Renewed anger made her lips tighten. How dared he? They'd only met a few hours earlier, and he seemed to think. . . How *could* she have let him?

'Men!' she spluttered, wiping shampoo out of her eyes. Why couldn't he have been a little less blatant on his first day? Now she had to face him this morning as though nothing had happened. And he'd probably be laughing at her for behaving like a prudish schoolgirl, with less sophistication probably than his own daughter.

For the first time since she had been on Bauhinia Island, Nicole slipped on her uniform with reluctance. For the first time she wasn't looking forward to the day's work. She was a little late for a start, having gone back to sleep after her alarm went off, and having been re-awakened when her breakfast tray had been shoved through the hatch.

Now she hurriedly swallowed orange juice, cereal

42

and toast and half a cup of black coffee. The dish of paw-paw and mango slices she put in her fridge, intending to eat them later. She was only ten minutes behind time when she closed the door of her unit and marched briskly across to the Lodge, but she found Sloan Reilly already in her office rifling a filing cabinet. At once all her antagonism came into play.

He looked up as she came in. 'Good morning, Nicole.' His tone was pleasant, but Nicole did not miss his quick glance at the clock on the wall near the door. To her it was like an accusation, which she deeply resented. What right had he to take her to task for being a few minutes late? Even though he said nothing, she seethed resentfully.

'You were looking for something?' she enquired, trying to sound perfectly normal.

'Just browsing through the case history files, that's all.' He pushed the drawer in. 'As you weren't here, Jan unlocked the cabinet for me. You don't mind?'

'Why should I mind? You're the doctor. You're in charge.' She regretted the surliness in her tone, but couldn't seem to help it.

Sloan's facial muscles tensed and his eyes narrowed slightly. He owed her an apology, and the best thing to do was to get it over with. He still wasn't sure what had come over him last night. He wasn't usually so impulsive. Heaven knew what might have happened if she hadn't been the kind to show outrage at a pass from someone she'd only just met. He might have found himself in a situation he would be well advised to avoid at present. He looked at her speculatively for a moment. Was she really as cool and aloof as she seemed? Was the sultriness in her green eyes a figment of his imagination?

'Nicole. . .' For the sake of their working relationship, he took the plunge. 'I'm sorry about last night. I. . .' Her look killed the words on his tongue. She'd damned him to hell and no mistake. A mere apology wasn't going to win her over.

With a tremendous effort, Nicole kept up a pretence of nonchalance. 'Oh, it's amazing what a little moonlight can do.' She tried to give the impression that his advances were no more than all in a day's work for her.

'I just don't want you to think. . .'

She waved a hand airily. 'It's forgotten, Sloan,' she said, forcing her eyes to meet his. 'It was nothing terrible. There's no need to make an issue of it.' She smiled forgivingly.

Her dismissive tone riled rather than reassured him. It was a put-down. Well, what had he expected? Surely not that *she'd* apologise for running off like a prim schoolgirl. He was uncomfortably aware, however, that, while she was as cool as a cucumber about it, his feelings were maddeningly confused.

Not feeling in the least cool, although managing to sound it, Nicole told him, 'The patients will have had breakfast by now. Our previous doctor usually visited them in their rooms after breakfast, and, as I mentioned last night, they can see the doctor in his office between eleven and twelve.' She lifted an eyebrow briefly. 'You may of course want to change that routine.'

'And surgery for the resort guests is at two,' Sloan recalled.

'Two-thirty,' Nicole corrected.

His mouth twitched. 'Yes, of course. Well, I'd better do my round of the patients.' He strode to the door, pausing to look back when she didn't follow. 'Aren't you coming too?'

'Do you need me to?' Nicole asked. 'Dr Granger preferred to see them on his own. I think they prefer that too. And I do have quite a lot of paperwork to do.' She added, 'This isn't quite the same as a hospital, Sloan. Our patients don't like too much regimentation. They're paying for peace and quiet and the security of having medical care on hand if they need it, but we keep the medical atmosphere as unobtrusive as possible. You can buzz me from any room if you need me.'

Sloan frowned at her little speech. He found her aggravating, yet intriguing too. He was sure she wasn't as starchy as she seemed, but he deplored the urge in himself to prove it. Under the ice, she was too attractive, damn it. She might not be aware of it herself, but there was a suppressed sensuality about her that made him want to take her and shake her and kiss her relentlessly. He made a hurried exit before fantasy overwhelmed reality.

Nicole watched the door close behind him with mixed feelings. She still wasn't sure whether she liked him or not. Some perverse part of her nature made her want to dislike him because he wasn't Bob, but honesty forced her to acknowledge that this was unreasonable. Nevertheless, he made her feel edgy. Once he had gone she relaxed. Give it a few days, she thought. He'll settle in, and we'll all start taking him for granted.

Some time later Jan came in. She looked weary. Nicole commented and teased, 'Up all night with Terry, I suppose.'

Jan sighed. 'The conference ends tomorrow, two days early. I thought he might be staying on, but he isn't. He has to get back to the States—urgent business, apparently.'

'Jan. . .' Nicole laid a sympathetic hand on her shoulder.

Jan forced a smile. 'He says he'll write, but I'm not that much of a fool, Nic. No, it's just a case of goodbye, nice knowing you, I'll call you some time.' She sighed wistfully, then declared with renewed spirit, 'Well, there's plenty more fish in the sea.'

Nicole crossed the room to look out of the window at the sparkling ocean. She knew how Jan felt. You gave a part of yourself to someone, and then when they walked off with it, you could only wait for the protective covering to grow over the wound.

Jan changed the subject. 'Everyone thinks Dr Reilly—Sloan—is very handsome, and has a wonderful bedside manner. All the women are practically swooning over him, regardless of age. Even that rich old biddy, Marcia Tate. You should have seen her rattling her bangles and rolling her eyes. Disgusting!'

Nicole laughed. Jan's rather acid view of humanity belied her obvious nursing skills and kind heart.

Jan went on, 'She needn't think she's any chance of throwing her hat over the windmills, though. He spent two minutes with her and half an hour with Mrs Mason.'

Nicole felt it was OK to tell the nurse what Sloan had told her about Mrs Mason, alias Coralie Mitchell, and Jan whistled through her teeth.

'So that's it! Why didn't we guess?' She slapped her forehead. 'It falls into place now—why she won't even take a sleeping pill, why she gets the shakes and seems so vague at times. Poor woman!'

'It takes courage to try and kick the habit by yourself,' Nicole said. 'I know it's not the same as giving up heroin, but the side-effects of prescription drugs can be pretty awful. I don't think she realised how awful.'

'Why didn't she tell us?' asked Jan. 'We could have helped.'

'The less we know the better, I guess.'

They were still talking when Sloan came in. 'I suppose you two have had coffee?' he queried.

Nicole said, 'We were just going to.' She gave him a look that said he needn't expect to be waited on all the time.

'I'll put the kettle on,' he offered.

'Now here's a man I could look up to,' said Jan, with a flirtatious look. 'I'll have black tea, and Nic has black coffee with lemon.'

Sloan looked a little startled, but he backed out, and the two girls laughed.

Nicole said, 'You've got a cheek!'

Jan tossed her brown hair. 'I'll have him tamed in a week!'

'Somehow I doubt that,' said Nicole. 'He strikes me as a volcano that might erupt any minute, and don't forget we're the ones likely to cop the lava flow.'

The phone on her desk rang, and she answered it. Jan frowned at the sudden alarm on her face.

'Right, get him up here as quickly as you can,' said Nicole, and dropped the receiver back on the cradle, rising as she did so. 'There's a coronary down at the resort. You'd better come too.'

She ran out into the corridor and along to the kitchen. Her eyes cursorily took in the tray set with three mugs and a plate of biscuits. Sloan had just switched off the kettle and was standing with it poised in hand ready to pour boiling water on the instant coffee and tea-bag.

'Hold it!' Nicole told him. 'Emergency—a heart attack down at the resort. They're bringing him up as quickly as they can.'

Sloan put the kettle down, caught his finger against the hot metal and swore succinctly. 'Better be ready, then,' he said crisply, and followed her out. They almost collided with Jan.

Heart attacks were common enough among Bauhinia guests to have persuaded Toff Barrett to equip an intensive-care ward with up-to-date life-saving technology. One of his top managers had died when on holiday, he had told Nicole, which wouldn't have happened if there'd been proper modern equipment available. And as Bauhinia Sands hosted many conferences of executives, it was an essential precaution—a good selling point, Murray had often said, quite seriously.

Sloan moved swiftly, checking ventilator, defibrillator, the ECG equipment and oxygen. Almost before Nicole and Jan could set up a drip, lay out instruments and the drugs which might be needed, the special ambulance buggy with the patient aboard had arrived. No attempt had been made at CPR; they had just transported the victim as quickly as possible. Nicole caught her breath at the sight of the patient. He was unconscious and dangerously cyanosed. She heard Sloan suck in a sharp breath too at the sight of the blue tinge suffusing the man's skin, particularly around the mouth. He pressed his fingers into the patient's neck, seeking the carotid artery which would tell him whether the heart was still beating or not.

'Defibrillator,' he said tautly.

Nicole tensed. How long was it since the man had collapsed? Unless a heart could be restarted within three or four minutes of an arrest, irreversible brain damage might occur because of lack of oxygen reaching the brain cells.

Moving swiftly at Sloan's commands, she assisted him to apply the electrodes for administering the electric shocks that would, they hoped, revive the heartbeat. What only took seconds seemed to her like minutes. Her usually nimble fingers seemed to her to fumble as she adjusted the oxygen mask over the patient's nose and mouth, and her throat felt as dry as dust. She caught a grim look from Jan, who was inserting the drip which would intravenously deliver the drug which would help stimulate the heart muscles. The other nurse raised a hand with fingers crossed, and as the shocks were applied, they both looked anxiously at the ECG monitor.

Sloan was muttering, 'Come on. . .come *on*. . .' under his breath, anxiety and impatience combining. Nicole sensed he would take it as a personal defeat if the man could not be revived.

For the first few interminable seconds there was no response, but when Nicole had all but given up hope, there was a change. She stared unbelieving at the faint signals on the monitor that meant life restored. She heard Sloan say softly, 'Ahhhh. . .' and their eyes met for a moment in a glance that conveyed the rapport that came with successful teamwork. Nicole caught Jan's eye too, and felt, as strongly as if it had been said, that success was theirs.

'I think we've got him,' Sloan said quietly, only the rigidity in his jaw muscles betraying the tension he was feeling. He leaned towards Nicole and whispered, 'Relax, baby!'

The pseudo-American accent and the humorous twinkle in his eyes broke her up. She laughed, and Jan, whose back had been towards them at that moment, turned round sharply, her eyebrows raised.

'We've done it!' said Nicole in a breathless but elated voice, her eyes darting back to the ECG monitor.

'Hurray,' said Jan, laconic even in crisis. 'I hope he's grateful. These past minutes took years off my life!'

'And you a nurse!' Sloan exclaimed.

Jan pulled a face. 'I should have been a secretary.'

The inconsequential banter was merely the release of tension. Nicole laughed again. She felt elated, as though she'd just won a prize. But she was still conscious that it wasn't over yet; the patient was by no means out of danger even though his colour was improving, a faint glow suffusing the formerly bluish skin.

Sloan's hand brushed hers as he reached to examine the man's eyes at the same time as she touched the oxygen mask. In this special moment of shared victory there was no room for antagonism, and Nicole did not feel any. In fact, what she did feel at the touch of his hand on hers shocked her.

Sloan grunted satisfaction at what he saw, then looked from one nurse to the other. 'I guess we skip the coffee break now and have lunch.' And *I've* done it, he thought. I made Nicole laugh.

'They send ours up from the restaurant,' Nicole said. 'Patients have theirs in their rooms or the dining-room. We have ours in the staff-room.' She threw him a challenging glance. 'You can eat with us if you like. It's only Jan and me and Danny, the orderly-handyman.'

Sloan said, 'Someone will have to special this guy. What's his name, by the way?'

'I forgot to ask!' Nicole exclaimed, and turned her head away at the look of mock severity she received from Sloan.

'I'll stay with him,' Jan offered. 'You can keep my lunch and I'll microwave it later.'

Nicole nodded. 'I'll be back as soon as I can.'

Sitting across the table from Sloan in the staff-room, Nicole was sure he felt as she did the drained feeling that always came after the release of adrenalin had subsided. They were alone. Danny was apparently eating elsewhere today and Sharon must still be busy. There was no domestic staff. Maids and waitresses, and cleaning staff, were all part of the hotel staff. They came and went according to whatever tasks they were needed for.

Nicole was not hungry and neither apparently was Sloan. Each toyed with the food and sipped iced water.

Finally Nicole asked, 'Are you going to fly him out right away?'

Sloan nodded. 'There's still a risk factor. Better he's in a general hospital in case of complications.'

Nicole pushed her chair back. 'I'd better go and relieve Jan.' She added, 'Don't forget surgery.'

'With you constantly reminding me, how could I?'

He sounded irritated and she wished she hadn't spoken. 'Sorry. I just thought, with all the excitement . . .and your not being used to the routines yet. . .'

'Yes, well, thanks.'

The dark eyes were inexplicably hostile all at once. Nicole left him, puzzled and a little hurt.

What was the matter with the woman? Sloan thought tetchily. Just when he thought the crisis had been a catalyst, breaking down her reserve, there she was back in her prim strait-jacket again. He gulped the rest of his iced water, nearly choked on a lump of ice, and strode out of the room to make arrangements for the transferral of the patient to the mainland.

When he looked into the ICU, Nicole was standing at the window, looking out across the bay, a dreamy look on her face. She started guiltily, her lightly tanned skin flushing. Sloan found himself hooked on her green eyes and wishing her lips would part and show him a smile, that she'd laugh with that pure, natural sound he'd heard from her earlier when he'd made the joke about relaxing.

'Everything OK?' he asked, crossing to the patient's bed.

'Fine. He woke up a while ago, but he's sleeping again now.'

'How did he seem?'

'Just tired. And a bit confused.'

'He's probably got pretty sore ribs as well as angina pain. If he wakes again, and needs it, give him paracetamol.' He paused, surveying the patient, then Nicole. 'Well, I'd better get along. I see we have quite a few appointments today.'

'Yes. Jan will help you.'

'I don't think that will be necessary,' he said stiffly. 'I imagine I can cope with a few run-of-the-mill consultations. It's not so long since I was a GP.'

'I wasn't suggesting you couldn't,' Nicole said evenly. 'But the run-of-the-mill medical problems we have here tend to be the kind that need some assistance, for dressings and suchlike. I always helped Dr Granger. Jan or Sharon helped me.' She added, 'There's also the paperwork.'

Sloan grunted, half turned as though about to go, then fixed her with a dark stare and said drily, 'Then perhaps you'd better see me through my first trial by paperwork and bandages. Jan can keep an eye on our patient here.'

'I'm sure Jan. . .' Nicole began to object because she suddenly felt it might be preferable to stay where she was and let Jan cope with Dr Reilly, but he would have none of it.

'I would prefer *you*,' he said, and left before she could argue.

As the last patient departed that afternoon, Nicole put away stethoscope, sphygmomanometer and other instruments, and then started cleaning up the treatment-room. After a few moments she became aware that Sloan lounged in the doorway, watching her.

Unnerved by his scrutiny, she glanced at him and said, 'It wasn't too bad, was it? Less taxing than your average suburban surgery.'

'That coral wound should have been reported days ago,' he remarked, sounding as though it were her fault. 'Then it wouldn't have turned septic.'

'You can't make people come to you,' she answered. 'I suppose you could say the same about the ear infection. It would have been less painful if the boy had been given an antibiotic right away.'

'Does that sort of thing happen often?' he asked. 'People failing to take advantage of the medical service offered them?'

Nicole had a feeling he was getting at something she had not realised yet. 'Sometimes.' She closed the door on the elctric autoclave and faced him. 'Look, people are on holiday. They get a minor injury or illness and they can't be bothered wasting time coming all the way up to the Lodge for treatment, especially if it isn't bothering them too much. Time's precious when you're on holiday. Expensive too.'

'Sure,' he agreed, 'and now the girl with the infected coral graze on the ball of her foot can hardly walk. She's going to be hobbling with a crutch for the rest of her stay, antibiotics or not.'

Nicole inclined her head. 'So what do you suggest? A notice on the back of the hotel doors—all injuries and sickness, no matter how trivial, must be reported to the MO? Toff wouldn't agree to that, Sloan. As I said before, we avoid any form of regimentation.'

He moved his position, to stand leaning against the door-jamb, arms folded across his chest in a stance that conveyed a stubborn determination.

'It's quite simple,' he said. 'We move the surgery down to the hotel.'

Nicole's mouth fell open and her eyes widened. 'Now, just a minute. . .'

'People would be more likely to drop into a surgery on the spot,' he went on. 'It's too much of an effort to trail up here for something that seems to be just trivial.'

'But. . .'

The dark eyes flared. 'I anticipated that you'd object,' said Sloan, his voice gravelly. 'You're a stickler for the status quo, aren't you? You dislike change on principle.'

'That's not——'

'You even resent a change of doctor,' he accused. 'I'm an intrusion in your domain, that's the trouble, isn't it? You enjoyed managing the Lodge by yourself, didn't you? It gave you a nice sense of power. But you must be realistic, Nicole. You were lucky you didn't have a crisis like today's.'

Nicole was stiff with annoyance. 'Jan and I could have coped. We're both trained in resuscitation techniques.' She added tightly, 'I resent your remarks, Dr Reilly. You've no right. . .' She moistened her suddenly dry lips and clamped her tongue between her teeth to prevent the hot words that welled up in her throat. The trouble was, he wasn't entirely wrong, and it hurt to have to admit it. She wasn't going to admit it to him, though!

'Give me one good reason why we shouldn't conduct surgery for the hotel guests at the hotel?' he asked, his dark eyes piercing.

Nicole felt her mind going blank. 'Where? I mean, there'd have to be space available, facilities. . . You couldn't just dismantle the surgery here, because we need it for the Lodge patients too.' She felt she was on solid ground again.

But Sloan was unfazed. 'I dare say the space could be found, and equipped. I intend to speak to Toff about it.'

She said defensively, 'I suppose you want to shift the ECG and other equipment down there too. Then what do we do if there's an emergency up here? Some of our patients have actually had heart attacks and open-heart surgery. They're in as great, if not more, danger than executives at conferences.'

Sloan let a half-smile escape. 'I dare say we could prove your point or mine by taking out some statistics, but that isn't the point. Take today, for instance. We were lucky—or rather, I should say, our patient was lucky. But he almost died. We ought to be able to provide resuscitation more quickly.'

'It would take nearly as long for us to get down to the hotel as for the ambulance buggy to bring the patient up here,' Nicole pointed out. 'You wouldn't gain much.'

Sloan strolled into the room and perched on the bench she had cleared. 'Enough sometimes, perhaps, to make the difference between life and death, total rehabilitation or permanent brain damage.'

'You don't think Mr Sheridan. . .?' Nicole demanded in dismay.

'No, I don't think he'll have suffered brain damage. At least, I hope not. Now, he collapsed in the guests' lounge, but supposing he'd been out on the golf course. First they'd have had to get him to the hotel, then up here. Precious minutes would have been lost, whereas if everything had been on the spot his chances would have been improved at once.'

'He'd still have had to wait until we could get to him,' Nicole reminded him.

'During which time, CPR could be started by trained operatives. I'm sure there are staff members, even guests, who could be alerted. You can't apply heart massage in a buggy!'

Sloan finished on a triumphant note which made Nicole's antagonism flare, even though she could see the sense of what he was saying. 'It'd be a huge expense,' she pointed out, 'just for those rare occasions when someone has a heart attack.'

He smirked. 'I hardly think Toff would notice it. He's just bought himself a new boat, all computerised, for close on a million bucks. And besides, he trades on the slogan of caring for his customers.' He regarded her steadily. 'How much is even one human life worth, Nicole?'

The reproach torched her anger. 'I'm as anxious to save lives as you are, Dr Reilly!'

His gaze was steady. 'Of course.' He paused, then added more fuel to the fire. 'I also intend to make a few other improvements while I'm about it.'

'Such as?' she queried in alarm.

He shrugged nonchalantly, and ticked off his proposals on his thumb and forefinger. 'We definitely need to upgrade our surgical instruments and other equipment generally—obstetrics, for instance. And the range of anaesthetic drugs you keep is a bit limited.'

Nicole gave a short derisive laugh. 'Isn't that going a bit far?' she said. 'This isn't a general hospital.'

'But Bauhinia Sands caters for a constant flow of guests, hundreds at a time.'

'Nevertheless, I think what you're suggesting is unnecessary. We're only an hour or two by air from Mackay. What's the Flying Doctor for?'

He remained unmoved by her opposition. 'A couple of hours can be too long in a real emergency,' he pointed out. His chin jutted stubbornly. 'I'm sure Toff will appreciate that.'

Which she didn't, he implied. Nicole seethed.

'Besides,' he went on, smiling at her, but piercing her with his dark eyes, 'I've noticed quite a few pregnant women staying here.' His brows lifted. 'You haven't?'

She bit her lip. He was baiting her now. Through tight lips, she answered, 'You don't waste any time, do you?'

There was a slight pause before Sloan said decisively, 'Well, I'll talk to Toff about it.'

He smiled with satisfaction, as though he'd won her over—which he hadn't, she thought rebelliously, drawing herself up to her full height and looking him straight in the eye. He'd just ridden roughshod over her.

Strong-willed but vulnerable, Sloan told himself, and said, 'I believe in getting things done if they need to be done.'

'So do I,' Nicole shot back. '*If* they need to be done.'

He half smiled. 'Think how reassuring it will be, Nicole, to know you're able to deal with emergencies which now, with inadequate means, might prove fatal.'

She had no answer to that. Of course she would like the Lodge to have better equipment. 'Well, I hope Toff's in a generous mood when you suggest it,' was all she said, turning away to finish her task.

She didn't hear him move, but strong hands gripping her shoulders made her jump. He turned her to face him. 'What's the matter with you, Nicole? I thought you were thawing out today, but now you're back in your igloo again. What have you got against me, for heaven's sake?'

Nicole felt his warm breath fan her cheeks, which were suddenly drained of colour. His verbal attack was unexpected and she tilted her head back to avoid his dark accusing gaze. Her lips trembled and, horror of horrors, she felt tears start in her eyes.

'N-nothing,' she faltered. 'There's no need to be so touchy.' To her chagrin a tear escaped and ran down her cheek to the corner of her mouth. There was such turmoil inside her as she had never experienced, and if it hadn't been for Sloan's restraining hands she would have fled. 'You're hurting me,' she murmured plaintively.

A corner of his mouth quirked and he gave a half chuckle, half snort. 'Nicole, I'm sorry!' He lifted a hand and brushed the teardrop from her mouth. 'I

didn't mean to be so abrasive. I'm quick-tempered, I
know. But I wish I knew why you seem so antagonistic
towards me.'

'I'm not.'

He ran his finger up the path of the tear and then
wiped away the one on the other side. Nicole swallowed hard. She felt embarrassed, angry, guilty and
totally confused. So confused that she could only stand
there trying to regain her control and salvage what
little of her dignity was left.

'It's been a draining day,' he said gently. 'You're a
bit overwrought. And so am I, I guess. I shouldn't
have spoken to you like that. I do tend to go at things
like a bull at a gate.'

'Please,' she begged, 'don't apologise. It's all right—
really.'

He resumed his grip on her shoulders. 'What we
both need is some real relaxation,' he said, nodding his
head in agreement with himself. 'I prescribe that after
dinner this evening, we dance a little, maybe gamble a
little. . .' He smiled. 'What do you say?'

Nicole felt the pull of his dark eyes, the charm of his
smile, and recognised the dangers. 'Thanks,' she said,
'but I still have my book to finish.'

He cupped her face in his hands, shaking his head
admonishingly. 'Nicole, why are you fighting me? I
only want to be friends with you, to establish a harmo-
nious working relationship. If you're worried because I
made a pass at you last night, you needn't be. I promise
I won't do that again.'

Colour rushed back into her face. 'I'm rather tired. I
think I'd rather go to bed early tonight.'

He let her go. 'All right, I get the message. Maybe
I'd better join Toff and his friends tonight after all.'

'Yes, you want to talk to him about your plans,' Nicole reminded him, unable to keep the edge completely out of her voice.

He inclined his head slightly. 'An ally would have been nice.'

She drew in a long breath. She was smarting from having behaved, as she knew, churlishly, yet she could not quite bring herself to capitulate. He'd only been here two days. Who knew what mad ideas he might come up with next? The fact that what he had suggested was sensible, and practical, only made it all the harder. In the end, it was always what was best for people that should be her motivation in medical matters.

'I'd like to think about it,' she hedged.

He had to be satisfied with that. 'All right.' He turned to go, saying over his shoulder, 'Enjoy your book!'

As the outer door to the surgery closed behind him, Nicole beat the bench with her clenched fists.

CHAPTER FOUR

JAN joined Nicole at dinner that night. As it was Terry's last night, Nicole had not expected to see her.

Jan answered her unspoken query briskly. 'There's a farewell party in the Reef Room for all the conference delegates. And friends. I declined.'

'Why?' Nicole was surprised.

Jan leaned towards Nicole, her vivacious face fierce. 'Want me to make a fool of myself?' She laughed in her laconic way. 'No way, Nic. I said cheerio to Terry this afternoon on the phone, and I shan't be waving him off. It was fun, but I don't expect phone calls or flowers or anything glittering in a small velvet-lined box. Terry was just another ship that passed in the night.'

Her voice had a husky timbre and her accent was more marked than usual. Jan was more upset than she was letting on, Nicole knew. She didn't know what to say. It brought back so many painful memories for herself.

Jan said brightly, 'So, where's our dreamboat doctor tonight?'

'Dining with his friend Toff, of course.' Nicole jerked her head back without looking round. The boss's regular table was on the far side of the restaurant in a secluded niche.

Jan craned her neck. 'So he is.' She stared for a moment. 'Good-looking devil, isn't he? Sexy!' She brought her gaze back curiously to Nicole. 'Were you two having an argument, Nic? I thought I heard voices raised after surgery this afternoon, when I was passing.'

Nicole chose her words carefully. 'Dr Reilly tends to speak loudly when he gets carried away with an idea.'

'Which in this case you didn't approve of?' Jan guessed. 'What's he trying to do, bring big-hospital management to a small-time nursing home?'

'Not exactly. But he's only been here two days and doesn't know much about the place yet. He seems rather impetuous.' Nicole explained Sloan's ideas.

Jan ate her meal and listened, nodding now and then. Finally she said, 'The man's quick on the uptake, I'll say that for him.'

'You think it's a good idea?' Nicole was a little disappointed.

'Definitely. If Toff's willing to foot the bill, why not? Even if it saves only one life, it'd be worth it, wouldn't it?'

'Yes, I suppose so. . .'

Jan forked the last of her French fries into her mouth. 'You don't like him, do you?' She sounded surprised.

'I don't know. He moves a bit too fast for me. I like time to consider, evaluate.' Nicole broke off a piece of bread and nibbled it. She had left her meal half eaten. She still wasn't very hungry.

'The trouble is, he's not Bob Granger,' said Jan flatly. She pointed a finger at Nicole. 'Nic, you've got to get that man off your mind. He was just another Terry. You can't moon after him forever.'

'I'm not!'

Jan poured the rest of the wine from the carafe into their glasses. 'Look, Nic,' she said, 'you weren't really in love with Bob. It's just your pride that's hurt. Bob left a big dent in your ego, just as Terry's done in mine, curse him. But don't take it out on Sloan. He seems like a great guy to me. Don't be petty.'

Nicole flinched. 'Am I being? Yes, I suppose I am a bit.' She sighed. 'You're right, Jan. It's just self-indulgence, but I can't seem to help myself. I've gone all bitter and twisted.'

Jan laughed. 'Why don't we go and dance afterwards? Let our hair down a bit.'

Nicole gave the same excuse she had given to Sloan. 'I'm a bit tired. It's been a hectic day.'

Jan yawned. 'You're right, and I'm tired myself. Maybe I'll have an early night too.'

Nicole was hardly surprised when next morning Toff Barrett phoned.

'Hi, sweetie,' he greeted her. 'Everything under control?'

'As usual.'

'Ah, it's good to have staff you can rely on,' said Toff, as though he really meant it. 'How are you getting on with Sloan?'

'Fine.'

'He's told you what he wants to do?' Toff's voice was cautious, and Nicole wondered if Sloan had warned him about her opposition.

'Yes.'

'That's Sloan,' said Toff. 'He sees the problem and the solution almost in the same breath. I knew he'd want to shake things up a bit.' He paused, then said quickly, 'You don't mind, do you?'

'Mind?' she echoed.

'Well, new broom and all that.'

'There's nothing to stop anyone having ideas for improvements,' she heard herself saying stiffly.

'You agree with what he wants, then?'

Nicole could not avoid the direct question. She had to answer. She thought about her conversation with Jan the previous night, about the hours she'd lain awake trying to put things in perspective. She took a deep breath. 'Yes. I can't imagine why we didn't think of it before,' she said, and it wasn't as difficult as she'd expected.

'I'll tell you why Dr Granger never thought of it,' Toff said with bite. 'He didn't give the job a lot of his thoughts, period. Sloan's different, Nicole. I know the guy, and he's one of the best. He won't stay long, I know that. This is no place for a man of his talent and dedication, but although it's only a favour to me and a stopgap while he sorts out a few personal problems, he'll treat it as seriously as though it were a permanent position. That's the way he is, and we might as well make the most of his professional advice while he's here.'

'Of course. But why are you. . .?'

'Asking your opinion?' Toff laughed. 'Sweetie, you're a treasure, and I wouldn't want to lose you just yet. I just wanted to be sure you were happy about the changes. Sloan does kind of spring things on people.'

'I think what he plans is an excellent idea,' Nicole said, and was surprised at her own sudden enthusiasm. 'How soon can you get the new equipment?'

'No problem. I dare say I can pull a few strings and have us set up in a week, ten days. Let's hope we don't have any more touch-and-go coronaries in the meantime.' He paused, then, apparently deeming that subject closed, asked, 'How's Coralie?'

'I think finding Sloan here has cheered her up,' Nicole told him. 'He understands her problem.'

'Great. I had a hunch Sloan might be good for her. They're old friends. Maybe something will come of it this time.' He paused again. 'Right—well, I just thought I'd check you were happy with things, sweetie. How about you and Sloan joining me for dinner tonight? We can finalise details. I'm off back to Sydney tomorrow.'

Nicole heard herself agreeing to the invitation, and then Toff had rung off and she was half wishing she had not. She looked up and Sloan was standing in the doorway.

'Was that Toff?' he asked.

'Yes, it was, and I told him I was totally in agreement with your plans. He reckons to have everything we need within a week to ten days.' Nicole held her chin high, waiting for his response.

He looked steadily at her for a moment, but he didn't allude to her former reluctance. 'He fancies himself as a miracle-worker,' he said, coming in and perching on the edge of her desk. 'We're having dinner with him tonight, so, if there's anything you want to add to his shopping-list, now's your chance.'

'I can't think of anything.'

'I can.'

Nicole felt a quiver of alarm. He had a very determined look in his eye. 'Now what?' she asked.

'I dare say you won't like it.'

'I won't?'

'Not one bit.'

'Try me?' she smiled.

He laughed aloud. 'I'm going to ask Toff to get us a computer.'

'A computer!' Nicole felt like a parrot repeating daft phrases.

'Yes. There's far too much paperwork for you nurses to do, the MO too. I know some of the official stuff can't be avoided, but we can make the records more efficient and less time-consuming.'

'Are you sure it's necessary? The Lodge is only the equivalent of a small nursing home.'

'So? I use a home computer to do my tax returns! I'm amazed you aren't using one here. The hotel's full of them! You should have been given one as a matter of course.'

'I suppose Toff thought the work didn't warrant it,' Nicole shrugged.

'Because nobody told him it did,' said Sloan. 'Toff takes advice; he doesn't concern himself with detail. Whoever set up the records and accounting system for the Lodge was probably shy of computers and refused to have one. I doubt that Toff's even aware you haven't one.'

'That could be the reason,' Nicole said. 'It was all set up by my predecessor, who was rather elderly. I believe she resented any interference from the hotel management, so Dorothy, the office manager, told me.'

Sloan gave her a sly look. 'Territorial jealousy,' he murmured.

Nicole flinched at what was surely a dig at her. 'I believe she was Toff's aunt.'

'Yes, he mentioned her. He was very fond of her, it seems, so, although she was retired, he gave her the job because she wanted something to do, and left her to it. Well, she might have been a very competent nurse, but that doesn't necessarily make people a whiz at systems.'

Nicole said drily, 'And in taking over from her, I seem to have overlooked a number of obvious things. You must think I'm very old-fashioned too.'

Sloan leaned towards her. 'I think you're very competent. When you run on oiled wheels, nobody notices you. They take you for granted. The Lodge is splendidly run, Nicole, but you don't have to stick with the status quo. You'd like a computer, wouldn't you?'

'Of course.' Now that he had suggested it, Nicole felt very inept for not doing so herself.

'Good, we'll put it to Toff this evening.'

A few days later, Nicole found herself supervising the installation of the computer and also helping Sloan set up the new surgery down at the hotel. In spite of herself, she was excited at the changes. She could hardly wait to transfer all her records to the computer. Dorothy Rayner, the office manager at the hotel, had promised to help her with the programme, so she expected to be able to do the job quickly and smoothly.

Jan, of course, was characteristically sceptical. When it arrived, she patted the monitor condescendingly. 'If you don't live up to your reputation, mate, you get tipped over the cliff!'

Nicole laughed. 'Computers are only as good as the people who operate them.'

'And I'm one of those who generate hate in inanimate objects,' said Jan. 'Best I keep well away from it, Nic.'

Nicole didn't press the issue then, but she was fully determined that Jan and Sharon should learn to use it too. Sharon, she felt sure, would have no problems. She was young enough to have used computers at school.

The new surgery at the hotel took shape rapidly. As anything Sloan Reilly had a hand in was bound to, Nicole realised. Two adjoining rooms used for storage of sporting equipment were allocated to the surgery, at first much to Murray Peterson's dismay.

'But, darling,' he complained to Nicole, 'where am I going to put all the gear?'

Nicole grinned. 'I suggest you ask Sloan. He'll know!'

Murray's mouth turned down. 'This is all very disruptive. We've got another big conference. . .' He wandered off, muttering.

Sloan, of course, had been ferreting about on his own, and, as Nicole had predicted, he had found some spare space which was adequate for the storage, and in fact more conveniently situated for people wanting to borrow tennis racquets, golf clubs, snorkelling gear and other equipment.

'They don't need all this space,' he told Nicole as they surveyed the rooms. 'It's a waste, but ideal for our purpose. This room will be quite big enough for you, and the other for consultations and treatments.' He looked at her for confirmation.

'Yes, fine,' she agreed.

So the very next day the sports gear was shifted and carpenters, plumbers and painters moved in to transform the vacated rooms into a surgery.

'When Sloan wants something done,' Nicole said to Jan, 'it's a case of "yesterday". Fortunately Toff's able to get things done at that sort of speed.'

'He won't be with us long—Sloan, I mean,' said Jan. 'A man with his energy will get fed up when he's turned the place on its ear, and there's nothing more he can do.'

'I don't think he ever intended to stay long,' Nicole remarked. 'He's just filling in for a while as a favour to Toff. Until Toff can get someone else, I suppose.'

'Anything to do with Mrs Mason?' Jan asked with a meaningful smile.

'What do you mean?'

'Oh, come on, Nic, you know as well as I do that those two are more than just good friends.'

Nicole raised an eyebrow. 'Are they? I know Mrs Mason is greatly improved lately, and I suppose that could be due to Sloan's treatment.'

'Which is mainly TLC of the most welcome kind, if you ask me,' said Jan. 'You don't suppose he was the cause of her breakdown and over-use of medication in the first place? And now they're making up.'

'I don't suppose anything,' Nicole said shortly. 'I don't think we should gossip about it.'

Jan grinned. 'I do believe you're beginning to like our new doctor!' She fled before Nicole could retort.

The first day that surgery was held in the hotel brought in enough patients to prove Sloan's point—that people would use the service more if it was closer. Nicole had to agree. She didn't really mind that the appointment sheet was filled the night before or that a few patients dropped in without appointments and had to be squeezed in. Sloan's insistence on holding surgery in the morning instead of the afternoon had also proved a popular change. It had meant a slight rearrangement of routine at the Lodge, but nothing that inconvenienced the patients there.

Nicole was tidying up as usual after the surgery had closed, Sloan having vanished, when the door opened and he came back bearing a tray with coffee-pot and cups and a plate of delicious-looking cakes.

'Reward!' he said, grinning at her. 'For both of us. That was a hectic two hours, wasn't it?'

'Busier than usual, yes,' she admitted.

'But not just a string of whingers and hypochondriacs?' His look was a challenge.

'No. You were quite right—it's better to hold surgery down here.'

Sloan poured her a cup of coffee and pushed the plate of cakes towards her. 'Sit down, Nicole. You've been on your feet all morning.'

'Nurses usually are. We have strong feet and legs.'

He perched on the corner of the desk. 'And some are very shapely too,' he murmured, his eyes dropping to hers as she sat in his chair, her uniform skirt riding up to give him a glimpse of smoothly rounded knees.

'I hope that woman with the skin cancer will seek treatment as soon as she gets home,' said Nicole, selecting a rich chocolate cake.

Sloan swallowed a mouthful of the confection he had chosen. 'Mmm, that's delicious, but not good for my waistline, I'm sure.' He considered Nicole's remark for a moment. 'Perhaps we ought to do more about warning people about skin cancer. A few posters. . .'

'Yes, why not?' she agreed at once. 'There's plenty of space on the walls in the ante-room.' She paused, then said eagerly, 'And what about somewhere everyone can see them? I know Toff won't want posters stuck up all over the place, but we could put one up in the pharmacy, and in the new sports equipment store— just about everyone goes there at some time or other.' she tapped her lip thoughtfully. 'We could ask Murray about the main office. They have travel posters there.'

It was a moment before she realised that Sloan was quietly chuckling.

'What are you laughing at?' she demanded.

'You! Two weeks ago you'd have killed me with a look if I'd suggested anything else innovative. Now you're having ideas yourself.'

Nicole lowered her eyes and bit into her cake, which prevented her from speaking for a minute or two at least. It was all too true that Sloan's energy and enthusiasm were catching and he had motivated her. She had ceased being resentful of him because he wasn't Bob, but she was still wary, still keeping him at arm's length. Not that he'd made any attempt to approach any closer since that night he had kissed her.

He said, 'I'll get some posters sent over. After all, skin cancer is the most common form of carcinoma in this country, and more prevalent in Queensland than anywhere else. People should be aware that they're at risk when they sunbathe and engage in sporting activities in the sun.' Grinning at her, he added, 'Go on, have another.'

Nicole had been looking at the remaining cakes, wondering if she should. She glanced up guiltily. 'I shouldn't. . .'

'You can work it off swimming or playing tennis,' he said.

'Is that medical advice?'

Sloan laughed. 'No. Just giving you an excuse. You have one, I'll have the other, and we'll be bilious together.'

'Or get fat.'

His eyes slid over her approvingly. 'You'll never get fat—you're too active. And you have the body type that stays slim.'

'That's all I need to know,' said Nicole, reaching for the cake. She munched for a moment, then said, 'You made a terrific job of the plaster on that executive's broken finger. He'll even be able to wield a golf club—in a fashion.'

'But it was you who noticed the skin cancer first,' Sloan reminded her. 'Well done.'

They smiled at each other in an amicable way. Nicole, suddenly noticing, said, 'Your hand has healed up quickly, and the bump on your forehead has almost gone.' He was combing his hair back the other way again.

He inclined his head, laughing at her. 'A tribute to your TLC!'

Embarrassed by the intimacy of his look, Nicole rose, collecting the few crumbs that had fallen into her lap and depositing them on the plate. 'I'd better get back to the Lodge.'

'I'll come with you,' said Sloan. 'Because of preparing for our first day here, I didn't get around to seeing the Lodge patients this morning, and I wouldn't want them to feel neglected.'

'I'm sure they understand,' Nicole said. There was one, though, who might have been disappointed, she thought. Mrs Mason.

Sloan picked up the tray. 'I'll find a pair of hands to shove this into—you lock up.'

He was gone in a flash, cups rattling on the tray. Nicole hoped he wouldn't crash into anyone. She pushed the chair back tidily into the desk and then noticed that he'd left his beeper behind. She shoved it in her bag. She was just turning the key in the lock of the new surgery when a rather distraught young man in skimpy shorts and thongs came running along the corridor.

'Sister. . .'

'We've just finished for the day,' Nicole told him. 'Unless it's urgent?' He didn't look ill or injured, just suntanned and vibrantly healthy.

'It's Julie,' he said, a note of panic in his tone. 'I think she's going to have the baby!'

Nicole was instantly back on full alert. 'Where is she?'

'In our cabin. Is the doctor. . .?'

'He's still here somewhere,' said Nicole. 'I'll look, you go to the office and get them to page him on the PA system. He's not carrying his beeper at the moment. What's your cabin number?'

'Ten.' Already moving off, he pointed back over his shoulder. 'That way. Last one nearest the beach.'

Nicole hesitated. Sloan had possibly already gone to the buggy rank where he would not be able to hear the PA call, so she'd better check it out first. No, she decided, she'd best get to Cabin Number Ten as quickly as she could. In the foyer, which she had to cross to reach the exit to the cabins, she saw a staff member and sent her off to find Sloan and organise a stretcher in case it was needed.

She ran down the ramp from the hotel to the swimming-pool area, across the patio and along the pathway where thatched cabins were strategically placed for privacy and scenic appeal. She found Number Ten without any problem. The door was open and the sound of a woman groaning came from inside.

Nicole dashed into the bedroom and found a prostrate figure on the double bed. The woman was very young, with long fair hair and pretty features, but at the moment the agony of labour had changed her prettiness to pain and her hair was damp with perspiration. As the spasm passed, she managed to smile. 'Where's Tim?' she muttered.

'He's getting the doctor. I'm Nicole Gardiner, the resort nurse.'

'Sorry about this! The baby's not due for another couple of weeks. I suppose it was mad to come away on holiday so near the end, but I was feeling so washed out. . .'

Nicole grasped her wrist, feeling for her pulse. One glance had given her cause for worry. The girl's legs were puffy and she had dark smudges under her eyes. 'Dr Reilly will be here in a minute,' she soothed. 'Your husband's having him paged.'

'Tim's not my husband,' the girl said. 'We—we're not married. . .' Tears started to course down her cheeks. 'I—I wanted to get married, but Tim's not sure, he doesn't want to be tied down. . . He didn't really want me to have the baby. I'm so afraid he'll leave me now.'

'That can happen whether you're married or not,' Nicole reminded her. 'Now, how close together are your contractions, Julie?'

Julie did not have time to tell her, because the next spasm came and she cried out, clinging desperately to Nicole's hand, digging her fingernails deeply into her palm. With her free hand Nicole reached for a handful of tissues from a box on the bedside table and gently wiped the girl's forehead as she murmured encouraging words.

It was with relief that she saw Sloan enter the room. His assessment of the situation was rapid, and Nicole saw by his frown that he was as worried about the girl's general condition as she was.

Tim came in right behind him, and after him Danny and another man carrying a stretcher.

'I don't think we've got time to take her up to the Lodge,' Sloan said.

Nicole was already halfway to the door. 'I'll go and open up the surgery.' She flew back into the hotel, closely followed by Sloan and the patient.

A few minutes later, she watched anxiously as Sloan carried out a further examination in the treatment-room. It wasn't hard for her to interpret his deep frown, and she wasn't surprised when he drew her far enough aside to be out of earshot, and said in a low, urgent tone, 'The baby's in the breech position, and I can't turn it. And what's more, we've got pre-eclamptic toxaemia with a real risk of renal failure. She ought to be in a proper hospital!' The seriousness of the situation was clearly written in his face.

Nicole sucked in a sharp breath. 'You mean she'll have to have a Caesar?' she murmured hesitantly, although knowing there was no alternative.

His expression grim, Sloan nodded. 'Right away.'

With a shock Nicole realised that he meant to do the operation himself, right there. 'But. . .wouldn't it be better to fly her to Mackay?' she blurted out, because she could not help the fear that there might be complications too great for them to cope with.

Sloan said flatly, 'No. There isn't time.' He gave her a half-smile. 'This is one time we can't pass the buck. Don't worry, Sister, I'm a competent surgeon!'

'Of course. I didn't mean. . .' Nicole felt she had insulted him.

His face relaxed briefly into a grin, and his glance was a trifle sardonic. 'Just as well we got all that *unnecessary* equipment, eh?' As Nicole flinched at the dig, he went on briskly, 'Get the instruments we need down here quickly. And for the anaesthetic, bupivacaine. I got some ampoules of Marcain, luckily.'

Nicole's eyebrows shot up. 'But that's for. . .'

'An epidural. Yes. I think it would be best for several reasons medically, including the fact that I shall have to be surgeon and anaesthetist, and also because I suspect immediate mother-and-baby bonding will be of paramount importance in this case. And it'll be good for the father too!'

Nicole was amazed at how much he had read of the situation. She glanced back into the room at Tim, standing rigidly near the examination table where Julie lay, holding her hand. Would he care if the baby died? Or would he be relieved? And Julie herself—how would she react? A Caesarean section under general anaesthetic meant that the mother would not see or hold her baby until some hours after the birth. This often meant difficulties with mother-and-baby bonding, breastfeeding, and even more post-operative pain. In a case like that of Julie and Tim, parents who had not really wanted to be parents, a more 'normal' birth could make a huge psychological difference. Sloan had seen that at once.

'You'd better tell them,' she whispered. 'I'll ring Jan and ask her to bring what we need.' In case he didn't know, she added, 'She's a midwife.'

'Tell her to hurry!' Sloan said urgently. 'We might not have much time. . .either for the baby or Julie.'

Nicole ran to the phone. Jan did not waste time on questions. 'I'm on my way!' she replied instantly to

Nicole's urgent request, and crashed the phone down. Nicole went back to Sloan and the patient. Tim was looking pale. She pushed a high stool across to him.

'Sit down, Tim.' She gave him a smile. 'You're staying?'

He had a tight grip of Julie's hand and gave a faint smile. 'She won't let go!'

'Don't leave me, Tim. Please don't leave me!' Julie begged, clutching his hand all the tighter.

He bent his head to hers, running his fingers through her tousled hair. 'I won't, Jules, of course I won't.' To Nicole, he said, 'Dr Reilly has explained what's going to happen.'

Nicole glanced at them as she set up a drip, and hoped they loved each other enough to stay together, whether the child survived or not. She gave Tim a small towel so he could wipe the perspiration from Julie's face when needed.

It was the first time Nicole had assisted in a delivery, let alone a Caesarean section, for all of three years, and as the moment arrived she suddenly felt nervous. But Sloan seemed to read her mind, and in a moment when they were far enough away for Tim and Julie not to hear, he bent close and whispered, 'Don't worry, it's a while since I did a Caesar too! But like riding a bike, you don't forget!'

'Sloan. . .' Nicole felt herself relax at his joke. Or was it? Was he as nervous as she was?

She relaxed even more when Jan joined them, bearing instruments, sterile gowns and other paraphernalia. 'Oh, boy!' she exclaimed. 'I do so love delivering babies.' She beamed at Tim and Julie. 'Congratulations, folks. You're the first in the new Bauhinia Sands

maternity wing! But please don't call the baby
Bauhinia!'

And then the jokes were over. They helped each
other into gowns and masks, Tim included, and swiftly
prepared the patient. Jan and Nicole gently moved
Julie on her side and Sloan slowly pushed the needle
into the epidural cavity between the membranes protecting the spinal cord, careful not to enter the subar-
achnoid space. Julie groaned.

As he withdrew the needle, Sloan smiled at her.
'Sorry! But now you'll have no pain for several hours,
and I hope not too much afterwards. It's a fact, as I'm
sure Jan here will confirm, and Nicole, that Caesarean
section this way, with you anaesthetised only from the
waist down, will mean a lot less pain and discomfort
afterwards. Write and tell me if I'm wrong!' He chatted
casually while the anaesthetic took effect, reassuring
Julie that everything was perfectly normal and would
soon be over. If he was anxious or nervous, it was not
showing, Nicole thought, admiring his cool, calm
demeanour.

She brought pillows for support, and placed them
under Julie as Sloan directed to tilt her slightly downwards at the head. She arranged the drapes and
checked the IV drip and oxygen. Jan was the one on
this occasion to directly assist, and she was deftly
setting up the instrument tray ready for Sloan.

There was tension in the small room, but also, Nicole
felt, confidence. Sloan had the ability to calm nerves
and imbue confidence without appearing to make any
conscious effort to do so. Her own initial panic had
subsided and she could see that, although apprehensive, even Julie and Tim were quietly accepting.

When, with swift precision, Sloan made the incision

in Julie's abdomen, Nicole momentarily held her breath. When the baby emerged and was held up by Jan, who shot her a triumphant glance, she felt a smile breaking all over her face. Moments later, the familiar reassuring wail of the infant brought a sigh of relief from everyone. Jan thrust the baby into Nicole's waiting hands, and turned to help Sloan close the wound.

'It's a girl!' she announced with a certain pride.

'Is she all right?' It was a chorus from Julie and Tim.

'She's fine,' said Sloan, and the taut lines in his forehead slowly eased out. Nicole found herself looking across the table at him with admiration and a strange fluttery feeling inside her.

'Well done!' she whispered, mimicking his earlier remark to her.

His eyes smiled back at her and for an instant there seemed to be a special kind of personal rapport that made Nicole want to leap across the table, fling her arms around his neck and kiss him. But that was only a foolishness engendered by the relief and joy she felt because a new life had just been brought into the world successfully despite less than perfect circumstances. The new baby was a shared triumph for all of them.

CHAPTER FIVE

NEXT day, when Nicole was preparing Julie and the baby for their trip back to the mainland, which Sloan had told Nicole, but not the new parents, was a matter of urgency in view of Julie's condition, the young mother suddenly said,

'I'm sorry we caused so much trouble, Nicole, but I'm really glad the baby came early.'

Nicole looked down into the soft pink face of the sleeping child. 'Why's that?' she asked.

Julie held out her left hand, and Nicole saw with amazement the ring sparkling there. Julie's smile was pure bliss. 'We're engaged! Isn't it marvellous? I can hardly believe it, Nicole. Tim went and bought the ring last night—he got he got the manager to open up the jewellery shop specially. He said being with me at the birth had made him realise he was truly in love with me and that all he wanted in the world was me and the baby. He went through agony, he said, terrified I might die or the baby would.'

Nicole felt tears smarting her eyes as Julie's misted over with happiness. 'I'm so glad,' she said, squeezing the girl's hand. 'He's a nice man, Julie. I'm sure you'll be happy. Worriers make good husbands!'

Julie laughed. 'I love him so much, and I was so afraid he'd leave me, but I don't think he will now. He's really a very kind and loving person.'

'And a very proud father!' Nicole added, 'By the way, have you decided what to call her yet?'

Julie grinned. 'I was never game to suggest choosing a name. Last night we talked, and we think Nicole is a nice name. Would you mind?'

Nicole was surprised and touched. 'I'm honoured,' she smiled.

'Well, it'll be Nicole Ann. Nicole Ann Roberts,' Julie said proudly. 'As soon as I'm out of hospital, we're going to get married.'

'Who's getting married?' Sloan came in to give Julie a final check, and had to be told the story. He nodded approvingly.

Sloan and Nicole saw the new parents and their baby safely aboard the aircraft, then returned to the surgery for the morning consultations.

'Let's hope we have a quiet day,' said Sloan. 'We've had a little too much excitement around here recently.'

'Unless crises go in threes,' said Nicole, pulling a face. She opened the appointments book. 'Any minute now!'

There were no crises that morning. There were, in fact, very few patients, and Sloan had little more to do than write prescriptions for stomach upsets, a sinus attack, an ear infection and Tenormin tablets for a woman with hypertension who had lost hers. Nicole was as little pressured, only needing to assist Sloan a couple of times in the treatment-room. It was a welcome relief.

They lunched together, and Nicole felt more at ease with him than she had so far. They were, she felt, beginning to build a good professional relationship. That they had got off on the wrong foot was, she knew, partly her fault, but Sloan seemed to bear no grudge over it.

* * *

When Nicole took her next full day off, she decided to get right away to a quiet cove that was rarely used by the hotel guests and enjoy some snorkelling. Drifting along on the surface of the water, looking at coral and shells, fish and seaweed, was her idea of complete relaxation. Jan was assisting Sloan in the surgery, and, although she did not expect to be needed, Nicole took her beeper just in case. That third crisis hadn't cropped up yet, she reminded herself, laughing at her own superstition.

The cove was on the other side of the island, and to give herself some exercise, she chose a bicycle instead of a beach buggy to transport her there. The day was warm, with low humidity and a light breeze, the ocean calm and ideal for her purpose. She was pleased to find her cove deserted and quickly established herself in a shady spot under a rocky overhang before entering the water.

The water was deliciously soft and cool and so translucent that even at some depth the sulight dappled the pale sand of the ocean floor. Floating above it, taking the occasional dive over outcrops of coral reef, Nicole spent a fascinating morning observing sea creatures and collecting one or two empty shells.

After eating her packed lunch, she lazed for a while, then, drawn by the ocean again, went back for another spell of exploring. The cramps in her right leg came so suddenly that she spat out the mouthpiece of her snorkelling gear as she gasped at the pain. She sank, swallowing a fair amount of seawater, and then, endeavouring to tread water, she realised that she had drifted further than she had intended. The beach was a long way off. There were rocks closer at hand, but

Nicole was afraid she wouldn't be able to reach them either.

How am I going to get back? she thought in sudden panic as the pain in her leg almost paralysed it and she kept going under. She tried to massage her calf, but could not manage this and stay afloat.

Then she saw a figure on the beach. She waved madly, trying to swim towards the shore, but she was breathless now, losing energy fast. Eventually, all she could do was to float on her back and hope that whoever was back there on the beach had seen her and would come to her assistance.

It seemed like forever, but must have only been a few minutes before she heard a man's voice calling, 'Hang on! I'm coming!'

It sounded like Sloan, but it couldn't be. . . It was, and all at once she was in his arms, clinging to him, nearly drowning them both.

'Cramp. . .' she spluttered. 'In my leg. Can't swim properly. . .oooh!' The pain knifed again and she doubled up, nearly dragging him under.

Keeping her head above water, Sloan said, 'I think we'd better take a rest on the rocks rather than try and get back to the beach right away. You need to get your breath back.' He hooked his arm around her neck and executed a strong back-stroke which brought them close to a large flat rock which was easily accessible. He hauled her up on to it.

'Crisis number three!' he said.

Nicole clutched her leg and rested her head on her knee. She felt nausea. She had never suffered quite such a crippling cramp before.

'Here, let me. . .'

Sloan placed himself in front of her, caught hold of

her leg and pulled it out straight. He removed both her
flippers and began to massage the knotted calf muscles
gently but firmly. Water dripped off them both, but in
moments their skin was drying in the sun. Nicole
watched with a curious kind of fascination as Sloan's
large strong hands manipulated her muscles with practised ease. It felt wonderful. Slowly the paralysis ebbed
and she felt the life coming back into her leg. She
wiggled her toes.

'That's better,' she sighed. 'I've never had such a
severe attack before, not in my leg. Thank you, Doctor,
you've done the trick!' Embarrassed by the intimacy of
his touch, and the realisation that she was sitting there
in a very skimpy bikini while he was scarcely any more
modestly clad, she pulled her leg up. 'It's OK now—
really. Thanks.' She smiled and knew she was blushing
from the faint amusement on his face.

'Sure?' he queried.

'Yes. The warmth helps.' She drew both knees up
under her chin and looked at him over them. 'You
found me in the nick of time.'

'I dare say you'd have made it back to shore
somehow.'

Nicole glanced towards the distant curve of beach. 'I
shouldn't have been out so far, but it was so interesting
I got carried away. I was following a pair of butterfly
fish.'

'Do you do this often?' he asked.

'Fairly often. It's very relaxing. I go scuba-diving
sometimes too—not alone, of course—only if there's a
goup going out on my day off. Life under the sea
fascinates me.'

'You look a bit like a mermaid, especially with
flippers on,' Sloan observed, and his dark eyes were

more enigmatic than ever in the bright light. 'But you're not, and you shouldn't go snorkelling alone. Anything could happen. And did.'

'Well, it wasn't fatal.' Nicole was surprised at his concern, which, from his tone, was obviously sincere, but she wished he would stop lecturing her. 'Hadn't we better get back to shore?' she suggested. 'We'll be getting skin cancer exposed out here!'

'No rush. . . It's a low UV day today,' he murmured, and clasped her ankles, pulling her legs out straight again.

Nicole was startled, and fell back to rest on her elbows. 'Hey, what are you doing? It's OK now.'

Sloan moved closer and slid a hand across her waist. His touch burned her skin and caused a worse knotting up inside her than the cramps in her leg. 'I thought I might just be eligible for a small reward,' he said softly, and stretched out alongside her, deftly turning her into his arms and matching his lips to hers before she could even gasp her amazement.

His kiss was salty, and sweet, the warmth of his mouth tantalising on hers and his bare skin meeting hers in numerous places so intoxicating that Nicole found herself tilting her head back and pressing herself closer in spite of herself. The cloudless blue sky seemed to whirl above her head and the cries of gulls were like the echoes of scolding voices far, far away.

Breathless from the length of the kiss, they finally drew apart, looked in startled wonder into each other's eyes and then came close again. Now Sloan's embrace was harder still, and Nicole was in no doubt that he desired her. She was shocked to find her own desire reaching uncontrollable limits, and when his hand slid between her thighs, burning her skin, it was only with an effort that she pushed him away.

'Sloan. . .no. . .' A sob flecked her voice.

He rained kisses on her face, her neck, her breasts, heedless of her small cries of protest. 'You're so lovely,' he murmured, his voice husky and low. 'Nicole. . . I want you so much. . .' He raised his head, looked down into her face while his hand now slowly caressed one erect nipple. 'You're beautiful. . . You drive a man crazy just looking at him. It drives me crazy just looking at you!' His gaze strayed down the length of her and his fingertips caressed her arms, her waist, her stomach and her thighs with almost irresistible temptation.

'No. . .' Nicole breathed weakly, trying to turn away from him, yet wanting desperately to lose herself in his arms.

Sloan turned her round and held her face in his hands, kissing her mouth, her nose, her eyes, with fierce possessiveness. He stretched out and held her close to him again, every move calculated, she knew, to break down her resistance. She wasn't angry with him. He was obeying age-old impulses that caused desire to spark between a man and a woman, especially when they were both more than half naked. She was vulnerable and he knew it. She could hardly blame him for wanting to take advantage. But did she want it to happen?

For Nicole the decision never had to be made. A loudhailer suddenly shattered the moment. 'Hey there! Do you need help? Are you stranded? Do you want to be rescued? Or do you just want to be alone?'

A yacht with a man and a woman aboard was fifty or so metres away. Hastily adjusting her top, Nicole jumped up and yelled, 'We're stranded!' She glanced down at Sloan and saw the unspoken curse in his eyes. But he smiled in defeat and hauled himself up, to wave to the boat.

'Saved by the loudhailer,' he said, rubbing his fingers sensuously across her waist again and massaging the end of her spine until she shivered involuntarily, and stepped aside.

'Stop it!' she told him, trying to sound grim, and failing.

The boat came in as close as possible and they jumped into the water and clambered aboard. The couple on the yacht, who introduced themselves as Wendy and Richard, were from the resort. Nicole explained what had happened. The couple exchanged an amused look but tactfully did not comment on the intimate scene they must have witnessed at least partially.

'We decided to have afternoon tea at this cove,' Wendy explained. 'Sorry if we're butting in. . .' She was wearing a see-through green shift over a white swimsuit. She tossed her dark hair and gave Sloan a slow smile.

'Not at all,' Sloan said. 'And thanks for rescuing us.'

Wendy extended the provocative smile. 'You're the resort doctor, aren't you?' She glanced briefly at Nicole. 'And you're the nurse.'

'Sister Gardiner's in charge of the Lodge,' Sloan told her.

'I suppose that keeps you very busy,' the woman said without interest, except in Sloan. 'You'll join us for a cuppa?'

When Sloan smiled back, Nicole felt a twinge she preferred not to identify. She saw Richard frown.

'Thanks,' said Sloan. 'That would be nice, eh, Nicole?'

Wendy linked her arm through his, dancing her fingers lightly on his wrist. 'Let's go below, shall we? Richard, you can drop anchor without me, can't you?' She laughed. 'I'm not very good with boats!'

For Nicole it was a painful hour. She should have been glad that Sloan's attention was drawn away from her, she knew, yet she wasn't reacting that way. She shocked herself by being jealous of the looks he was giving Wendy. And to make matters worse, Richard, also jealous presumably, decided to flirt with her. Nicole was glad when Sloan said they must be going.

They waded ashore from the yacht, and Nicole raised a polite hand in farewell as the boat glided out beyond the cove.

'Phew!' exclaimed Sloan, flinging an arm around her shoulder.

She tried to shake it off, but he caught both her shoulders and drew her close, his dark eyes burning into hers. 'Poor Richard—he won't keep tabs on that young woman for long!'

'Not when other men seem to enjoy themselves so much flirting with her,' Nicole responded tartly.

Sloan's arms closed more tightly around her and he chuckled. 'I do believe you were jealous, but you seemed to be finding Richard rather interesting.'

'I. . .'

Nicole's reply was lost in the dry warmth of his mouth on hers, the firmness of his lips which quickly became soft and searching and moist. She could feel her heartbeat thrumming against his chest, slightly out of step with his, and the hardness of his body against hers stirred her emotions to a fever pitch. She felt the catch on her bikini top snap and the scrap of material fall to the ground, and there was a small satisfied groan from Sloan as her breasts were erotically teased by the sprinkling of hair on his chest.

'Nicole,' he breathed, 'you're wonderful! You have such a beautiful body, so warm and supple and. . .'

She stood transfixed as he trailed hot kissses down her neck and shoulders, his hands sliding down her arms as he sank slowly to his knees, kissing the swell of her breasts and lingering on her nipples before caressing with his lips the sensitive skin of her midriff, the projections of her hipbones, until he held her small buttocks cupped in his hands and his head was pressed against her belly.

'Sloan. . .' She moved slightly, and he held her closer, pulling her down until they toppled over on to the damp sand. Behind them the ocean caressed the beach with light foaming fingers, just like Sloan's fingers on her body, reaching across the sand the way his fingers reached further and further, seeking possession. The incident with the yacht had been no more than an interruption, with Wendy's provocativeness serving merely to heighten his ardour. With his fingers threading through her hair, his mouth devouring her, his legs twining with hers, Nicole was losing the battle of wills.

'I want to go back. . .' she whispered.

Sloan raised himself on one elbow. 'Back? Back to the beginning, you mean? Like this. . .' He was kissing her again, starting with her lips, then her eyes. And laughing softly at her.

'No! Back to the resort.'

He pinned her arms to the sand. 'Nicole. . . Not

yet. . .' He looked longingly into her face. 'Don't you want to. . .?'

'No!' She struggled under him, and all at once he rolled away.

'OK, let's go.' He got up, held out his hand to her and dragged her up the beach to where she had left her towel and wrap, the picnic basket and other belongings. He had left a rolled-up towel, hat and a satchel beside them.

As Nicole grabbed her own hat and clamped it firmly on her head, she was shivering, but not with cold. Then a sound she didn't at first register rang in her ears. Only when she heard Sloan's expletive and saw him dive at the satchel did it dawn on her that it was his beeper.

He silenced it and looked at her. 'The loudhailers and beepers are all on your side today, it seems!'

'I wonder what the emergency is,' Nicole said worriedly. She tucked her own appliance into her bag.'I wish we had those units the police have that you can use like a telephone.'

Although he had voiced no anxiety, Sloan was hurrying. The doctor would not be called back from an afternoon off unless there was an urgent reason. They ran up the beach to where Nicole had left her bicycle, and there she saw the buggy he had brought.

'We'll stow your bike on board and you can come back with me,' he said, acting at once on his own suggestion.

Nicole didn't argue. She climbed in beside him, and Sloan turned the buggy round and headed back to the resort as fast as the electrically powered vehicle was able to go. Back at the Lodge, Sloan jumped down from the buggy and strode inside ahead of Nicole. He went straight to the office to find out what the emergency was, whether it was at the Lodge or the hotel, and Nicole followed, carrying their gear.

She headed straight for the office too, and met Jan in the corridor.

'What's the emergency?' she asked.

'You'll see,' said Jan, with a dark, disapproving look.

Puzzled, Nicole went into the office. Sloan was already there, and so was someone else, a small dark-haired girl in a red quilted jacket over a T-shirt that said 'I'm all yours' above pouting lips, and underneath, 'At a price.' She was also wearing blue jeans and a wide blue bandeau around her elbow-length hair. She was pouting almost as much as the lips on the T-shirt.

Sloan was saying angrily, 'And you don't insist on them calling me on the beeper. That's for emergencies.'

The girl waved a slender hand at him, and Nicole noticed several chunky rings and tinkling bangles.

'What should I have done?' she answered cheekily. 'Concussed myself or cut my wrists? Is that the only way you can get attention around here?' She caught sight of Nicole. 'Oh, I see. Is this what was grabbing your attention all afternoon? Is she another one of your women?'

'That will do, Lucy!' The force of Sloan's voice made even Nicole jump, and she was sure she saw his hand begin to rise involuntarily, but he clenched his fist instead. His glance at her was apologetic. 'Nicole, this is my daughter Lucy. She isn't usually so rude, but she was a bit put out when she arrived and I wasn't here. Unfortunately, I didn't know she was coming today.'

Ignoring the contempt in the girl's look, Nicole held out a hand to Sloan's daughter. 'Hello, Lucy. I'm the charge sister at the Lodge. How did you come, on the boat or plane?'

Lucy looked her over disdainfully, instant dislike burning in dark eyes that were her father's. There was a hint of him in the rest of her features, but something else too, an elfin beauty that was disguised at the moment by truculence and bad temper.

'I walked,' Lucy said deadpan. 'On the water. You can do anything you want, you know, if you try.' She angled her head and gave Nicole further appraisal. 'Did you seduce him, or did he rape you?'

'Lucy!'

'It's all right, Sloan,' Nicole said quietly. The girl was very uptight and she was sure the rudeness was a defence mechanism. She went on, 'Shall we have some coffee? I'm dying for a cup.'

Lucy held her gaze for a moment and Nicole refused to be the first to look away. Lucy eventually averted her eyes, and mumbled, 'Actually I came over by boat, not the ferry, though. I was waiting for it when these guys offered me a lift on their yacht. . .' She rolled her eyes and twisted her mouth provocatively.

'Lucy. . .' Sloan's tone was more anxious than angry now.

She pulled a derogatory face, and mimicked his tone. 'Da-ad.' She shot a defiant look at Nicole. 'They were real cute.' She grinned wickedly and looked for a moment astonishingly like her father. 'We sat in the saloon drinking gin and shooting smack.'

Sloan took a menacing step forward. 'That's enough! I think we'd better go to the house.'

'Why don't you make us some coffee first?' Nicole suggested. 'You'll find some biscuits in the big tin.'

Sloan looked belligerent as though he resented her

interference, then indecisive, and finally he stomped off.

Lucy was admiring. 'Wow! You've got his measure, haven't you? I never heard anyone speak to him like that.' Then she looked sullen again. 'What am I doing here? I could be having a great time. . .' She sighed theatrically. 'It's a pretty daggy dump, isn't it? Aren't you bored out of your mind?'

'No, I rather like it here,' Nicole said calmly. She went on, 'I thought you weren't coming until the holidays.'

Lucy's face closed up, then she said defiantly, 'I couldn't stand another minute of that revolting school. I quit.' She gave a shrug. 'Dad's off the deep end about it, of course.' She stared at Nicole with scorn. 'Which is hardly surprising, I suppose. He doesn't want a daughter stuffing up his sex life, does he? I'm used to being in the way. I'm just a millstone round his neck.'

Nicole skimmed idly through some messages on her desk. 'Oh, I don't think you'll stuff anything up, Lucy. There's enough room on Bauhinia Island for both of you. You'll find plenty to do once you look around.' The rest of the girl's comments she ignored.

'Is he any good?' Lucy demanded, her full lips sneering a little.

Nicole bit back a sharp retort. The girl was deliberately trying to shock. 'He's very good at his job,' she answered, meeting Lucy's stare unwaveringly. 'You should be proud of him. He did a first-rate Caesarean section the other day, and not under ideal conditions, I can tell you.'

'That wasn't what I meant,' said Lucy, still baiting.

'I'm sorry. I thought. . . What did you mean?'

'In bed, of course!'

Feeling it was time, Nicole hardened her tone and said, 'That, Lucy, is none of your business.'

As she finished speaking, Sloan returned with the coffee. Nicole immediately started talking about the joys of snorkelling, and after a few minutes she was gratified to see the scorn in Lucy's face diminish a little. In spite of herself, she was interested.

'You can come with me one day, if you like,' Nicole offered. 'When you've nothing better to do, of course.'

'I guess I'll need to fill in time somehow,' Lucy said in a bored tone.

Nicole glanced at Sloan and knew that he, like her, was controlling a strong desire to slap the girl's face or shake her. Finally she said, 'I'll ask one of the maids to make up the spare room in your house, Sloan. And now, if you'll excuse me, I must go and shower and change.'

Lucy gave her a supercilious glance, and Sloan looked exasperated. 'See you later,' he said.

'Much later, I bet,' muttered Lucy, as Nicole went out the door.

Nicole heard Sloan's voice rise in anger, but there was nothing she could do at that point but slip away. Poor Sloan, she thought, he's got a bag full of trouble there. She also thought, Poor Lucy—she's so unhappy.

In the shower recess, she turned the water on full pressure and for a moment or two enjoyed the force of the tiny jets from the shower head battering her skin. She closed her eyes and the whole day rotated before her like a movie. It had been quite a day. She had experienced fear, pain, insult and a kind of fierce joy that had astonished her with its intensity. And she had experienced frustration too.

Be careful, she told herself. Don't let Sloan Reilly

get under your skin just because he's pretty smooth at making love. You can be sure he's had a lot of practice.

In the bedroom she pressed her damp hair into shape and slipped into underclothes. She paused to survey herself in the mirror. '"Another of his women",' she said scornfully, echoing Lucy Reilly's cruel remark. 'No way, Lucy. I'm not one of the Wendys of this world.' Then she rolled her lips into a tight grimace. 'Except I started behaving like one this afternoon.' Nicole paced the room several times, then wrenched a dress from her wardrobe. 'Damn! Damn him and damn every male. They can all go to hell!'

Ready to go to dinner, she walked across to the Lodge to have a few words with Lindy, the night nurse. Lindy was not in the office, so Nicole went to look for her. She caught up with her as the girl was leaving Coralie Mitchell's room.

'Everything OK?' she asked.

Lindy nodded. 'Now it is, I hope. Mrs Mason hasn't been very well today. She vomited twice and Jan said she had a crying fit earlier, so she asked Sloan to see her. He's with her now. She looks terrible, Nic, really drained. I think Jan was worried about her blood-pressure too.'

Nicole said, 'I hope he'll persuade her that she needs specialised hospital treatment. Even he can't give her the care she needs here.'

Lindy agreed. She left Nicole to go and see another patient, and Nicole strolled back towards the entrance. Remembering something she wanted to check in the office, she went in and was looking through a file when she heard low voices outside. She looked up and through the glass pane saw Sloan, with Coralie Mitchell hanging on his arm. They paused at the Lodge entrance

and Sloan said something Nicole did not catch, but
assumed he was saying goodnight and urging her to go
back to bed.

Coralie withdrew her arm slightly, but gripped his
forearm and looked up at him with what seemed to
Nicole like desperate appeal. Then she flung herself
into his arms and they kissed. Nicole looked away,
shrinking down into the shadows as far out of sight as
she could, glad that the main lighting was off and only
the desk lamp was on.

When she finally looked up, Sloan and Coralie had
gone. Nicole sat rigidly in the chair for a few moments.
No, she vowed silently, she was definitely not going to
let Sloan Reilly cause her any pain. She was not going
to let him even get to first base. The fact that her skin
still tingled from his touch was a physical phenomenon
that would quickly fade.

Sloan and his daughter joined Nicole and Jan for
dinner. Lucy was bizarre in a low-cut hot pink top and
tight black mini-skirt. She was decked in jangling
bangles with chains around her neck and her hair was
spiked with mousse in front, and twisted into a rope at
the back. She teetered on ridiculously high thin heels.
Nicole guessed she was still out to shock her father and
anyone else around.

Sloan introduced his daughter to Jan, and although
the girl kept a bored and sullen expression pinned on
her face, she did not deliver any more insults like the
ones she had hurled at Nicole earler. She picked at her
food, drank a glass of wine too quickly, and sighed
heavily several times to underline her contempt for the
scene, her boredom with the conversation.

Nicole tried to draw her into the conversation, as did
Jan, but Lucy seemed unwilling to participate. Sloan

looked strained, Nicole thought. They had finished and were getting up to leave, when Lucy announced,

'I'm going dancing now. See you later.'

Sloan put a restraining hand on her arm. 'No, you're not—not tonight. We've got some talking to do, young lady.'

Lucy gave him a look of pure dislike. 'So it's all right for you to have fun, but not me. Well, hard cheese, Dad. I told the guys who brought me over here today I'd see them after dinner.'

'Lucy! Who are these men?'

She shrugged. 'Just businessmen, I guess.' She preened a little. 'Loaded, I expect. You might even get me off your hands.'

'Don't talk rubbish. All right, go and dance, but I want to meet these friends of yours first. OK?'

Lucy exploded. 'No, it's not OK! What are you trying to do, make me look like a ninny of a schoolgirl?'

'You still are a schoolgirl!' Sloan reminded her.

'I'm sixteen. And I've left school.' She gave a brittle little laugh. 'They won't have me back now, you know.'

'In that gear you look more like twenty,' Sloan told her. 'For heaven's sake, Lucy, don't you know the dangers? Are you completely naïve?'

'I'm not a child!' Her dark eyes flashed in response to her father's own anger. 'So what's it to you? What do you care? Like father, like daughter, eh?' Her pretty lips curled in a sneer and Nicole flinched for Sloan. She glanced at Jan, who was shocked.

'I think we'd better go,' whispered Jan.

Nicole realised that they had been standing there transfixed by the argument when they should have tactfully departed. She said, 'See you later, Sloan. 'Night, Lucy.'

Sloan muttered something, but Lucy ignored the two nurses.

'Nasty little brat!' exclaimed Jan as she and Nicole walked to the buggy park.

'Troubled young woman,' Nicole said slowly.

Jan chuckled. 'Trust you to make excuses for her! Well, all my sympathy is for Sloan. She'll send him grey with worry.' She sighed. 'You're probaby right, of course. Perhaps her behaviour stems from her mother's death.'

'Yes, that's probably it,' Nicole agreed.

'Adolescence is a tough time for some,' said Jan. 'She'll no doubt grow out of it, and come to terms with reality.' She sighed deeply again. 'That's what we all have to do in the end.'

Back at the Lodge they chatted for a while in Nicole's unit, then Jan went off to hers, saying she wanted an early night. Nicole did not comment, but she had noticed that Jan was more subdued lately and not so keen to socialise in the evenings down at the hotel. For all her bravado, she was suffering some heartache over Terry, Nicole felt sure.

Nicole wrote a couple of letters and read a magazine, then decided to turn in herself. Having undressed, she then decided she wanted a supper drink, so she put the kettle on to make decaffeinated coffee. She was just about to pour water on the grounds when there was a knock at her door.

Warily she called out, 'Who's that?'

'Sloan.'

Nicole frowned, threw on a cotton dressing-gown and opened the door. 'It's very late. . .'

He looked a bit distraught. 'Yes, I know, but I

wanted to talk to you.' His eyes begged her not to refuse.

'Come in.' Nicole stood aside and he almost staggered into her unit. 'I was just making myself a cup of coffee. Want one?'

'Thanks.' He slumped into a chair.

She went into the tiny kitchen annexe and made the coffee, saying, 'What's trouble? Lucy?'

He leaned forward and buried his head in his hands. 'Lucy! I don't know what I'm going to do, Nicole. She's totally out of control. I can't do a thing with her.' He looked up as she brought the coffee in and took the mug from her. 'I came to apologise, Nicole—for all the rude, crude things she said. I can hardly believe it's my own daughter I hear saying such things. It's as though the devil's got into her.'

Nicole sat down in the other chair and sipped her coffee. 'Not the devil, Sloan. Unhappiness.'

His mouth twisted. 'You're right, of course. But what can I do about it? I can't bring Helen back. . .'

She put her mug down on the table and reached out to touch his arm. 'Time, Sloan. Lucy just needs time. And you don't have to apologise. She has to vent her misery on someone.'

'But what she insinuates isn't true. . .'

Nicole took a deep breath. 'That's not the point. She's out to shock you and me and anyone else she can, to embarrass you. You rise to her bait too readily, Sloan. You should ignore her.'

'As you did.'

She smiled. 'I certainly wasn't about to argue with her. She was jealous, Sloan. Couldn't you see that? You weren't here when she arrived. She was nervous because she'd quit school again and she knew you'd be angry. In spite of that she was also disappointed because she had to wait for you. She's a pretty mixed-up kid, Sloan.'

'It was my tragedy as well,' he said quietly.

'But you're a man, an adult; you should be able to cope more easily.'

He buried his face in his hands again. 'What am I going to do, Nicole?'

'Take it as it comes,' she told him. 'That's all you can do. Don't antagonise her, but be firm too. Where is she now?'

'In bed—I insisted. She carried on for a bit after you left, but in the end she came back with me.' Anguish showed on his face. 'She hates me.' Nicole's hand was still resting on his arm and he clasped her hand and held it to his lips. 'I'm sorry about today.'

Nicole wanted to take her hand away, but she didn't. 'Why?'

He stood and caught both her hands, pulling her up. Smiling, he said, 'Because I made a bit of a mess of things.'

'You saved me from drowning,' she reminded him.

'And then upset you by trying to make love to you.'

'It's probably better that we didn't,' Nicole whispered, feeling heat flood her face and limbs, and a dangerous churning deep inside her. What if he wanted to make love to her now? Would she have the strength to turn him out? Would her resolutions just be so much hot air?

Sloan kissed her mouth gently, without passion. 'You're probably right.' He smiled down into her face. 'Not that I don't still want to.' He ran his hands across her shoulders and down her arms. 'But. . .'

'You'd better go,' Nicole urged. 'I don't want to get

involved either, Sloan. We have to work together, remember.'

For an answer he slid his arms tightly around her, holding her close while he kissed her hungrily, arousing the same flame of passion as had flared earlier in the day between them. Then, reluctantly, he lifted his lips from hers, let his arms slide away from her, and turned towards the door.

'Goodnight, Nicole. Thanks for the coffee. And today.'

Nicole managed to wait until the door closed behind him before she let the tears fall.

CHAPTER SIX

FOR several days Lucy ignored Nicole, looking through her when they encountered one another, which was seldom, or avoiding her altogether. Nicole attempted once or twice to strike up a conversation, but Lucy seemed stubbornly determined to give her the cold shoulder.

'You're competition,' said Jan, after witnessing a snub. 'She'd hate anyone who even remotely looked like being a rival for Sloan's affections.'

Nicole's colour flared. 'But I'm not!'

Jan smiled. 'Attention, then. You were with him when she arrived. You were the reason he wasn't around.'

'Only because he happened to choose the same cove as I did that afternoon. It wasn't prearranged.' Nicole was appalled at the construction Jan had put on the incident.

'And why do you think he chose that cove?' Jan enquired with a sly smile. 'Why do you think he asked me where you'd gone, and whether you were alone?'

'You told him?'

'Well, it wasn't confidential, was it? Besides, I don't think you should go snorkelling alone, and I was proved right, wasn't I? You ought to have more sense, Nicole.'

Nicole knew Jan and Sloan were right about that. 'Yes, I suppose so. It's just that sometimes it's nice to be totally alone. And I did tell you where I was going.'

'You nearly drowned yourself,' Jan reminded her.

Nicole bit her lip. 'I doubt if I'd have drowned. I'd just have floated on my back until the cramp eased. I wasn't totally incapacitated. But you're right, and I won't do it again. It was risky.'

Jan grinned. 'Bet you enjoyed being rescued, though!'

'Not particularly,' said Nicole stiffly. 'Sloan scolded me as much as you.' She finished counting some dressings, then said, 'Don't get any ideas about Sloan and me, Jan. I'm not interested and neither is he. If he's interested in anyone, it's Coralie Mitchell. I saw them kissing the other day.'

Even as she spoke, she regretted revealing that fact, but Jan was not surprised.

'That doesn't surprise me. She told me they're old friends, and I got the definite impression that she was hopeful of renewing the friendship on a permanent basis. She thinks he's wonderful, and the fact that he's now free and so is she probably means they'll get together.'

'I wonder how Lucy will react to that,' Nicole said thoughtfully.

'Not favourably, is my guess. To my knowledge, she hasn't visited her.'

'Maybe Sloan knows her, but Lucy doesn't,' Nicole pointed out.

Jan agreed that was probable. 'Expect fireworks when he tells her,' she predicted.

'I dare say he'll wait until they're all back in Sydney, and Coralie is well, and Lucy more amenable,' Nicole surmised. 'He's bound to want to keep the peace here.'

Surgery that morning was brisk. They treated the usual crop of minor injuries and ailments, and Sloan offered reassurances to one or two over-anxious guests who suspected illness but were loath to cut short their holiday. The worst they had to contend with was a case of mild concussion in a young man who had fallen while water-skiing and managed to hit the boat, and an elderly woman who had suffered an attack of tachycardia while playing the poker machines.

It was one of the other patients, however, who unintentionally gave Nicole a further insight into Lucy's behaviour.

'I chatted to Dr Reilly's daughter on the ferry coming over,' the woman told Nicole while she was waiting her turn. 'Delightful little girl, so polite. Her mother's dead, she told me. She said she wants to be an actress, but her father doesn't approve. I think she's hoping to persuade him to change his mind.' She paused, looked a bit put out, and said, 'You won't tell him I told you, will you?'

Nicole had to reply, 'No, of course not.' So Lucy had been play-acting when she'd said she'd come over with some men in a yacht. Nicole had not believed the rest of what she'd said, but she had thought half of it might be true.

Because she thought Sloan might still be worried, she told him that much, but not the rest of what the woman had said.

Sloan groaned. 'She just wants to aggravate me. She'll make up anything to get me mad.'

'Or to make her life seem even a little bit more glamorous and daring than it really is,' suggested Nicole.

He nodded. 'But I don't know when she's lying and when she's telling the truth. I'm out of my depth,

Nicole. I'm no good as a substitute mother for a sixteen-year-old.'

'It's never easy,' she told him.

He sighed. 'She'd resent anyone I married, anyone I even had a relationship with. You've seen how appallingly she can behave, even when there's no. . .' He shrugged helplessly.

Nicole turned away so he wouldn't see her face. She was angry with herself for being hurt. Of course there was nothing between her and Sloan. She didn't want there to be.

On her way out of the hotel later, she glanced down towards the swimming-pool and caught a glimpse of Lucy. She was lying on a banana lounger under a beach umbrella, reading a magazine, alone. Nicole regarded the girl thoughtfully for a moment, then went on her way.

That evening, after dinner, there was another scene between Sloan and his daughter. Nicole heard it from her unit. Sloan was remonstrating with Lucy just outside. She wanted to go to a party on board one of the yachts, and Sloan said no. He was apparently aware of the people concerned and knew there would be unlimited alcohol available.

'Well, I'm going whatever you say,' Lucy said stubbornly. 'You can't stop me.'

'I can!' Sloan threatened.

Lucy's voice became shrill. 'You lay a hand on me and I'll report you for child abuse! Don't be such a mouldy old killjoy. Can't I have any life of my own?'

'Not the sort that might get you into trouble,' he insisted. 'You're not old enough to cope with people like that.' There was a pause which even to Nicole behind her door conveyed a highly charged atmosphere. Then Sloan said grittily, 'OK, if you want to go, all right. But I come with you.'

Lucy's shriek of outrage echoed down the covered pathway in front of the units.

'Keep your voice down!' snapped Sloan. 'There's no need to make a spectacle of yourself!'

'You're not coming with me,' Lucy said flatly. 'And if you dare, I'll tell them all what a brute you are. I'll tell them what you did to Mummy. . .'

Sloan lost his temper. 'All right, go! But don't come whining to me when things go wrong. Go your own way. Do what you want. But don't expect me to treat you as a daughter.'

There was a clatter of heels as Lucy fled, and Nicole held her breath, wondering if Sloan was still standing outside or if he had retreated. She was so horrified at what she had heard that she just stood there rigidly, wondering if she had imagined it. Then, tentatively, she opened her door. There was no one outside. On an impulse, she dashed back inside, grabbed her bag and a wrap and set off after Lucy. Somehow she was going to have to try and talk some sense into the girl.

'You shouldn't interfere in other people's domestic problems,' she muttered as she headed for the buggy park. But a stronger conviction made her go on regardless.

There was one vehicle left. Still feeling a bit guilty because she ought to have told Sloan what she was doing, Nicole headed down to the resort. If she had, he might have stopped her from going, accused her of interfering, and she hadn't wanted to risk that.

She wasn't quite sure what she was going to do when she reached the hotel. The chances were she would be too late to intercept Lucy before she joined the party on the yacht, and, even if she weren't, she might not be able to cope with Lucy's reaction any more effectively than Sloan. Nevertheless she felt she had to do something. Impossible though Lucy seemed to be, there was a vulnerability about the girl that touched a chord in Nicole and made her feel that all was not as it seemed.

When she entered the hotel, there were a lot of people about, some just finishing dinner, others going to the nightclub and discothèque or other entertainments. Nicole made for the reception desk and asked about the party on the yacht.

'There's a dinghy ferrying guests from the pier,' the receptionist told her, raising an eyebrow just a fraction.

Nicole raced along the jetty to where there was a small group of people. There was a fair degree of inebriation among them already, she noticed. Lucy, however, did not appear to be there.

'Hello, darling!' A tall man in a tuxedo flung his arms around her, then shouted to his friends, 'This one's mine! Hands off, see!'

Nicole squirmed in his grasp. 'Has anyone gone over to the yacht yet?' The yacht was moored a few hundred metres out in the bay, lights blazing, and the sound of loud music drifted across the water.

The man ogled her, smiling drunkenly. 'Not yet, darling.' He held her tightly. 'How about a little kiss to warm up while we're waiting?'

'No, thanks,' said Nicole, averting her head. 'I'm not going to the party. I was just looking for a friend who is.'

'Well, why not join in and come along too?' said her captor. 'All the more the merrier. Andrew won't mind.'

'But I might,' snapped Nicole, and brought both hands up to give him a push. He wasn't expecting it, and surprise made him let go. He stumbled back, swearing, and overbalanced. Nicole watched horrified as he teetered on the edge of the jetty, then fell backwards into the water, a couple of metres below.

A shout of laughter rose from the rest of the gathering as they all rushed to the edge. Nicole peered over anxiously. Had he injured himself? Then to her relief he was being hauled out by two of the other men, amid further laughter. She shut her ears to the unpleasant name he called her, and, satisfied that he didn't need urgent medical attention, she fled.

But where was Lucy? Reaching the hotel end of the jetty, Nicole paused. She glanced over her shoulder, half expecting a belligerent partygoer bent on revenge for a ducking, but there was just the darkness between her and the group at the far end of the pier. An outboard motor cut the silence and she saw a dinghy approaching. No doubt the owner of the yacht would lend his guest some dry clothes.

A couple of people passed her, presumably more guests, who would be ferried on a second trip, but there was no sign of Lucy. Nicole frowned. Surely, if she was going, she would be here by now. She might have gone to the powder-room first, but she'd had ample time. Of course, that man might have been mistaken and a boatload had already gone across to the yacht.

Nicole debated in her mind what to do. She didn't like the idea of Lucy being at the kind of party which her own recent experience had suggested it might be, any more than Sloan had, and the only way to find out if the girl was already on the yacht was to go with the next trip. If Lucy was not there, she'd come back. And if she was there already? Nicole took a deep breath. She'd try to persuade her to leave, and if she refused, rather than cause too big a scene, she would stay and keep an eye on her. Which might be easier said than done. Especially as she was a gatecrasher and had already made an enemy of the man in the tuxedo. He would no doubt take great pleasure in having her thrown out—even literally! Nicole shuddered.

How did I get involved in this? she asked herself ruefully, perching on a bollard while she decided what to do. She didn't have much time to make up her mind.

Beyond the jetty the beach was deserted, in the moonlight a long graceful curve of silver sand. The fringing palms moved gently in the breeze and the scent of frangipani wafted on the air, mixed with the sharp salty smell of the ocean. Nicole was about to take her courage in both hands and join the party on the yacht, whatever the consequences, when she noticed a small figure walking along the beach away from the jetty. A figure with a long swinging pony-tail, dressed in a pink mini-skirt and fringed shawl and carrying her shoes. Surely it was Lucy?

Nicole peered into the night, straining her eyes. Yes, she was certain it was. But what on earth was she doing there? Trusting she had not made a mistake, Nicole raced down the steps to the beach and, removing her own shoes, sped after the solitary figure.

'Lucy!' she called, and gave a sigh of relief when the girl turned and she saw that it was Sloan's daughter. 'Thank goodness!' she breathed, glancing at the illuminated yacht and thankful that Lucy was not there after all.

Lucy did not run, she stopped and waited for Nicole

to catch up. Nicole half expected a tirade of abuse, but Lucy said nothing except, 'Hi,' in a small flat voice, then, 'What are you doing here?'

Nicole sensed the misery in her voice, and knew she was too close to tears to put on an act, especially as Sloan was not there to be aggravated by it.

She smiled. 'I was looking for you.'

'Why?' Lucy scuffed the sand.

Nicole slipped her arm around the slim shoulders. 'Because I thought you were going to a party on that yacht, and we could go together.'

Lucy's voice was shocked. 'You! You mean you're going to that party? But. . .' She shrugged off Nicole's arm and took a step aside as though to distance herself from her. 'They're a rough crowd, you know. There's a guy. . .the guy who asked me to go. . .who thinks he's just the greatest. He made a pass at me at the swimming-pool today. He—he tried to touch me. . .it was disgusting!' Her look said she was also disgusted with Nicole.

Nicole listened with more relief than she had ever felt in her life. 'Lucy. . .oh, Lucy, my dear!' Impulsively she hugged the girl. 'You mean you never had any intention of going? You just pretended you were to upset your father?' She held her at arm's length, and, when Lucy said nothing but just nodded, she went on, 'I wasn't going either, Lucy. I was going to gatecrash to keep an eye on you. As a matter of fact, I think I might have met your Don Juan. I'm afraid I repulsed his advances so heavily, I pushed him off the jetty into the water. He called me a rather rude name.'

Lucy looked disbelieving. 'You're kidding!'

'I am not! I had to run hell for leather back along the jetty before he throttled me. I was sitting there wondering how I could keep out of his way when I actually got to the yacht. I was going to take the next trip. You see, I thought you must have already gone over.'

Lucy burst out laughing. 'I wish I'd seen him fall in!' Then she said wonderingly, 'You mean you'd have gone to that party, in spite of that creep, just to look after me?' There was an incredulous as well as admiring note in her voice.

'I thought you might not be fully aware of the kind of party it might turn into. Sometimes it can be a bit tricky getting out of situations you wish you'd never got yourself into. There's nowhere to run on a yacht, is there?'

'But why?' asked Lucy suspiciously. 'I'm nothing to you. I suppose you did it for Sloan? You fancy him, don't you?' A touch of the familiar resentment and jealousy had returned.

'There's nothing between Sloan and me,' Nicole said.

'Except you're lovers.' Lucy was scathing.

'No. You can believe it or not, but it's true. Sloan and I are colleagues, that's all.'

Lucy hesitated, eyeing her warily. 'Well, you must be the first not to be a sucker for his charm. Boy, that must make him mad!' She laughed again, then queried, 'So you were just doing him a good turn coming after his rebellious daughter? I suppose he put you up to it.'

Nicole kept her temper. 'No. You may not have noticed, but you were arguing right outside my unit. I couldn't help hearing you. Sloan had gone when I opened my door, and if I was to catch up with you there wasn't time to tell him where I was going. There was no need anyway. I was concerned about you, Lucy, that's all, as I'd be concerned about anyone I thought might be going to do something foolish that maybe I could prevent.'

Lucy walked a few paces, then turned round. 'I suppose you think I'm pretty stupid,' she muttered.

'I'd like to know why you pretend to be,' Nicole said. 'I think you're probably a pretty bright person, but you're also very sensitive and emotional, and I think you're a bit mixed up. Look, why don't we go and have a coffee up at the hotel and talk there?'

For a moment Lucy looked as though she would rebel against that idea, but eventually she said, 'OK.'

The coffee-shop was not crowded and they found a secluded booth against the wall where they could talk privately. Nicole sensed that Lucy was ready to pour out her troubles, and she was only too glad to listen. She knew she had gained a very fragile acceptance and that it could be easily lost again, so she proceeded carefully.

For a few minutes they did not talk about Lucy herself at all. Nicole made small talk about the island, the resort, about nursing, and a number of other things, until finally she was able to mention the woman who had chatted to Lucy on the ferry.

'You enjoy making up stories, don't you, Lucy?' she said quietly. 'Especially if what you say shocks your father. You want him to think you're worldly and rebellious and smart and sophisticated, don't you? So you make up things, like going to that party tonight.'

Lucy nodded. 'I—I can't seem to help it. It sort of slips out. He treats me like a kid. . .and. . . Well, as soon as I'm grown up and off his hands, he can marry again, can't he? That's what he wants to do. Meanwhile I'm just a millstone round his neck. He doesn't care. . .'

'Of course he cares,' said Nicole. 'That's why he gets so angry. You worry him half to death, you know.'

Lucy bit her lip. 'I know. I suppose I want him to worry. I want to see him worried about me. And I want him to be angry with me, because that proves he doesn't care. . .'

'No, it doesn't. Quite the opposite. I heard what he said to you tonight,' Nicole murmured, 'but he didn't mean it, Lucy. You provoked him beyond endurance. I'm not surprised he lost his temper.'

'Like he used to with Mummy,' Lucy said. 'I used to hear them quarrelling, shouting at each other, and I'd put my head under the pillow to shut it out. He killed her!'

Nicole placed a hand over Lucy's which was shaking as she picked up a spoon to stir her coffee. 'You don't mean that,' she said gently.

The girl's features suddenly showed a terrible bitterness. 'Yes, I do. He drove her to it. He isn't quite the hero you think he is, Nicole. He was carrying on with other women all the time, and he—he was with one of them the night she died. That's why she. . .' Her pale elfin face was racked with pain. 'She drove her car into a tree on purpose because she knew he was going to leave her. He killed her, and I hate him!'

'Lucy,' said Nicole, 'is this something else you're making up?'

'No! No, it's true. He drove her to do it. He made her life a misery with his affairs. She told me.' Tears began to roll down Lucy's cheeks.

'Oh, Lucy, I'm sorry,' Nicole said gently, clutching her hand tightly. The girl was so upset that it was unlikely she was not telling the truth. And this truth certainly explained her bad behaviour and her sense of rejection.

Lucy found a handkerchief and mopped up. Then she smiled wanly. 'I don't often cry,' she muttered.

'Maybe you should more often. It helps sometimes to ease the tension.' Nicole felt close to tears herself.

'You won't tell him I told you. . .?'

'Of course not. But you can't go on like this,' Nicole told her. 'You'll have to work out something. Whatever he's done, he's still your father and I believe he does care deeply for you, Lucy. You're his daughter. It doesn't help to bait him, to embarrass him and worry him. Revenge is never sweet, you know.' She could see that the girl was exhausted emotionally, so she suggested, 'I think it's time we went home. If you want to talk to me about it some more tomorrow, or any time, Lucy, you will, won't you? Maybe if you talk about things to someone like me who isn't involved, you'll eventually be able to talk to your dad about them too. You're both a bit too uptight with each other at the moment. You need time to simmer down.' A sudden thought occurred to her. 'Look, brooding never did anyone any good, so, instead of just lying around the pool, would you like to do something useful, like helping at the Lodge?'

Lucy looked uncertain. 'Like what?'

'Nothing very glamorous, I'm afraid. Just paperwork, or sorting laundry, or running errands for patients. Really, just being there in case you're needed. Not all day. Let's say for a couple of hours in the mornings when we're busiest.'

Lucy twisted her dark hank of hair and said diffidently, 'OK.'

'You can start tomorrow if you like,' Nicole told her.

'And now, let's go. I don't know about you, but I'm worn out!'

To Nicole's amazement it was almost midnight. They left the coffee-shop and strolled through the main foyer to go to the buggy park. It was a shock when the exit door flew open and they found themselves confronted by Sloan.

He stared at the two girls for a moment, as stunned apparently to see them as they were to see him. Nicole flinched at the fury that darkened his face, and she sensed Lucy go rigid beside her.

'Where the hell have you been?' Sloan's eyes flashed from his daughter to Nicole.

CHAPTER SEVEN

IT WAS a moment to shatter glass. Nicole felt as though she was splintering into a million fragments. Speech failed her, and Lucy too was so taken aback that she had nothing to say.

'I said where the hell have you been?' Sloan repeated, with a thunderous look at Lucy, and one hardly less so at Nicole.

'Please,' said Nicole, at last finding her voice, 'don't shout—people will hear. Why don't we go back to the Lodge and talk there?'

'Just tell me where you've been,' Sloan repeated, lowering his voice a fraction while still glaring at his daughter. Then he glowered again at Nicole. 'And what you're doing here!'

'Daddy, please. . .' Lucy added her plea, glancing over her shoulder. 'Don't make a scene!'

'Since when has a scene bothered you?' he snarled. 'You've embarrassed me often enough!'

'Sloan, listen, please,' begged Nicole. 'I can explain, but let's get out of here, shall we?' She linked her arm through Lucy's and headed for the exit.

Defeated by her determination, Sloan followed. They picked up a buggy and, with Sloan at the controls, headed for the Lodge. On the way, Nicole said nothing. Lucy also was silent, but Nicole, sitting close beside her, could feel the young girl's body shaking as though she was trying not to cry. Lucy had had just about as much emotional strain as she could endure tonight.

Sloan did not speak either, and his rigid profile told Nicole that his anger had not abated one iota. They parked the buggy in the Lodge car park and walked towards the staff units and the doctor's residence.

Nicole said, 'I think you'd better go to bed, Lucy. I'll see you in the morning, right?'

Lucy, pale in the moonlight, nodded, and looked grateful.

'Now, just a minute. . .' Sloan put a restraining hand on her arm.

'Let her go,' Nicole pleaded quietly. 'I'll tell you what happened.'

To her relief, Sloan did not argue. He watched his daughter go, then followed Nicole to her unit. Once inside he prowled angrily, saying, 'Now, what's all this about? How do you know about that party?' He turned his back on her and stared at a picture on the wall.

Nicole took a deep breath. 'I heard you and Lucy quarrelling—perhaps you didn't realise you were outside my door. I was worried, so I went after her.'

Sloan wheeled round, new fury in his face. 'Without telling me? Who gave you the right to meddle in other people's affairs?'

Nicole was hardly surprised at the reproach. 'I'm sorry, but I had to move fast if I was going to catch up with her.'

'You did?' His anger subsided a little.

'Eventually.'

'And talked her out of going to the party?'

She shook her head. 'I didn't have to, Sloan. She'd had no intention of going.'

'What? Don't be ridiculous! She'd do anything she knew I'd disapprove of.'

She said, 'Sit down, Sloan. Would you like a drink?'

He nodded absently as he sank into a chair. Nicole poured him a whisky, perched on the arm of the couch and told him exactly what had happened. He listened impassively, but she was sure there was a glimmer of a smile when she told him how she had pushed the man in the tuxedo over the edge of the jetty.

'I think I know the guy,' he said with disgust. 'He was prostrate on the deck when I got there—dead drunk.'

Nicole's mouth fell open in amazement. She leaned towards him. 'When *you* got there? On the yacht, you mean?'

Sloan swirled the liquid in his glass and took a deep gulp of it. 'I couldn't let her walk into what was surely going to be trouble. She's only a kid. She's my daughter, damn it! I cooled down and went after her. I was in time to catch the last trip to the yacht, but she wasn't there. I made myself a bit unpopular looking for her in the cabins, but I didn't care. I was afraid she was hiding somewhere. I was desperate, Nicole. . .' He buried his face in his hands. 'Desperate!'

'I think you should tell Lucy you went looking for her,' Nicole said, filled with relief and admiration.

He looked up, anguish still distorting his features. 'She'd kill me most likely!'

'I don't think so. She needs to know how much you care.'

'It'll only prove what a killjoy of a father I am.' He looked up at her, his face still stricken. 'How am I supposed to know what's just pretence with her? When she's lying deliberately to shock me and make me angry.' He raked his hands through his hair and finished the whisky in one gulp. 'Why does she do it?' he groaned in despair.

Nicole was loath to break a confidence, but she had to try and help Lucy. Sloan too. 'She's a young girl on the brink of adulthood. She's torn between needing security and wanting freedom. Maybe if you try talking to her like an adult instead of a naughty child, you'll find out why she fights you, Sloan. It's a cry for help, and she's still desperately unhappy because of what happened to her mother.'

'I can't bring Helen back.' The anguish is his voice tore at her heart.

'No, but you can talk about it to Lucy. She has to learn to come to terms with what happened. She'll only go on blaming you and hating you otherwise.'

'I know she hates me. But blames me?'

The pain in his face was almost too much for Nicole to bear. She wanted to have it out with him herself, to tell him what Lucy had told her about his affairs and Helen's suicide, but she checked herself. She must respect Lucy's confidence that much at least.

'Of course she blames you,' she said. 'And she's rather young to know how to forgive.'

'Forgive?' He stared at her, as though uncomprehending, then shook his head when she offered him another whisky. He rose. 'I'd better be going.' He stood near her, looking down into her face. 'Thanks for what you did, Nicole. I'm grateful. I apologise for ranting at you.'

'At least we found out a little bit about Lucy's behaviour. Things aren't quite as bad as you imagined,' she said. 'Maybe things will be different now. She won't be able to fool you so easily with her fantasies.'

For the first time, he smiled. 'Maybe.' He cupped her face in his hands and kissed her lips. 'Thanks again.' He let her go and quickly left.

Nicole did not see him to the door. He let himself out, and as the door clicked shut, she looked at the empty space where he had been, and Lucy's words echoed in her mind like a funeral bell. Sloan had had affairs with women and had finally driven his wife to suicide. She didn't want to believe it, hated to believe it, but surely it must be true. Lucy wouldn't have pretended about a thing like that. It was the whole underlying reason for her wilful behaviour and her desire to torment and hurt her father.

She dragged her own fingers lightly down her cheeks and jawline, following where his had trailed, and her heart was full of anguish.

The next morning there were two new convalescents arriving, so Jan went down to the hotel to take surgery with Sloan, while Nicole remained to welcome them and settle them in. One was an elderly man recovering from a stroke which had not incapacitated him too much, but had curtailed his activities to the point where his family had suggested he have a spell away. The other was a woman suffering the trauma of a car accident in which she had lost her husband. Nicole also wanted to be on hand when Lucy turned up, if she did.

Nicole half expected the girl not to. In fact she would not have been surprised if Lucy had given her the complete cold shoulder again after last night. In the cold light of day Sloan's daughter might well regret having let her defences down, and, because Nicole had found her out, she might well be even more antagonistic.

Nicole also wondered if father and daughter would have talked yet. She thought it unlikely, since Sloan would have been up and about long before Lucy. When he had come into the Lodge earlier, he had said nothing to her, and she sensed that he preferred to forget the whole unpleasant interlude. He had thanked her for what she had done, but clearly he resented her interference.

Just as she was having a cup of coffee, Nicole suddenly found herself with two arrivals. One was a bouquet of flowers for Coralie Mitchell, the other was Lucy.

Nicole was delighted that Lucy had not reneged. She looked scrubbed and shining, and only faint smudges under her eyes, which were a little puffy, betrayed the emotion of the previous night.

'Good morning,' Nicole said cheerfully. 'Am I glad to see you! We've got two new patients today, and it's Sharon's day off, so I can do with some help.'

'Hi,' Lucy said diffidently. Her T-shirt today was a message one, saying 'Free battery hens' with a picture of a large white hen with her head poking through the bars of a small cage. She shoved her hands in the pockets of her jeans. 'What do you want me to do?'

'What about some coffee first?' Nicole wondered if the T-shirt also demonstrated how Lucy felt—caged.

'No, thanks. I just made myself some breakfast. Where's Dad?'

'Taking surgery down at the hotel. Jan's assisting today.' Nicole paused, hoping Lucy might say she had talked to her father, but the girl revealed nothing.

Lucy perched on the edge of the desk and fiddled with the Cellophane on the flowers. 'Somebody thinks of lot of somebody. Orchids!' She smiled a little wistfully.

'They're for Mrs Mason,' Nicole told her, and a daring idea began to form in her mind. If Lucy got to like Coralie before she discovered that her father was involved with the woman, it might make a lot of difference, especially as Lucy would be bond to recognise Coralie, who would surely talk to her about acting as a career. Nicole made an instant decision.

'Would you like to do the flowers, Lucy? It would be a great help.' Lucy continued to look glum, but she didn't actually refuse, so Nicole went on, 'Show the bouquet to Mrs Mason and give her the card, then arrange them in vases for her. I expect the ones in her room will be ready to be thrown out, but, if not, you can sort them and make up a display for the lounge. I'll show you where the vases are kept. Then you can check all the other rooms—some will be occupied, some not, so just knock fairly loudly before you barge in—and say you've come to change their flowers. I'll ring down to the florist for some fresh ones.' She smiled hopefully. 'Are you any good at flower arranging?'

Lucy made a face and laughed. 'Not really my scene, Nicole! But I get As for art, so I guess I can do a fair job.'

'Good girl!' Nicole led the way to the kitchen and showed Lucy where the vases were kept. They laid the flowers on the bench, and Nicole said, 'Right, I'll leave you to it. Mrs Mason is room eleven. I'll be in the offfice if you want me.'

Nicole had barely sat down at the computer to enter the details of her two newest patients when she heard running footsteps and Lucy flashed past her window, heading for the entrance.

Rising involuntarily, Nicole exclaimed aloud, 'Lucy! What on earth. . .?' She burst out of the office. 'Lucy. . .!' But the girl had already vanished. Her first instinct was to follow, to find out what had precipitated such a headlong flight, but patients came first, so she hurried along to room eleven to find out what had happened.

Coralie Mitchell was up and dressed, as she was most days lately, although she still rarely left her room. From the scattered newspapers, it seemed she had been sitting on her balcony, reading. Now she was standing in the middle of the room wringing her hands. On the parquet floor near her lay the abandoned bouquet of flowers, some of the blooms shattered and scattered across the floor.

'Whatever's wrong?' Nicole ran to her, found her trembling all over, and gently guided her to a chair. 'What happened?'

'I don't know! I don't know!' wailed Coralie. 'I had no idea she was here—Sloan never said—and she didn't know I was here.' She covered her face with her hands. 'Oh, my God, it was awful! The shock! Why was she so hostile?'

'What exactly happened?' asked Nicole, perplexed, and feeling guilty because she had precipitated the whole thing. Her desire to help had turned into a disaster.

Coralie's eyes overflowed with tears. 'I just don't understand it. We used to be such good friends, Lucy and I. I haven't seen her for a couple of years, of course, not since her mother died. I got married and lived interstate for a time. But why would she. . .? She screamed at me, awful words. She called me a bitch and worse, and she flung the flowers in my face and ran. What on earth can have got into her?'

'She's very upset,' Nicole conceded. 'I'll go and talk to her and maybe she'll tell me why she behaved like

that. I'm sorry. Perhaps you'd better rest on the bed
for a while. I'll bring you a cup of tea.'

'Yes—yes, thank you. I can't understand it. She
sounded as though she *hated* me!'

'Lucy's at an age when hate comes easily,' Nicole
said. 'Adolescent emotions tend to be pretty dense.
Everything's either black or white; there are no shades
of grey.'

Coralie was getting over the shock and her annoyance began to show in a hardness of tone. 'Well, I hope
Sloan takes the child in hand a bit more firmly. I
suppose he's spoiled her and she thinks she can gain
attention by throwing tantrums. What's she doing here
anyway?'

Nicole did not answer. Let Sloan explain. For once
her sympathy for Coralie Mitchell was not automatic,
and, despite the girl's apparently execrable behaviour,
she was more anxious about Lucy. However, she
hurried away to make tea for the actress, and by the
time she had also dealt with a couple of phone calls
and seen to other patient needs, it was nearly time for
Sloan and Jan to return. Nicole wanted to talk to Lucy
before Sloan did, but she couldn't very well leave the
Lodge unattended.

She paced restlessly, and finally decided to ring the
surgery. Jan answered. Nicole asked her if she could
come back as soon as she had finished, rather than stay
down at the hotel for lunch.

'What's wrong?' asked Jan, sensing her anxiety.

'I'll tell you later. Just come, please, Jan.'

'Is it medical? Do you want Sloan?'

'No! Don't let him come too. It's Lucy. I want to
talk to her without him around.'

'Oh, I see. All right. I'll be about half an hour.'

It was nearly an hour before Nicole left the Lodge and hurried over to the doctor's residence. She crossed her fingers that Lucy would have gone to her room, not rushed off somewhere else. The door was ajar, so it seemed likely the girl was in the house.

'Lucy! It's Nicole.' There was no answer, so Nicole went in. A glance into one bedroom told her immediately that it was Sloan's and she felt like a trespasser even just looking. The door to the other one was shut. She tapped on it. 'Lucy, it's Nicole. I want to talk to you.'

'Go away,' came the muffled voice from behind the door.

Nicole took a deep breath, and turned the handle. The door was locked. She called out again, 'Lucy, please let me in. I'm not angry—I just want to talk to you, like we did last night. . .'

She waited, was sure she heard a sound in the room as though someone was moving around and then the door opened. Lucy's eyes were red from weeping and her face was sullen. She did not try to prevent Nicole entering her room. She flung herself on the bed, knees drawn up under her chin, and stared morosely at the wall.

Nicole closed the door and sat on the bed at a distance. 'Mrs Mason is very upset,' she said, 'and I think you owe me an explanation. Why did you throw the flowers at her and run away?'

'She's a bitch!' Lucy said venomously. 'A right bitch. She's not Mrs Mason. She's Coralie Mitchell, the actress.'

'Yes, I know. She has a right to her privacy, Lucy, and I hope you'll respect that.'

'Respect her? That's a joke!' Lucy almost spat the

words out. 'No wonder he wanted to come here! No wonder he didn't want me to come before the holidays.'

'I don't think he knew she was here,' Nicole said. 'He had quite a shock when he saw her.'

Lucy sneered, 'I don't believe that. I bet they've been seeing each other—all the time. Probably even when she was married to that other guy. She's a cow!' She clenched her fists. 'I suppose he thought I wouldn't find out as she wasn't flitting about the place. If you hadn't asked me to help. . .'

Nicole fervently wished she hadn't; it had led to complications she could never have imagined. She said, 'Is it true you used to be friends?'

'Huh! Friends! She was all sweetness and light, said she'd help me become an actress, but it was just for show, because she was having it off with Dad!'

Nicole was appalled. 'You mean when your mother—died?'

'Yes,' Lucy said dully.

'How do you know that?'

'Mummy told me. He was with her the night Mummy —the night Mummy crashed the car. She *knew* he was with Coralie. She knew they'd been having an affair for ages and she was afraid that this time he was going to leave her, so she. . .so she killed herself. The irony is that Coralie married someone else, but now she's divorced and it's obvious they're at it again. God! Now he probably will marry her!'

Lucy looked at Nicole for a moment, then flung herself across the bed into her arms and burst into a storm of weeping. Nicole rocked her gently until she stopped. There was nothing she could say. She felt a strong irrational anger against Sloan, a deep compassion for his daughter, and a sense of utter helplessness.

She was also aware that her own feelings were becoming deeper and deeper involved.

She made Lucy a cup of tea, and presently left her. The words of comfort she offered sounded trite, because mere words could not solve what seemed an insoluble problem. She could not even say she thought Lucy was wrong about Sloan and Coralie Mitchell. If, as Toff hoped, they were taking up where they had left off two years ago, the chances were that now they would marry. And that would mean misery for Lucy, who saw them both as the instruments of her mother's death. Even if Sloan talked to Lucy, it wasn't going to do much good.

'You bastard, Sloan,' Nicole muttered under her breath, and the knowledge of what he had done hurt so deeply that she almost cried out in pain. She had begun to admire the man, she realised; she had let him get under her skin, and break down part of her defences. But not completely. She had found out about him in time.

Back at the Lodge, she told Jan a little of what had happened, but not everything Lucy had said, especially not about her mother.

Jan was philosophical. 'Poor kid! Girls never like their fathers to marry again. But she'll get over it. If she was a friend of Coralie's once, she's bound to come round—especially if Coralie helps her start an acting career.'

Nicole felt it was unlikely. Lucy's hurts were too deep, and Coralie was not likely to be helpful to her after the way Lucy had treated her.

Jan had brought up the mail, and was sorting it. 'One for you, Nic, from the Robertses.' Suddenly her face drained of colour as she picked up a long white envelope, stared at the address on it, then the sender's address in the top left-hand corner. She looked up at Nicole.

'What's the matter?' demanded Nicole, slitting open her own letter. 'You look as though you've seen a ghost.'

'Nearly as incredible,' Jan said. 'Just as well I'm sitting down. It's from Terry.'

Nicole noticed the airmail sticker and American stamps. She grinned. 'Well, what do you know? He's not a creep after all!'

Jan's fingers were shaking and her face was grim. 'Let's not be hasty, Nic. It might just be a thank-you note.'

'Shall I make a tactful exit while you read it?'

'Don't be daft!' Jan slit the envelope open and removed several thin pages of typescript. Her eyes scanned the beginning and then the end. She looked at Nicole. Colour was flooding back into her face. 'Wow! I think I was wrong about the guy after all. He's asked me to marry him. And he's coming back in a couple of months.'

'Jan!' Nicole hugged her. 'Oh, Jan. . . I'm so happy for you! I knew you were in love with him.' She tossed the note and photograph of a baby with its parents in front of her. 'And here's another happy ending. Tim and Julie and Nicole.' She glanced at the photograph again, wistfully, and at Jan's flushed and happy face as she read her own letter. A wave of envy almost engulfed her.

She was forced to snap out of it when the phone rang. It was Sloan. 'We have a perforated appendix and I'll have to operate,' he told her. 'Get the theatre ready, will you? We'll be there in a few minutes.'

Nicole relayed the message to Jan, who sprang into action alongside her without query, so that by the time Sloan arrived they were ready. Nicole prepared the patient and Jan helped Sloan into a gown and mask.

The patient was a young woman of twenty-two, sun-bronzed and healthy, and she had been out water-skiing when the pains had struck.

'She'd been having symptoms for a couple of days,' Sloan said, after he had administered the anaesthetic and the girl was unconscious, 'but she'd put it down to indigestion, or the water. She was shocked to discover the real reason.'

'She looks the healthy, outdoor type,' Jan remarked. 'Probably she's never had a day's illness in her life. No wonder she was shocked.'

'Evidently she's a champion water-skier,' Sloan told them as he contemplated the array of instruments Nicole had ready beside her. 'She wasn't too happy when I told her she'd have to miss the competition she's in next week.' He nodded at Nicole. 'Ready?'

'When you are,' she answered.

He made a small adjustment to a finger of his surgical gloves, and the operation began. Nicole had assisted at countless appendicectomies. It was one of the common-est surgical procedures in the book, and complications were rare. The only differences were in individual surgeons' particular techniques, and though the basics were the same each had his own way of doing things. A nurse had to be aware of this, and trying to anticipate the needs of a man she was unfamiliar with was not always easy.

Today it was more difficult than it might have been. It was hard to concentrate when her mind was churning with what Lucy had told her last night and today, what had happened this morning. But worst of all was the knowledge that Sloan was not the man she wanted him to be, that he had been unfaithful to his wife and his infidelity had sent her to her death. The knowledge was like the cut of the knife Sloan was using, without any anaesthetic to dull the pain, and Nicole could no longer escape from acknowledging why it hurt so much. She was in love with Sloan.

'Well, we got there in time,' Sloan was saying with satisfaction as he removed swabs and Nicole automatically counted them. 'She'll be fine.'

As the last suture was inserted in the girl's abdomen, Jan gave a little grunt of approval. 'I do like to see a neat row of stitches.' She glanced up at Sloan, grinning. 'Don't you ever feel tempted to do lazy daisy or snail trail?'

He laughed, and caught Nicole's eye, but she could only bring herself to force a faint smile. How could he lean against the table like that, relaxed and responding to a joke, when his selfishness had cost one woman's life and made his daughter's a misery?

'I'd better get the ward ready,' she said.

Jan broke in, 'I'll do that.'

She was off before Nicole could object, leaving Nicole to wheel the patient into the small recovery annexe and tidy up the theatre. She expected Sloan to leave, but he lingered. He pulled his mask down and peeled off his gloves, then stood for a moment watching her.

'I haven't had a chance to speak to Lucy yet. Last night we were both too emotional and this morning I didn't want to wake her.'

Nicole's lip curled a little. 'Or perhaps you just

wanted to put it off.' She bundled up the disposable drapes and marched off to stuff them in the bin.

Sloan followed her out. Automatically she untied his gown, wanting him to go, yet wondering if she should tell him what had happened this morning. Coralie undoubtedly would.

'Sloan,' she said resolutely, 'I've got something to tell you. Coralie's going to tell you anyway, but you might as well be forewarned.'

He looked startled. 'What? Nicole, you look angry. What's the matter?'

'I know it's none of my business,' said Nicole, 'but I've become involved because of Lucy.' She explained in clipped tones what had happened that morning, and almost felt sympathetic as she witnessed the shock in his face. 'You've behaved despicably,' she finished. 'Absolutely despicably!'

The colour had drained from his face and he just stared at her for a moment. 'It isn't true,' he said quietly. 'Oh. God, Nicole, you can't believe. . . Lucy. . .' He raked his hair wildly. 'Nicole, that's not what happened. Let me tell you the truth.'

She refused to let the surge of hope she felt be born. 'I don't think Lucy was lying this time,' she said.

'But, Nicole. . .' His face was desperate.

'I don't want to be involved,' she said emphatically. 'Your private life is nothing to do with me. I don't know how you're going to work out such a terrible dilemma, but I hope you'll give some priority to Lucy's feelings. You've made her suffer enough, Sloan. Don't speed her on the same downward path as her mother.'

His eyes flashed with fury. 'How dare you say that?'

Nicole moistened her lips, regretting the impulse that had made her accuse him so directly. 'She's a nice girl, Sloan,' she said, avoiding his gaze. 'Intelligent, sensitive, and at the moment very, very unhappy. I don't think you'll win her round with excuses.'

'Excuses! Good God, Nicole, is that what you think? That I just want to make excuses?'

'I don't think anything——'

He grasped her shoulders. 'Yes, you do! You think I drove my wife to kill herself. Well, it isn't true, Nicole. I'll tell you what really happened.'

Nicole bit her lip. She mustn't believe him. 'Tell Lucy,' she said, and added bitterly, 'See if she believes you. I suppose you'll get Coralie Mitchell to deny there was ever an affair between you, that all that's just something new since you and she came here.'

His hands fell to his sides. 'Coralie and I have never had an affair—not before, not now,' he said grimly.

Nicole wanted to believe him, but she couldn't. 'Why didn't you tell her Lucy was here? Why didn't you tell Lucy she was here? It seems pretty obvious why.'

He raked his hair agitatedly. 'Coralie's here under an assumed name. I was protecting her privacy as I would protect the privacy of any patient.'

'The other patients know who she is. She's recognisable,' Nicole pointed out. 'And as you both know her. . .'

He glowered angrily. 'Are you suggesting I'm a liar?'

Nicole refused to answer, and he went on less harshly, 'All right, I didn't tell Coralie that Lucy was here because of the frame of mind both of them were in. I didn't want Coralie involved in my problems; she has enough of her own. I thought it unlikely they'd meet since Coralie keeps herself to herself most of the time. How was I to know you'd persuade Lucy to do volunteer work?'

'I thought it would give her something to occupy her instead of brooding,' Nicole explained. 'I'm sorry.'

He slumped wearily. 'It wasn't your fault.'

She moved away. 'I must check the patient. She'll be coming round soon.'

Sloan nodded. 'No, you mustn't neglect the patient,' he agreed wearily. He turned to go, then said over his shoulder, 'I can't believe you'd think so badly of me.'

Nicole just shrugged. She felt as though someone had drained all the blood from her body and forgotten to give her a transfusion. She felt some of the despair that Helen Reilly must have felt when she discovered that her husband was having affairs. But she wasn't married to Sloan; she did not have to suffer the humiliation as well as the hurt. She wasn't so deeply involved with him that she couldn't break free.

CHAPTER EIGHT

'I'M LEAVING.'

Lucy's bald statement jerked Nicole's head up. She had not heard the girl come into the office. In a sleeveless yellow top and white shorts, her hair in a pony-tail, Lucy looked very young and vulnerable.

'Lucy. . .' Nicole was at a loss, and her heart constricted at the misery in the young girl's face which she was valiantly trying to hide.

Sloan's daughter shook her head vigorously. 'It's no use, Nicole. I'll never forgive him for what he did to Mummy, and, if he's going to marry Coralie, then that's the end. I couldn't live in the same house. I despise her!' Her mouth was a hard, determined line, but, in spite of her resolution, her lips trembled. Nicole felt a wave of pity and helplessness.

It was the following morning and Nicole had spent a sleepless night and was herself feeling drained. If only I hadn't sent her in with the flowers, she kept thinking, if only I hadn't interfered. 'He says he's never had an affair with her,' she murmured.

Lucy's expression was derisive. 'Believe that and you'll believe in fairies!' She flattened her palms on the desk-top and leaned towards Nicole. 'Mummy told me, Nicole. She knew he was having an affair with Coralie and wanted a divorce. He can't crawl out of it by lying now. *I'm* not likely to believe him.'

'Has he spoken to you—about yesterday?' Nicole asked.

'No—he doesn't dare. What is there to say? He knows I won't believe his lies. I'm not a child now. Oh, I was a fool to come here. I didn't dream Coralie would be here too.'

'Why did you come?' asked Nicole.

Lucy shrugged, and her eyes filled with tears. 'Where else was there to go? The house in Sydney is all locked up, and I hate that place anyway. He's the only family I've got. . .and I thought it might be fun, with lots of other people. I just couldn't stand that school a minute longer.'

Nicole rose. 'You always cut and run when things look grim, don't you, Lucy?'

'What would you have done?' Lucy countered, eyes flashing.

Nicole smiled. 'At your age, probably the same thing. But impulsive acts are sometimes regrettable. Before you rush off again, be sure you know what you're doing. You're still his responsibility, you know.'

Lucy sank into a chair and drummed her fingers on the desk-top. 'I know—that's the worst part. I just want to go away and be myself. I don't want to have anything to do with him, or her, ever again.'

Nicole felt her anguish. 'But he's your father, and you love him——'

'I hate him!'

'Maybe if you talked to him, listened to his side of the story. . .' Nicole was astonished to hear herself saying it. She had refused to hear Sloan's side of the story. But that was different. For Lucy the past was something she had to come to terms with or she would suffer for it all her life. Whatever Sloan had done or caused, Lucy had to face up to it, to recognise that he was a fallible human being, not just someone to arbitrarily pass judgement on. For her peace of mind she must try and salvage something of her natural feelings for him. She had to learn to forgive.

Lucy clasped her hands over her ears. 'I don't want to!'

Nicole put an arm comfortingly around her shoulders. 'Try,' she urged.

Lucy looked up at her, with sudden insight. 'You're pretty rapt in him, aren't you?'

The unexpectedness of the remark made Nicole flush. 'Me? Don't be ridiculous!'

Lucy's smile was wry. 'It's hardly surprising. He takes everyone in.' In a sudden gesture she squeezed Nicole's hand. 'Don't get hurt, Nicole.'

Nicole dredged up a smile. 'Thanks, but you've no need to worry. I'm not even remotely involved, and I'm not "one of his women", as you so explicitly put it when you arrived!'

Lucy had the grace to blush, then looked at her thoughtfully. 'You know, I wouldn't mind if it was you he was keen on,' she said. 'You'd make a pretty cool stepmother.'

Nicole was astounded and flattered. 'How would that change anything?'

'I don't know. . .' Lucy got up and paced the floor. She stopped suddenly, hands on hips, facing Nicole defiantly. 'How can I ever forget what he did to Mummy?' Her voice was tearful, her face a picture of woe. 'How can you love and hate someone both at the same time?'

'You can't. Sooner or later one emotion must overwhelm the other. And if you don't want to destroy yourself, it has to be love.' Nicole reached out to her instinctively. 'Lucy, you're only torturing yourself. . .'

Lucy spread her own hands helplessly but did not touch Nicole's. 'Well, as I said, I'm leaving. You won't tell him till I've gone, will you? I've got friends in Sydney, I'll go to them. They'll understand.'

Nicole was worried. She wasn't sure whether what the girl was saying had substance or was just bravado. 'Are you sure, Lucy? You're not making this up, like the other stories? Have you really got somewhere to go?'

Lucy's tongue flicked over her lips and her eyes wavered. Then, as she had done the previous day, she flung herself into Nicole's arms and burst into tears. 'I don't know what to do!' she wailed. 'I wish I were dead!'

Nicole waited for the outburst to subside, then said gently, 'When you don't know what to do, the best thing to do is nothing. Something will work out. There's only one thing I can see that will help, Lucy, and that's you and Sloan having a sensible heart-to-heart talk. No histrionics, no recriminations. You have to reach a compromise. You're too young to go off on your own, and you don't really want to do that. Somehow you've got to make the best of a bad job, and you can only do that if both of you are honest with each other. Sloan's nervous of talking to you, so you'll need to make the first move.'

'I can't. . .'

Nicole said it again. 'Try. You don't know how you'll really feel unless you do. Give him a chance, Lucy.'

'Does he deserve one?' Lucy asked bitterly.

'Yes, of course he does. He's your father,' said Nicole, and knew that whatever the truth she would still love him. Love didn't need forgiveness.

Jan came in looking anxious. 'Have you heard the news?' she demanded.

'What news?' Nicole's heart quickened.

'That cyclone which has been hanging around is heading this way. It's the one that's been dodging about further north for a week, and suddenly it's on a direct path for the Whitsundays. They're announcing it to all guests so that anyone who wants to go can get off the island.'

Nicole glanced at the chart on the wall which listed all the precautions that needed to be taken in the event of a cyclone. 'I suppose we'd better start battening down and carrying out instructions.' She glanced at Lucy. 'Do you want to lend a hand? We could do with all the help we can get.' She left the invitation with the unspoken question attached: 'Unless you still want to leave?'

Lucy seemed to waver for a moment, then she said, 'Sure, I'll lend a hand. I've never been in a cyclone. It might be fun.'

'Neither have I,' said Nicole, 'and I'm not sure I relish the thought. Somehow I don't think it'll be fun.' She glanced at her watch, then at Jan. 'I'd better go down for surgery. Lucy can help you, Jan. You'd better warn everyone and find out who wants to leave.'

'Mrs Mason's leaving this morning anyway,' said Jan without looking at Lucy, but exchanging a meaningful look with Nicole, who felt instant relief. 'I think most of the others will want to go too.'

Nicole nodded. 'I'll check with Murray and let you know what the arrangements are. I'll be back as soon as I can.'

Sloan was already in the hotel surgery when Nicole entered. He looked up from his desk unsmilingly.

'Good morning,' she said as cheerfully as the tension between them would allow. 'I hear we're about to be struck by a cyclone. Murray's organising transport for everyone who wants to leave.'

He lifted an eyebrow. 'You?'

'Of course not. None of the nurses is going. What about you?'

'Hardly. We might be needed,' he said. 'I'd like Lucy out of the way, though. But I don't know where to send her.' His brow creased with worry.

Nicole gathered her courage and said, 'Is Coralie leaving today because of Lucy?'

'Yes. She was ready to go anyway. I've persuaded her to see a psychiatrist friend of mine in Sydney who can help her, as well as a physician. She's over the worst, but she'll have side-effects for some time, I'm afraid.' He paused, then asked, 'Have you seen Lucy this morning?'

'Yes. I've just been talking to her. She's helping Jan at the moment.' Nicole paused, then took the bull by the horns. 'Sloan, you've got to talk to her, explain everything to her. You've got to establish some kind of understanding.'

'Easier said than done,' he shrugged.

Nicole forced herself to ignore his tight expression, which conveyed his resentment of her interference. 'In the circumstances, I have to agree. But the past is the past, and both of you must come to terms with it some time.'

He looked at her steadily. His voice was low, emotionally charged, when he said, 'Nicole, it wasn't the way Lucy believes. . .'

'You must tell her, not me.' Nicole's own emotions

were making her edgy. 'It's Lucy you have to make your peace with.'

He stood up and approached her, putting his hands on her shoulders. 'Nicole, listen to me. . .'

'Not now,' she said, breaking away. 'Our first patient has just arrived.'

The outer door had opened and closed. Nicole hurried out to see who it was, took down details, then ushered the man in to see Sloan.

There were only a few patients, mostly guests with minor problems, and one of the kitchen staff with a bad burn on his arm.

'Mmm, nasty,' murmured Nicole when he showed her. 'How did you do that?'

'Slipped on a banana skin!'

'You're pulling my leg.'

'No, truly. I knew you wouldn't believe it. Someone dropped a piece of banana skin on the floor and I slipped on it. I happened to be carrying a pan of hot oil at the time.'

'You're lucky it wasn't worse,' Nicole told him. 'No burns on your body, feet?'

The man shook his head, and as Sloan's previous patient came out she ushered the new one in. As she expected, Sloan called for her assistance in dressing the burn. It was the only time he did call for her that morning, and she found it unsettling. I'm like Lucy, she thought, I want to be here, but I also want to run away.

She did not bother with lunch, but went for a short walk along the beach instead, with an apple and a banana in her pocket. The sky was leaden, a peculiar kind of greyish bronze, and the water had the same metallic glaze. There was a stiff breeze, and to Nicole it felt different somehow, perhaps only because she knew it was a precursor of something much more lethal.

Watching a plane come in to land on the small airstrip south of the resort, she sighed. It was definitely time she left Bauhinia. As soon as this crisis was over, she would go. She ought to have gone before. Maybe she could go to Sydney and get a job at the Southern Cross again. And if Lucy needed a place to stay—well, maybe they could share a flat. And perhaps she could persuade her to finish school, even if not at the same boarding-school she had been attending. She laughed at her fancies. What a cheek! Imagining herself involved in Lucy's life. But she could not help feeling concerned about the girl—or was it just a subconscious need to keep in touch with Sloan, however remotely? What good could that possibly do?

'I'm a fool,' she said, and her words were carried away on the wind.

She reached the jetty and climbed the steps, to sit on one of the bollards to eat her fruit. A plane took off, and she wondered if Coralie Mitchell was on board, if Sloan had seen her off. She could have sat there all day gazing morosely into the water, but Jan was probably rushed off her feet even with Sharon and Lucy to help. She was just leaving to go back to the Lodge when Sloan appeared. She sank back on to the bollard.

'Wind's getting up,' he remarked. It was blowing his dark hair about untidily, but he was still the handsomest man she had known. Even with his brow troubled, his dark eyes withdrawn, he had the power to make her ache with longing. And nothing he had done could make any difference.

'What's the latest news on the cyclone?' she asked.

'Heading this way still.'

'What's she called?'

He laughed. 'Not she—he! Cyclone Damien.'

'Oh, that's trendy.'

Sloan squatted down beside her and placed a hand on her knees, a hand she knew to be gentle and caring, a hand that could also arouse unsuspected desires in her. 'I have to square things with you, Nicole. You've got to listen to me.'

'Please, Sloan, I don't want to be involved.'

'You *are* involved,' he insisted.

'I've got to get back to the Lodge to help Jan and Sharon.'

'Five minutes,' he begged.

'All right. Tell me, but I'm not going to persuade Lucy to believe you. You have to do that yourself.'

Sloan looked grateful. 'I need to rehearse.'

He sat down on the edge of the jetty, staring at the sea which slopped noisily against the wooden piles. 'Lucy's got it all wrong. I was not having an affair with Coralie when Helen supposedly killed herself.'

'I think Coralie might deny that,' Nicole told him.

'Only because now she wants people to think that we're old flames,' said Sloan. 'But the truth is we were never lovers.'

'So you said before, but do you deny you were with her the night Helen died?'

'No.'

'Well, there you are——'

'I met her to talk about Lucy,' he said quietly.

'Lucy!' Nicole exclaimed sceptically.

'Yes. She's had a bee in her bonnet for years about becoming an actress. No doubt she's talked to you about it. I wasn't keen on the idea, so I decided to ask Coralie's advice before Lucy got too set on the idea.'

'Without Helen?'

His face darkened and the muscles were rigid. 'Helen had something else to do that evening—something that came up after we'd both arranged to see Coralie. Helen always had something else to do, was always breaking appointments. So I had dinner with Coralie and she promised to talk to Lucy and warn her about the problems and pitfalls, to try and find out if she was really determined and if she had any talent. She was seeing Luke then, Nicole, the man she married. He was with us the whole time.'

Nicole let his words swirl around her brain. It sounded so convincing.

'Helen evidently was convinced you and Coralie were having an affair,' Nicole said slowly.

Sloan shook his head. 'This is the hard part, Nicole. This is why it's so difficult for me to talk to Lucy about it. I've never wanted to shatter her illusions.'

'What do you mean by that?'

His voice was low, barely audible in the rising wind. 'It wasn't me who was having affairs, it was Helen. I'd known about it for some time and turned a blind eye. Our marriage had been on the rocks for years. We stayed together because of Lucy and because it suited Helen. Helen was beautiful, sexy and liked the glamorous, sophisticated life. I was too mundane for her. At first our marriage was OK, but I wasn't socially ambitious enough for her.

'She didn't commit suicide. She was on her way to a lover the night she died. I even knew who it was, but of course I said nothing. I didn't want anyone else involved. I didn't want Lucy to find out. Helen's death was an accident. She wasn't the kind of woman to take her own life.'

'But she told Lucy. . .'

'That I was the one having affairs. Maybe she even half believed it—I don't know. Maybe believing it made her feel less guilty, or perhaps she just wanted to hurt me by alienating my daughter. We were coming to the point of divorce, you see, and had already been through some bitter wrangling.'

'Lucy will never believe that,' Nicole said.

Sloan pushed the hair out of his eyes and stared hard at her. 'Do you?' he asked directly.

Nicole bit her lip. 'I don't know. . .'

He stood up abruptly. 'It's the truth! I never wanted Lucy to know the truth. I didn't know Helen had been poisoning her mind against me. I thought she believed Helen's death was an accident. It *was* an accident.'

'But you can't prove it. Lucy trusted her mother.'

He paced up and down in front of her, distraught. 'I know. So did I—once. Oh, it wasn't all her fault, of course not. We simply weren't compatible. I didn't blame Helen for seeking consolation elsewhere. Mostly I blamed myself. . .' He looked down at Nicole in despair. 'There's no cliché solution, Nicole. I can't produce someone who'll vouch for me as they do in fiction, no lover of Helen's to tell Lucy the truth. Either she believes me or she doesn't.' His mouth twisted ironically. 'If you believe me, she might. She thinks you're pretty cool, to use her jargon.'

Nicole felt the burden was too much. 'You have to tell her, Sloan. You have to let her make up her own mind.'

'You don't believe me, do you?' He turned his back

and she caught only the tail-end of his next words. 'Fool to imagine you would.'

Impulsively she jumped up and ran to him, throwing her arms around him. 'Sloan, I *want* to believe you. I—I think I do. But I'm not Lucy.'

He turned in her arms and held her tightly. 'Nicole . . .oh, Nicole. . .' Suddenly his mouth was warm and hard on hers, and his kiss was searing, but not with desire, .more with a fierce need for something more than mere physical love. The wind whipped their clothes with a noisy flapping and the water sucked at the jetty piles as though to draw them down with it.

Sloan slowly let her go. 'I'll tell her,' he said, but his face had a look of grim despair. He looked at the sky. 'We'd better be going. They'll need all the help they can get to batten down ready for the big blow.'

Nicole looked around. The yachts had gone from the bay, probably to more sheltered anchorages or to ride out the storm where they could not be battered to bits on the reef. The palm trees were already bending with the force of the wind and swirls of sand were eddying along the beach. At the end of the jetty the waves were smashing against the framework in clouds of spray.

'It could do this for hours,' said Sloan, 'before it makes up its mind to strike, or to veer off somewhere else.'

Nicole felt the wind tug at her and stumbled. Sloan caught her and prevented her from falling. She clung to him, panicky all at once. 'Sloan, I'm scared!'

He held her close to his side and half dragged her up to the hotel. 'We'd better go back to the Lodge,' he said. 'Before it's too late.'

There were men helping to batten down at the Lodge. Storm shutters on the windows had been fas-

tened and garden furniture secured. Jan was distribut-
ing candles and oil-lamps as the power was almost
certain to go off. Not all the patients had gone. Those
who were left would gather in the big windowless
storeroom which was supposed to be cyclone-proof.
All the medical equipment and other fragile items were
to be taken there too.

'We've got emergency rations,' Jan said, still able to
smile. 'In case it goes on all night. We can make tea on
the Primus.'

Sloan said, 'We'd better be prepared for injuries.'
As he spoke, Lucy appeared, having finished some
task, ready to do another. She looked once at her
father, then deliberately turned her back on him. He
exchanged an agonised look with Nicole, and she knew
then that she believed what he had told her. She had
to. It was the word of a living man against that of a
dead woman, and she was in love with the man. She
could not believe evil of him.

The cyclone struck with full force late in the afternoon. While the wind howled and roared outside,
Nicole swallowed her fear and forced herself not to
panic. A dozen times she felt sure the roof would lift
off and the whining wind would whirl them all into
some black vortex in the sky. The whole building shook
and several times there was the sound of breaking glass
and other ominous sounds of destruction. The power
failed, and Jan made tea on the Primus and kept up a
cheerful chatter, although she was probably as terrified
as Nicole. Lucy huddled in a chair, wide-eyed and
fearful, and Sloan prowled.

When the silence came it was eerie, and they did not
even notice it at first. It was Jan who said, 'Have I gone
deaf, or has the wind dropped?'

Sloan said, 'It could be just the eye of the storm. We might be in the calm centre now. Just for a while.'

'You mean there's more to come?' Jan's face was still white with strain.

He nodded. 'I'm going down to the hotel in case there are any casualties.'

Nicole said automatically, 'I'll come with you.'

For a moment she thought he was going to forbid it, but he didn't. He glanced at his daughter, his mouth rigid, but a small muscular movement in his neck betrayed his emotion. 'All right, Lucy?' he asked.

Her eyes flicked to him briefly. 'Sure, I'm OK. I'll come too. I might be able to help.'

Nicole thought Sloan was about to forbid it, but he didn't. She guessed he wanted to be near Lucy as much as she wanted to be near him in this crisis. 'Let's get going,' he said briskly.

Emerging from the safety of the windowless 'bunker', which had allowed them no view of the cyclone's capacity for destruction, Nicole was unprepared for the devastation that confronted them.

'Oh, God!' she gasped, her hand to her mouth. 'Oh, Sloan—look at it!'

Lucy, beside her, was speechless, and Sloan just stood and stared, momentarily rigid with dismay.

Half the roof of the Lodge had vanished and one end of the building had collapsed completely. The office was a heap of rubble. There was shattered glass everywhere and beyond the buildings palm trees lay uprooted and shrubs had been stripped of every leaf. Some of the big trees were still standing, but they looked like skeletons. Nicole had never seen such devastation, never imagined how appalling it could be.

'Our units!' she exclaimed, horrified. 'Where are

they?' All she could see were piles of debris, with some walls astonishingly still standing. But there was no time to worry about personal belongings.

'It's like a battlefield,' murmured Lucy, her face white with shock as she held tightly to Nicole's hand.

Sloan's shock was dissipating the fastest. 'Come on,' he urged, 'we'd better see how the hotel fared. By the look of things, we'll have to go on foot. The track will be covered in debris. We might have a job getting through.'

'And it could start all over again soon?' Nicole asked, as the three of them half ran, half stumbled down the hill.

'Very soon,' Sloan said grimly, catching her arm as she almost tripped and fell. He caught her close to him for a moment and their eyes met, his anguished, then he let her go and plunged on ahead.

It took them half an hour to reach the hotel. The track was almost obliterated and they had to detour across the golf course, which was littered with debris. Halfway they were hailed by shouts, and two men from the hotel ran up to them.

'Thank heavens you're OK, Doctor!' said one with relief. 'We've got a few casualties, I'm afraid.'

'The damage looks pretty bad from here,' Sloan commented. The jetty appeared to have vanished and high waves were pounding the shoreline. A curtain of spray concealed part of the resort, but it was obvious that the hotel had suffered like the Lodge.

'Anyone badly hurt?' asked Nicole.

'I don't think so,' said one of the men. 'What about up at the Lodge?'

'They're all OK,' said Sloan. 'The storeroom proved its worth. We sat it out inside, and it held.'

The second man was scanning the sky. 'We'd better get a move on—we're going to be in for it again shortly.' He glanced at Lucy's frightened face. 'It probably won't be so bad. The radio says she's deteriorating into a rain depression pretty fast.'

Lucy gave a faint smile. 'It's a "he"!'

Everyone laughed and the tension eased a little. The two men from the resort led the others back to the hotel by the route they had taken, but it still seemed an age to Nicole before they arrived and were able to attend to the patients.

Despite the whole complex seeming to be a total shambles at first glance, it was soon apparent that the buildings had in fact suffered less than the Lodge, which was in a more exposed position on the hill. Part of the hotel had been unroofed, most of the cabins were badly damaged and the swimming-pool was full of debris. The beach was littered with debris and uprooted palms and other trees, and the jetty had collapsed in the middle and was being pounded by a still angry sea. But being in the lee of the island's 'mountain', from which direction the cyclone had arrived, had provided some protection. Part of the main building was still, miraculously, standing.

The surger, to Nicole's relief, had survived, apart from a broken window through which a tree branch was jammed and a pattern of large cracks in the ceiling.

'I hope that isn't going to collapse on us,' she said, giving it a wary glance.

Sloan looked as dazed as she felt. He raked a hand through his hair. 'We'll just have to cross our fingers. The maintenance guys are checking, but there's not a lot they can do until the big blow's over. I'm told we'll have emergency lighting shortly.'

A small knot of people appeared in the doorway, their faces strained. Murray Peterson, looking the most worried of all, was with them. He glanced anxiously around the surgery.

'Looks as though you've got off fairly lightly here, folks.' There was fleeting relief in his smile. 'And no serious injuries, thank goodness.' He turned to the casualties. 'Back to the shelter as soon as you can. You know where? Good. And you too, Doc, Nicole—as soon as she starts to blow. Take no chances. Right?'

Nicole caught Lucy's eye and they both grinned as Lucy mouthed, 'It's a "he"!'

Nicole noticed that Murray was absently rubbing his chest. 'You all right, Murray?' she asked, following him out and detaining him for a moment.

He glanced sharply at her. 'Yeah, why?'

'The way you were massaging your chest, I thought you might be having pains.'

He dropped his hand to his side. 'Me? Oh, just a touch of indigestion, darling. It's my old duodenal ulcer, flares up when there's too much stress.'

'You ought to let Sloan take a look at you,' she told him.

'Maybe later,' he said. 'It's nothing, Nic. You'll have your work cut out to see everyone else before we have to batten down again.'

Nicole went back. The patients drifted into the waiting area and Sloan rapidly reviewed them to see who needed attention first. Lucy was eager to help, so Nicole showed her how to take the patients' details, then joined Sloan. By then the emergency power was on.

Most of the injuries were minor cuts and bruises, with one case of possible concussion. The man had been unconscious for several minutes but had come to and now complained of a throbbing headache. Another had a sprained ankle and one a broken finger. They had been injured while trying to shift debris.

A particularly nasty splinter took some time to remove, and it was while Sloan was doing this, with Nicole holding a light as steady as she could, that she realised it was growing darker again and that the wind was rising once more. Almost at the same moment she became aware of it, so did Sloan and the young man on the treatment couch.

'Second helpings coming up,' the man said.

Sloan swore under his breath, and said edgily, 'Hold the light closer, Nicole! Stop waving it about.'

She tried to keep her hand steady, but it wasn't easy. Her mouth was dry and she felt, if anything, even more frightened now she knew what the wind could do.

'We'd better give you a tetanus booster and an antibiotic,' Sloan said, as he completed removal of the splinter. 'I don't think there's any left, but just in case——' A loud explosive sound cut off his words, and the light in Nicole's hand went out, leaving them in deep gloom. Nicole stared at the lamp as though she had caused the power failure herself.

Fortunately, she was still able to see to prepare the necessary injections. There was only one more patient to see and she, fortunately, did not require any delicate procedure. She had slipped and fallen on her elbow, which was now swollen and painful.

Sloan examined it carefully. 'Nothing broken,' he said. 'But we'll X-ray it later—if we can—just to be sure. Meanwhile a support bandage—and have we got a sling, Sister?'

Nicole produced the required bandage and arm sling,

and the patient hurried away. The noise of the wind was now rising to a continuous roar and they could feel the vibrations through the buildings. The fact that she had already experienced it once made it no less frightening for Nicole.

Sloan looked around the surgery and at the broken window and sagging ceiling. 'I guess we'd better go.' He turned to his daughter, whose face betrayed a mounting panic. 'Come on, Lucy.'

She stared at him, a wild look in her eyes, and Nicole caught her breath. She recognised hysteria in the girl, born of panic and fear and her emotional turmoil. She was clearly at breaking point.

'Lucy, you can't do any more here,' she said gently. 'We'll be along in a minute too.'

Lucy's face was white in the gloom, her pupils distended. Lips parted and trembling, she yelled at her father, 'You killed her! You killed my mother!'

Sloan stepped back as though she had struck him, and Nicole went forward, hand outstretched to console the girl, but Lucy thrust her away. 'You wouldn't care if I was killed too! You probably hope I will be! Well, I don't care either. What have I got to live for? Nothing!'

Sloan went to her and tried to put his arms around her. 'Lucy, for God's sake. . .'

She managed to break free and ran to the door. 'Will you be satisfied if I kill myself like she did? You'll be free then, won't you? Totally free to do what you want. You can marry that bitch Coralie. . .'

Nicole felt a new kind of fear. She realised that Lucy had cracked under the strain, and that, with a cyclone raging about them, her irrational behaviour was potentially dangerous. She moved towards the girl again. 'Please, Lucy. . .we'll talk about it later. . .'

Sloan tried again to grab his daughter, but she eluded him, and, sobbing, 'Leave me alone! I hate you! I don't want to be near you for another second. I'm going back to the Lodge,' she fled.

Sloan gave Nicole a brief agonised glance. 'She'll never make it!' he said, and sped after Lucy.

Nicole picked up his medical bag and raced after them. She almost bumped into one of the staff who was checking that everyone was in the maximum shelter building, and thrust the bag at him. 'Look after this for me, Eric,' she said urgently.

'Where are you going?' he asked.

But Nicole did not answer. She had glimpsed Sloan going through the shattered exit doors at the far end of the corridor and she flew after him. By the sudden change in the note of the wind, she knew they had to catch up with Lucy before she got too far. In the open, with the wind blowing debris around, it was dangerous, especially for someone in as highly emotional a state as Lucy. Nicole did not even think that it might be highly dangerous for Sloan and herself too.

CHAPTER NINE

OUTSIDE the hotel it was a maelstrom. Nicole halted in
fascinated horror at the sight of a boiling sea, at the
spectacle of leaves, branches, pieces of buildings being
tossed about the sky as though by the frivolous will of
some child in a tantrum.

A mist of spray from the ocean drifted across the
resort, cutting visibility, and the trees and palms that
were still standing thrashed in the wind like maniacs
trying to escape their fetters. In the fading light it was
weird, theatrical, and terrifying. Back at the Lodge,
secure in the protected storeroom, Nicole had not
actually witnessed much of the actual storm, but now
she was caught up in it.

She paused for only seconds as the elemental display
hit her senses. Through the gloom she saw Sloan
running and assumed he could see what she could not,
the fleeing Lucy. If that was so, then Lucy was not
heading for the Lodge. She was fleeing in the opposite
direction, off into the bush. In her distraught frame of
mind, she probably had no idea where she was going.

'Sloan. . .' Nicole's cry was swallowed by the wind,
a pitiful shriek in the midst of shrieking that reminded
of hell. 'Sloan!'

She ran after him, not questioning why she did, why
it seemed imperative for her to follow. She just felt
more strongly than anything else she had ever felt in
her life that she must be near him, that in case he
should need her she must be there. It was an emotional

response, not a rational act, and there was no way she could have controlled the impulse. Wherever Sloan was, she had to be too. She had to share his danger, his anguish, his problems whether he wanted her to or not.

Nicole ran headlong, dodging flying debris, stumbling over obstacles, her eyes seeing only the dark figure of Sloan Reilly as he searched for his daughter in the storm. She sobbed aloud, and her tears were whipped away by the unmerciful wind. She felt the sting of flying twigs scratch her face and arms, the tangles of debris trying to bring her down, but she kept on, bruised and buffeted by the power of the cyclone, not even sure where she was going, desperate to keep Sloan in her sight, fearful of what might happen to Lucy.

I love them both, she thought once in a kind of frenzy. Please don't let anything happen to them!

Once she thought she had lost sight of Sloan, but a fragment of sound came to her—'Lu—ceee!'—and she caught sight of him again and was spurred on. If he had lost the girl then together they might have more chance of finding her. That he had lost sight of his daughter was soon confirmed. She caught up with him, found him standing dazed and uncertain, clinging to a tree, buffeted by the wind, his clothing torn as hers was, his face as scratched and muddied as her own.

'Sloan. . .oh, Sloan. . .where is she?' Nicole fell into his arms and for a moment there was blessed comfort as his tightened around her and the horror receded. But it was a false security. The wildness all about them was unrelenting.

'I don't know!' he yelled. 'She must have fallen somewhere. Maybe knocked over by flying debris, a falling tree. . .oh, God, Nicole, where is she? I have to find her!' He held her close, his cheek against hers as though to find comfort in their contact. 'Nicole, help me find her. . .please.'

'That's why I'm here,' Nicole said, probably too softly for him to have heard above the roar of the wind. Louder she asked, 'Where did you last see her?'

He pointed. 'There. . .then she vanished.'

'Come on! She must be somewhere. She must have to stop soon. No one can run for long in this.' She tugged on his hand. She was almost out of breath herself, and a stitch in her side made her grit her teeth.

Sloan did not move. Nicole turned her head, puzzled at his immobility. If she was not yet spent, neither should he be.

'Look, we're near the edge of a cliff.' He spoke so quietly she could not hear the words, but she could read his lips. 'Oh, God, Nicole, she must have gone over. . .'

Nicole left him, battling her way against the force of the wind, to the edge of the steep drop which she had not noticed before. Everything looked the same in the half-light. As it would have looked to Lucy.

'Lucy!' she called. 'Lucy, where are you?'

A faint cry seemed to come from somewhere close by, but Nicole thought it must be imagination. Then, as she stood near the edge of the cliff looking down into the valley, digging her heels into the earth to prevent being blown over the edge, she heard it again. Sloan reached her side and gripped her arm. 'For God's sake, don't go so close!'

'Over there!' Nicole shouted, and dragged him along the edge with her.

They found Lucy crumpled in a heap just below the

lip of the cliff. She had fallen a few yards and been caught up in a tangle of tree roots and branches. There was an ugly weal on her temple and she was moaning.

Sloan almost threw himself on her. 'Lucy, my darling, are you all right?' Automatically, his skilled hands probed for broken bones while Nicole checked her pulse and brushed the debris off her tear-stained face. Lucy looked at her briefly and then passed out.

Sloan lifted the inert body in his arms, steadying himself against the gale.

'You can't carry her. Not in this,' Nicole told him. 'Not all the way back to the hotel. We must find shelter somewhere until it's over.' She looked desperately around her, and almost wept when the miracle happened. 'Sloan, look. . .a cabin!' she yelled. 'Over there!'

It was one of the small picnic huts where bushwalkers could shelter in bad weather, but it hadn't been constructed to weather cyclones. It was in a state of collapse, but it was better than staying in the open. Nicole stumbled towards it, and Sloan followed. One side of the hut had been blown in, but there was still enough shelter for the three of them.

Sloan carried Lucy into the dim interior and laid her gently down on the floor. Nicole, searching, found a plastic cushion and pillowed the girl's head on it.

'Is she all right?' she asked urgently.

Sloan was pulling down the pale eyelids. 'She must have taken a heavy blow on the temple.'

'She'll be all right,' Nicole heard herself saying. 'She's not injured otherwise, is she?'

'I don't think so.'

Nicole found her face was close to his, and the pain

in his eyes was like a knife in her own body. 'Oh, Sloan,' was all she could say.

It was impossible to talk above the roaring of the wind, so they sat in silence, crouched beside the unconscious Lucy, as the darkness intensified until they could no longer even see each other's faces. Time might have been passing slowly or quickly. Nicole could not judge, and she could not see her watch. All she knew was that they must have been there for some considerable time, because her body was growing stiff with sitting in a cramped position. From time to time, small movements from Sloan—checking Lucy's pulse, Nicole guessed—were all that indicated he was still there. Once he tried to strike a match, but it quickly went out. Nicole saw his face, drawn with anxiety as he looked at Lucy in the brief flash of light.

'I wish we had a torch,' he said. 'I've only got a small packet of matches, and I'd better not waste them.'

'I wish we had a blanket for Lucy,' sighed Nicole.

'It's not cold,' said Sloan. 'That's one thing to be thankful for.'

Suddenly it dawned on them that they were talking without having to shout, and that the wind had a different sound.

'It's dying down,' Sloan said, his voice flooding with relief. 'It's nearly over.'

Nicole put her hands over her ears. She felt deafened, as though the roaring had burst her eardrums.

But it wasn't quite over. The wind gradually died away, but on its heels came the rain, heavy driving rain that thundered on the partially collapsed roof they were sheltering under like an advancing army. Damp and miserable, tense with worry, Nicole and Sloan could only sit in the darkness with Lucy and wait.

Nicole knew how helpless Sloan must be feeling, but there was no way they could move the girl until morning. It would be impossible to find their way back to the hotel in the dark, and dangerous. The cyclone had obliterated the tracks and it would be foolhardy to try and pick their way over the debris, even without an injured girl to carry.

Now that the wind had dropped, every now and then Sloan struck a match and peered into his daughter's ashen face. With her own fingers on the girl's wrist, Nicole could only feel relief that Lucy was still breathing. Every other feeling seemed to have been crushed out of her.

As each match Sloan struck flamed and then died, the darkness seemed to press in even more like a suffocating blanket, and the sound of the rain was a relentless drumming on the roof.

Once, a flickering match burning down to his fingers, Sloan looked at Nicole, then glanced at his daughter's still form. 'It's not being able to do anything. . .' The flame went out, but he was still speaking. 'That's how it was with Helen. . .a feeling of utter helplessness, not being able to save her, wondering if I could have prevented it. . .'

'You mustn't blame yourself,' Nicole said gently, her hand touching his arm.

'That's the trouble,' Sloan said in a grating tone. 'I don't! Oh, some of the fault for ending our marriage must have been mine as much as hers, but what happened after that I couldn't have prevented. Sometimes I wish I could blame myself, as Lucy does. Maybe then I could forgive myself and she could forgive me. . .' His voice shook and Nicole felt his hand cover hers. 'I couldn't tell her the truth about Helen. I couldn't shatter her illusions. Oh, God, Nicole, if she dies without ever knowing how much she means to me. . .'

Nicole moved closer and put her arms around him. His shoulders were shaking and she knew he was crying. In the darkness, unable to see each other, it didn't seem strange to be holding this man in her arms, comforting him.

'Lucy isn't going to die,' Nicole said firmly. 'Her pulse is good, her colour's reasonable. You've examined her yourself, Sloan. She's had a nasty bump on the head and she could be out cold for a while, quite a while in fact, but it's just concussion and she might even come to before morning.'

'I wish she would,' he said fervently. 'I think I'd die if I lost her. That *would* be my fault.'

'You're not going to lose her,' murmured Nicole soothingly. 'You're letting your emotions override your medical expertise. Pull yourself together, Sloan. Lucy's going to need all your strength in the morning.'

His head dropped wearily on to her shoulder and she settled herself as comfortably as she could with him leaning against her. They sat in silence for some time, then Sloan stirred, struck another match and looked at Lucy.

'She's moved!' he exclaimed. 'Nicole, she's turned her head!'

Nicole reached automatically for the girl's wrist. 'Lucy,' she said in a low tone, 'Lucy, are you awake?'

'Lucy! Lucy, for God's sake speak to me!' Sloan ran his fingers gently down the pale cheek, but there was no response. The match flickered and went out. 'She's still unconscious,' he said despairingly.

'At least she's moved,' Nicole murmured. 'She's going to be all right, Sloan.'

As she sat back, trying to make herself comfortable in the awkward situation they were in, Sloan slid his arms around her and held her close. 'I don't know what I'd have done without you, Nicole.'

Nicole felt tears welling in her eyes and swallowed hard. She hoped he could not feel her racing heart.

Sloan's hands slid up to her shoulders, touched the cool flesh of her neck and, like a blind man exploring a new face, he cupped hers in his hands. 'Nicole. . .' His voice was rough, emotional, and full of need.

Nicole did not turn away from his lips as they met hers. She needed the contact as much as he, and they clung together in a frenzy of shared emotion for long minutes, parting breathlessly once or twice, only to fall into each other's arms again.

Nicole did not remember falling asleep, but when she woke there was a faint grey light in the sky and she was lying with her head on Sloan's shoulder. He had one arm flung around her protectively, and his other hand held Lucy's in a firm grip. He had probably not meant to fall asleep, but exhaustion had taken its toll and he was sitting with his head slumped on his chest, still deeply asleep. Nicole touched his cheek wistfully. She had slept beside him, but not as a lover. That she would never do. Briefly, Sloan had turned to her with passion because he was at the end of his emotional tether, and, loving him, she had not be able to deny him some solace. But she was not the woman he wanted in his life.

'My darling. . .' she whispered, and laid her head against his chest for a moment. He did not wake.

But a small sound made Nicole glance up. Lucy's eyes were open and she was staring at the gap where the dawn light was filtering through.

'Lucy, you're awake!'

Lucy slowly brought her gaze to Nicole's face. 'Hi! What happened?' she whispered.

But Nicole was momentarily speechless with relief and joy. Then she turned back to Sloan, shaking him. 'Sloan, wake up! Wake *up*!'

He stirred and sat up, looking desperately at her. 'What's the matter?' he muttered.

'Lucy's awake!'

But before she had finished speaking, he was bending over his daughter, saying emotionally, 'Lucy—thank God!'

Then the girl was gathered into his arms, held close, rocked like a small child, and through her tears, Nicole saw Lucy's arms clasp her father tightly. She thought she heard her murmur, 'Dad, I'm sorry.'

Nicole scrambled outside, leaving them. The sky was clear again, the rain gone, the wind stilled. Only the appalling devastation all around them reminded that the nightmare had been real.

Lucy wanted to walk back to the hotel, but Sloan vetoed that idea, and when she tried to stand and defy him she swayed giddily and had to give in.

'My head aches,' she said, holding it in her hands.

'You've got a very colourful bruise coming on your temple,' Nicole told her, as she looked in at them through the gap in the hut wall.

'I'll give you a piggyback,' Sloan said. He helped Lucy out of the hut. 'You're not steady enough on your feet to walk. Come on, up you get.'

'Dad! Really! There's no need,' Lucy protested.

'Do as you're told! There was a time when you'd beg me to give you a piggyback!'

Nicole heard the light-hearted banter with amazement, relief and some hope, but under it lurked her own sense of loss. She wanted with all her heart for Sloan and Lucy to be reconciled, and some sixth sense told her that it now might be possible, but in their reconciliation there would be no place for her. Despite what he had said, she felt that once everything was sorted out he would still turn to Coralie. He might not have been in love with her before, or her lover, but Nicole felt sure he was now, or, if not, certainly on the brink of it. Lucy had liked Coralie in the beginning, and once she accepted the truth she would do again.

Lucy climbed on to her father's back and they staggered and stumbled back to the hotel. From a distance it looked like a ghost resort, and Nicole momentarily caught her breath. Then the closer they came, she saw moving figures and allowed her taut nerves to relax.

As they reached the hotel, picking their way over broken glass and other debris, a figure hurried towards them. It was the office manager, Dorothy Rayner. She was as rumpled as they, and clearly in a panic.

'Sloan! We've been searching everywhere. They hadn't seen you up at the Lodge, we couldn't find you anywhere here. We didn't know where you were.' Her eyes flicked swiftly and curiously over Lucy and Nicole, but there was no time for explanations. 'Sloan, it's Murray. I think he's having a heart attack!'

'What?' Sloan eased Lucy from his back and set her down. She swayed slightly and Dorothy caught hold of her. 'Take care of Lucy, will you, please, Dorothy? She's suffering from concussion. She needs to go to bed, if there is one. Where's Murray?'

'In the surgery. I thought that was the best place.'

Tears suddenly filled her eyes. 'I didn't know what I was going to do if I couldn't find you.' The strain was telling on her too. 'Oh, what a terrible mess everything is! How are we ever going to clean it up?'

But only Lucy heard her. Sloan and Nicole were running as fast as they could to the surgery. Nicole saw with relief that the two rooms were still more or less intact. She gasped when she saw Murray Peterson prostrate on the floor with two people bending over him trying to resuscitate him.

She heard Sloan shout to her, but she did not need to be told what to do. The two employees who had been trying to revive the hotel manager stood by, silent and tense, watching as Sloan and Nicole took over. It was minutes before Nicole would admit it, but she knew instinctively that they had been too late. A terrible choking sensation gripped her throat as she looked at the inert form of the man who had undoubtedly worn himself out yesterday and last night coping with the storm. It wasn't fair that he should pay such a high price, that he should survive the fury of the elements to die like this. Her eyes smarted with tears she refused to shed and she swallowed hard. Poor Murray, she thought, he didn't deserve to die. But sometimes people didn't. People didn't die because they deserved to, but because sometimes it just happened. Like Sloan's wife. . .

For the next twenty-four hours Nicole felt like a zombie, doing what was required of her, but in a dazed state. Everyone else was the same, she knew, which accounted for the strange disconnected looks people sometimes gave her. No doubt she unconsciously looked at them the same way. It was a case of mass shock, and in some it was more pronounced than in others.

Murray Peterson's death cast added gloom over the resort. It seemed to make the destruction which the cyclone had wrought even more devastating. But gradually people rallied as the need to restore some kind of normality became imperative. Power was again restored, debris was cleared from the interior of the hotel and courtyards, water pipes repaired, and meals were prepared. Emergency services help from the mainland, which had not been so badly hit, began to arrive by air and sea, and an air of cheerful optimism began to grow. People even began to joke about their experiences.

Nicole and Sloan were kept busy treating, fortunately, mostly minor injuries and shock, and there was little spare time for talking. When Sloan was satisfied that she was only suffering from concussion, Lucy had been taken to the Lodge where Jan was looking after her. Although the Lodge had been very badly damaged, some of the rooms were habitable and makeshift facilities were installed.

However, the damage was such that the few remaining patients from the Lodge and guests from the hotel had to be transported to the mainland. Among the first arrivals was Toff Barrett, who was devastated to learn of Murray Peterson's death.

Nicole was bandaging a sprained wrist when he walked in. She had never seen him look so shattered. The debonair entrepreneur was also shocked to the core by what he had seen on a reconnaissance flight around the island, and he seemed to have aged ten years since she had last seen him. But there was a glimmer of determination in his eyes.

'We'll rebuild,' he said. 'I'm quite determined about that.'

'Brave words, Toff!' It was Sloan, seeing another patient out. He paused to run an eye over Nicole's handiwork, gave her an approving smile, and added a word or two of advice to the young kitchen hand, who then left. He turned to his friend. 'Bit of a mess, eh?' Then soberly he added, 'I wish we could have saved Murray. We had the means, but we didn't get to him in time.'

'Not your fault,' Toff said.

Sloan exchanged a glance with Nicole and she felt a sharp stab inside her. She knew what he was thinking. If he and Lucy hadn't been at loggerheads, she wouldn't have run off into the storm, and he would have been on hand, or could have got there more quickly, when Murray collapsed. Sloan was blaming himself.

'Have you told his family?' asked Sloan, his face showing pain.

'Yes. There's only a brother in Brisbane. He's coming over to take him back today.'

They were silent for a moment or two, then Nicole said, 'Shall I make some coffee?'

The men nodded, and began talking about the clean-up that had already commenced, but which in reality would take some time. It would be months before rebuilding could begin. Busy with kettle and mugs, Nicole could not hear everything that was said in the other room, but she did hear Toff say to Sloan, 'Good thing Coralie left before the storm hit. I'm glad you two met up again. You'll be seeing her in Sydney, of course?'

Sloan answered, 'Yes. I'm hoping she'll have Lucy

to stay with her for a while. I think they'll be good for each other.' He gave a short, wry laugh. 'And I'll be able to keep an eye on them!'

'As they say, it's an ill wind that blows nobody any good,' said Toff drily. 'I'm glad you've sorted things out with Lucy, Sloan. She's a great kid, a bit of a chip off the old block.'

'And a lot like Helen in some ways,' said Sloan ruefully.

'Well, I grant you she's beautiful like Helen,' was Toff's reply. He added, 'It's time you married again, Sloan. Give Lucy a taste of secure family life before she flies the nest. She likes Coralie, doesn't she?'

Nicole bit her lip so hard she tasted blood.

'They've had their differences. . .' Sloan said, and stopped when Nicole entered with the tray of coffee. Before they had a chance to drink it, Dorothy came in, saying Toff was wanted on the telephone. He went out with her.

Nicole felt hurt that Sloan had not told her himself that he and Lucy were reconciled, but, despite her curiosity, she gave no sign that she had overheard. He looked steadily at her, then said, 'I'm taking Lucy back to Sydney tomorrow.'

Nicole prayed she would be brave. 'I thought you'd want to get away as soon as you could. I suppose you'll want a specialist to look at Lucy, just in case.'

He smiled faintly. 'Fussy father syndrome.'

'It's perfectly understandable.' As was his need to be with Coralie.

Again he studied her for a long uncomfortable minute before saying, 'I've been wanting to tell you, Nicole, but I haven't had a proper chance before. . . Lucy and I have had that talk at last, and she—she understands. I told her everything. I was afraid that in her low emotional and physical state it might have had a negative effect, but it didn't. It seems that deep down she knew Helen was lying, but she didn't want to believe it. She didn't want her mother to be the kind of person she suspected she was, so she refused to accept it. I think—I hope—she's come to terms with it now. She's realised that you can still love a person even if he or she has faults, that she can love Helen for all her good points, she doesn't have to condemn her because she wasn't perfect, because none of us is perfect.'

Nicole impulsively touched his arm. 'Sloan, I'm so glad! So relieved. I hope everything will work out wonderfully for you both now.'

'Nicole. . .' he drew her into his arms with a tenderness that made her weak, 'you helped more than you know.'

She looked up at him, trying to smile. 'Don't. . .' She was at breaking point, and his dark, speculative look seemed to unmask her. It was a highly charged moment, and Nicole was at a loss to know how to end it. But the arrival of a new patient saved her the anguish.

The next morning Lucy came to say goodbye to Nicole who, having rescued what she could of her personal belongings from her wrecked cabin, was back at the Lodge, trying to help salvage papers and equipment. Lucy hugged her warmly. Sloan's daughter was pale, but more relaxed now, and there was a different look in her eyes. The misery had gone and there was, Nicole saw with gratitude, the beginnings of happiness.

'I was a stupid idiot,' Lucy admitted ruefully. 'I was pretty rotten to Dad, but it's all sorted out now. You were right, of course.' She gave Nicole a rather old-fashioned look. 'You know, when I was unconscious out there in the bush, I had a strange dream. Dad was talking to me about Mummy and I knew it was all true, so when he did tell me it sort of confirmed what I already knew.' She paused. 'In the dream, he said he'd die if I did. It was so real, Nicole. And I felt so good, because I knew he really cared.'

'It was real. He really did say it,' Nicole told her softly. 'You weren't dreaming, Lucy. You probably regained consciousness briefly and heard us talking. He was distraught. He loves you very much—you know that now, don't you?'

Lucy's eyes filled with tears. 'Yes. I wish I hadn't been so hateful to him. I know he was only trying to protect me from the truth. Nicole, when I woke up and found he was holding my hand, that he'd been watching there beside me all night, afraid I might die, I felt so awful. . .and about Coralie too. I always liked her. I couldn't believe it when Mummy said. . . I felt betrayed by both of them, Dad and Coralie, and yet I also felt that somehow it was all my fault. . .'

Nicole gave her a little shake. 'Now, Lucy, you mustn't blame yourself. Nothing was your fault.'

Lucy hugged her. 'Are you coming to see us off?' she asked.

Nicole could think of no excuse. When Sloan kissed her she thought she would break down, but she managed to keep control.

He said, 'You ought to be coming with us.'

Nicole shook her head. 'Toff wants Jan and me to stay for a while in case we're needed.'

'Yes, I know. . .' He seemed reluctant to go suddenly.

Nicole forced a bright smile. 'After all, we managed very well on our own for weeks before you came!'

He cracked a small smile. 'Indeed you did! And now you've got all that new equipment I dare say you can cope with anything.'

'Yes, we were lucky not to lose any of it,' she agreed.

The small talk continued for a couple of minutes and then he had to go. He kissed her quickly again and was gone. Nicole watched the plane take off from the runway, which had been one of the first areas to be cleared, then she ran to hide in the surgery, where she locked the door and let the tears flow in private.

CHAPTER TEN

'REBUILDING this place is going to be a long job,' Toff Barrett said gloomily as he swirled the whisky around in his glass. 'Expensive too. Maybe I'm mad to even contemplate it.'

Nicole, who was having a drink with him as he had, rather to her surprise, invited her to do most evenings since he had come back this time, was startled. Toff was an optimist, an entrepreneur who enjoyed challenges. After the cyclone had practically destroyed his island, he had been full of determination to rebuild, and the work was going ahead. He'd come and gone several times, always seeming enthusiastic about his new plans. Self-doubt wasn't like him at all.

'This isn't like you, Toff,' she told him. 'I thought you were keen to rebuild. After all, it isn't really a greater challenge than when you came here and started from scratch in the first place.'

His gloom lifted. 'You're right—I shouldn't have said that. Just a moment of self-doubt, Nic.' He laughed. 'Not something I ought to let my staff see! But I don't really think of you as staff.' He stood up. 'Come on, let's see what our innovative chef has for us tonight.' He flung an arm across her shoulders. 'It's good of you to stay on, Nic. I thought you'd have taken the opportunity to explore pastures greener.'

Nicole shrugged. 'Well, to be honest, I had decided it was about time for a change, but I'm lazy, Toff.' She tried to make light of what was inwardly a heavy burden. 'I couldn't think what to do next, and when you asked me to stay on that seemed the easiest thing to do. After all, I was on the spot, and medical help is needed here.'

'Was that the only reason?' He looked down at her, smiling.

Nicole was puzzled by his mood. He wasn't at all like the Toff Barrett she was accustomed to. If she hadn't known him better, she would have said he was nervous. 'Well, yes. . .' she said.

They went into the restaurant. There was hardly any of the old hotel staff left now. Teams of workmen had moved in and slowly the debris was being removed and the damaged buildings demolished. Soon rebuilding work would commence. The original kitchen staff had mostly gone, and temporaries replaced them. There was hardly a familiar face on the island. Of the office staff, Dorothy had remained to monitor communications with the outside world and deal with the inevitable paperwork. She had an assistant, but he was a stranger too.

Nicole had intended to leave when Jan went, but Toff had asked her to stay on to look after the demolition crews and building workers who would be swarming over the resort for months to come. She had agreed to stay, but had not promised a definite period. Toff had been content with that.

The restaurant, which had been only partially damaged, was not earmarked for immediate demolition. It seemed empty and bleak without the crowds of holidaymakers and conference delegates, and their voices echoed unless they spoke in low tones.

They continued to talk about Toff's plans for the reconstructed resort, but all the time Nicole felt that

Toff had something on his mind, that what he wanted to say was something quite different. Finally, he did.

'I won't be able to come up here quite so often for a while, Nic. I've got to go overseas on business soon. I have to remember I've got other commitments besides Bauhinia Sands.'

'Of course,' she agreed. 'I was wondering how you could afford to spend so much time here. I know how you feel about the place, but you do have a good man handling the reconstruction. You told me that yourself.'

He nodded, smiling directly at her. 'I didn't have to fly up quite so often. But when Sloan said. . .'

'Sloan?' she queried. The mention of his name made her tense. Sloan was part of the reason she had stayed on, deluding herself that staying was the best way to get him out of her system, just the way she had Bob Granger. She had begun to believe she was beginning to until this moment when Toff's saying his name, right out of the blue, had touched a nerve that was still as raw as ever. 'You've seen him?' she asked, her voice more controlled than her heartbeat.

He nodded. 'We have a couple of drinks together about once a week. We're old friends. . .'

'Yes, I know. . . How is he? How's Lucy?' Nicole had known that Toff would probably have been in touch with them, but she had been unable to ask of her own accord. 'I've had a couple of letters, but she doesn't say a lot.'

'Sloan's fine—working at the Southern Cross again. Lucy's doing a business studies course, at his insistence, but she's still hoping to get accepted into drama school eventually. Evidently Coralie thinks she has a good chance.'

Nicole gathered her courage and asked the question the answer to which might be the most hurtful. 'How is Coralie?' Lucy had not mentioned her, but no doubt she had persuaded Sloan to let Lucy go to drama school.

'She's fine,' said Toff. 'She's been seeing a specialist Sloan put her in touch with, and I believe her problem is more or less solved. She was at a crossroads in her life and took a bit of a wrong turning, but she seems to know where she's going now.'

'Which will include marrying Sloan, I suppose,' Nicole remarked, as though it was only of academic interest to her.

'I haven't been invited to a wedding yet,' Toff answered, and went on at once, 'Talking of weddings . . .that's what I was going to talk to you about when you started quizzing me about Sloan and his womenfolk.'

Nicole raised an eyebrow. 'Are *you* getting married?' She was delighted and beamed at him. 'When, Toff? Who to? Are you inviting me to the wedding?'

He reached for her hand and covered it with his. 'Yes, I am inviting you,' he said, meeting her eyes with an earnestness she had never seen before. 'I want you to be the bride.'

Nicole was stunned. She drew her hand away as though his touch had burned her. 'Toff, you can't mean that——'

He captured her hand in mid-air and held it tightly. 'I do mean it, Nicole. I very much want to marry you. And Sloan gave me the distinct impression that you wouldn't say no.'

'Sloan did?' Nicole felt weak. Why would he have

said that? 'But you're not in love with me,' she said dazedly. 'We've never. . .'

'I've never even kissed you,' Toff said, a mischievous smile playing about his mouth. 'Well, that can be easily remedied.' He half rose as though to go, and held out his hand to her, but Nicole sat firm.

'Toff, I can't believe you mean it. I mean, I'm just one of your employees.'

He subsided back into his chair. 'You're a lovely woman, Nic,' he told her, reaching across to stroke her cheek. 'You're beautiful, intelligent, kind. . .'

'You must meet a lot of women like that.'

He shook his head. 'I meet a lot of women who regard me as eligible, but most of them are shallow and self-interested. That's why I haven't married. I've been waiting for someone like you.'

Nicole knew she should tell him that she did not love him, that Sloan had been joking—more cruelly than he realised—but rejecting Toff was not as easy as it should have been. 'I'm very flattered,' she told him. 'You've completely bowled me over asking me to marry you. I still think it's a joke.'

'I was never more serious in my life.' He stroked her cheek again. 'Come back to Sydney with me tomorrow. I'll get someone to take your place here—I have to employ an assistant anyway, and a new doctor. There'll be quite a big workforce here over the next few months, and I've got a reputation for looking after my employees.' He went on eagerly, 'My mother will take you in hand, don't worry. You two will get along fine, I'm sure, and she'll take you shopping for clothes and——'

'Toff, stop!' Nicole looked hard at him. 'Toff, I can't. . .you can't. . .this is ridiculous!'

'Nicole. . .?' he queried.

'I'm sorry, I can't marry you. I'm not in love with you, Toff. I *like* you, but. . .'

Disappointment darkened his eyes. 'Sloan was only guessing? Wrongly?'

'Yes. I don't know what gave him the idea. . . Oh, Toff, I'm sorry. I'm immensely touched, but. . .'

'There's someone else?'

Nicole lowered her eyes. 'There was. But it's not just that, Toff. It's just that. . .' She ran her tongue over her lips.

'It's Sloan, isn't it? I thought it might be.' He sighed deeply. 'It's no use, Nic. He and Coralie. . . Hell, I was a fool, matchmaking—interfering. Serves me right, I suppose.' He laughed hollowly. 'You know, Nic, we might make a go of it. We're in the same boat, aren't we? Both wanting what we can't have. But that doesn't mean we have to spend the rest of our lives alone, does it? We might even fall in love. What's love anyway?'

His meaning was plain, and after a moment's astonishment, Nicole smiled sadly. 'You know, Toff, as well as I do. A special feeling you have for one person and no other. With you it's for Coralie, isn't it?'

He nodded. 'It didn't really hit me until I saw her back in Sydney. I guess I've had strong feelings about Coralie for a long while, but she went and married Luke, and I suppressed them.' He gave Nicole an apologetic smile. 'You must think I'm a bit of a jerk, proposing to you.'

She reached across the table to touch his arm. 'Of course not! I like you a lot, Toff, but I don't think it would work.'

A small spark of anger flashed in his eyes. 'You'd

stay single all your life because one man didn't return your feelings?'

'I don't know,' she said. 'I only know how I feel right now. It would be wrong to marry you, or anyone, Toff, when I feel that way. How I'll feel in the future, I don't know.'

'Well, if you change your mind. . .' he said, smiling at her.

The meal was finished and, feeling suddenly tearful, Nicole got up rather abruptly. 'I'd better go. . . Goodnight.'

Toff rose too. 'I'll see you to your cabin.'

Nicole was living at the hotel now in one of the repaired cabins. She protested, but he insisted on seeing her to her door, where he said goodnight and left her.

During the next ten days, the momentum of work on the shattered resort increased. Workmen arrived almost every day and Nicole found herself kept busy attending to injuries and ailments. There was only one serious case in that time, an acute appendicitis. The patient was flown to the mainland, and, after she had seen the plane off and was having a cup of tea with Dorothy, Nicole sighed and said, 'Lucky it wasn't critical, seeing we haven't got a doctor now.'

'One's coming, I believe,' said Dorothy. 'Didn't Toff tell you he was arranging it?'

'Mmm, he did,' Nicole remembered. 'But it's not easy to get someone for a place like this, especially in the state we're in now. Do you think it will ever be the same again, Dorothy?'

Dorothy was confident. 'I'm sure it will. Toff's not the sort of person to jack it in, and this place means a

lot to him. It's kind of been his pet project ever since
he bought the island. I reckon it'll be bigger and better
than before, if I know Toff,' she laughed. 'And it'll be
as cyclone-proof as he can make it. I've been looking
through some of the specifications, and he's got the
very latest materials and construction methods. It won't
be a case of "I'll huff and I'll puff and I'll blow your
house down" next time.'

'He's certainly one determined guy,' Nicole said
admiringly. 'Now I'd better get back to the surgery.
I've got some sorting out to do. A delivery of pharma-
ceuticals came on the plane.'

She did not say that she was anxious to see what
might have come in the mail. She hadn't had a card
from Lucy for a while. Sloan had not written at all, but
then she hadn't expected him to. And Lucy's hastily
scribbled missives had told her very little anyway. Lucy
was busy with her changed life and no doubt Sloan was
preoccupied with Coralie and his job at the Southern
Cross. Would she bother to look them up when she
went back to Sydney? she often wondered. It would be
nice to see Lucy again. No, be honest, she told herself.
You want to see Sloan just once more. . . But not in
his house, with Coralie as hostess. No, it would be
better not to contact them at all.

A couple of days later Nicole was having a very quiet
morning, with only two patients wanting attention
having come and gone, when there was an emergency.
Assisted by two mates, a workman staggered into the
surgery, his face bleeding profusely.

'What happened?' Nicole sprang up from the kneel-
ing position she had been in, sorting out a bottom
cupboard.

Both the men helping the patient looked white and

shocked. One said shakily, 'He's got glass in his eye. It was so stupid. He just dropped a bottle on the concrete and it exploded. I never saw that happen before. Bits flew everywhere, and he got some in his eye.' They sat him on the chair Nicole indicated.

Nicole frowned as she examined the man's face. That he was in pain was obvious, although he was controlling himself well. 'She'll be right,' he muttered.

'Leave him here,' Nicole said quietly to the other two. She walked to the door with them. 'Just do one thing for me. If this is as bad as I think it might be, I'll want him to go back on this morning's flight. Let Dorothy know, will you? I don't want the plane going without him.'

'Is he going to lose his eye?' one of the men asked.

'I mightn't be able to tell that,' Nicole said. 'I'm not a doctor.' If only Sloan were here, she was thinking. This was just the kind of emergency that made having a doctor on the island so essential. Prompt, skilled treatment could sometimes mean the difference between life and death, or recovery and permanent injury. She felt lost without his strength and expertise.

She went back to the patient, who told her his name was Chris.

'I guess it's pretty painful,' she said. 'And I'll tell you straight, Chris, I might not be able to do much for you. I'll clean you up and see if I can assess what the damage is, how much glass is in your eye, and then we'll get you on the plane.'

'I reckon I'm going to lose my eye,' he said morosely. 'I can't see anything. . .'

'There's a lot of blood,' she told him, applying a pad to the flesh wound at the edge of the man's eye where most of the blood was coming from. 'Now, if I can just

have you in here where there's a good light.' She
guided him into the treatment-room.

'Maybe I'd better take a look at this one.'

The voice made Nicole spin round. 'Sloan. . .!' Her
heart leapt in an extraordinary way, as though she was
seeing a ghost. But Sloan was real—tall, handsome
and still with a still pinkish scar where he'd cut his
forehead on his first day and she'd dressed it. The
room tilted and she felt as though she might faint.

'What are you doing here?' Her voice was a whisper.

He didn't enlighten her. His eyes were swiftly assess-
ing the situation. 'Just in time to lend a hand, by the
look of it,' he said, so calm, so casual, so authoritative,
taking over even as he was speaking. 'Dorothy told me
you had an emergency.'

Nicole closed her eyes and gave herself a mental
shake just to convince herself he really was there. 'It's
glass,' she explained briskly. 'From a bottle which
exploded on impact with concrete. There are probably
slivers. . .'

Sloan was not listening. Of course not. He didn't
need her prattle. He was already washing his hands.
His examination of the patient's eye was swift, and
from his expression Nicole could tell he was worried.

'There's one sliver of glass rather too close to the
cornea for comfort,' he said finally. 'I think we'd better
try to remove it right away before it moves of its own
accord and does more damage than it has already. Just
blinking could shift it.' He turned to Nicole. 'You'd
better tell Dorothy the plane'll be held up a bit longer
than anticipated.'

'You're going to operate?' Nicole couldn't help
surprise.

Sloan met her anxious gaze with calm confidence. 'Yes.'

Nicole looked away, afraid she had implied that he might not be capable. 'Have we adequate instruments?' she muttered.

His strong, steady fingers closed briefly around her arm, and he said quietly, 'I wouldn't do it unless it was necessary.'

The delicate operation on the man's eye was one of the tensest Nicole could remember. Eye surgery was not an area in which she had had much experience. She watched Sloan with admiration as he extracted the sliver of glass that could, if it dislodged or were ineptly removed, cause the patient to lose the sight of his eye. His hand was as steady as a rock, and the job was not easy with so much blood in the eye.

When it was over he glanced at her with a gleam of triumph in his own eyes. 'I think that's got it,' he said. 'They'll be able to give it a more exhaustive examination in hospital. There could still be tiny specks embedded in the eyeball. You can hand me the dressing now, Nicole.'

Nicole felt as though she had been put through a wringer. 'I'm glad you were here,' she murmured. 'Although I still don't know why you are.' Her hands, which until now had been as steady as his, were shaking as she handed him the dressing.

He did not answer her question, but said, 'Well, we'd better ship him out right away, and alert the hospital in Mackay. You still have a stretcher, I suppose?'

Nicole nodded. Within minutes Chris, still unconscious, was aboard the plane, and the ambulance service had been alerted to meet it at the other end. It wasn't until they were back in the surgery and Nicole was making the cup of coffee Sloan had asked for that he did get around to explaining.

'I offered to come back for a while,' he explained. 'Toff hasn't been able to get anyone else.'

'But I thought you were at the Southern Cross?' Nicole felt as though a million butterflies were rioting inside her.

'You don't mind?'

'Mind? No, why should I mind?' She was in heaven.

'My charging back in and stealing your thunder. You didn't care very much for that the first time.'

She flushed. 'That's not true!'

Sloan laughed softly. 'You're a hard one to read, Nicole. You don't wear your heart on your sleeve, do you?'

'How's Lucy?' she asked.

'Fine. I thought she was keeping in touch.'

'I've had a couple of brief letters. She sounded happy. Is everything all right now?'

'I hope so. We understand each other better. And Coralie has helped. They're good friends again. Coralie believes Lucy has talent and will get into drama school. I'm not sure I wholly approve, but it's what she wants to do. So long as she gets some other qualification first, so she won't starve when there's no acting work.'

'I hope she sees the sense of that.' Nicole had to pretend it was just casual conversation, but it was breaking her apart inside. 'And how's Coralie? Toff said she was much better.'

Sloan looked grave for a moment, then said, 'Yes, she's much better. It did her the world of good up here, but she still needs help. I'm glad to say she's agreed to proper medical attention, and my fingers are crossed. I hope there'll be no lasting side-effects of what she's been through with prescription drugs. We're both hoping she'll be able to start work again soon.'

It sounded like togetherness. 'That's good news.' Nicole wondered what Coralie felt about his return, but she did not want to talk any more about the actress. The trouble was, she couldn't think of anything else to say. She shifted nervously, leaning against the bench a little further away from him, looking desperately around for something to do.

Sloan put down his coffee-mug, stood up and moved to face her. He looked deeply into her eyes. His arms slid around her, pulling her close to him, and he brought his mouth firmly to hers, kissing her hard until her lips softened under his and she began to kiss him back. She felt her whole body melting against him, and her arms seemed to lift of their own accord to hold him even closer, her fingers clasped behind his neck as she let the ecstasy of what she had never expected to happen again envelop her.

But it was madness. She had no right to be kissing Sloan, he had no right to be kissing her, no right to show that he desired her. Was this the kind of man he really was? Like Bob, never able to resist a woman? With a sudden surge of anger, she pulled away.

'That wasn't called for!' she said furiously. 'You ought to be ashamed of yourself!'

He grasped her wrist and hauled her back into his arms, winding his arms tightly around her. 'Why? For loving you?'

'You don't love me!'

'Want a bet? You'll lose!'

Nicole was dazed. 'You don't know what you're saying. Stop it, Sloan! Please stop it. It's not fair. . .'

His dark eyes were challenging. 'Why, Nicole? Toff

told me he asked you to marry him and you turned him down. I want to know why you turned him down.'

She bit her lip. 'That's none of your business.'

'I thought you were pretty keen on Toff. Murray said so, and Coralie thought so. And you told me you had your sights set on a millionaire.'

Nicole flushed deeply. 'I only said that for a joke. Surely you didn't think I meant it?'

His face was stern, accusing. 'It's not an uncommon ambition among young women.' He paused, looking at her closely. 'If it's not Toff, is there someone else?'

'There was,' she confessed. 'I don't want to talk about it.'

'But I do,' he insisted. 'It's important. I want to know whether you're still eating your heart out for another man.'

Nicole turned hastily away. 'Sloan, please. . .'

He grasped her arms and turned her back to face him. 'You didn't want to get involved again, did you? And neither did I. I had too many problems. How could I even think of marrying again? With Lucy the way she was it wouldn't have been fair. And even when we left I couldn't be sure the changes would be permanent.'

'I thought all you wanted was a casual affair.'

He smiled. 'I have to admit you were a big temptation!'

Nicole pushed her lips tightly together. 'What's the point of all this, Sloan? You're going to marry Coralie, aren't you? Toff said——'

'Did he?' Sloan interrupted sharply. 'Did he indeed? Well, like me, he's been barking up the wrong tree. There's never been anything between Coralie and me except friendship. I told you that before, but evidently you didn't believe me.'

Nicole looked sceptical. 'Why should I? I saw her in your arms once up at the Lodge.'

His mouth hardened and he frowned. 'You did? Ah, yes, I think I know when that was. Coralie was very distraught, Nicole. She knew her bid to cure herself wasn't working, and when I arrived she clung to me for help. Perhaps for a while she did entertain some wild ideas about me, but she knows the score now.'

'Does Toff?' asked Nicole quietly.

Sloan looked quizzical. 'Meaning?'

'It's Coralie he wants, Sloan, not me. He's been in love with her for years. He asked me to marry him only because he thought she was going to marry you. He got you together, then realised he loved her.'

Sloan looked aghast. 'I never guessed! One day when we were having lunch back in Sydney, Toff started saying it was about time he got married. I told him you were just the kind of wife he needed and that you were crazy about him.'

'I'm not!'

Sloan looked sheepish. 'I feel guilty about it now. It must have been humiliating for him to be rejected. But I thought if I couldn't have you myself I'd rather you were married to a good mate of mine who'd treat you properly. I was as jealous as hell, but it was a good second-best solution.'

'You're mad!' Nicole told him, with a lightness growing in her that she hardly dared to believe in.

'A bit,' he agreed. 'Do you know, Nicole, when he came back and said you'd turned him down, that was the best news I'd heard in my whole life?'

Her tongue moved nervously over dry lips. 'I—I don't know what you mean.'

He was smiling now. 'You ought to!' He gripped her

hard. 'I offered to fill in again here until he gets back from overseas. I couldn't wait to get up here and find out for myself. . .if there was any chance for us. . .' He looked deeply into her eyes. 'This other fellow you were in love with? Did you say that because you thought Coralie and I. . .?'

'Yes.'

'There's no one?'

'No one at all.' It was true. It had been true for quite a while. Bob was just a dim and unimportant memory. He had never been very important anyway, not in any real sense, as she'd always known deep inside her. Her longings for Bob had been superficial physical ones. Her longings for Sloan were deep and abiding.

She felt Sloan's arms tightening around her. His mouth covered hers and for some moments there was no need for mere words.

At last Sloan lifted his lips and said softly, 'Nicole, I love you. I want to cherish you and take care of you forever. Please say you'll marry me.'

Nicole's knees were threatening to give out again. She sagged against him, thankful for his strength. 'Oh, Sloan, there's nothing in the world I want to do more. . . I didn't think it was possible. I thought I'd have to learn to forget you. . .and I knew it wouldn't be as easy as it was in the end with Bob. . .'

'Who the hell's Bob?' His gaze was fiercely jealous, and he gripped her hard, giving her a shake.

Nicole could only smile and tell him. She ended, 'I never loved anyone as much as I love you. . .'

'And I thought you were only interested in millionaires!'

She smiled. 'Like Lucy, I'm good at fantasising.'

He tilted her chin and kissed her lips. 'Lucy doesn't fantasise any more.'

'Neither do I. There's no need now.'

Sloan stroked her cheek, sending tingles of fire along her veins. 'So here we are stuck together on a cyclone-devastated island and we've both promised Toff to hang around until he gets back from overseas. Three months at least.'

'Is that so bad?' Nicole hardly dared look directly at him.

He twisted a strand of her hair in his fingers. 'Not if we slip over to the mainland and get married one day, just so Dorothy won't be outraged.'

'For Dorothy's sake, any day you like,' Nicole said, laughing. 'After all, this is a honeymoon island!'

'Did you ever hear of newlyweds working on their honeymoon?' Sloan exclaimed. 'We ought to get penalty rates at least.'

'I expect we'll have a lot of spare time,' she said with a shy smile.

He crushed her tightly against him. 'We'd better,' he said fiercely. 'And now let's go and tell Dorothy we're engaged and would she mind organising a wedding in double quick time. She'll love it! We could also tell the chef we want a candlelit dinner tonight.'

Nicole laughed happily at his enthusiasm. 'Sloan, darling, you're so romantic!' she mocked. She detained him a moment, winding her arms tightly about him. She lifted her face, and, standing on tiptoe, kissed his forehead, then his eyes, and finally his mouth, whispering, as she did so, 'Oh, Sloan, I never knew it was possible to be this happy.'

He chuckled softly as he returned her kisses. 'And neither, my darling, did I!'

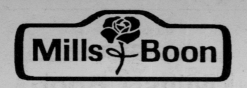

Discover the thrill of 4 Exciting
Medical Romances – FREE

BOOKS FOR YOU

In the exciting world of modern
medicine, the emotions of true love
have an added drama. Now you can
experience four of these
unforgettable romantic tales of passion
and heartbreak FREE – and look forward to
a regular supply of Mills & Boon
Medical Romances delivered direct to your door!

🙦 🙦 🙦

Turn the page for details of 2 extra
free gifts, and how to apply.

An Irresistible Offer from Mills & Boon

Here's an offer from Mills & Boon to become a regular reader of Medical Romances. To welcome you, we'd like you to have four books, a cuddly teddy and a special MYSTERY GIFT, all absolutely free and without obligation.

Then, every month you could look forward to receiving 4 more **brand new** Medical Romances for £1.60 each, delivered direct to your door, post and packing free. Plus our newsletter featuring author news, competitions, special offers, and lots more.

This invitation comes with no strings attached. You can cancel or suspend your subscription at any time, and still keep your free books and gifts.

Its so easy. Send no money now. Simply fill in the coupon below and post it at once to -

Mills & Boon Reader Service, FREEPOST, PO Box 236, Croydon, Surrey CR9 9EL

NO STAMP REQUIRED

YES! Please rush me my 4 Free Medical Romances and 2 Free Gifts! Please also reserve me a Reader Service Subscription. If I decide to subscribe, I can look forward to receiving 4 brand new Medical Romances every month for just £6.40, delivered direct to my door. Post and packing is free, and there's a free Mills & Boon Newsletter. If I choose not to subscribe I shall write to you within 10 days - I can keep the books and gifts whatever I decide. I can cancel or suspend my subscription at any time. I am over 18.

EP20D

Name (Mr/Mrs/Ms) _____

Address _____

_____

_____ Postcode _____

Signature _____